"Scarily good."

— BESTSELLING AUTHOR, LEE CHILD

"Sharp is part of a very small group of writers who actually talks the talk and walks the walk. She really knows this stuff and so when she writes it, it feels more real than most non-fiction books. Sharp deserves a genre all her own."

— JON JORDAN, CRIMESPREE MAGAZINE

"Zoë Sharp is one of the sharpest, coolest, and most intriguing writers I know. She delivers dramatic, action-packed novels with characters we really care about."

— BESTSELLING AUTHOR, HARLAN COBEN

"Male and female crime fiction readers alike will find Sharp's writing style addictively readable."

— PAUL GOAT ALLEN, CHICAGO TRIBUNE

"Zoë Sharp is a master at writing thoughtful action thrillers."

— BESTSELLING AUTHOR, MEG GARDINER

"This is hard-edged fiction at its best."

— MICHELE LEBER, BOOKLIST (STARRED REVIEW) FOR
FIFTH VICTIM

"I loved every word of this brilliant, mind-twisting thriller and even yelped out loud at one of the genius twists."

— BESTSELLING AUTHOR, ELIZABETH HAYNES, ON THE
BLOOD WHISPERER

"Sharp is a writer of extraordinary skill."

"Superb."

"Zoë Sharp has an apt last name. She delivers yet another sleek, sharp thriller."

"If you don't like Zoë Sharp there's something wrong with you. Go and live in a cave and get the hell out of my gene pool! There are few writers who go right to the top of my TBR pile—Zoë Sharp is one of them."

"Well, holy sh*tballs! What a book!...an intense, compelling and totally engrossing read."

BAD TURN

CHARLIE FOX BOOK 13

ZOË SHARP

First published in Great Britain 2019
ZACE

Registered UK Office:
Kemp House, 160 City Road, London EC1V 2NX
Copyright © Zoë Sharp 2019

ISBN-13: 978-1-909344-56-3

For Gillie Goodman
actor and friend
(1941-2018)

ALSO BY ZOË SHARP

For more information on Zoë Sharp's writing,
see her website: www.ZoeSharp.com

1

I DON'T LIKE SURPRISES. More often than not, they're the nasty kind and experience has primed me to react accordingly. Jump out of a cupboard with a birthday cake or a bottle of champagne when I'm not expecting a party, and you're liable to get smacked in the mouth.

Up until a couple of months ago—back when I still had a job that came with both the requirement and the authorisation to go armed most of the time—I might even have shot you. These days I have to improvise with whatever is at hand.

On a backwoods route in rural New Jersey, all I had at hand was the old GMC pick-up I was driving, when I rounded the next bend and stumbled into a full-blown ambush.

I had only a split second to take in the scene. A Lincoln Town Car, incongruous outside of the city, sat halfway onto the dirt shoulder, nose-down at an angle, its chauffeur-black paintwork speckled with bullet hits. Two dark SUVs had been slewed across the narrow road in either direction, effectively boxing-in their target.

Three men were using the SUV closest to me for cover. I marked them as aggressors from the body armour and assault weapons. The two men I could see near the Lincoln both wore ordinary suits. They were doing their best to repel the attack with semi-automatic pistols. A losing bet, whichever way you squared it.

My right hand had snaked toward the small of my back before I remembered I didn't have a weapon of my own.

The moment I appeared, two of the men crouched behind the SUV stopped pouring fire into the stricken Lincoln and switched their aim to me. Nothing personal, I figured, just standard operating procedure—leave no witness behind. The third man didn't flicker. He stayed on target, trusting his pals to deal with the new threat.

Which meant I was dealing with pros.

I braked hard and just had time to duck down behind the pick-up's dash before the first rounds punched through the windscreen. They thudded into the back of my seat where my head had been, moments earlier.

Yeah, definitely bloody pros.

Well, if they were playing for keeps, so was I.

I jammed my foot onto the accelerator again, heard the heavy V8 growl in response, the steering wheel vibrating under my hands as the transmission kicked down a gear. For once, I was glad I wasn't on a motorcycle as all four tyres bit and the front end of the vehicle lifted.

Sprawled across the front seats, I braced as much as I could. A second later, we smashed into the driver's side of the SUV. The pick-up's airbags deployed with an explosive whumph. It almost drowned out the shriek of graunching steel and breaking glass, ending with a scream chopped short by a soggy thump.

I pivoted onto my back and kicked the airbag out of the way. It was already beginning to deflate but the driver's door was bent and buckled. I scrambled for the passenger door, which had suffered less in the crash. It opened at once. I spilled out onto the road and rolled to my feet, keeping low.

More by luck than design, I'd struck the SUV directly amidships, ripping the driver's door off its hinges and tenting the roof as the pick-up buried its front bull bars deep into the B pillar. The driver had been using his part-open door as a firing position and I realised he was the reason for that wet thump. I forced myself to remember he'd been aiming for my head…

One down.

The gunman towards the rear of the SUV had come off better, but not by much. The nearside front corner of the pick-up was embedded in his door. The man—muscles, buzz-cut, olive skin, clean-shaven—was now pinned between door and frame at the chest. He flailed weakly, eyes screwed shut in pain and shock.

I leapt for the weapon already dropping from his grasp—a Colt M4 carbine. I'd seen plenty of those over the years. I jerked it out of his weakened grip and slammed the stock into the side of his skull just below his left ear. The blow cannoned his head into the roof of the SUV and he slumped.

Two down.

I spun with the M4 pulled up into my shoulder, looking to acquire the front-seat passenger, but he had dropped from sight.

Rounds zinged past me. I didn't wait to confirm if they were fired by the occupants of the other SUV in retaliation. For all I knew, the two guys from the Lincoln were taking no chances, either.

I flung myself behind the SUV's rear tyre, which at least offered a little protection from stray rounds passing underneath the vehicle, took a breath and checked the M4's thirty-round magazine. It was about two-thirds full. *Could be worse.*

Behind me, the pick-up's engine had dropped to tickover now, patient as a dozing cab horse waiting for the return fare. So, it ran, but I had no idea if it would still drive. A puddle was forming around the front end, and at first I thought I'd busted the radiator until I realised the fluid was not the piss-yellow of coolant but instead a dark, sticky red. I looked away.

On the far side of the vehicle, the firefight continued. I didn't stick my head up to see who was winning. Instead, I dropped to my belly and squinted through the darkened slot between the SUV and the road.

The first thing I saw was the body of the driver. He'd fallen partly on the ground and partly back into the vehicle, the M4 close to his open hand. His leg was badly broken, the knee joint operating in reverse. I couldn't tell if he was alive or dead, but he was certainly unconscious or he would have been screaming.

Beyond him, the twin yellow stripes of the road's centre-line led directly to the other SUV. I could see part of the passenger side, the lower edge of an open door and the legs of one of the attackers from about mid-calf downwards, booted feet braced.

I dropped my eye to the M4's optical sight, right thumb feeling for the safety lever and flicking it to three-round burst as I did so. Another breath, trying to slow my heart rate, steady my aim.

I squeezed the trigger, stitching across the man's ankles. Half a dozen rounds spat from the barrel in the time it took me to release my finger. *What the—?*

I swore under my breath and flicked the safety back to single shot, knowing I didn't have that kind of ammo to waste. My target was already falling back inside the vehicle.

One of the men shouted but I didn't catch what he said. I couldn't even swear to the language he used.

I squirmed sideways, tried to get a bead on the other men from the second SUV. They were staying out of sight. A moment later, the vehicle took off backwards, performed a pretty credible J-turn, and disappeared around the next bend in the road, engine screaming.

A deafening silence greeted its departure.

2

"Hey, you in the Lincoln—I'm coming out," I shouted, loud above the ringing in my ears. "I'm here to help. So, don't shoot me, OK?"

Nothing.

I rose cautiously, ready to duck down again at the first sign of movement, never mind trouble. Still nothing.

So far, so good...

I edged out around the back end of the SUV, flicking my eyes across the fallen driver as I did so. Yup, he was definitely dead. Nevertheless, I toed his M4 a little further away from his hand. Old habits.

The front passenger door of the Lincoln stood open, but there was no sign of the guy in the suit who'd been standing next to it when I first appeared.

I stepped round the rear of the car, eyes everywhere. I was still keeping the M4 up into my shoulder but let the muzzle drop a fraction in an attempt to convey, if not friendliness, then at least a little less outright hostility.

The driver of the Lincoln was down and appeared dead, something I confirmed with two fingers against the side of his neck. I swore under my breath—I hated getting shot at without affecting the outcome. As I started to rise, I caught a glimpse of something inside the back of the car. When I yanked open the rear door, I found a woman on the back seat, huddled into the corner as far away from me as she could get. A man was crumpled up on the floor, wedged between the front and rear seats. The legroom was generous in a Town Car, but he was a big guy and it was a tight fit.

"No closer!" the woman snapped, grabbing my attention as much by the iced fury in her tone as by the 9mm suddenly in her hands. Something cold pooled at the base of my skull.

Shit...rookie mistake. I should have been paying her more attention from the start. I rectified that now—better late than never. She was small, with a Mediterranean complexion that tanned easily. Her hair was ashy blonde, about shoulder length, a tribute to her hairdresser's art. The gun looked too big for her hands but I could tell by her grip that it wasn't her first time. Her clothes were obviously expensive—they went with the car. She wore gold rings on both hands and a watch studded in diamonds.

Slowly, I lifted my left hand away from the stock of the M4, palm open and fingers spread placatingly.

"I'm here to help," I repeated. "Are you injured?"

For a moment the woman stared at me almost without comprehension. She made the slightest motion with her head, which I took to mean no. The man on the floor of the car shifted a little then, groaning. It seemed to twitch her back to right here, right now, and took the last of the fight out of her.

"My God," she said shakily, lowering the gun. "Illya!"

"He needs treatment." I put the M4 down outside the car, but still within reach, and knelt half inside. The man she'd called Illya had a pulse but it was weak and erratic. "Do you have a phone? If so, you should call for help."

She nodded, eyes still on the big man as I began to loosen his clothing enough to find out where he was hit. There was nothing visible on his head or back and I struggled to turn him in the confined space.

When I finally managed to roll him onto his side, I saw the front of his shirt was soaked with blood. Good job the interior of the Lincoln was all black, or it would have looked like a scene from a Quentin Tarantino movie in there.

I pulled a knife out of my jeans pocket, flipped it open and sliced the shirt up the centre, ignoring the buttons. I used the remnants to wipe a path and found entry wounds in his shoulder, chest and stomach. All were bleeding faster than I could clear them.

"Do you carry a first-aid kit?"

The woman shrugged helplessly. "I–I don't know."

"OK. In that case, do you have sanitary towels on you?"

The woman, fumbling in a large Louis Vuitton handbag, looked up at me as if I'd grown another head.

"Wha—?"

I bit back a curse. "Sanitary napkins—pads? Whatever the hell you want to call them. Or tampons? Anything."

She reached into the bag again, pulled out a discreet drawstring bag and handed it over without a word. I looked inside and found half a dozen slim tampons.

I smiled my thanks, ripped the wrapping off one, teased out the strings, and inserted it into the first of Illya's bullet wounds with great care. He seemed too far out of it to notice or care. Gradually, they expanded to plug the wound and the flow slowed to an ooze. He might not make it, even so, but at least he wouldn't die of blood loss before they could get him to a hospital.

When I finished and sat back on my heels, I found the woman staring at me again but with less suspicion this time.

She had a smartphone with a huge screen pressed against the side of her face, making her appear all the smaller by comparison. "I never would have thought of…" she began, voice sombre. "How did you know what to use?"

"It doesn't *matter* what you use, as long as it's absorbent and sterile."

She looked about to say more, but ducked her head as the other end of the line was finally picked up. "It's me," she said, not meeting my eyes. "Trouble. You will know where. No, I'm OK! But…*hurry*." And she ended the call, stabbing at the screen with a thumb that had started to tremble.

"Well, either you have a *really* close relationship with the local cops around here," I said, "or I'm guessing that wasn't them you've just called."

She didn't answer.

I sighed and nodded to Illya. "I hope you have just as close a relationship with a local trauma surgeon as well, otherwise your guy here isn't going to make it."

"He will take care of him," she said, without going into specifics.

I shrugged, doing another scan of the surrounding area. We were lucky nobody else had arrived on-scene in the meantime, but this area to the far west of New Jersey was farming country and sparsely populated. As long as it remained beyond an easy train ride into Manhattan, it was likely to remain that way.

I nodded to the open front passenger door. "Where's the other guy?"

She frowned for a moment, following my gaze. "Ah, I had only two men with me. Illya got in back with me when he was wounded…to give me his weapon."

I glanced at the wounded man with renewed respect. He'd lived up to the slang term for bodyguard—bullet catcher. Now all he had to do was survive the experience.

Minutes later, I heard a thudding engine note over the top of the faithful GMC, which was still ticking over on the other side of the wrecked SUV. I climbed out of the Lincoln and checked the road in both directions. For the moment, I left the M4 propped against the rear tyre, close by but not actually in my hands. No point in asking for more trouble than I probably had already.

A shadow flitted across the sun overhead, and the branches of the trees began to shiver. I looked up, shielding my eyes against the light above the canopy, just as the dark shape of a helicopter swung low and came in for a fast landing in the field next to the road.

The woman got out of the Lincoln and stood at my shoulder, her eyes skimming briefly over her dead driver. She kept any feelings she might have had about that out of her face by pure effort of will.

I jerked my head towards the car. "GPS tracker?"

She nodded. We both kept our eyes on the helo. It was a Sikorsky S76D in dark red livery with gold detailing. Top of the range and classy—not to mention expensive. It went with the Lincoln and the handbag and the watch.

As soon as the helo was on the ground, the doors were flung open and half a dozen men jumped out, armed to the teeth. Two of them carried medical packs. They had the woman hustled across the downdraft-flattened grass and the wounded man loaded in on a stretcher inside seven minutes.

I turned away from the scene, found one of the men standing behind me. He also carried an M4 carbine—coincidence? He held the weapon not quite aimed at me, but near enough to be suggestive. I glanced at it pointedly.

The man didn't speak, just gestured that I should head for the Sikorsky with the woman and the stretcher. When I hesitated, his grip on the weapon tightened.

I shrugged, jogged across the grass ahead of him, automatically keeping my head down, and climbed inside. The cabin was kitted out in cream leather and deep carpet, executive style.

My guard climbed in behind me and slammed the door shut. The pilot goosed the collective and the Sikorsky rose smoothly into the air. As it climbed, it rotated onto its new heading. Through the trees below I caught a last glimpse of the pick-up, still embedded in the side of the SUV, the bodies sprawled on the blacktop, and the stricken Lincoln, before the scene was lost from view.

3

NOBODY SPOKE to me during the short flight. I stared down out of the helo's starboard window, trying to gauge roughly where we were going. It distracted me from thinking about the guy I'd pancaked between the pick-up and the SUV. Instead, I tried to remember the way his rounds had ripped into my seat, right before I'd run him down. It seemed to balance the scales just a little.

I'd been shot before and had been lucky to survive. It wasn't an experience I was in a hurry to repeat.

After only a few minutes, at a guess, the aircraft's forward momentum slowed, nose lifting as the pilot flared the rotors. We swung into position for landing and I saw acres of rooftop and glass, barns, and white-fenced paddocks with grazing horses apparently unfazed by our arrival.

As we touched down and the engine note died back, the doors were flung open. The stretcher was unloaded first onto a waiting gurney. I half-expected to see an ambulance waiting, but instead a middle-aged man with a stethoscope around his neck hurried forward, otherwise dressed as if he'd come straight from the golf course. The doctor pulled on latex gloves, already bending over his patient as he was wheeled away.

The woman got out next, surrounded by a tight phalanx of

four men. A phrase containing the words 'stable door', 'horse' and 'bolted' sprang to mind, but I kept such thoughts to myself.

I warranted only one guard, probably enough considering he was armed and, if you discounted the folding knife in my pocket, I was not. We followed the woman into the house through an impressive double-height front door. Inside, it opened out into a massive entrance hall with a sweeping staircase leading up to a galleried landing above.

The woman's heels clicked on the Italianate marble floor. Everyone else was wearing soft-soled boots, myself included. I looked down at my dusty jeans and bloodied shirt and got the feeling they really should have hosed me down and taken me around to the tradesman's entrance at the back of the house.

She disappeared into a room to our right, the door closing firmly behind her. Her bodyguards stayed outside. Two flanked the doorway, the others disappearing along a corridor at the rear of the hallway. My guard, sadly, was not among them. He gestured again, this time towards a baroque-style buttoned chair near the foot of the stairs.

"Wow, you just can't stop jabbering, can you?" I murmured, and saw the merest flicker of amusement in his stony features. "I think I'll stand, though, thanks."

Partly to get away from the stare-out competition we seemed to be having, and partly just to see if he stopped me, I wandered to the far side of the room to study the artwork on the walls. It was mostly modern—I recognised works by Jackson Pollock and Mark Rothko, which, if genuine, gave me a good ballpark figure for the income bracket of the owner. Not that the executive helicopter, and the mansion, and the private army hadn't pretty much done so already.

We waited. Maybe a quarter of an hour passed, during which time a young man in a black suit brought out a tray of coffee served in a Limoges pot, which he put down on a side table, also without speaking. I was beginning to wonder if everyone here had taken a vow of silence. None of the bodyguards touched it, so I helped myself, if only because it allowed me to hold something I might be able to use as a weapon—either the cup itself or the coffee it contained.

Finally, the door opened to the room the woman had entered. A man stepped out. From the way he was dressed—the same casually expensive style as the woman—and the way the guards stiffened slightly, I guessed this was the boss.

He was maybe mid-thirties, tall, broad, and light on his feet in the way that martial artists are. Something about the way they walk, the way they put their feet down. His hair was darkish blond and his jaw was square. I bet he'd played football in college, the kind that involved padding and helmets. But I didn't mistake him for a meathead, by any means. There was a calculating brain behind his narrowed eyes that made me instantly wary.

He came into the hallway unsmiling, but with his right hand outstretched. Mixed messages.

"Ms Fox?" he said, his grip firm without attempting to crush my knuckles. His hands were long-fingered and broad but well-kept, neither soft nor calloused. "It would seem I owe you my thanks." He didn't sound happy about that state of affairs. Maybe it explained the stony face.

Clearly, he'd spent the time between our arrival and now running background on me, although it was interesting how quickly he'd learned my name without much to go on. He couldn't even have run the plate on the pick-up, because it belonged to the owner of the farm where I was house-sitting.

Yeah…very interesting. And maybe a little worrying, too.

"I'm sorry I couldn't do more," I said, ignoring the stark mental image of that greasy red puddle under the front of the pick-up again. "How is your guy—Illya, was it?"

"Being well taken care of," the man said smoothly. He stepped to one side and indicated the open doorway behind him. "Please, will you join us?"

Unable to think of a good reason to decline, I put down my now-tepid coffee and obliged. Inside, the room was a little less imposing and a lot more lived-in. A huge flat-screen TV hung above the open fireplace, in front of which was a low marble table boxed in on three sides by a comfortable-looking sofa and a pair of armchairs, their cushions misshapen by regular use. It lacked the interior-design magazine, staged look of the hallway.

The only thing conspicuously out of place in the room was the small, slim man lounging against the wall just behind the open door with his hands in the pockets of his jeans. I caught a glimpse of him in my peripheral vision as I entered and couldn't prevent my head jerking round in that direction. He gave me a fractional nod, like I'd passed some kind of test.

Something about him made the skin prickle across the top of my shoulders. I had to force my arms to stay relaxed by my sides when instinct tried to form them into a defensive block, just in case.

He was dressed in uniformly dull-coloured clothing that didn't look either new, or originally bought for him. A baggy jacket over an open shirt and T-shirt topped off the jeans and suede boots. His reddish-brown hair was collar-length, and he sported a droopy moustache and goatee, and small wire-rimmed glasses.

It took a moment for me to realise he was another bodyguard, but from a very different mould to the men in the hallway outside. More subtle, more sinuous, and ultimately far more deadly.

The boss paid him absolutely no attention as if the man was a fixture, the same as the curtains.

The woman from the Lincoln was sitting on one of the sofas. Her shoes lay on the floor and she'd curled her bare feet up beneath her. She was clutching a glass of liquid the colour of a ripe conker that might have been brandy, or bourbon. Dutch courage, either way.

"You've been doing your homework," I said. At his silent invitation, I sank onto the sofa opposite where I could keep the slim bodyguard in view. "You know my name, but I don't know yours."

They exchanged the briefest of looks, then the woman cleared her throat. "I'm Helena," she said. "Helena Kincaid. And this is my husband, Eric."

She paused, as if expecting the name to resonate. I kept my face neutral. "I would say it's a pleasure to meet you, Mrs Kincaid, but under the circumstances…"

That provoked a smile. She was not conventionally pretty,

but the smile lit up her face from the inside, made it more than the sum of its parts. Kincaid sat alongside her, closer than he needed to for convention's sake. I picked up no tension between them. In fact, they were a well-matched couple—outwardly at least.

"I understand you're staying out at the Stephensons' property," Kincaid said. It was a statement rather than a question.

"Just taking care of the place while they're away. Europe, I believe," I said vaguely. I pulled a rueful face. "Speaking of 'taking care' of things, that reminds me—I need to do something about Frank's truck—"

"It's in hand," Kincaid said, using that same smooth, almost bland tone as before. "The vehicle will be returned to you as soon as it's been…sanitised."

I grimaced. "Yeah, that might take some doing. I admit that using it as a battering ram wasn't quite in the game plan."

Helena's head came up quickly. "You had a game plan?"

"Just a figure of speech."

"Really?" she demanded, her voice sharp now. "Well, figure of speech or not, what kind of a person just so happens across an ambush on a road-to-nowhere in Hicksville and has any kind of a *game plan* in place for dealing with it?"

Kincaid put his hand on her leg, to reassure rather than threaten, I judged. Her own hand—the one holding the glass—trembled slightly, but I put that down to shock. She wasn't afraid of him. That was something, at least.

"We know what kind, Helena," he said gently.

For the first time, she glanced at the bodyguard by the doorway, as if checking something by comparison, although I hoped I didn't give off the same kind of vibe. Then she nodded, the fire going out of her.

"Like I said—you've been doing your homework," I repeated.

"Nobody sets foot into our home without that happening, Ms Fox," Kincaid said. "Particularly after the events of today."

He paused, as if waiting for me to jump in with questions I had no intention of asking.

Eventually, I sighed. "OK, I get that you don't want to take anything about me on trust, and I suppose I can't blame you for that. If someone had just made that kind of attempt on me, I'd be as suspicious as hell of anyone and everyone—especially someone who *just so happened* to be on-scene at the time."

I rose, stuffed my hands into my pockets and gave each of them a level stare. They didn't do a bad job of maintaining eye contact, either of them. "But I'm not after anything from you other than the repair and return of the truck I was driving."

"Nothing else?" Helena demanded, unable to keep a note of incredulity out of her voice.

"Well..." I let my gaze travel around the room, as if pricing up the cost of the furnishings. "As your guys insisted I leave my vehicle behind, I wouldn't say no to a lift back to the Stephensons' place, if you wouldn't mind? It doesn't have to be by helicopter."

Out of the corner of my eye, I saw the bodyguard by the door break into a smile. It was not reassuring.

"Dude, I like this girl," he said, speaking for the first time. He had a soft voice, his accent difficult to place. "Seriously, she's cool."

Kincaid ignored him and reached into his inside jacket pocket, the action making me twitch reflexively. When he withdrew his hand, however, the only thing in it was a chequebook. He flattened it out on the table between us, laid a gold pen on top.

"Please, don't get me wrong, Ms Fox, I—*we*—are very grateful for your...intervention today. But you must realise that people in our position find trusting in strangers...difficult."

"You're very cynical, Mr Kincaid."

"I'm a realist," he returned. "Anyone successful in kidnapping my wife could have legitimately asked for a substantial ransom for her safe return, as I'm sure my associate, Mr Schade will confirm."

The slim bodyguard shrugged. "I'd have opened at twenty million, maybe accepted ten as a kind of early settlement deal."

Kincaid uncapped the pen, opened the book to the next blank cheque and started filling in the day's date.

"What do you think you're doing?"

He paused. "How much will it take, Ms Fox, to ensure your…discretion in this matter?"

"I've already told you my price," I said roughly. "Give me back Frank's truck—preferably in the same condition it was in before I used it to hit that bloody SUV, and we'll be even."

"Nothing else?"

"I assume, from what you've said, that you're going to make all the evidence out there on the road simply…disappear?"

Kincaid looked to the bodyguard again.

"Oh yeah, already in hand," Schade said. "Clean as my conscience before nightfall."

"Then that will do for me," I said. "All I'm trying to do is get by."

Kincaid sat back slowly, recapped the pen and laid it back on top of the chequebook. "When you say 'get by' I take it you're referring to your current…employment status?"

I gave a short laugh. "Lack of it, you mean?"

"In that case, I'm sure we could offer you something that would suit your…unique skill-set. I want to—"

I shook my head before he could get any further down that particular line of thought.

"I'm sorry," I said quickly. "But I don't do that kind of work anymore."

"Is that so?" He gazed at me. He had blue-green eyes that were focused and intense. "From what I heard about you today, Ms Fox—driving unarmed into the middle of a firefight—you just can't help yourself."

4

MY LACK of current employment status was a situation entirely of my own making. I was the one who handed in my notice, after all.

If only that had been the end of the story.

The circumstances that surround my telling Parker Armstrong to take his job and shove it, are too long and complicated to go into here. Let's just say that things happened while I was over in the Middle East a few months ago that made me view my boss in a somewhat different light.

What I hadn't quite taken into account, however, was the fact that not only did Parker pay my salary, but his family owned the building where I'd been renting my heavily subsidised apartment, and he had rubber-stamped the work permits that allowed me to remain in the States, and my firearms licences. He was also a major player in the relatively tight-knit world of close protection.

All of which were major obstacles to my future career prospects and general wellbeing.

He let me get back to New York and settle in for a few days before he came to see me. It smacked of unseemly haste, but I reckoned I was probably getting special dispensation, even so. Anyone else would have been out on their ear the moment they handed their kit in.

"There's no easy way to say this, Charlie…but I'm gonna have to ask you to vacate the apartment."

It was put baldly enough to make me stare at him, not quite open-mouthed, but damn close to it. We were sitting in the living area, apparently relaxed and friendly. I'd just made him a cup of coffee—the real stuff. He'd asked me, without tension, if I'd changed my mind about remaining with his agency. Equally without tension, I'd told him I had not.

Then he pulled the pin on that little conversational grenade and rolled it across the floor at my feet.

There were plenty of things I could have said at that point. I could have sworn and stamped and yelled at him that this mess was as much his fault as mine. Instead, I took a last calming sip of coffee and put down my empty cup, quietly and carefully, on the side table next to my chair.

"O–K," I said slowly, drawing out the word. "How much notice do I have?"

"By the end of next week would be good."

"The rent's paid monthly," I pointed out.

"And the lease is directly related to your position with the agency, which you relinquished two-and-a-half weeks ago."

I did a quick mental calculation. He was giving me one month to the day. Nobody would be able to accuse Parker of not playing strictly by the rules.

Well, in this case, maybe…

We sat for a moment longer, eyeing each other while the bustle of the city carried on in the street far below us, the rasping exhaust of a motorcycle going up through the gears, the wail of a police siren.

Parker always was a good poker player. I could read nothing in his face now. It was a stern face under hair prematurely greyed and still kept clipped military short. There was a time, when Sean had been out of the picture, that I'd thought there could be something beyond a professional relationship between us. Parker certainly wanted more than I could give. More than would have been good for either of us, in all kinds of ways.

"What about Sean?" I asked.

"As far as I know, he's not coming back, either."

"*As far as you know*? You mean you haven't heard from him since…Bulgaria?"

"Not a word."

If me handing in my notice was bad, Sean leaving was worse. For both of us, probably. Parker had taken Sean on as a partner—his name was over the door. As soon as the Manhattan firm Parker started became Armstrong-Meyer, whatever Sean did had direct consequences for Parker's hard-won reputation.

"I'm sorry it's come to this between the two of you," I said, and meant it.

"Thank you," Parker said, and sounded like he meant that, too.

I had come to the States with Sean Meyer almost as part of a buy-one-get-one-free deal. I'm sure Parker initially took me on only because if he hadn't, he knew he wouldn't get Sean. Since then, I reckon I'd more than proved my worth—earned his professional admiration, even his trust.

Shame he hadn't done the same for me.

Parker drained the last of his coffee and we both rose. Out of habit, he eased the jacket of his dark suit so it wouldn't catch on the Glock he wore behind his right hip, but made no immediate moves towards the door.

I said nothing, just cocked an eyebrow in his direction.

He let his breath out slowly down his nose. "And…I need you to surrender your weapons."

I nodded without speaking. *Of course you do.* Officially, my own SIG, and the back-up Glock in the safe under the bedroom floor, both belonged to the company.

I fetched the weapons and the two boxes of 9mm hollow-point rounds that had been stored with them in the safe—also company property—and presented them to him with the slides locked open and magazines out alongside, very formal and correct.

Still he hesitated.

"What else, Parker?" I kept my tone dry. "It's not as though I have a badge you can demand I hand over as well."

His eyes narrowed a little at that, the only outward sign of emotion he displayed.

"I don't know what you intend to do next, Charlie, but I hope you weren't looking to take a position with another agency?"

"Oh?" A noncommittal response. In truth, I hadn't given it much thought. About time I did—especially as I now needed to find new digs as a matter of some urgency.

Parker cleared his throat. "There's a non-compete clause in your contract. You can't go get a job with anyone else in the same line of business."

"For how long?"

"A year."

I stared at him blankly. "A job with anyone else in New York, you mean?"

"With anyone in the United States."

We both knew I could have argued against the restriction in court—if I had the money or the will to do so—just as we both knew that the resultant bad publicity would make me practically unemployable anyway.

"Well, bloody hell, Parker, you're just the anti-fairy godmother today, aren't you?" I said, finally letting a bitter note creep into my voice.

He turned away, reached the door to the hallway and paused again with it held half open.

"I'm sorry, Charlie," he said then. "But leaving was *your* choice, not mine."

And with that he went out. Behind him, the solid click of the door seemed to take on a far greater significance than it should have done.

You know what they say—as one door closes, another one slams shut in your face.

5

THE RIPPLE of planks on the old wooden bridge leading to the Stephenson farmstead alerted me to the approach of several vehicles. The farmhouse was a sturdy timber-framed building with a covered verandah all round and external shutters on the windows.

I moved to the living room window and looked out, keeping far enough back to be invisible from beyond the glass. The farm was isolated, set in its own woodland. The mailbox was at the end of the driveway on the road, and visitors were not a regular occurrence while I'd been in occupation.

It was the morning after the attempted ambush on Helena Kincaid. Her husband's men had delivered me back, as requested, the previous afternoon. I hadn't expected to hear more from any of them so soon, never mind receive what looked like a state visit.

I went out onto the screened porch at the front of the house and watched the small convoy of vehicles curve around the pond and pull up on the hard standing between the house and the main barn. A couple of top-spec Range Rovers, followed by the old GMC pick-up I'd been driving the day before. That image of an old carthorse came back to me, now trailing behind a pair of fancy thoroughbreds. Still, it looked in remarkably better nick than the last time I'd seen it.

I waited until everyone who was getting out had done so before nudging open the screen door and advancing as far as the top step, keeping my empty hands in view. Three guys from the point vehicle, two from the second car, including the slim bodyguard, Schade, and the guy driving the pick-up. I recognised the latter as my chatty guard from the day before. None of the men had their jackets buttoned up. I guessed that meant they had weapons close at hand, even if nothing was on view at the moment.

When they'd glared into the surrounding trees long enough to make the local bear population do a runner, one of them opened the rear door of the second Range Rover and Eric Kincaid got out.

"Ms Fox," he called across in greeting as I stepped down from the house. "I hope I haven't caught you at an inconvenient time."

"You brought back my transport," I said, nodding to the pick-up. "I'd call that fairly convenient at any time."

I accepted the keys from Chatty and took a good look at the front of the pick-up. As far as I could tell it was better than new —not because it appeared factory-fresh, but precisely because it didn't. The damage had been repaired to match the age and condition of the rest of the vehicle seamlessly. Even the replacement driver's headrest was the same faded velour as the original. The only thing they hadn't replicated were the scratches on the old windscreen from grit caught under the wiper blades. I wasn't going to complain about that.

"Clever." I patted the front bull bar with something akin to affection for the old bus.

"And forensically clean, of course," Schade added. "If the local LEOs check this baby out they won't find a trace of anything—or any*one*—that shouldn't be there."

"I'm glad to hear it," I murmured, although I hoped things wouldn't get to the stage of involving any Law Enforcement Officers, never mind what they might or might not find. "Thank you."

Kincaid inclined his head. "It was the least I could do, Ms Fox."

There was a moment's awkward pause while I waited for him to make his excuses and leave. He didn't, which was instructive in itself. He was not the kind of man with time to fritter on social conventions.

"Can I offer you coffee or something?" I asked without much expectation.

"Coffee would be good, thank you." He smiled, making me blink. He was more overtly good-looking than his wife but, like Helena, the rearrangement of his features transformed them. It also made him seem deceptively harmless.

He followed me into the house with Schade at his heels, leaving the rest of the posse outside.

As soon as we were indoors, Schade slipped into the hallway and disappeared on silent feet. Checking the place out. In his position, I would have done the same.

I was halfway through spooning fresh grounds into the filter machine when he joined us in the kitchen. He smiled at his boss. "She even makes the bed in the morning when there's no-one else here to see it," he reported. "This one's a keeper."

I scowled across at him. "You want to drink coffee or wear it?"

Kincaid took a seat at the Shaker pine table, its original blue stain softened by age. Schade leaned his hip against the counter near the doorway, folded his arms and seemed to fade into the background hum of the room. Much the same way he'd blended into the décor when he stood behind the door at the Kincaids' place. More like a hunter than a protector for the hunted.

As for Kincaid, I could feel his eyes scanning the comfortable country décor of the kitchen, the box near the stove containing a female cat nursing half-a-dozen kittens, and lastly me.

I gestured to the kittens. "One of the reasons Frank and Lorna wanted to have somebody here while they were away."

He didn't speak until I'd finished assembling milk, sugar, and a pair of the slightly deformed mugs that were products of Lorna's abandoned pottery classes—a wise move on her part since it was something for which she clearly showed no aptitude. I thought of the Limoges coffee service and hoped he didn't mind slumming it.

"So, I've been doing a little more of that 'homework' you mentioned," he said at last.

"Oh?"

"Yes indeed." Another pause while he took an experimental sip of coffee, drinking it black and apparently finding it to his liking, wonky mug notwithstanding. "You used to work for Parker Armstrong in New York."

That threw me. "You know him?"

"Only by reputation."

He glanced at Schade, who stirred himself long enough to say, "They reckon he's one of the best."

"He is," I agreed.

"And yet you left a couple of months ago." Kincaid again. Half statement, half question. "Playing mama to a bunch of kitty cats seems a waste of your talents."

I shrugged. "Maybe I needed some time off."

"Well, you're going to get your wish. I understand you signed a contract that precludes you getting another job in the industry for a year."

"It's a standard clause." Yeah, but it still stung that Parker had chosen to enforce it.

"Still not going to be easy for you—financially, at least. And when that year is up, let's just say you're not going to find it a cinch to step back in."

I said nothing, but no doubt my face gave me away.

"Your former boss has put the word out," Schade supplied helpfully. "You're on some kind of blacklist."

I did react to that one, swearing under my breath.

Kincaid acknowledged my response with a twitch of his lips. "What did you do to upset him so much?"

"I resigned."

"And that's not allowed?"

"Let's just say, not under circumstances that Parker would wish to become widely known."

He raised an eyebrow. "That likely?"

"No-one will hear about it from me, if that's what you mean. But since when has that ever stopped anyone being paranoid?"

"He must be," Schade said cheerfully. "He's also whispered in the right ears to get your firearms ticket cancelled."

I sighed into my own coffee. "Yeah, that figures, I suppose."

Another short silence ensued. The mother cat, a tabby with a white bib, stood up, arched herself into a twanging full-body stretch, and climbed out of the box, shedding kittens as she went. She padded over to her food bowl and sat, staring up at me with unblinking yellow eyes.

I put down my coffee, fetched a plastic container out of the fridge and spooned some of the contents into the bowl. She tucked in as if she hadn't seen food in a month.

"What's that?" Kincaid asked.

"Hard-boiled egg and canned tuna. And watch yourself—she'd mug you for it."

He shook his head as if unable to understand how or why people kept pets that didn't run fast or bite hard.

"Frank and Lorna will be back from their trip in a week," he said then. "What else do you have lined up?"

"It's good of you to be so concerned for my welfare, but I'm sure something will turn up."

"Must be a worry, living from week to week, not knowing where the next paycheque is coming from."

"I'll survive. I can always go home." *And it might just come to that.*

"To England, you mean?"

I nodded.

"Not your first choice, I gather."

"That obvious, huh?"

"Accepting an offer from me would make that more of a choice and less of a necessity," he pointed out. "Think of this as a temporary solution to your problems, if you like—just until that non-compete clause expires."

"Ah, but I'm not sure working for you would be any better for my long-term job prospects than going home would be."

His turn to raise an eyebrow and say, "Oh?"

"You've been doing your homework, Mr Kincaid, but I've been doing mine, also. You deal in armaments in the kind of quantities that can start a war—or finish one." I let my gaze drift over Schade. He returned it without blinking. "That means you run with an...interesting crowd, shall we say."

Kincaid said nothing. I gave him a wry smile. "Just because I'm prevented from working in the industry here anymore, doesn't mean people in it aren't still willing to talk to me."

"You wouldn't be working for me," he pointed out. "You'd be working for my wife. She plays no part in any of my...business dealings." His face tightened, and the dangerous undertone was back in full force, like the sudden tidal bore on a river. "It seems there are some people I do battle with in the boardroom who are not prepared to view her as a civilian outside of it."

"It's been my experience that the first casualties in any battle are usually the civilians, Mr Kincaid."

He shifted, restless in a way that made me suddenly wary. "That doesn't make it right—or acceptable, Ms Fox." He flicked his eyes in Schade's direction and the slim bodyguard twitched away from the counter, almost glided further into the room. When he reached the box of kittens by the stove, he stopped and looked down, nothing in his face. "Are you going to tell me that the life of Mrs Kincaid is of less value to you than these cats?"

I'd moved without thinking, not towards Schade, which something told me might be a painful waste of effort, but closing to within a few feet of his boss. I ran through a fast mental checklist of the man's height and weight and point of balance and what he was likely to be carrying and where the weak points might be in his levels of expertise, all in the time it took to blink.

And he did blink, just once. I suppose I've had plenty of practice at overturning other people's expectations of me.

Kincaid turned his head and we stared at each other. His eyes, I noticed for the first time, were a mix of not just pale green and hints of blue, but were flecked with amber and moss, like verdigris on old copper. After a second or so, he looked away. The tension went out of him. Schade bent to fuss the mother cat as she curled around his ankles on her way back to her brood. And I thought cats were supposed to be good judges of character.

The moment passed.

With my eyes still on Schade, I said, "You must have other bodyguards on your payroll?"

Kincaid shook his head. "Not women. No-one at that kind of level—your level." He hesitated. "Helena said you made her feel safe, almost the moment you arrived, and I will do anything to ensure she stays that way."

"I admire your devotion to your wife," I said. "But why me? There are plenty of other qualified women out there. I can probably suggest a dozen names off the top of my head. Good people, working for top-class outfits, who would have the backup and support needed to do the best possible job."

"She wants you."

"Oh, and what she wants, she gets?"

He inclined his head, more at my tone than my question. "Helena is no spoiled princess, Ms Fox. She's a strong-minded, independent woman who has made a decision based on what she witnessed with her own eyes yesterday."

Yesterday. Was it really only yesterday?

"How *is* Illya, by the way?"

"Still with us," Kincaid said. "Which is, I gather, also largely thanks to you."

"Yeah, the doc sends his compliments," Schade put in. "Says he's never seen gunshot wounds plugged by such *unusual means*."

I couldn't suppress a brief smile. "I think you'll find most women are familiar with the absorbent effectiveness of a tampon."

"That's my point," Kincaid said. "First you used your truck as an available weapon, then improvised with whatever was at hand." He stopped, took a breath. "I have some delicate negotiations coming up. I cannot afford to be distracted worrying about Helena while all that's going on. You have the right mind-set— the right skills—to protect her. And for that I am prepared to pay."

I opened my mouth to protest, deny, whatever, but he cut over the top of me, naming a figure that made my head spin.

"Wait a minute." I glanced at Schade for confirmation. "Is he talking…per *month*?"

"Hell, no. I wouldn't get out of bed for that kind of money per month. He's talking per week."

Holy shit…

I'd thought Parker Armstrong paid well, but it was practically a subsistence allowance compared to what Eric Kincaid was offering.

I went very still, mind racing. If Parker really had blacklisted me, then it was either this or…?

Or nothing.

I held out my hand.

"OK, Mr Kincaid. Consider me hired."

He reached to clasp my hand in his own and there might have been just a sliver of disappointment in his face. But, like an eel in shallow waters, it was gone too fast to tell.

"Just like that?" he queried.

"Yeah. Just like that."

I agreed to stop by his place to tie up the paperwork as soon as Frank and Lorna were back. He didn't try to push me to start sooner, accepting that I'd given them my word, and that was worth more than any amount of monetary incentive.

After he and Schade had gone, I moved through to the living room to watch the pair of Range Rovers rumble back across the planked bridge. As they picked up speed where the driveway disappeared into the trees, I switched on the burner phone I'd been given for just this eventuality. When it had gone through its start-up routine, I dialled a memorised number. The line rang out twice before being picked up. Nobody spoke at the other end.

"It's me," I said. "Tell him I'm in."

6

SIX WEEKS after Parker Armstrong came to the apartment and gave me notice to quit, I found myself working security at a BDSM nightclub in the Meatpacking District, not far from where the old Pastis restaurant used to stand—a New York landmark, long since defunct.

It wouldn't have been my first choice of job—or my second or third choice, come to that—but living in Manhattan was not cheap at the best of times. When you're an unemployed and therefore barely legal alien, that just complicates things. I'd managed to cadge temporary accommodation from a friend-of-a-friend in Washington Heights while they were working on a play down in Atlanta. But the run had ended early and the friend's friend was coming home at the weekend, so that left me looking for yet another place to stay.

Still, at least now I had work. The pay wasn't good—not compared to what I had been earning with Parker—and the hours were terrible, but it was a job, with a paycheque, and that would have to do. Besides, this wasn't the first time I'd worked club doors. As I recall, I hadn't liked it any better then, either.

It was a Saturday night and the place was heaving with bodies writhing to the amped-up beat of music so loud it practi-cally qualified as an offensive weapon. At least I didn't have to get any closer to it than the main entrance, complete with waiting line and velvet rope stretched between chrome posts.

The smell of sweat laced with alcohol and pheromones was enough to fell a bull elephant. It billowed up the narrow stairwell and out into the street around us.

My job was to pat down the girls if we were suspicious they might be trying to bring anything into the place besides drinking-age ID and a credit card with a lot of headroom on it. This being the kind of club it was, though, most of the clientele were likely to complain only if you *weren't* rough enough doing the body search. I swear, if one more half-cut, giggling twenty-something begged me to hurt her, I was probably going to do exactly that—in far more inventive and permanently disabling ways than she had in mind.

The club shut down at four in the morning. Without anything notable to report to the security chief, I was soon shrugging into my jacket and saying my farewells to the other door staff. At least the guys treated me as an equal without making me prove it by breaking any of them.

It had started to rain about midnight. Now it settled in as a steady downpour, the bumps and hollows in the sidewalk filling rapidly into ankle-deep traps for the unwary. A lot of the Meatpacking District still boasted the old cobblestone streets. Where asphalt had been laid over the top, the blocks were intermittently visible as the surface cracked away. I reckoned the local authority claimed leaving them on show constituted some kind of Historic Monument and were glad of the excuse to cut back on road repairs.

There are times when I like walking in the rain, but 4 a.m., after an eleven-hour shift—most of it on my feet—was not one of those times. Still, it was only two blocks to the nearest subway station where I could pick up an Uptown A-train. New York, as the song claimed, really was the city that never slept—at least so far as the Metro Transit Authority was concerned.

Unfortunately, this meant they had to carry out maintenance work on the system 24/7 as well. They'd been digging up part of the track north of 168th for weeks. I was just calculating if the walk at the far end would be longer or shorter if I hopped across onto the 1-line at Columbus Circle, when my spidey-sense tapped me on the shoulder.

You are not alone.

Not the first time I've got this message from some primitive, swamp-dwelling part of my psyche but I found it impossible to ignore, even if I wanted to.

I kept walking without a moment's hesitation in my stride, aware that the air around me was suddenly sharper, the darkness more vivid. From falling in solid curtains of water, the rain separated into individuate droplets, through which the city was all the more clear.

I didn't carry a bag, so had nothing to tangle me up or slow me down, and no strap to be grabbed by. I always wore gloves to avoid the temptation to stuff my hands into my pockets. The warmest ones I owned were my motorcycle gloves, with the moulded carbon fibre section across the back of the knuckles. I was wearing them now—protection for my hands, and not just from the cold.

I headed north on 9th Avenue, which was one-way. Behind me on the far side of the street, keeping pace, was a dark Chevy Suburban. The way the overhead light was hitting the glass, I couldn't tell how many were inside and I had no real desire to find out.

The most straightforward route to the subway would have been straight up to 14th and then one block east. Instead, I turned right onto W 13th. That was one-way, also, but the traffic flow was east to west and the Suburban couldn't legally follow.

I lengthened my stride a little, keeping the cadence the same so it was harder to tell that I'd begun to cover more ground. As the Suburban drew level with the cross-street, I turned slightly and stepped off the kerb, checking both ways as my mother had taught me.

That brief glance was enough to tell me the Suburban had stopped. Doors opened.

I abandoned all pretence and ran.

Behind me, I heard the screech of tyres spinning up on wet asphalt as the Suburban took off, then feet pounding through the rain in pursuit. It was hard to hear much else beyond the hammer of blood in my ears.

I hoped for shouts identifying my pursuers as law enforcement—hell, identifying them as anything. Men only want to remain anonymous when they're doing something they don't want to come back and bite them in the arse later. Something they might have to one day stand up in court and defend or deny.

I dived left on the next cross-street, purely because corners allowed for more uncertainty in a pursuer. Unless they want to risk running into an ambush, they have to slow down. Besides, I didn't want to give them a straight shot at my unprotected back. It wasn't until I'd made the decision that I realised my mistake.

I was now on Hudson—another one-way street, but this time with the traffic-flow heading south only, towards me. Sure enough, a moment or so later I saw the Suburban come barrelling in from the W 14th end, rolling hard in the turn and almost drifting sideways through standing water.

I stopped. No point in running into trouble that could flatten me without even putting a dent in the paintwork.

I turned. Two men were bearing down on me. Big men in dark clothing, fists pumping as they thundered on. The one on point faltered slightly when he saw I was no longer running away.

Because now I was running full-pelt *towards* them instead.

I hit the first guy hard in the throat, allowing his weight and forward momentum to do most of the damage and the carbon fibre reinforcement in my gloves to do the rest. His legs were still carrying him forwards even as his upper body snapped to the rear.

He landed flat on his back with enough force to blast the air from his lungs—even if I hadn't half-paralysed his larynx first. He stayed down, clutching his throat and gasping.

The second guy was just far enough back to take in what happened. He braked hard, feet slithering on the slick sidewalk, and spun into a roundhouse kick that would have taken my head off at the shoulders if it had connected.

It didn't.

I learned a long time ago that fancy high kicks may look very impressive, but trying to use them in a street fight is a foolish manoeuvre. Anticipating the arc of movement, I stepped in, grabbed the guy's leg and clamped it tight against the side of my body.

Then I punched him in the fleshy vee under his ribcage, putting my weight behind the blow and rotating my fist as it landed. I felt the power of it jar all the way up my arm into my shoulder.

I shoved him backwards and let go. He dropped faster than the first guy. Neither of them was getting up in a hurry.

I began to turn, but by this time the Suburban had skidded to a halt alongside us. The passenger window was down and I saw the clear outline of a semiautomatic pistol in the driver's right hand, pointing firmly in my direction.

You have to know when to fight and when to yield. I dropped out of flight mode and half-heartedly raised my hands. I was suddenly aware of the rainwater sliding down my face and dripping from my chin. My hair was flattened to my scalp and my lungs were burning.

The Suburban's limo-black rear window buzzed down. The interior courtesy light was on, illuminating the face of the man who sat inside. I recognised him immediately. After our last encounter, I had hoped we'd never meet again. But I always knew that one day we would.

"Ah, Ms Fox," Conrad Epps said, as though he'd just bumped into me at the park rather than running me to ground with his human attack dogs. "Please, get in. I believe we may be of mutual benefit to each other…"

7

IT HAD BEEN a while since I last set eyes on Conrad Epps. I never quite pinned down exactly which shady part of the government he worked for, except that it was most likely one of the alphabet agencies—CIA, NSA, DIA—something connected to Homeland Security. In any event, it was an organisation with a long arm and deep pockets.

He still looked exactly the same as he had at our last meeting, in California, what seemed like a lifetime ago. Straight-backed in the ex-military mould, with steel-grey hair cropped so close to his head it looked like he'd been flocked. I'd never noticed the colour of his eyes, only the coldness in them.

It was impossible to see the colour of them now, as I climbed into the back of the Suburban. The overhead cabin light threw his deep-set eye sockets into shadow.

"You may shut the door behind you," Epps said mildly, his voice a resonant rumble. I glanced back at the two men still squirming on the wet sidewalk behind me. He added, "They won't be joining us."

I did as I was ordered and sank back in the leather upholstery, pushing sodden hair out of my eyes with hands that were remarkably steady, all things considered. The driver took off far more sedately than he'd arrived, leaving his fallen comrades behind without a murmur. If he'd worked for Epps long, I guessed he'd be used to such behaviour.

"The price of failure?" I asked. "That's a little harsh, don't you think?"

Epps shrugged. "Think of it as a consequences-based training method."

We sat in silence while the driver took the next two right turns. I assumed he was in a one-block holding pattern until he turned left on W 14th and began cruising slowly in the direction of the High Line. I leaned forwards and tapped the man on his shoulder. To his credit, he barely flinched.

"Washington Heights, please," I said cheerfully. "Since Mr Epps knows where I work, no doubt he also knows where I live, so you'll have the address."

"Does this *look* like a cab to you?" Epps demanded.

"You have something you want to discuss with me—something that's so important it couldn't wait until a more sociable hour. If you want me to hear you out, I think a ride home is the very least you can offer in return, don't you?"

Epps considered for a moment, caught the driver's eye in the rear-view mirror and gave him a curt nod. I spared a brief thought for his two heavies, abandoned in the rain. Tough. Especially the one who'd launched the abortive roundhouse kick right at my head. A long—I hoped—as well as soggy and uncomfortable train ride home was no more than they deserved.

Epps seemed in no hurry to start the ball rolling, and I didn't try to push him. The longer he took, the further up Manhattan Island we were likely to get before I told him what he could do with his proposition. It would probably involve a procedure he hadn't contemplated since his last prostate examination.

"I know you have no intention of giving due consideration to what I have to say," Epps said at last. So, the man had added mindreading to his list of accomplishments. "But I trust you'll do me the courtesy of evaluating all the implications before you make a decision you might regret."

"I have not forgotten our…history," I said, maintaining as much neutrality as I could manage. Epps had played a significant part in my personal and professional life on two previous occasions. Neither had ended well. Whatever debt to him I might have racked up in our first encounter had been well and truly cancelled out by events of the second. I didn't feel I owed him anything, but having the positions reversed—particularly the way things stood at the moment—might not be all bad.

I should have known that a man like Epps was not going to be manoeuvred into owing anybody favours.

"I never thought I'd see you employed as a bouncer in a sex club," he said then.

I frowned at the apparent change of tack.

"It's a BDSM club—you must be familiar with those. And I think you'll find I *suggest and persuade*. I don't bounce. I leave that to the heavy mob." *Much as you do yourself.*

"Nevertheless, it is not the professional occupation under which you applied for your permanent residency here in the United States." He let that one sink in for a moment. "Is it?"

Oh shit. So that's *how it's going to be…*

I sighed. "OK, let me save you a little time here and cut to the chase, shall I?" We were heading north on 12th Ave now, six lanes of sparse traffic with industrial buildings on one side and, on the other, not much between us and the river. We passed under the overhead sign for the Lincoln Tunnel exit.

"By all means."

"The US Customs and Immigration Service and border patrol and God knows what other agencies, now fall under the purview of the Department of Homeland Security, which I'm assuming is where this part of the conversation is going, yes?"

"You're very astute," he agreed.

"So, just as a wild guess, if I don't agree to do whatever it is you want me to do, you'll have me deported."

"Succinctly put."

"And?" I prompted.

"And correct in almost every detail."

"So, what *is* this job that's so nasty you'd prefer to blackmail a freelancer into doing it, rather than simply assign one of your own people?"

"There are dangers inherent in all kinds of security work, as you are well aware. In this case, the problem we have is more one of…information integrity, one might say."

"Meaning?"

"We have a deep-cover agent in place inside an arms dealing operation that has ties to organised crime on an international scale."

"Aren't your people more concerned with domestic terrorism?"

"When they are capable of arming factions or even govern-ments who may harbour hostile intent toward the United States, then it *becomes* my concern."

I'd rarely heard him sound so focused, so intense. There had always been a latent violence to Epps. I'd once thought of him as a more soulless version of Parker. After recent events, however, I was struggling to differentiate between the two of them.

"O–K," I said slowly. "What is it about this undercover agent that you think I might be able to help you with?"

The driver took the left sweep for the 9A. As we climbed onto Henry Hudson Parkway, north towards the Bronx, six lanes became eight. There wasn't much opportunity for him to pull over and tell me to walk. I doubted even Epps was prepared to toss me from a moving car, although I wouldn't have put money on it.

Epps let out a long breath, the most unsettled I'd seen him. "This agent has been in so deep, for so long, that we feel we can no longer entirely trust their…judgement."

"So pull them out and can the operation."

"Things have reached a delicate stage. There's a complex transaction in the offing that may have serious ongoing repercus-sions for national security. Our agent—if he or she can be trusted —is in a position to ensure the outcome is…favourable."

"I'm sorry, I don't speak spook. Could I have that again in English?"

Epps glared. "There is a limit to how much I am permitted to tell you."

"Just as there's a limit to how much consideration I can give your…offer." I paused, watching the mask of his face as it cooled and hardened. A peace offering seemed sensible at this point. I sighed, forced a placatory note into my voice. "Even the basics would do."

He glanced at me, something cynical in his eyes. Oh yeah, he knew exactly what I was doing.

"This organisation—" he began.

"Who are?"

The scowl was back. "You're going to have to give me a lot more assurance before I can read you in further than that."

I said nothing and waved him on. We'd picked up signs for the Boat Basin at 79th Street, moving through Riverside Park. *Probably about halfway home.*

"This organisation," he repeated, pausing pointedly for a beat in case I was foolish enough to interrupt him again, "has, in the past, supplied weapons to the Syrian government, who are using them, with the support of the Russians, against sections of their own population opposed to the existing regime."

"I'll stick my neck out and suppose that you disapprove?"

"Of the use of arms against the people, or of the regime itself?"

"Either," I said, "Or both."

"Both." Something about the way he snapped out the single terse word was illuminating. I'd never suspected Conrad Epps might feel strongly about anything that didn't apply to the safety and security of his home country. Look up 'patriot' in the dictionary and I'd bet the entry had his picture underneath, that he pledged allegiance to the flag every morning and slept in his medals every night.

But this…?

"What is your undercover agent *supposed* to do—if they're still following the game plan, that is?" I asked, genuinely curious now. "Halt supply to the regime? Or *start* supplying the rebels?"

"We are *not* about to reignite the Cold War by proxy by weaponising the opponents of an internationally recognised government," Epps bit out. And while his tone was starchy, I'd learned that when he sounded like he'd swallowed the official manual, that was when he was burying things deepest.

"So you're trying to halt the supply."

He inclined his head in agreement. "That objective has already been attained."

I shrugged. "Then…where's your problem?"

He sat without fidgeting in the rear seat, eyes on mine never wavering. "We've heard whispers that another shipment is being prepared, and that this time it involves chemical weapons."

"What kind of chemical weapons?"

Epps shook his head and for once I didn't get the feeling he was giving me the brush off. His frustration was too genuine for that.

"We don't know, and we've had no confirmation from our agent. Indeed, they are ignoring our requests for clarification on this matter."

"And you think, therefore, that they've been turned?"

He nodded, a single, stiff jerk of his head, and raised one hand, briefly rubbing his thumb across the tips of his fingers. "These deals are worth millions of dollars. Anyone could be…tempted."

"What are the consequences?"

"It would be disastrous for peace and stability right across the Middle East region and Europe."

Don't overstate it, Epps, whatever you do.

"And what is it you want from me?"

"I need to insert another operative—one who is completely unknown to our agent—to keep a watching brief on the situation from the inside."

"What else?"

"If, indeed, it seems that dealings have been resumed and chemical weapons—of whatever type—are about to be delivered —then I need to know about it in as much detail as possible."

"And?"

"That is all I need from you."

I shook my head. "Oh, come on. Are you really trying to tell me that, with the whole of the security services to draw from, you've come up empty and have to coerce some displaced Brit to do your dirty work for you?"

"This agent has worked on a number of different inter-agency operations in the past. They led courses at Langley, Quantico,

Washington. If we put in another agent from almost anywhere, there's a chance of him—or her—being made."

I picked up on the unconscious emphasis on gender and was silent for a moment. Then I said, "I seem to remember you once telling me you didn't approve of using female operatives for undercover work. That we weren't temperamentally suited for it."

"Times change."

"Don't they just," I muttered.

And just when I thought he'd finally dragged his dinosaur mind-set kicking and screaming into the twentieth century—if not quite the twenty-first—he went on, "The timeframe necessitates moving quickly. It would be difficult to put in place a legend for anyone else that would stand up to extensive…pressure testing. Not in the time we have available."

"So, what were you planning to do for me by way of a cover story?"

"Nothing is required. This is why we're having this conversation right now. Your history with Armstrong-Meyer is already out there and has the advantage of being one hundred percent genuine, as far as anyone is aware."

I glanced at him. "What's *that* supposed to mean?"

"It means, Ms Fox, that while there is no suggestion that you jumped ship before you were thrown overboard, as it were, there's enough uncertainty surrounding your departure from that agency to allow room for manoeuvre."

"Thanks, I think," I muttered. "*If* I agree to do this—and it is only an 'if' at this stage—how will it work? How do you intend to get me in?"

"We have covert surveillance in place on the organisation. I'm confident there will be no difficulty in creating an opening."

The driver took the tightening turn for the W 178th Street exit and Yeshiva University and we plunged into the cluttered shadows beneath one of the flyovers, all industrial steelwork pockmarked with rivets. He was smooth through the bends, progressive with brake and accelerator. No doubt he was also deaf, dumb, and blind when his boss required him to be.

"*If* I get inside and *if* they accept me at face value, what exactly do you expect me to do?"

"Watch and report. No more than that."

"One last thing—who is this agent?"

"That's strictly need-to-know," Epps said. "And you don't."

I stared, smarting as much from the dismissive tone as the implication. "How the hell can I be expected to tell if anyone has gone native if you won't tell me who it is so I can distinguish your agent from the genuine natives?" I demanded. "That's absurd."

"Don't get your panties in a wad, Ms Fox. Withholding that information is a purely practical, operational decision."

In other words, what you don't know can't be tortured out of you.

He didn't say the words out loud. Then again, he didn't need to.

8

"IF YOU'LL PARDON me for saying so, dear, you don't look like much, but I guess in your line of work that's a blessing."

The speaker had just been introduced as Kincaid's personal assistant, Mo Heedles, and if there was a certain irony to her statement, she didn't appear to be aware of it. Because, to be honest, *she* didn't look like much, either.

The word that sprang to mind when I looked at Mo was... brown. Dark brown hair, neatly styled into a single-length bob level with her pale jawline, brown suit, dark leather slip-on shoes. Even her jewellery—a ring on her right hand and a pendant on a slim chain around her neck—was decorated with pale brown amber. The only thing about her I could see that wasn't brown were the frames of her Wayfarer-style spectacles. They were grey.

She had an aged-yet-ageless look that meant she could have been anywhere between a haggard fifty and a youthful seventy-five, and was almost undoubtedly the smartest person in the room. I bet both Eric and Helena Kincaid loved her—for very different reasons.

As for her opinion of me, she clearly had yet to be convinced.

"A little convenient, wasn't it?" she said. "That you just-so-happened to be driving along that particular road, at that particular time?"

"You think so?" I shrugged. "I've been out here looking after Frank and Lorna's place for a month. It's the same road I took whenever I needed to go into town for anything. I'm not sure there *is* another route."

She eyed me shrewdly and didn't respond.

In truth, I'd worried about that aspect of the whole operation myself. The insertion point was always going to be the weakest spot. It relied entirely on apparent coincidence rather than the coded tip-off I'd been waiting three weeks to receive. Even so, I'd had no concept of the situation I'd be walking into—or driving into, in this case.

If the men who'd ambushed Helena Kincaid were part of some covert government team at Epps's disposal, I didn't want to think of the consequences I might face for having killed one of them and seriously injured two more. Was the threat of chemical weapons falling into the hands of the Syrians really worth that?

Taking a life was bad enough but, under fire, it had been a clear-cut choice of him or me. I remembered again the way those rounds had ripped into the headrest of my seat. There was making it look good, and then there was playing for keeps. The guy I'd run down with the pick-up had not been fooling around.

I'd been expecting questions about that at some point, but not from such an unlikely source. Kincaid's bodyguard, Schade, struck me as a far more likely candidate for giving me the third degree.

Kincaid sent him over with a car on the morning after Frank and Lorna Stephenson returned from Europe, without me having to make contact. Either he knew the Stephensons' schedule or he'd been keeping an eye on me.

I'd seen Kincaid—with Schade in tow, of course—just once in the intervening period, to sign contracts of both employment and confidentiality. The former was in standard legalese almost unintelligible to normal humans. The latter was brief to the point of being lip service only. When I queried this, it was Schade who answered for him: "Well, all it really needs to say is that if you shoot your mouth off about any of Mr Kincaid's affairs, I'll be paying you a visit."

I eyed him for a moment, then switched my gaze back to Kincaid himself. "And how's that working out so far?"

His smile answered for him.

Now, though, as I faced Schade and the formidable Mrs Heedles in her office, I wasn't sure which of them might be scarier.

"OK, children, time for you to be someplace else. Go get her geared up, Mr Schade, and stop disrupting my schedule." She flapped her hands at him. "Go on—and get your butt off of my paperwork. Shoo."

Schade grinned at her, uncoiled himself from the edge of her desk and rose. He was maybe an inch or so taller than me, and then only because he was wearing heavy duty boots with Cuban heels.

"After you," he said.

"I don't know the way, so…after you." I smiled. "I insist."

"Oh, just go do your job, the pair of you. She's hardly going to shoot you in the back on her first day, Mr Schade. She doesn't know you well enough yet to hate you that much."

"And she doesn't have a gun."

"Exactly. Maybe you should take care of that," she said pointedly. "And then maybe *she'll* take care of *you*."

He was still laughing as he led me out of the office and to the doors of an elevator just along the hallway. We were in the opposite wing of the house from the private sitting room where I'd first met Eric Kincaid and been formally introduced to Helena. The décor was more restrained here, bland and anonymous like an office block or a hotel.

"So, is Shade your real name?" I asked.

"'Course. Only, my family's from Germany, so you spell it with an S-C-H."

The elevator dinged and the doors opened.

"Ah, as in Schubert?"

He shrugged as we stepped inside. "Close enough, although he was Austrian. More like Robert Schumann."

I flicked him a sideways glance. "There are no bonus points for showing off."

"Oh, there are always points for showing off." The elevator

doors slid shut behind us. The smile was gone. He was all business. "OK, let's talk weapons. You got any preference?"

I shrugged. "I like the SIG P226, if you have one, but as long as it goes bang when I press the trigger, I'm not too fussy."

"I believe we may be able to accommodate you on that."

The doors slid open again. We'd gone one floor down, or maybe two. There was no lurching start/stop and no indicator lights. We were in another corridor, this one even more utilitarian than the last. Bare walls in institutional cream with scuff marks nobody had bothered to paint over.

Schade stretched a set of keys from his pocket on a retractable chain and unlocked a reinforced door. When he pushed it open, the smell of gun oil and powder filled my nostrils.

Inside, the room was lined with lit gun racks displaying assault rifles, handguns, machine pistols and shotguns. A scarred steel workbench stood along the back wall, a vice clamped to one end and shelves of tools above. Schade moved over to the bench, started opening drawers and pulling out gun cases.

"OK, here's your basic P226. Here's one with a DAK trigger, if you want to try that."

I glanced at the SIG with the double-action-only Kellerman trigger, but reached for the standard double-action/single-action weapon instead. "I'll stick to something I know I can shoot."

He nodded again, as if I'd passed some kind of test. "Okey-dokey. We prefer to standardise with 9mm—you're more likely to get a reload when you need it—although we got 'em in .40 and .357 if you can't live without?"

"Interesting choice of words," I said. "No, I'm happy with 9mm."

"Cool. There you go, then. All yours. Just do me a favour and don't name it."

"Name it?"

"Some of the guys like to name their guns. It gets kinda personal." He put up a hand to stop me cutting in. "But if that's your thing, I won't ask."

"Really?" I raised an eyebrow. "Well, some guys like to name their dicks as well, and I definitely don't ask about that."

"Yeah, there are some clubs you are just never gonna be allowed to join, huh?"

I picked up the SIG, worked the action, checked the chamber and dry fired it. It was smooth, predictable and familiar. Both weapons had a barrel threaded ready to take a suppressor, which was an interesting modification for Kincaid's armoury to offer right from the off. It made me wonder exactly what my role as Helena Kincaid's latest bodyguard might entail.

Schade put down two fifteen-round magazines and a Kramer belt-scabbard holster.

"You cool with the Kramer rig? Designed for chicks to keep the grip at low-waist level, rather than riding so high it interferes with your"—he gestured to my chest with palms facing upwards, fingers cupped, before coming out with—"person-alities."

The holster looked already worn in, which was a good thing. Brand new, the leather tends to be so stiff I would have needed both hands and a chisel to pry the gun from it.

"Yeah, I'm cool," I said, straight-faced. "And just for the record, I don't name my ah, *personalities*, either."

"Good to know. Now we move on to the fun stuff. How are you with tactical shotguns?"

"It's a blunt-force instrument. I'll take whatever you've got handy."

"You're gonna love the Mossberg 500. Nine-shot pump for when things get real up-close and personal."

"Things were fairly up-close and personal back there on the road last week," I said as Schade lifted the Mossberg out of the rack. "Why didn't Helena's driver and Illya have a couple of those?"

I'd asked him about Illya's ongoing condition on the way over to the Kincaids' place. "Stable" was the most he would say and I didn't push him for more.

"They did," Schade said shortly. "Had 'em in the trunk. May as well have left 'em at home. You can't access a weapon when you need it...well, it's like Mark Twain said: 'The man who doesn't read has no advantage over the man who cannot.'"

"Profound."

"For Ellis—the driver—it turned out to be just that, huh?"

He moved over to the assault weapons, which I noted were Colt M4 carbines—as used by the men who'd ambushed Helena Kincaid.

"We tend to stick with the M4 as a kind of everyday item, across the board," Schade said. "Reliable, durable, ammo and clips are interchangeable, and everybody knows where they are. Plus, it cuts down on showboating. And trust me, around here that *is* a plus."

"My weapon's bigger than your weapon, you mean?"

"Oh yeah."

He took one down, dropped the empty magazine out and handed the carbine over. I checked the chamber was empty anyway, just out of habit, and gave the weapon a cursory inspection. One thing struck me immediately.

"The men who ambushed Mrs Kincaid's Lincoln were using the M4A1 full-auto model," I said, remembering the way I'd clicked the fire selector onto what I thought was three-round burst. Then I'd aimed for the guy's lower legs and got more than I bargained for. "And they were using thirty-round magazines."

"So?"

"So, where did they get them? You can't legally buy that kind of weapon for civilian use, even in this country."

The look Schade gave me was calculating. What I'd said clearly was not news to him, but the fact I'd pointed it out had either raised flags or won me brownie points. With him, it was hard to tell.

"We ran the serial numbers on the weapons they left at the scene—part of a batch that were apparently shipped out to 'Stan. As far as US Army records show, they're still there," he said after a moment. "Looks like some fat quartermaster has gotten himself an equally fat retirement fund sitting in an offshore account somewhere."

"Any leads yet on who they were? Was it a kidnap attempt or a kill?" *Either way, they botched it.*

"Those are questions for Kincaid." He nodded to the SIG and the waistband holster. "Soon as you're dressed, I'll take you up there and you can ask him yourself."

9

LESS THAN TEN MINUTES LATER, I was sitting in a steel-framed leather chair on one side of the desk in Eric Kincaid's inner sanctum. The room was huge and the furniture on a scale to suit. Artwork that displayed the wealth of its owner by the sheer amount of wall space it commanded, a ceiling twenty-odd feet up with chandeliers dangling from it. You could have played full-size billiards on the surface of the desk and still had enough room left over for a cocktail bar and a finger buffet.

There were four large flatscreen TVs mounted flush to the wall opposite where I sat. They were tuned to various news channels with the sound off and subtitles on. The main stories centred round a European summit, a suicide bomber in Kabul, and the increasing humanitarian crisis in Yemen, cycling round and round in never-ending, depressing circles.

Kincaid sat in a high-backed black leather swivel chair behind the desk. The chair must have been designed with a Bond villain in mind. All he needed was a fluffy white cat and a wardrobe of grey Chairman Mao suits. To my surprise, he sat with his back to the window, which I assumed was some kind of anti-ballistic glass. It certainly had a film layer on it that probably helped shield against eavesdropping.

"So, do you have any intel on who those guys were?" I asked, glancing from Kincaid to Schade, who sat opposite. His seat was identical to mine, his stance more laid back.

"You're asking the wrong question—or maybe the right question but in the wrong order."

I had a feeling I knew what I should have asked first, but I wasn't willing to reveal anything by admitting that so I played the game.

"OK, what *should* that question have been?"

Kincaid eyed me for a moment as if still expecting me to come up with the correct answer. He had a very direct gaze. Your first impression was of a total lack of guile. Followed shortly afterwards by the realisation you had absolutely no idea what was going on inside the man's head.

He leaned back in the chair and rotated it gently from side to side a little. "The 'who' is not as important as the 'how'." He spoke to a point over both of our heads, more to himself than either Schade or me. "Whoever they were, how did they know exactly where Helena would be?"

I frowned, aware of a rushing noise inside my head as my adrenaline surged. This was not the first time I'd gone undercover, in one form or another, but nevertheless it was not something I'd been trained for. Not something, perhaps, for which I was particularly well suited. *Ah, well...*

"We're agreed this was a kidnap attempt rather than a kill?" Schade said, part question, part statement. I watched a muscle tense in Kincaid's jawline.

"If they'd wanted to...kill my wife, one guy in the treeline with an RPG would have got the job done a hell of a lot more easily," he agreed finally.

"But six guys in two vehicles is nothing like enough for a foolproof abduction plan," I said. "Not against two professionals. They should have known it would turn into a gunfight at the OK Corral."

"If they weren't trying to kill her, and they weren't seriously trying to snatch her, what the hell *were* they trying to do?"

"Maybe it was a warning," I suggested.

"Yeah, but who from?"

"We're back to the 'who' again. How difficult would it be for someone to find out Mrs Kincaid's schedule?"

Kincaid's expression tightened. "Harder yesterday than it was last week."

"Oh yeah," Schade agreed. "Her new cell is all decked out with the latest end-to-end encryption, anti-surveillance alerts, location tracking countermeasures—"

"But is it hack-proof?" Kincaid interrupted.

Schade eyed him for a moment, then said gently. "You know as well as I do, nothing ever is, dude. All I can say is, it's more hack-*resistant* than anything out there. 'Bout the only things that baby doesn't do is eject chaff and return fire."

Their eyes locked, something fierce in Kincaid's. Something relaxed as a sunbathing cobra in Schade's. I wouldn't have liked to step on either.

I cleared my throat, bringing their attention round slowly. "If it's not an awkward question, why no such precautions until now?"

Kincaid sighed. "You may think I work in a dirty business, Fox, but that's what it is—a business. So, a couple of years ago, we reached an understanding—"

"Wait. Who's 'we'?"

"Most of the major players in the arms dealing industry. Almost all of them, as a matter of fact. We held a kind of summit over in Europe and came to an agreement on non-combatants. You got a problem with me, you bring it to my door, with whatever firepower you want to use to make that problem known. But my family? Those closest to me? They're off-limits. And for me, with my competition? Same rules apply."

Had Epps known about this apparent multilateral accord before he played whatever part he had in the hijack of Helena Kincaid's Lincoln?

"All off-limits?" I murmured, just to give myself more time to think. Much as it went against my instincts as far as Epps was concerned, I couldn't rule out that he *hadn't* known. I tried to remember who had said that when it came to government agencies, cock-up was always a more likely scenario than conspiracy.

Schade was slouched sideways in his chair. I'd already begun to realise that 'rumpled' was a state of mind for this guy. "Yeah," he said now. "Wives, girlfriends, kids, racehorses…Nobody lays a finger on any of them. Think of it as a kind of reciprocity."

"I take it there are no women in actual positions of power themselves in this game, then?"

Schade gave a brief chuckle. "Oh yeah, the chicks have *all* the power. They're the ones with the money, but they don't have to keep looking over their shoulder the whole time. What's not to like?"

"Only, maybe now they *do* have to look over their shoulder," Kincaid said, no humour in his voice or face, but no sign Schade's flippant attitude irritated him, either. "If someone has violated this agreement, it could start a war."

"And the one group of people you do *not* want to start a war with," Schade put in, looking at me over his glasses, "are arms dealers."

10

It was my old friend Chatty—the silent man who'd stood guard after the ambush—who showed me to the quarters I'd be using. I was expecting a room in the staff wing. What I got was an entire suite next door to the Kincaids' own.

All the lights were on when we walked in, as in a hotel. I almost expected to see a welcome message playing on the huge flatscreen TV that hung above the fireplace. Chatty handed over a set of labelled keys and departed without a word. As the door latched behind him, I dumped my small backpack on the floor in the hallway and looked around.

The main area was set out as a living space with a cream leather corner sofa facing the TV. The fire turned out to be a real-flame gas fire—instant atmosphere operated by remote control. Over to one side was a kitchenette with microwave and coffee maker. There was even a kettle that still had part of the packaging attached. Somebody knew that Brits tended to drink their tea hot rather than iced, and made sure to accommodate me. I wondered who had gone to the trouble.

In the far corner was a study area with desk and chair. Not quite on a par with Eric Kincaid's cavernous domain, but more than adequate for my needs.

I poked my nose into the other rooms. The bedroom sported a bed that would have lodged Snow White and all seven dwarves with mattress to spare. One wall was lined with built-in wardrobes and drawers I'd never own enough clothes to fill, although when I slid back the centre doors they revealed another TV set, only slightly smaller than the one in the living room, taking up part of the space. There was a heavy-duty safe at one end of the wardrobe, too, tall enough to take the shotgun and M4 that Schade had equipped me with, plus a smaller safe for personal items. Both were bolted to the sub floor.

Thick curtains completely covered the wall opposite. When I cracked them open, I found the floor-to-ceiling glass looked out over a view of horses grazing in lush, shady paddocks surrounded by immaculate white post-and-rail fencing.

I let the curtain drop on this rural idyll and stuck my head into the bathroom. It was all marble and chrome, with a rain head in the shower cubicle and a bath that was actually deep enough to soak in.

When I was done, I went around the room again, looking underneath and behind things. If there were hidden mics or cameras, they'd been placed by someone better at concealing such things than I was at finding them. Even so, I didn't intend to have any conversations anywhere inside the house that I didn't want the Kincaids or Schade—especially Schade—to overhear.

And that was a pity. Because after the revelations of the morning I really *needed* to speak to Conrad Epps. Either he was playing a far more dangerous game than he'd prepared me for, or he had only half an idea of what was going on.

Either one of which did not bode well for my short-term health or long-term survival.

I found Helena Kincaid in one of the horse barns adjacent to the main house, brushing down a beautiful palomino mare.

She was wearing full chaps over jeans, and a stylish looking western shirt. The style of clothing matched the horse. Helena's fair hair was pulled back into a single plait at the nape of her neck, and she wore no jewellery or make-up. Everything about her, from her appearance to her movements, suggested brisk competence.

If she'd lost her composure in the back of the Lincoln, out there on the road, she had regained it now in spades.

She was grooming the horse with a body brush. Every few strokes she scraped the brush against a metal curry comb in her other hand to clean it. She worked in utter concentration, her eyes fixed on the task. It didn't take a genius to work out that she was doing so to avoid having to meet my gaze.

"I didn't thank you," she said, not pausing in her labours. "For coming to my aid. Please don't think I'm ungrateful, because I'm not."

I hear a "but..."

I leaned on the door frame, watching her work. The stable was roomy, one of maybe a dozen laid out on either side of a central walkway that was wide enough to lead a horse down the centre without having to run the gauntlet—or the teeth—of the other animals in occupation.

The construction was like something from the Royal Mews, which I'd toured years before, all immaculately varnished planks between the stables, clean wood shavings and rubber non-slip mats on the floors. There were even ceiling fans and a mist system in case of a summer heatwave.

As Helena evidently caught a ticklish spot, the mare stamped and swished her tail. Helena stopped her vigorous brushing and glared in my direction. The resentment in it took me a little by surprise.

"Let's be real clear on this, right from the get-go," she said. "You are not my mother—and you are certainly not my father. OK?"

I blinked. "I think we can agree on that." I said after a moment. "Were you expecting that I might try to be?"

She didn't answer that, but went back to her brushing, still not looking me in the face.

"You are *not* going to restrict my movements, interrogate my friends, or veto my plans. Do you understand?"

"Yes, ma'am." I pronounced it the same deadpan way I had done back in the army when addressing female senior officers —"marm" rather than the more American "may-yam" —and resisted the urge to come to attention before her.

That brought her up short. Finally, her gaze snapped across to me, searching for insubordination. There was nothing for her to see. I'd had quite a bit of practice at that, too.

She took a deep breath and said in a lower voice. "I will listen to you but only if you will show me the same courtesy. I *will not* be suffocated in security."

I raised an eyebrow and she flushed a little.

"I get the impression that hiring me was not exactly your idea?" Which was weird, because Kincaid himself had stated clearly that my employment was at his wife's insistence, more than simply at her request. So, he'd lied to me—the question was, why?

"No, it wasn't my idea." She shook her head. "Nothing personal, I just don't want anyone baby-sitting me."

"What about Illya? And…Ellis, was it?"

Mentioning the dead driver was a calculated move. Most people rejected close protection because they couldn't, or wouldn't, accept that the threat towards them was real. The price paid by both men—and Ellis in particular—proved beyond a doubt that it was.

Her flush deepened, as did her defiance. "What about them?"

"You were, presumably, happy to have *them* looking out for you?"

She shrugged. "Happy? Not exactly. But they'd both been with me forever and, besides, there were plenty of places they… *couldn't* accompany me. I still had a measure of privacy."

She turned back to the mare, untied the lead rope attached to her halter and turned her around in the stable so she could groom the other side. I was glad of a moment to analyse what she'd just told me—and what she hadn't.

Privacy to do what? It could have been anything, from a gambling habit, an affair she didn't want Kincaid's men to report back to him, or simply the need to get out from under a microscope every once in a while.

Or it could be that she needed the seclusion occasionally in order to check in with her handler, Conrad Epps.

Helena retied the palomino to a ring set into the wall on the other side of the stable. As she did so, the mare lipped at the sleeve of her shirt and nudged her shoulder, eager for titbits. Helena smiled, rubbed the top of the horse's neck just behind her ear. By the way the mare tilted her head and leaned into it, I guessed it was a favourite spot.

"She's in beautiful condition," I said. "What's her name?"

"Sunrise," Helena said, affection in her voice. Then she glanced at me sharply. "You ride?"

I nodded, thinking back to a job on Long Island when having half a ton of horse on hand had proved very useful as a kind of improvised weapon. "It has been known."

Her first response was pleasure, but her expression quickly clouded. I guessed she was realising belatedly that this could be yet another piece of alone-time I'd just removed from her grasp.

"I don't go off of the property when I ride out," she said. "We have two hundred acres, so there's no need. If it makes you feel any better, I'll steer clear of roads and boundaries." *But I don't want you with me.*

That part of the message came across loud and clear, even if she didn't say it aloud.

I tilted my head slightly. "How difficult do you intend to make life for me, Mrs Kincaid?"

She stiffened. "Well, I understand my husband is paying you a *lot* of money to put up with a little inconvenience."

I shook my head. "No, actually. He's paying me an *obscene* amount of money to keep you alive." I paused a beat, watched the flush reappear in her cheeks. "Do you have any objection to that?"

She lifted one shoulder, let it drop. "It's his money."

"No, I mean to the 'keeping you alive' part?"

That provoked a reaction, just not the one I'd been expecting.

I saw the flash of anger sear across her face a split second before she threw the metal curry comb straight at my head.

I ducked in reflex. The curry comb whizzed over the top of me, a little too close for comfort. It clattered into the wall of the stable opposite, gouging a jagged chunk out of the varnished top layer. The horse inside the stable skittered in fright. Even the palomino mare bunched up into the corner, snorting. Panic gleamed white in her eye.

I straightened up slowly, allowing no expression onto my face, even though my mind was spinning.

Helena was staring at me, her own eyes as wild as the mare's. Her chest heaved as though she'd just run a marathon. She rushed for the door to the stable and I stepped back, letting her past. She still had the body brush in her hand, although that one was only wood and bristle.

"I'm…sorry," she muttered as she fled. "I'm… I can't… Please, excuse me."

I stood and watched her half-walk, half-run along the length of the horse barn. She disappeared through the main door at the end, still clutching the forgotten grooming brush in her hand.

I stepped into the stable and stroked the palomino mare along her silky neck. She quivered beneath my hand for a minute, then calmed.

"Well, Sunrise," I murmured. "You know her better than I do, so what the fuck was that all about?"

12

WITH AN EFFICIENCY that came naturally to her, it was Mrs Heedles who supplied me with access to Helena's diary. Not her private journal—if she even kept one—but a schedule of appointments, social engagements, and a note of her general routine.

If I'd waited for the lady herself to furnish me with the details, by the time the information arrived I reckoned I would probably be too old to act on it.

For someone apparently not involved in her husband's line of business, and without the necessity to go out and make the rent money every month, she still kept to a busy timetable.

Her day began a little after 6 a.m. with a run. Accordingly, when she stepped out of the master suite the following morning, she found me already in the corridor. I was dressed in similar sweats to her own.

The only major difference between us—or so I hoped—was that I wore the Kramer rig clipped to a leather belt underneath the drawstring waistband of my sweatpants. It wasn't the most comfortable option, but the only way to guarantee the SIG would remain firmly in position, exactly where my hand expected it to be.

Helena didn't try to keep the annoyance out of her face when she saw me waiting for her. But there was a hint of underlying embarrassment, too, for the way she'd reacted—or maybe over-reacted—the day before.

I kept my expression totally bland. "Morning, ma'am."

"Oh, for heaven's sake," she said, more weary than exasper-ated. "If I can't shake you, then you may as well at least call me Helena. 'Ma'am' is for my grandmother."

"OK…Helena."

"Better." She walked past me and I fell into step alongside, felt rather than saw her cast me a sideways glance. "I don't suppose there's any use in me pointing out that I'll be staying on the trails inside the property?"

I already knew from talking to Schade that the extreme boundaries were covered by a range of electronic and automated security measures that made the CIA headquarters at Langley seem as wide open as a public park on the Fourth of July.

"Not much," I agreed cheerfully. "And anyway, I could do with the exercise."

She set off at a pace she couldn't hope to sustain. More to the point, one I hoped she couldn't. I was more than capable of a half marathon at a steady jog, or a flat-out dash over a hundred metres or so, but I wasn't much good at combining the pace of the latter with the distance of the former.

Fortunately, after the first half mile or so she throttled back to a more reasonable speed. One I was able to manage without the disgrace of going into a full cardiac meltdown.

Helena didn't go much for small talk while she ran. A good thing, since I didn't have the breath to spare. Every now and again, I flicked my eyes across at her set features. The fixed line of her mouth told me this was one occasion when playing dumb would serve me better than any other strategy I could come up with. I said nothing.

As we reached the home stretch, Helena lengthened her stride. Maybe she was hoping to leave me floundering in her wake at a moment where her husband was likely to see us and decide I wasn't up to the job.

I kept pace.

I stayed half a step behind and to her right, with my eyes on the treeline and any possible chokepoints in between. We were moving slightly uphill now, along a sandy path that separated two of the paddocks and provided a convenient lane to separate the groups of horses and walk them to and from their grazing unmolested.

Each of the paddocks had a wooden structure next to the fence to provide shelter for the animals from the weather, hot or cold. One was coming up on our right and I instinctively moved a little closer to Helena, forcing her further over to her left.

"You're crowding me," she snapped. They were the first words she'd spoken since we left the house.

And right at that moment, as her attention was on me, a man stepped out from behind the shelter with a gun in his hand.

I'd reacted before I had time to think, to blink, to draw breath. A visceral response that went straight from optic nerve to muscle.

I grabbed Helena's shoulder with my left hand, yanking her backwards as my right went for the SIG behind my right hip.

As I cleared the rig, I piled my weight sideways, twisting so Helena was flung behind me, swung off her feet, while I put myself between her and the threat. Aiming low centre mass as an extension of my arm, I had taken up half the poundage on the trigger when my brain finally caught up with what was happening.

I froze, breathing hard—not simply from the running—and waited a beat longer before uncoiling my finger from the trigger and laying it alongside the guard.

Behind me, Helena picked herself up, slapping sand from her clothing.

"God*dammit*, Schade," she barked. She glared at the man, who calmly put away his weapon with apparently no concern for how close he'd come to being gut-shot. "What kind of an idiot game was that to play?"

Schade, meanwhile, had not taken his eyes from mine. He stood entirely relaxed. It was hard to read what was going on behind those wire-framed spectacles.

"Big on idiot, clearly," he admitted. "Just wanted to check the girl knew how to dance."

"And?" Helena demanded, moving up beside me, her eyes

scanning from my face to his. I kept my gaze on Schade a moment longer, then broke away, lifting the side of my T-shirt and tucking the SIG back into its holster. I tried to keep my face neutral, to suck the air deep into my lungs without gasping for it, to will my hands not to tremble from the nitrous shot of adrenaline punching through my system.

When Schade spoke again, his voice was low with a kind of wonder. "And, damn me if she can't do a mean tango…"

13

I TAPPED the back of my knuckles lightly on the open office door and stuck my head through the gap. Mrs Heedles' eyes never shifted from the screen of her computer, fingers dancing over the keyboard with the finesse of a concert pianist.

"Yes, dear, how can I help?" She must have great peripheral vision.

"Mr Kincaid didn't mention anything about me taking time off."

She did glance up then, a twist of amusement to her features.

"You putting in for vacation time already, huh? Well, after that stunt Mr Schade pulled yesterday, I can't say I blame you."

I shrugged. There was plenty I could have said about that, but thought it best to go with diplomatic for now. "He just wanted to be sure I was up to the job."

"Uh-huh," she said, too ladylike for it to have been an actual snort. "What do you need?"

"Frank and Lorna Stephenson have invited me over for supper—as a thank you for house-sitting for them."

"The Stephensons are good people, from what I gather." She reached for the mouse and clicked something open on her computer desktop—presumably a day-planner. "Well now, I don't see him having a problem with you taking a few hours to yourself, dear. And if he does, tell him to go to hell and back, the long way," she said. "When?"

"Tomorrow evening. There's nothing in Mrs K's schedule—I already checked."

She nodded. "Then have at it. You need me to have someone drive you over there? You're aware, naturally, that getting caught DUI would mean instant dismissal."

"Not if you've a spare vehicle about the place that I could use?" I said. "I don't plan on drinking."

That *did* provoke a snort, no doubt about it, but whether at the request or the statement of intent, it was hard to tell. She reached into a desk drawer and brought out what looked like a garage door remote, tossing it over to me. I caught it one-handed, held it up with a raised eyebrow.

Mrs Heedles grinned in response and there was a certain amount of relish to it. "If the keys are in the ignition, then it's fair game," she said. "Enjoy."

———

I DIDN'T APPRECIATE the true meaning of her words until I found my way to the garages in an annexe at the rear of the property. I'd studied the floorplan for the place, so I had a rough idea of direction. As soon as I opened the personnel door at the side, the lights blinked on automatically. They revealed a huge space with gleaming white walls and glossy black tiles on the floor.

And, parked in a neat line, at least a dozen cars that were collectively worth at least seven figures, and possibly eight.

"Holy cow, Batman," I murmured. I thumbed the button on the remote to open the large doors at the front, just to be sure I hadn't wandered into the wrong garage by mistake. They parted in the centre almost at once, sliding back noiselessly in sections like an aircraft hangar.

I closed them again and walked along the row, the soles of my boots squeaking on the tiles. It was like a *Who's Who* of the automotive world—a Bugatti Veyron, McLaren Senna, and an Aston Martin Lagonda sat alongside a new model Bentley Continental GT. The paintwork was showroom fresh. Even the tyres looked unworn.

"Kid in a candy store, huh?" said a voice from the doorway.

I looked back. Eric Kincaid stepped into the garage. He wore jeans and a tailored Oxford shirt with the collar open and the cuffs folded back to reveal an ultra-thin Jaeger-LeCoultre wristwatch. On his feet were loafers that didn't make a sound on the tiles.

"So, you're a bit of a petrolhead?"

"Not really," he admitted, hands in pockets as he surveyed the gleaming display of collective horsepower. "More of an investor, I guess."

"Ah. Then I suppose that me taking any of this lot up a bumpy track, through a forest, at night, might not be on the cards."

He shrugged. "You want to try it, be my guest," he said, with the indifference to potentially expensive damage that only the truly rich can afford to overlook.

"I'd be happier in one of the Range Rovers you were using the other day, to be honest," I admitted. "If you don't need them both yourself."

"I'll have Schade leave one out front for you. Take it whenever you need to."

"Thank you." I ran my hand casually along the paintwork of the Aston Martin Lagonda. It was a four-door Taraf model, sporting the discreet Q badging that showed bespoke customisation on top of the standard spec, and no doubt also sporting a price tag to match.

"So, if you're not into cars for what they are, rather than their return on investment, what *does* float your boat?" I asked, suddenly curious. "And I assume you have a boat stashed away somewhere as well?"

"Nassau," he said with a smile. "And a Gulfstream 650, before you ask. It's a nice little family plane."

"Of course it is," I agreed.

Another shrug. "At the end of the day, they're simply tools to make more efficient use of my time. Why travel to someone else's schedule when you can do it at your own convenience?"

We stared over the cars in silence for a moment before I tried another prompt. "So, if you don't mind me asking, why do you do this? Why do you work so hard, generate so much wealth, if not to then enjoy the fruits of your labours?"

"Who says I don't enjoy them?" He lifted an eyebrow. The guarded edge was back, the shutters down behind his eyes.

"OK, wrong choice of words," I said. "I've been around a lot of very rich people over the last few years. In this job, it's par for the course. And some of them are driven by having come from nothing and never quite being able to forget it. They need possessions—endless expensive *stuff*—as a constant reminder to themselves as much as to others, of how far they've come." I paused but he wasn't giving me anything to work with, one way or another. I took a breath and plunged on. "But for you, I get the impression materialism is not what motivates you."

He nodded then, and all hint of humour had gone from that stone-cold gaze. "Life is one big game and it's one I'm in to win. There is no second place, as far as I'm concerned," he said. "But you're right—I don't do it for the money. That's simply how we keep score."

14

SUPPER AT THE STEPHENSONS' farmhouse the following evening was a relaxed and enjoyable affair—for the most part, anyway.

I heard all about their European travels, from the olive groves of Tuscany to the monasteries and ancient castles of Spain, and the vineyards of France. When they recounted, laughing, a story of late connecting flights, and escorted dashes through various airports, I couldn't help but recall Eric Kincaid's comment on the advantages of private jet ownership. Someone I'd once guarded had said much the same thing. That one of the first things that changed when he started making serious money was the style in which he was able to travel. You begin to look forward to the journey almost as much as the destination, he said. Or at the very least you no longer view the prospect of flying with the same kind of weary forbearance.

We ate at the big table in the kitchen. The tabby cat with the white bib was still in her box by the stove with her kittens. The last of the evening light shifted gently around the room, like it was touching on mementos. Afterwards, Lorna took me through to the sitting room while Frank—at his own insistence—pottered through the tidying up and clearing away.

He joined us perhaps ten minutes later. He was bearing a tray loaded with real tea they'd picked up from Fortnum & Mason during their brief stopover in London, in a china teapot. Lorna poured cups for each of us while Frank went through the ritual of drawing the heavy curtains to block out the star-sprinkled sky above the trees.

"Well," Lorna said with a distinct glimmer in her eye as she handed across my cup. "I think that should satisfy any Peeping Toms out there in the woods, don't you?"

"It should," I agreed.

As if on cue, footsteps sounded on the creaky wooden stairs, descending. A moment later, Conrad Epps stepped into the sitting room. He shook hands with Frank, who called him "sir" although he was clearly the senior—in years at least. I realised I hadn't given any thought to the relationship between them when I'd agreed to come out to the farm in the first place.

Lorna rose, taking her teacup and handing another to her husband. "We'll go catch up on some TV in the study," she said placidly, as if hosting covert meetings was an everyday occurrence for her. "Let us know when you're all done talking."

Then we were alone, with only the ticking of a long-case clock for company. Epps took the leather recliner opposite the sofa and fixed me with an interrogator's stare.

"So, what was so urgent you had to drag me all the way out here to hide out until dark?" he asked, with less heat than I might have expected, under the circumstances. His very calmness stirred a sense of irritation I couldn't quite squash. "Have you made any progress on the status of the chemical weapons deal?"

I ignored the question, asked one of my own instead, barely keeping my voice level. "What exactly were you hoping to achieve with that ambush on Helena Kincaid?"

Epps sat back, his feet flat on the floor and his hands on the armrests of the chair, but something in him relaxed a little, as if whatever he'd been expecting me to say, that wasn't it.

"Your insertion into the Kincaid household," he said. "Which was a successful part of the operation…unless you're about to tell me otherwise. Why?"

"Did you know about this summit he was a part of?" I kept my eyes on his face, tried to spot any minute signs that he was lying. He was as difficult to read as a shark. You knew he was going to bite your leg off at some point, it was simply a matter of when.

His only reply to that was a raised eyebrow. I hissed out a breath. "The agreement about not going after any family members who classify as non-combatants," I went on. "Kincaid was a party to it, and by orchestrating that attempt on his wife, you may well have just fired the first shots in a bloody war."

Epps's continued silence was ominous in itself.

"You think the attack on Mrs Kincaid was at my instigation?" he asked finally, his voice silky with threat. "You have a very poor understanding of my operating methods, Ms Fox, if you believe I would be prepared to sacrifice men in order to achieve such an objective."

"It could have been another of those *consequences-based training methods*—wasn't that how you put it?"

He glared without speaking. I stared right back.

"Yes, as a matter of fact," I said. "I believe you'd sacrifice men in a heartbeat if you felt you could justify it. And I'm fully aware that includes me."

"I am not in the habit of wasting assets until they have proven themselves...unreliable."

"So they weren't your men?"

His mouth twitched. It took me a moment to recognise the gesture as what passed for a smile. "Your tenacity is to be admired, but now it's your understanding of your own capabilities which is poor," he said. "I would not have pitted anyone I valued against you. I've seen you in action before, Charlie. Hell, at one point I thought I'd have to pull the damned trigger on you myself to force you to stand down."

An instant flashback opened up in front of me like snow dropping away into a crevasse, leaving a gaping chasm I almost tumbled right into.

I felt again the heat of the California sun beating down on me, heard the harsh reports of pistol shots, saw the blood spraying outward from the head wound that had almost killed Sean Meyer, and had certainly destroyed whatever relationship we might have been able to build together. And the sheer rage that had filled me then roared through my veins like fire. My hands gave a quick, convulsive clench I couldn't control, then the vision faded and a hollow calm returned.

I took a swallow of my tea, placed my cup down carefully, and looked up aware that Epps had missed nothing of the memory I'd just relived.

"So, if not yours, who were they?" I asked. "And how did you know what they were planning?"

"Let me simply say that Kincaid's communications network is not as secure as he'd like to believe. And because we have him under surveillance, we knew when someone else attempted to infiltrate his security, also."

"*Attempted*? Or succeeded?"

"Attempted," Epps confirmed, just this side of smug. "I have better expertise at my disposal."

"Who was it?"

"That is what we have been trying to ascertain. A new player. No other intel is yet...available." For that I read *'no intel I'm willing to share'*. "We know only that when they failed to crack the encryption on Kincaid himself, they turned their attention to a softer target."

"Helena."

He inclined his head slightly. "All we did was intercept the information they accessed, which suggested interest in the particular time and location we passed on to you. The rest you know."

My instincts about Helena, about her reluctance to accept 24/7 security and the reasons for her insistence on maintaining a level of privacy, prompted me to put out a feeler. "You were willing to possibly sacrifice a civilian to get me in there?"

Something shifted behind Epps's expression. Only a fraction, but enough for me to suspect there was more to Helena Kincaid than being the non-combatant wife of an arms dealer.

"I had every confidence in your ability to improvise, Charlie."

I gave a short, sarcastic laugh. "Oh well, *that's* all right then, or my parents would be hitting you up for the cost of a wreath about now."

"You know I'm good for it," he said, with such seriousness he probably *was* being utterly serious. It was a more feasible explanation than Epps actually being in possession of a sense of humour, however bleak.

He rose, abruptly indicating that, as far as he was concerned, my audience was at an end.

"What's her story?" I asked as he started to turn away. "Why is Helena so set against being protected? What happened to her in the past?"

Epps paused. If I didn't know him better, I'd almost call it a hesitation. "I think it best if you wait until Mrs Kincaid is ready to share that with you herself…"

15

HELENA KINCAID WAS CLEARLY NOT in a sharing mood. At least, not as far as I was concerned. On the plus side, if she wasn't exactly *happy* about having me to babysit her, after the first couple of days she stopped being actively unhelpful about it.

She seemed to accept the fact that I was going to run with her first thing in the mornings, and exercise a horse alongside her before lunch, as well as accompany her to see financial brokers, to her hair, nails, spa, and beauty appointments, on shopping trips, or to a surfeit of charity lunches. Everywhere up to and including the ladies' loo, although I drew the line at sharing a cubicle.

It was while we were attending one of the charity lunches that I saw the first slight thaw in the sub-zero temperature of our relationship. One of the fearsome Old Money ladies, who sat alongside my principal on yet another committee, inclined her head fractionally in my direction before telling Helena how fortunate she was to have a Personal Assistant close at hand to keep her diary organised for her.

Out of the corner of my eye, I saw Helena freeze, not with insult but, I guessed, with a kind of embarrassed fear that I might correct the woman, and the inevitable questions that would follow about the veneer of her apparent respectability.

Normally, I wouldn't have allowed the mistake to stand.

Nothing to do with thinking I was too good to be anybody's PA. Nothing to do with staying in a covert role, either, although there have been many times when preserving that element of surprise has been vital. As Mo Heedles pointed out, I probably didn't look like anybody's idea of a bodyguard.

But in most cases, it's as well for everyone present to be able to identify the close-protection officer right from the outset. Saves them getting in your way later if you suddenly find yourself in the position of having to earn your keep.

This time, on a hunch, I smiled politely and murmured something to the effect that Mrs Kincaid was so naturally efficient that she made the job of organising her almost superfluous. The woman laughed as though I'd said something terribly amusing and was instantly distracted by someone more worthy of her attention. As she turned away, Helena caught my eye and the corner of her mouth quirked into what might have been a smile.

Progress, of a sort.

After that, I made sure I dressed to fit the role I'd tacitly agreed to play—shirts with enough of a collar to hide the faint scar that still laced my throat, worn under suits that allowed me room to move without restriction and hid the gun behind my right hip.

For the first week after I joined the Kincaid household, the most exciting thing that happened was a violent thunderstorm that frightened one of the horses into barging through the post-and-rail fence of his paddock and hightailing it across country. He made it almost to the boundary of the property before we tracked him down in one of the Range Rovers, and Helena, jumping out into the downpour without a murmur, calmed and caught him.

She ordered me to keep back, something I wasn't happy to do when there was three-quarters of a ton of self-guided weapon on the loose around her. I recognised the frightened animal would not come to a stranger, but I climbed out into the rain anyway and stood near the front end of the Range Rover, leaving Schade behind the wheel.

Having coaxed the horse close enough to clip the lead rope to his headcollar, Helena grinned back at the pair of us. I just had time for my stomach to drop before she vaulted onto the animal's back. And I'd already started to swear under my breath even as she dug her heels into the horse's sides. He bounded forwards into a gallop, heading back up the sandy track in the direction of the horse barns and the house, with her bending low over his neck.

As I clambered soggily back into the Range Rover and slammed the door, Schade threw me a wry look that might even have been sympathetic at the cause of my disgust.

"Yeah," he said. "Sometimes Mrs K has too much spunk for her own good, huh?"

———

Then, just when I thought Helena and I had taken a couple of steps forward, we took half a dozen back again. And, this time, her husband joined in.

"No," he said firmly. "It's dinner, just the two of us. A quiet romantic meal. No way are you two doing a full roll-out, Schade, so suck it up."

Schade's eyes behind those wire-rimmed glasses were expressionless. So was his voice. "You're the boss, dude."

Kincaid stared at him for long enough that I felt I ought to offer to hold their coats while they took it outside. We were in his spacious office—me standing, Schade leaning against the nearest wall as if it was the only thing keeping him upright, and Kincaid perched on the front edge of the enormous desk. He'd called us in to announce his plans for an evening out, seemingly already prepared for the arguments he knew we'd throw against it. As security chief as well as Kincaid's personal bodyguard, Schade had seniority when it came to most of the arguing. His boss batted everything straight back, but Schade was dogged in his persistence.

Eventually, Kincaid sighed, rubbed a hand round the back of his neck.

"Look, it's our anniversary, for God's sake. You know how Helena feels about being spied on. Is it too much to ask that we be allowed some privacy for *one* meal? Or are you planning to watch us the whole night? Maybe give us marks for style?"

Schade's face didn't twitch. "I was gonna go with technical difficulty," he said. "Maybe a final round against the clock—"

"Enough! Minimum cover only. Is that clear?" Kincaid held the bodyguard's gaze until he received a brief, reluctant nod. "Just you and Fox, one chase car, two drivers. And that's it."

Schade gave a nod. "Like I said—you're the boss." Even if his tone suggested there might be some doubt about that.

Kincaid sighed again. "It's just a quiet anniversary dinner," he repeated wearily. "Not a gala at the Met, for fuck's sake."

He rounded his desk and sat behind it. The dismissal was loud and clear. Schade and I made the long trek to the office door and passed through. I closed it behind us with a lot less force than I would have liked to use. In the outer office, Mrs Heedles didn't look up from her computer screen, just held up a hand to forestall any pleas we might have been about to make.

"Save your breath," she said. "I've been trying all morning to talk him out of the idea."

Schade waited until we were in the corridor before he let out a long breath down his nose, the most emotion I'd seen him display. "Well, I'd give him a four."

"That's a little harsh," I said. "Is that for style or technical difficulty?"

"No," he said. "For conviction. He *knows* it's a bad plan—especially with what's happening right now. He's just being stubborn, and stupid, and hoping to get lucky tonight."

I raised an eyebrow, unsure if this was an aspect of the Kincaids' marriage I wanted, or even needed, to know about. It was hard to tell if Schade was ever being entirely serious in what he said. But if our principals had tired of each other sexually—and were satisfying that need elsewhere—it *might* explain Helena's aversion to having me cramping her style whenever she left the property.

"This anniversary," I said. "Which is it?"

Schade looked at me as if I should have known the answer to that one without having to ask.

"It's their first."

16

"QUIET ANNIVERSARY DINNER, MY ARSE," I muttered under my breath.

I stood at the back of a darkened hall, which was set with perhaps thirty or forty cabaret tables, each lit by shaded candles. On stage at the front, in the narrow cone of a single spotlight, a young Chinese woman in a long red dress played one of the Bach cello suites with what sounded to me like an exquisite touch.

Certainly, if the tilt of Helena Kincaid's head was anything to go by, she was transfixed by the music. Eric Kincaid sat alongside her, looking pleased to have pleased her. They held hands across the starched white linen.

I kept the couple's table in my peripheral view at all times, letting my gaze rove across the rest of the audience. The staff moved between tables with deceptive pace, never appearing to hurry but not obviously dawdling, either. I watched closely for dress or movement that didn't quite match, comparing faces against a mental database, straining my eyes in the low light.

"From what little I've seen of your ass, I wouldn't confuse the two." Schade's voice sounded in my ear. He was behind the stage somewhere, covering the entrances and exits back there, circulating through the kitchen at regular intervals. We'd done a quick walk-through when we arrived—and again before the performance began. The place was a rabbit warren, but at least he didn't need night-vision goggles to do his job effectively.

"If you want a turn out front, let me know," I said, hoping for a chance to emerge into the light for a change. "This girl is amazing."

"No thanks, I brought a book," Schade said, and once again I wouldn't have put it past him to be telling something close to the truth.

"If you're sure? But you're missing a treat."

"Yeah, sorry, this chick doesn't do it for me."

"Don't tell me," I murmured, still scanning constantly. "The kind of bands you go to see live have to play behind Plexiglas because of the flying bottles at the end of the night?"

"Not so much," he replied easily. "The reason I'm not into this chick is because she's all about the technical precision without any emotional connection to the piece. That and her bowing's slightly off. If I had to guess, I'd say she's most likely damaged the rotator cuff in her right shoulder."

"Schade, you are a constant source of wonder."

"Yeah." He paused. "Naturally, I *also* go to see those bands who play behind the Plexiglas—goes without saying."

"Oh, of course it—"

Movement over to my right caught my eye.

"What's up, Fox?" The lazy relaxation had disappeared from Schade's voice.

"New waiter." I frowned, unsure how to put a gut feeling into words. "He's...out of sync with the others."

"You sure?"

"Uh-huh."

"Yeah, 'course you are. Sorry. Force of habit."

I kept my gaze locked on the waiter. He was weaving smoothly between the tables—but he was doing it a little *too* smoothly. His eyes were everywhere. Not simply scanning table-tops for plates or glasses that might need his attention, but the angle of his head told me he was also checking out exits and blind spots. And he was spending a fraction too long checking on the other staff, who were people he should have known, and on the bystanders, of which I was one.

We made eye contact. He gave a slight nod and a smile. It was almost perfectly weighted, like he knew his job was to remain invisible and he was feeling a little guilty to realise someone could see him. Just like a skilled waiter should.

Or a skilled assassin.

The only way I could tell the difference for sure was when he didn't break the connection soon enough. A genuine waiter would have been more concerned with regaining his invisible status. This guy kept his eyes on me while he worked out if his cover was blown.

And by doing so, he blew it himself.

"Waiter," I snapped into the throat mic, already pushing away from the wall. "We need to get them out of here, Schade. Right now."

As soon as I started moving to intercept, the man dressed as a waiter registered that he'd been made. Even in the low light, I saw him hesitate, just for a second. That was all it took for him to calculate that he couldn't get to his target before I got to him.

The fake waiter altered course without apparent effort, movements still unhurried and even. He reached a door by the side of the stage, twisting as he went through to take a last look at me, and how far I was behind him. My stride faltered. The urge to chase, to attack and bring down tempered by the need to protect.

At the opposite side of the stage, the door opened and Schade came out onto the floor. He spotted me at once. I saw the question in his face and jerked my head in the direction the would-be assailant had taken. Schade stabbed a finger that way impatiently, his message clear: *Get after him!*

I knew I should stick with my principal, but the opportunity to go after the guy, to gather intel, was too tempting to ignore. Besides, I had few doubts that Schade was probably very good at his job. He was already ushering the Kincaids from their seats, heading for the exit.

I quickened my pace, not caring about the disapproving glances from patrons as I brushed between their chairs. By the time I reached the door where my quarry had disappeared, I was practically running.

I hit the door with my shoulder and spun through. Because of that, the blow that should have landed on the back of my skull glanced off my upper arm instead. I ducked, bringing my hands up on reflex to protect my head. As I turned into my attacker, his fist grazed past me again. Momentum had him overreaching. I darted past his guard, slid across the outside of his arm and plunged stiffened fingers into his right eye.

He jerked back with a grunt, then lashed out again. Short, vicious blows with his bodyweight behind them, any one of which should have finished the fight—if he'd managed to land it.

I crowded in on top of him, hands up by my head so I took the brunt on my forearms and biceps. My bent elbows stopped him getting close enough to grab my torso, but lured him in as far as I needed in order to pound his sternum and larynx—short blows with a twist at the end of them—then slice down under the side of his jawline.

He started to crumple, letting fly with his boot as he did so in a last-ditch attempt to put me down first. I hammer-fisted his ankle to one side. He landed off balance, staggering. I leapt, stamping into the back of his knee and grabbing the collar of his shirt to yank him off his feet. Stitching ripped, scattering buttons, but his head still cracked down hard enough on the solid wood floor to put him out.

I stepped back, breathing hard. "Schade, what's happening? Talk to me."

Nothing.

Then, somewhere outside the hall came the sound of gunshots. The cellist stopped playing in mid-stroke.

I started running again.

17

By the time I hit the front of the building, the SIG was in my hand. To hell with trying to keep things low-key and not frightening the other diners or the staff. As soon as the shooting began, any kind of subtlety went out of the window.

I'd taken a side door and legged it around the building. It seemed easier and faster than going back through the audience, who might be stampeding by now.

Since we'd gone in, the weather had turned and the heavens had opened. The rain gushed down, overflowing the gutters. It sat in a visible layer on the concrete path, pelting into my back. When I slowed at the front corner and dropped to one knee, it soaked instantly through the leg of my trousers. I edged my head around the brickwork just far enough to give one eye a clear view of the scene.

Schade stood in the centre of the driveway, oblivious to the rain, holding one of the tactical shotguns up to his shoulder. He was firing slugs from the Mossberg as fast as he could work the pump-action, into the back end of a Range Rover that was accelerating rapidly away from the scene. It was hard to tell in the dark and the rain, but the vehicle looked suspiciously like the one I'd arrived in with Helena Kincaid.

Alongside the bodyguard, not afraid of getting his hands dirty, Eric Kincaid poured semiautomatic fire from an M4 into the rear of the Range Rover. From the way both men were aiming for the tyres rather than the glass, there was only one conclusion I could draw.

"Helena?" I demanded. "Where's Helena?"

Neither man heard me above the gunfire and the sluice of falling water. I hardly needed them to answer, in any case.

Gaining speed, the Range Rover side-swiped one of the trees lining the drive as the driver misjudged a bend, kicking up a plume of spray. One of the rear lights splintered and went out. The vehicle shimmied from the impact, righted itself and was lost from view.

Schade ceased firing immediately. Kincaid carried on until the moving parts locked back on an empty magazine. Even then, he continued to grip the weapon like he could *will* more rounds into it. Schade slung the Mossberg onto its shoulder strap, reached across and very gently peeled the M4 out of his principal's nerveless hands. It steamed and hissed as the water droplets hit hot steel.

"We'll get her back, Kincaid," he said softly. "I promise you."

Kincaid barely looked at him. His hair was plastered flat to his skull, shirt soaked almost translucent. He was shivering and seemed utterly dazed.

"Helena," he muttered. "They took her…"

Then he dropped to his knees, threw his head back, and howled into the heavens.

18

"THEY CAUGHT us with our pants down," Schade said. "Almost literally."

I agreed with his assessment, but said nothing.

We had found Helena's driver—a replacement for the dead Ellis—out cold in the gents' toilet, his trousers still unzipped. After that, it was easy to put together what had happened.

I still wasn't sure if the man who'd been posing as a waiter had been a genuine threat, or simply a means to spring the trap they'd set for us. Either way, it had worked to drive the Kincaids out of the relative safety of the crowded concert hall and into the more exposed parking area. There, in the dark and the rain, Helena's Range Rover had been waiting for her exactly where it should have been. She was hustled into it without anybody stopping to check on the identity of the driver.

I'd run back for the fake waiter, only to find him already gone —whether under his own steam or scooped up by other members of his team, I wasn't sure. I certainly thought I'd hit him hard enough to stop him walking for a while.

Now, I was sitting squashed into the rear of the remaining Range Rover, with Schade on the other side and Helena's semi-conscious driver lolling in the centre between us. Kincaid had taken the front passenger seat. He was leaning forwards against his seatbelt as if in pain, one hand braced on the dashboard. Utter rage roiled off him in waves.

I knew the feeling.

Losing a principal—no, I corrected myself, Helena was 'temporarily mislaid' not lost as in *lost*—was making me feel physically sick. I could understand Kincaid's reaction. I'd responded in a very similar way myself on the day Sean Meyer was shot in front of me. It still surprised me that I hadn't killed the bastard who'd done it, right there and then.

Perhaps I would have found it easier to live with if I had.

Half a mile up the road, at a rural intersection, we found the Range Rover abandoned with the doors gaping wide in the continuing downpour. Both rear tyres were shot out and the alloy rims were distorted and scarred.

I gave the inside a cursory inspection, looking for blood. I didn't find any. Helena's purse, with her new all-singing, all-dancing smartphone inside, had been tipped out into the rear footwell.

Her driver, Lopez, had come round enough to be mortified at being so easily caught out. Or maybe he had a better idea than I did of what punishment awaited us. It was hard to get a read on what Kincaid might do. Either way, the man was pale and silent when Kincaid ordered him to stay with the vehicle until his collection team arrived. "And don't touch anything. We may get something we can use off of the interior."

I half-expected to be ordered to wait with him in the rain, but Kincaid jerked his head and I retook my seat in his car. He twisted in his seat to face me and I mentally braced myself.

"I'm…sorry," he said through gritted teeth, the reluctant apology taking me by surprise. "You were right—both of you. Trying to do this low-key was a mistake. But you know how Helena feels about being overwhelmed with security. I just…"

"We will get her back for you," Schade said, but there was nothing in his voice.

Kincaid turned away, gestured to the driver to get moving. When he spoke again, it was almost a growl. "We better had."

"Mo is putting the word out. Anybody hears anything—we'll know."

"Oh, somebody knows something, that's for sure," Kincaid said bitterly. "Otherwise, how the hell did they just-so-happen to find us? We just upped security on Helena's communications."

I remembered the last conversation I'd had with Epps. "And you're confident that all your comms *are* secure?"

Neither man spoke for a moment, merely exchanged a glance I didn't catch the meaning of. I was sitting directly behind Kincaid and couldn't see his face. There was no streetlighting to illuminate Schade's features alongside me, either.

"I'll get right onto that," he said, in such a way it could have any number of hidden connotations. He paused. "You realise we're gonna have to let her father know."

"Not until we have a better idea what we're dealing with."

"He's bound to find out. And when he does..." I sensed rather than saw Schade shrug.

"Yeah, well, let's just hope we have her back by then," Kincaid said. "Or we're all fucked."

19

Back at the mansion, we set up a war room in Kincaid's office. Schade slumped into a deep cushioned armchair and closed his eyes, apparently taking a nap. His boss paced. I took one of the upright chairs near the desk, within reach of the phone, and willed it to ring. At this stage, a ransom demand was better than any other alternative.

I tried not to think too much about Epps. He'd claimed he'd done nothing more than follow information others had already accessed and drawn logical conclusions from that about a possible attack on Helena. Now, I wished I'd pushed him further on who might be after her, and why.

About twenty minutes after we got back, Mo Heedles came in wearing a pair of latex gloves and a disposable apron over yet another brown suit. It was close to midnight but she looked as unflustered and unruffled as she did during normal office hours.

"I've checked over Mr Lopez," she said without preamble, peeling off the gloves. "There's a pinprick in the back of his neck —some kind of fast-acting sedative would be my guess, but I've taken a blood sample so we'll know soon enough."

"Thank you, Mrs Heedles," Kincaid said quietly.

"He should have known better," Schade said, without opening his eyes.

Mo threw him a stern glare, nevertheless. "That's twenty-

twenty hindsight, as you're very well aware." She unhooked the apron, folding it with neat precision. "Let's face it, standing there with his dick in his hands, the poor bastard didn't stand a chance."

"Exactly," Schade said, lifting his head and staring back without expression. "In this job, he shoulda learned to piss one-handed, kept his gun in the other."

Mo sniffed loudly but made no other response to that, one way or another. She glanced over at Kincaid, concern etching the lines deeper into her face. "I'll let you know the minute I've had a chance to go over the car, dear. It's been picked up and is on its way back now."

Kincaid nodded distractedly. She went out, closing the doors quietly behind her.

"Mrs Heedles has hidden talents," I said. "Where did you find her?"

"She's ex-CIA," Schade said. He'd closed his eyes again. It was hard to tell how serious he was being with his answer.

"Is she as good with electronic security as she is with every-thing else?"

Schade opened his eyes and sat up. "No, but I am," he said. "Why are you so concerned about that, Fox?"

"Somebody knew where we were going to be this evening." I gave a shrug that tried to be far more casual than I actually felt. "How else could we have been compromised?"

It was Kincaid who spoke up. "Any number of ways," he said, voice flat with tension. "Somebody at the restaurant, maybe?"

Schade shook his head. "Table was booked under a fake name, dude. Standard operating procedure. And before you ask," he added, flicking me a deadly glance, "no, we weren't followed and yes, I'm sure about that."

"For what it's worth, so am I. There's too little traffic on the roads around here," I agreed. "A tail would have stood out a mile—unless they were using satellite tracking. Or drones."

Epps, I reckoned, must have access to both.

Kincaid and Schade exchanged another look I couldn't read. It was getting to be a habit.

"Our system is the best available. We've more failsafes and tripwires than the Pentagon," Kincaid said then. "Whoever took Helena didn't get to us that way."

"Of course, the alternative to a data breach is a good old-fashioned tip-off." Schade uncoiled himself and sat up, his focus fully on me now. It was not a comfortable feeling. "An inside job —maybe from somebody new on the team."

I straightened in my chair, also. It was hard not to. I uncrossed my legs and placed both feet flat on the carpet.

"Someone like me, you mean?"

"Never did like happenstance, Fox, and you have to admit your arrival here has coincided with some…unfortunate events."

"Purely from a reputational point of view," I said, faking calm, "why would I agree to protect Mrs Kincaid and then arrange—or allow—for her to be taken?"

"Money, loyalty, fear. Those are the main reasons," Schade listed. "There are others, but usually it comes back to one of those three."

I glanced across the desk to where Kincaid had paused. He was gripping the back of his chair with both hands, eyes fixed on me, but he didn't step in. I knew I had to play this one out, so I sat back, leaned one elbow onto the desktop and forced my shoulders to relax.

"Oh? So, which category do you reckon I fall into?"

"Well, you can't deny you need the money or you wouldn't have taken this gig," Schade said easily. "I don't see it being fear —somehow, I don't think you'd be easy to scare into doing much you didn't want to."

I said nothing, just continued to stare him out. He nodded as if I'd spoken anyway.

"Yeah, thought as much." A faint smile touched the corners of his mouth. It did nothing to reassure. "But loyalty, now *that's* a possibility."

"Loyalty to what?"

"Or who." He shrugged. "Depends who's behind Mrs K's abduction, and what they want from it."

Kincaid shifted restlessly. "If it was money they were after, surely we would have heard something by now?"

"Not necessarily." I shook my head. "They like to make you sweat—give you time to let your imagination run riot before they hit you with the first demand."

Schade's eyes were calculating. "And you'd know all about that?"

My temper sparked. "Of course I bloody know about it! Close protection was—*is*—my job."

On the wide plain of the desk, the telephone buzzed, making Kincaid flinch. He stabbed a finger onto the base unit. "Yes?"

"We have movement by the west gate." Mo Heedles' voice was composed, even through the distortion of the speaker. "Single vehicle. Nobody got out yet—it's just sitting there, idling. You might want to have somebody go take a look."

20

Kincaid thanked Mo, started heading for the door. As he passed Schade, the bodyguard rose, turned and hooked a hand under his elbow, all in one smooth move. I saw the whitened knuckles and knew he'd gone in hard enough on pressure points to stop Kincaid in his tracks.

"Can't let you go out there, dude," Schade said, regret in his voice. "You know the rules."

"Fuck the rules," Kincaid said tightly. "I *made* the rules. Now I'm changing them."

He twisted out of Schade's grasp, revealing skill levels of his own. Schade let go, but only long enough to regroup. He struck again, swept Kincaid's legs half out from under him, then grabbed his wrist and forced it into a lock with one hand. This time, he used it to lever Kincaid to his knees and stood over him as he gasped around the pain. Schade's face was devoid of emotion.

"Like I said, I can't let you go out there."

I sighed and got to my feet. "Shame you didn't protest this much when they wanted to go out earlier this evening without adequate security, hm?"

Schade's eyes met mine. They glinted behind the small lenses of his glasses. "A mistake is only of value if you learn from the experience," he said. "After all, for something to happen once is misfortune—"

"But twice is carelessness. Yeah, I know. Oscar Wilde. He was a clever guy, but look what happened to him in the end."

"Good point, Fox. What do you suggest?"

At his feet, Kincaid had stopped struggling, but the sweat was beading on his forehead. "He's a big boy," I said. "Let him make his own decisions."

"Easy for you to say when you're not the one responsible for his safety."

"*Very* easy for me to say," I agreed placidly, then added, "when I'm not the one trying to break his arm."

Schade glanced down at Kincaid as if he wasn't sure how they'd ended up in that position. He released him and stepped back.

It took a moment for Kincaid to get to his feet, but he spoke without heat. "When this is over, remind me to fire your ass, Schade."

Schade made no reply, just gave him a feral smile and headed for the door.

———

OUTSIDE THE FRONT ENTRANCE, we climbed into the same Range Rover we'd used earlier. Kincaid got behind the wheel. Schade took the front passenger seat, with another of the security men—my old mate Chatty—in the back alongside me. Chatty slid a bundle of reloaded M4s butt-down into the rear footwell between us. The headlights of a second vehicle curved around the side of the house and slotted in behind. The driver pulled up sharply enough to make the front suspension bounce.

As we moved out from beneath the shelter of the portico, the rain hammered down onto the roof of the Range Rover. Visibility was maybe twenty metres. Kincaid leaned closer to the windscreen, as if that might help him see better. Schade took the assault rifle Chatty handed to him. He checked it over with movements that seemed almost entirely muscle memory—a kind of calming ritual, if he needed one.

I did the same with my own weapon, head cocked to look between the front seats as the main gate came into view. Most fences and gateways in the area were wooden, I'd noted, occasionally adorned with an old wagon wheel or plough.

The Kincaids lived behind a high brick wall. Substantial gateposts with iron gates slung between them. A pair of ornate lamps shed high-intensity illumination onto the semi-circular apron in front of the drive, where cars could turn off the road and stop for inspection by the hidden cameras before being admitted.

A dark panel-van sat in the centre of the space, throwing out twin shadows on both sides from the lights shining down. The rain rebounded a good six inches from the asphalt around it. The van's engine was running, its headlights on, making it impossible to see who might be sitting inside. I lowered my window a little to give my ears a chance.

Kincaid rolled to a slow stop before he reached the gates themselves. The chase car pulled up to the side of us. Nobody moved to get out of the van. The rain continued to sluice down onto all three vehicles. Schade reached up and pressed a switch in the headlining. It took me a moment to realise he'd done it to stop the courtesy lights coming on automatically when the doors were opened. Nice to be working with professionals.

Kincaid had not taken his eyes off the van on the other side of the gates. "OK, you got my attention," he murmured. "Now what?"

"One way to find out," Schade said, and operated the electric gates. They parted silently in the centre and began to swing inwards. As soon as they did so, I opened my door a crack and slipped out onto the driveway, keeping below the level of the Range Rover's glass. Not only less visible to the occupants of the van, but it also put something slightly more solid between me and any incoming rounds.

Moving away from the sound of our own engines, I caught a metallic scrape as the van's side door was thrown back. It was on the opposite side to the gates—the side facing away from us. No doubt a calculated move on their part.

I ducked, trying to scan the darkened space underneath the

chassis for feet, legs—signs of people getting out. I could see nothing. The beams of the lights didn't reach that far into the shadows.

The van's engine note rose to a sudden howl as a foot stamped down hard on the accelerator. By the time it began to move, tyres scrabbling for grip on the slick surface, I was already running. I skated through the narrow gap between the opening gates and out onto the apron with the M4 pulled up into my shoulder ready. My eyes strained to make out even one digit of the rapidly disappearing licence plate through the deluge. Zilch.

Shouts from the gateway had me spinning. Where the van had stood, there was now a crumpled shape on the ground. In the dark, and the rain, it was almost impossible to identify it, but gut instinct outlined it as the body of a woman.

And she wasn't moving.

21

HELENA WAS ALIVE.

Against my better judgement, we loaded her into the back of the Range Rover and took her up to the house. She was in a deeply unconscious state—chemical rather than natural, if I was any judge—and soaked to the skin, her body like ice.

I drove the return journey while Kincaid crouched awkwardly beside his wife in the rear. Schade, having instructed his guys, retook his place in the passenger seat. He made a series of calls on his smartphone, his demeanour very cool and unemotional. The first was to someone who was obviously a doctor, casually asking him to stop by the house when he was next passing.

As he ended the call and caught my eye, he said, "I say 'when you're next passing' but what I mean is 'get your butt over here right now or I will come around to your house and drag you out by your balls'. It's kinda shorthand. You never know who's listening in at his end, huh?"

"Is this the same guy who treated Illya?"

He nodded. "He's the best in the business, he's fast, and he knows how to keep his mouth shut. For what he's making on the side, he ought to."

Mo Heedles was waiting for us at the front entrance as Kincaid strode in carrying his wife. Helena looked small and bedraggled in his arms, her hair ratted and plastered to her face and her evening dress a ruin. They left a dripping trail behind them across the tiles. Kincaid headed, not for the staircase leading up to the master bedroom, but towards the more utilitarian area at the rear of the house. I knew they had rooms back there kitted out as a medical suite, and all the gear needed for a full examination.

Including, no doubt, a rape kit.

I would have followed, but Schade barred my way.

"Let them take care of her," he said quietly.

"We don't know what they did—"

"No, we don't. And finding out now—or finding out tomorrow, or the day after—won't make a deal of difference to what happens next," he said. "But it will make a difference to *her*. Leave her to the people she knows. People she trusts."

I winced at the last bit. "That's below the belt, isn't it?"

He shrugged. "Yeah, what can I tell you? I never did play well with others."

My eyes followed Kincaid as he disappeared through a doorway, careful not to catch Helena's head or limbs, and Mo Heedles closed the door firmly behind them. Then I let out a long, exasperated breath, glanced sideways at Schade.

"Just what the fuck is going on here?"

"You took the words right outta my mouth."

"What now? You don't honestly think I had anything to do with what happened tonight?" I waited, temper rising, but he stared me out. "Seriously?"

"Talk me through it again—you and the dummy waiter."

"I've been over this. I followed him through the doors to the side of the stage." *On your orders*. I didn't voice the thought. It would have come across as too defensive, as though I was trying to dodge the blame. "He tried to jump me. We fought. I put him down, then heard the shots. Sorry if I was a bit more concerned with backing you guys up than handcuffing him to a bloody radiator."

"Oh, I believe you," Schade said. "But I'm not the one you have to be worried about convincing."

———

It was the following morning before I was allowed to see Helena. By that time, she'd been given the all-clear by Kincaid's tame doctor and moved from the in-house medical facility up to their suite.

The same man who'd treated Illya had arrived, less than half an hour after Schade's apparently casual invitation, with a jacket thrown on straight over his pyjamas. A part of me rather envied Schade this fearsome reputation. It appeared to allow him to speak very softly while everyone assumed he also carried a big stick. With nails in it.

When Mo Heedles let me into the suite, not long after breakfast, I half expected to find Helena still in bed. Instead, she was on a foam mat out on the terrace, dressed in yoga gear and working through a series of advanced stretches. Last night's rain had gone and the early sun was burning through what was left of the cloud. She'd already built up a sweat.

Kincaid sat on a cane sofa nearby. After Schade's comments of the previous night, I eyed him warily. He had a thick folder of documents beside him, but his eyes were on his wife.

She didn't acknowledge my arrival right away. I didn't try to hurry her. I'd been focused on seeing her for most of the night but, now I was here, I'd no idea what to say.

Did I apologise to her? Or wait for her to apologise to me?

Eventually, she unfolded herself and came upright, breathing hard. Kincaid rose and handed her a towel from the back of the sofa. She draped it around her neck, using the ends to wipe her face.

"I'm glad you're OK...physically, at least," I said. Not my finest opening gambit, but the best I could do under the circumstances.

She paused, seeming as discomfited by the situation as I was, then she gave me a faint nod and moved to sit beside Kincaid. He reached for her hand, entwining their fingers, bringing hers up to his lips. I saw her throat work as she swallowed.

Feeling an utter intruder, I shifted my gaze out across the paddocks and the grazing horses. Anywhere but at the couple on the sofa. There was a time when that was Sean and me—so wrapped up in each other, so aware of every movement, every breath. So determined to make it work between us. So defiant of everything that tried to get in our way.

Maybe we'd tried too hard. Or not hard enough.

In the end, what difference had it made?

Kincaid was speaking. I reeled in my focus, turned to face him and caught the tail-end of what he said.

"A warning?" I repeated numbly. "What kind of a warning?"

Kincaid shrugged. He had not yet let go of his wife's hand. "We're still trying to work that one out."

With her free hand, Helena poured herself a glass of iced water from the jug on the low table in front of her. She seemed thankful for a reason not to have to meet my eyes.

"They told me to tell Eric that they'd proved they could get to me—to anyone—any time they wanted," she said. Her voice was low but level, as if the only way she could deal with this was to distance herself from it.

"For what reason?" I glanced from one to the other but their faces told me nothing. "Surely, you don't go to all that trouble and then fail to make any kind of demands?"

Kincaid shrugged again. I was beginning to really dislike it when he did that. "It could be said that it's good tactics," he said. "Fire your biggest guns right off the bat, just to show your opponent how serious you are."

"Yes, but serious about what?" I demanded. "And who *are* these guys?"

Before Kincaid could answer—even if he'd been going to—the doors to the suite opened abruptly and a man came in, with Mo Heedles on one side of him and Schade on the other. It was hard to tell if they were accompanying him or trying to slow him down.

At a guess, the man was older than Schade and possibly younger than Mo. He was as well-preserved as money could buy —liver-spotted hands but a tight jawline, his skin stretched shiny across his cheekbones. White teeth, black hair. He had on a very sharp Italian suit that did a great job of disguising his bulk, handmade shoes and a silk tie.

He paused in the doorway leading from the suite to the terrace and spread his arms with a greeting of, "Sweetheart!"

Helena got to her feet, letting go of Kincaid's hand with obvious reluctance. She shuffled forwards to be enveloped in a stifling hug. He kissed her on both cheeks, then held her at arms' length, ignoring her twitch of protest.

When still she tried to disengage, the man gripped her biceps harder while he inspected her face with ruthless diligence.

"Let me look at my little girl, hey?" he insisted softly. He had a voice like a handful of rocks thrown into a cement mixer. "You doing OK, kid?"

My eyes flicked to the others. Their expressions were guarded, but none of them made any kind of move towards Helena. I had no idea what was going on, but that didn't mean I was prepared to let it.

I stepped closer.

The man finally let go of Helena and turned. I could almost feel the weight of his gaze landing on me.

"Ah," he said. "You must be the bodyguard."

And then he punched me.

22

I PROBABLY COULD HAVE DUCKED it.

I didn't.

He was pretty fast for a big guy, but maybe I felt it was the least I deserved. So I tensed for all I was worth and took one to the stomach. His fist landed hard enough to blast the air from my lungs and double me over.

I fought back nausea. It took me a second to compute the damage, which fortunately was minimal. Another to see if he was going to follow it up—something to the face, perhaps, to really hammer home his point. Apparently, he decided that one was plenty to express his displeasure at my inadequacies.

I straightened up slowly, careful to keep everything out of my expression. Schade's influence was rubbing off on me.

The man was watching me as closely as he'd watched Helena. Only difference was the gun that had appeared in his left hand. He held it casually down alongside his leg. A Beretta M9. Most likely he was either ex-military or a wannabe. Either option was dangerous.

But, in some ways, though, I was strangely heartened by the sight of the Beretta. It told me he was not *so* convinced of my weakness that he felt confident taking me on for a rematch without weighting the odds in his favour. Whatever the punch to the gut took away from me, that realisation gave a small part of it back.

"And you must be the father," I managed.

"Heard all about me, hey?"

"No, not much," I countered blandly, and watched a flicker of annoyed surprise come and go in his eyes.

It was the truth, as far as it went. Nobody *had* said much, but fragments came back to me, fitting together to make a fairly comprehensive whole.

"You are not my mother—and you are certainly not my father," Helena had thrown at me, back when Kincaid first landed me on her as the new bodyguard.

"We're gonna have to let her father know… He's bound to find out. And when he does…" Schade had warned after the abduction. *"We're all fucked,"* Kincaid had responded.

And then, just last night, Schade again: *"I'm not the one you have to be worried about convincing."*

I'd thought he meant Kincaid, but now I realised he'd been talking about Helena's father. It all added up to a man used to power. The kind of power that meant he not only carried a gun— even in rural New Jersey, where gun ownership was common- place, carrying was not—but he had no qualms about drawing it in company.

From the lack of reaction or surprise from the Kincaids or Schade, I gathered this wasn't unusual behaviour. Anyone who dished out violence quite so readily, and backed it up with weaponry, was far too used to doing as he wished without fear of comebacks. Legal or otherwise. I could only hope that dick- waving was about as far as it went.

"You," he said pointedly, "failed to protect my little girl."

"Yes."

He raised an eyebrow, gestured with the gun as if he'd forgotten it was in his grip. "That's it? You got no excuses for me?"

I avoided even glancing over at Schade. He was the Kincaids' head of security. Last night, he practically ordered me to go after the man posing as a waiter, while he got the couple to the supposed safety of their vehicles. Still, nothing said I had to do as I was told…

"There *are* no excuses," I said evenly. "Mrs Kincaid was *my* responsibility. She was taken on *my* watch."

"Yeah, she was. So, what would you do about that, right now, if you were in my position?" he demanded, his gaze narrowed onto my face. "You think you deserve a second chance?"

"Everybody should know what failure feels like every once in a while," I said, aware of stepping out onto ice that was already cracking under my feet. "Or how else will they know how much they hate it? How else will they know they can't live with it happening again?"

Oh, good thinking, Fox. Mention "not living", why don't you? Give him ideas…

For the longest time, he seemed to be giving it serious consideration whether I should live to see much of anything happening again. Then he smiled. He showed his teeth the way I could imagine a shark doing when it realises the divers' cage is open and there's little to stop it taking a bite.

"OK, here's what I'm gonna do. I'm gonna give you your second chance, hey?" he said. "Because my little girl, she's taken a shine to you." The smile blinked out. "But you screw it up and you won't have to worry about living with it, 'cause I will *bury* you. You hear me?"

"Yes, sir."

"You hear that, Schade? 'Yes, *sir*' no less. I like this chick." The smile reappeared like a magic trick, sleight of hand. There, gone, back again. He turned back to me. "What's your name, kid?"

"Charlie," I said. "Charlie Fox."

He thrust out his hand—the one not still holding the Beretta. "Darius Orosco."

I mumbled something appropriate as he let go, lost interest. His attention now on his daughter and his son-in-law.

Although, making any connection between *law* and the man whose hand I'd just shaken was tenuous at best. A lot of things suddenly became clearer, the first of which was why Helena was so set against being smothered by security. And the second was that next time I came face-to-face with Conrad Epps, *he* was going to be the one on the receiving end of a punch in the gut.

There were a few salient points he'd failed to mention when he'd set me up on this job. Not least of which was the fact that the woman I'd landed myself a mission to protect was the only daughter of the Godfather of the East Coast Mafia.

23

"MY MOTHER WAS A WHORE," Helena said.

"Excuse me?"

"It's a name, Charlie, not an occupation. H-O-A-R-E."

"Ah, like the bank?"

"Exactly." Helena seemed perfectly familiar with the London private banking house, one of the oldest in the world. "The name means a man with white hair, so I believe. Anyway, rich old family in everything but actual cash. She never made any secret that she married my father for a life of luxury."

"There are worse things."

"Maybe, but you've no idea what it was like for me, growing up," she said. "Like being in prison—only worse."

"Worse, how?" I asked.

Helena threw me a sharp look, but I'd purposely spoken without inflection. I wasn't judging her. I was simply curious to get her take on an upbringing that was more privileged and luxurious than most people can dream about.

We were riding out. Helena was on the palomino mare, Sunrise, who seemed to be something of a favourite. I was on a twitchy, dapple grey Anglo-Arab gelding called Zoot, who shied and side-stepped at every flutter of leaves, snorting and goggle-eyed.

Eventually, Helena said, "Because…if you go to jail, you kinda know what you've done to deserve it."

"Most of the time," I agreed.

We reached a metal gate across the trail and Helena halted.

"OK, *most of the time*, but you also know when you're likely to be released." She gave a short laugh, harsh enough to make the palomino's ears flick back and forth, gauging her mood. "Me? I got life without any possibility of parole."

I nudged Zoot alongside the gate so I could reach down for the latch. At the clang of it disengaging, the gelding skittered sideways, nostrils flaring. I tried to ignore the histrionics—both from him and from Helena.

We rode through. Zoot decided that the gate had now become a scary monster and I had to half coax, half bully him near enough for me to close it. It all took longer than it needed to. Helena sat and watched the battle without impatience. I guessed it gave her more time to think.

When I fell in beside her again, she said, "My parents had another daughter before me. She died as an infant. No reason, no explanation. There one day and gone the next. A crib death—is that what they call it in England?"

"Cot death, but the same thing, I think," I said. "I'm sorry."

"It happens, so I'm told." She shrugged. "To perfectly healthy babies. Thing is, when I came along, it made them totally over-protective."

I thought of my twin brother who had not survived to term, and what I perceived to be my father's perpetual disappoint-ment that the wrong child lived to be born. "An understandable reaction, perhaps?"

"An *over*-reaction," she shot back. "You weren't *there*. You didn't have people watching you twenty-four/seven, even while you slept. *Especially* while you slept."

"No, I didn't," I agreed. I refused to play the game of who had it worse. Everybody's own story is as bad as it has ever been, without compare.

"They'd go crazy over every cough or sneeze after that—and Lord preserve us from letting me take any kind of a *risk*."

And yet she'd clearly been allowed—even encouraged—to

ride horses. Something with inherent dangers, which saw people both seriously injured and killed. When I pointed this out, she shook her head.

"I was doing dressage by the time I was ten, but no galloping across country, no jumping over anything but the smallest fences."

I remembered her wild ride back to the house a few days before, and Schade's comment about her having too much courage for her own good. Did he know how much of it was deep-seated defiance, I wondered?

"Everything I did was orchestrated, right from when I was a child. Who I came into contact with, who was allowed to be my friend. My father arranged for anybody who got close to me at school to be checked out and, if they didn't meet *his* standards, he either paid them off, or warned them off. *His standards*. I mean, can you *believe* that?"

"Maybe he thought that was the best way to keep you safe."

She pulled to a halt abruptly enough for the mare to throw her head up in protest and swing her quarters sideways. "Seriously? He *hit* you, and you're *defending* him?" Her voice rose in outrage. She shook her head, lips thinning into a line caused as much by upset as anger. "You're just like the rest. My father tells you to jump and the only thing you want to know is how high and when can you come down. He's controlling you just like he controls everybody else."

I didn't think she'd listen to explanations of my own sense of guilt, even if I felt inclined to share, so I said, "You can't hold your parents responsible forever for what happened as a child."

"You think it stopped when I got to be a teen? An adult?" she asked bitterly. She let out a long breath and looked up, blinking, at the clear sky above us. "I lost my virginity when I was fifteen to the boy who came to clean the pools. When my father found out, he had him beaten so badly he could barely walk."

I could have pointed out that, if she was fifteen, the pool-boy had committed statutory rape. I didn't think it would help my cause.

"I worked so hard in school. And when I was offered a place at a really good college I thought that might be my chance to finally be free of them. Then I found out the only reason I'd gotten that offer was because my father financed a new library wing."

I said nothing. She glanced at me, then continued, "If I'd worked hard in school, I busted my *ass* in college. I graduated top of my class."

There was no mistaking her pride. "What subject did you study?"

"Accountancy. I know, boring, right? But I was good with numbers and I just wanted so badly to be *normal*. My father talked about setting me up in business. I turned him down flat, sent out my résumé, and was offered a junior position at a great firm in Chicago. I met a guy there, who was being tipped for partner. He didn't seem to care who my father was. I began to think that, *finally*, they seemed to be leaving me alone. I should have known better."

"I'm guessing the firm didn't suddenly acquire a new library wing?"

She smiled in spite of herself. "Close enough. New investor, new clients, snazzy new building. Still, I didn't spot it. Dumb, huh?"

"What gave it away?"

"He did—the guy, I mean. Shall we move things up a little?" And without waiting for my response she pushed the mare forwards into a canter, then a full-blown gallop across the next field. Zoot immediately started jumping up and down at the prospect of being left behind. Muttering curses under my breath, I slackened my hold on the gelding's head and let him thunder in pursuit.

His breeding made him fast and competitive. We caught up with Helena's palomino before she reached the far gate.

"You were telling me about this guy you were dating," I reminded her once we'd settled back to a walk. Or in Zoot's case, a sideways jog, up on his toes.

"Yeah, things were going badly. He kept telling me he loved me, but seemed to resent spending time with me. And when I tried to call the whole thing off? Let's just say he didn't take it well, and then the *real* story came out."

"Which was?"

"How my father hand-picked him as son-in-law material, promised him the earth if he'd 'make an honest woman of me'— yeah, his exact words, apparently—and how he'd kill me if I took that away from him now."

"What a charmer," I said. "So, what did you do?"

"What else could I do?" she said, and for once the question didn't sound entirely rhetorical. "I called my father. Told him he'd created this mess, he could damn well clean it up."

"And what happened to the guy?"

"I don't know," she said, her voice hollow. "He disappeared a few days later. I never saw him again."

24

THE KNOCK on the door of my suite came later the same afternoon. When I checked the Judas glass before opening up, I saw Mo Heedles standing in the corridor outside. She looked as neat and competent as ever. Ah well, at least I'd showered and changed after riding out with Helena, so I no longer smelled strongly of horse.

I took a moment to compose myself. When I swung the door open I was able to offer a neutral smile.

"Before you ask, Mrs K is back safe and sound in the master suite. Was there something you needed?"

I still wasn't sure entirely where I stood with Eric Kincaid's strangely talented PA. It was difficult to get a read on her. Now, she tilted her head to look at me over the top of her glasses. They were on a decorative chain that looped round the back of her neck. I resisted the urge to shuffle my feet.

"I came to check you were OK," she said. "That was quite a hit you took this morning, dear."

I took a deep breath and let it out. I could now do so with discomfort rather than pain. No lasting after-effects. "Well, it's not the first time I've been thumped and it probably won't be the last. Don't let it worry you."

It suddenly seemed stupid and petty to keep her hanging around outside my door. I stood back and jerked my head. She stepped past me into the living area of the suite and turned around, arms folded.

"It's reckoned that a punch to the stomach was what killed Harry Houdini," she said.

"I thought he died of appendicitis?"

"He died of peritonitis caused by a ruptured appendix," she corrected. "The blow to the stomach was what ruptured it in the first place."

"Allegedly."

She nodded as if acknowledging my point. "Still, I'm sorry you had to go through that. He always was a mean bastard."

"Yeah, well, fortunately he punches like a girl."

That almost raised a smile. "Think yourself lucky he went for the personal touch instead of delegating it to Mr Schade."

"Was that a possibility?"

"Mr Schade was Mr Orosco's man—probably still is, for that matter. Mr K may be the boss day-to-day, but Mr Orosco has what you might call a controlling interest."

"Well, *that* little nugget wasn't included in the job description," I muttered. Or in the intel I'd been given, either. Epps hadn't mentioned anything about Mafia involvement, past or present.

"When you hide ownership behind enough shell corporations and finance houses, you'd need to be a forensic accountant to know for sure."

I shrugged, leaned against the corner of the wall next to the hallway. "Then why are you telling me this?"

"Like I said, you took a hit for something that wasn't your fault. As I understand it, Mr Schade instructed you to go after the waiter instead of sticking with Mrs K."

Something in her tone tipped me off. I regarded her, head on one side. "Yesterday, you—and Schade, for that matter—were acting as though I was in league with the bad guys. What changed?"

She reached into her bag and pulled out a smartphone, thumbing the screen into life.

"I managed to obtain this," she said and tilted the phone so I could watch the video clip that began to play. It was a little on the fuzzy side, and it took me a moment to work out that the closed-circuit camera had been sited high in a corner between two walls and a ceiling, distorted by the width of the lens.

As soon as a man dressed like a waiter burst through a door directly beneath the camera, I knew what I was going to see. He dodged to one side. A moment or so later, I watched myself push open the same door and he launched his attack. There was no mistaking the weight of his intent. He'd missed taking my head off by a fraction.

I hardly needed to see the fight that followed—I'd been there, after all. But what interested me was what happened after I'd reacted to something unseen on the footage—the sound of gunshots outside—and abandoned the man on the floor.

He certainly hadn't been capable of moving under his own steam, I noted with minor satisfaction. Instead, he'd been scooped up by two guys who entered from the rear of the building. They wore baseball caps, pulled low, and were careful to keep their faces averted from the camera.

When the clip finished, she blanked the screen again and dropped the phone back into her bag.

"It would seem I owe you an apology, dear, and I *hate* it when that happens."

"What else?"

For a moment she looked taken aback. "Well, you're not having it in writing, if that's what you mean."

"What I *mean* is that you don't actually owe me anything. You could have got away with saying nothing at all and I wouldn't have thought more about it. So, what else is going on?"

She sighed. "OK, I'm guessing that Mrs K has told you about her father—what he was like when she was growing up?"

"Yeah, she's said some things," I agreed carefully. "Where was her mother while all this was going on, by the way?"

"At home, being the perfect little homemaker in a ten-thousand-square-foot mausoleum in Bergen County. For years she floated around the place on a cloud of gin and prescription pain meds. She passed while Helena was in college."

She sounded scathing, but I remembered Helena telling me

about the cot death of her sister and couldn't bring myself to pass judgement.

"If that pained expression on your face is any kind of sympathy, then save it," Mo said. She sniffed. "She treated her daughter as nothing more than a fashion accessory, like one of those little yippy dogs some ladies like to carry around in their purses, dyed to match the furniture."

"I'm guessing you're not a fan."

"I'm more of a cat person," she said. "No, but we'll be leaving in a few days and I wanted you to understand—"

"Leaving? Leaving for where?"

"Europe. Mrs K was going to stay behind for this trip, but after everything that's happened, well, she's decided she wants to go along with her husband."

Epps had not mentioned anything about going overseas. "How long is this trip?"

"A few weeks, maybe a month," Mo said. "The point is, I wanted you to understand that you're not just protecting her from outside dangers, like last night, but potentially from the people close to her as well."

"Including Kincaid?"

"No! I'm talking about her father." She shook her head, emphatic. "Mr K is one of the few people who ever stood up to the old man. Why do you think she married him?"

25

I STOOD in the frozen vegetable aisle, thoroughly nonplussed. Over the supermarket's low-grade PA system they were playing mangled muzak. I tried not to grind my teeth as I wondered if the intended effect was to drive customers to the checkouts as quickly as possible. Just when I was debating running amok to make it stop, I was approached by a middle-aged woman wearing an apron bearing the store logo.

"Excuse me, ma'am," she said with a cheeriness that had no basis in the reality of her job. "Could I possibly take a few moments of your time to answer some questions about your shopping experience with us today?"

Her name badge read 'Tammy' but I doubted that her driver's licence read the same. I gave her a big smile. "I'd be absolutely delighted to."

Her eyes widened fractionally for a moment.

"Well, that is *so* nice of you," she said, as if I'd just agreed to let her firstborn have one of my kidneys. "First of all, if we could start with your name? Oh, would you look at that—my pen don't work. Would you mind stepping on back to the office with me while I grab myself another?"

"Of course. Lead the way."

I abandoned my shopping cart where it sat and trailed the woman's busy footsteps through home baking and past the deli counter. A pair of scratched plastic swing-doors led into the warehouse area at the rear of the store. We passed through without anybody giving us a second glance.

In the far corner, a small office had been knocked together out of stud partitions that nobody had bothered to box in on the outside. The woman was already divesting herself of the apron as she trotted to the door and rapped on it with her knuckles. A muffled voice from the other side called, "Come!"

She stuck her head round it just far enough to say, "Ms Fox, sir."

Then she winked at me and turned away. I watched her toss the clipboard onto a pallet of breakfast cereal and keep walking.

I pushed the door wider. Inside the office, behind the untidy desk, sat Conrad Epps. He was surrounded by paperwork—piles of what appeared to be shipping notes and staff rotas and promotional items. He looked about as happy as I would have expected him to in such a setting.

"Close the door and sit down," he said, not exactly welcoming. I obeyed the first part and ignored the second, leaning on the desk instead.

"You," I said, "have some explaining to do."

"Oh?" Epps managed to inject so much doubt into a single word.

"Why didn't you tell me that Helena Kincaid is the daughter of Darius Orosco?"

He sat back in the tatty swivel chair. If he was embarrassed to have been caught out, it didn't show. "Would it have made any difference, *had* you known?"

"It might have made me think twice about getting involved in your half-arsed scheme, yes." I straightened in realisation. "Ah, so *that* was the reason."

"Perhaps it was to stop you thinking too much about what you were doing," Epps allowed. "You are not an actor, nor are you a trained undercover operative. The less you had to pretend not to know, the better."

"Better for whom?" I demanded. "It didn't help me much when he turned up yesterday and belted me for failing to keep his daughter safe."

That got his attention. Just for a second, I thought I saw the flare of concern in his features. I never knew he cared.

"Were you compromised?"

Ah, so he doesn't *care.*

I ran through the events of the last few days, up to and including Helena's abduction and return, apparently unhurt.

"So, was it…taken as a warning?" he asked slowly.

"I don't know—you tell me."

He bridled. "I'm not sure I like your tone, Ms Fox."

"Tough. It's the only one I've got," I said recklessly. I leaned forwards, getting into his personal space. "Did you arrange Helena's kidnapping?"

"What possible reason might I have for doing that?"

I shook my head. "Uh-uh. Answering a question with another question is not an answer. There could be any number of reasons. To stir things up with Kincaid and Orosco? What better way to unsettle them both? After all, one's her husband and the other's her father. Not to mention that it puts pressure on your inside man—or woman. Reminds them that you have a long reach and they shouldn't forget who's pulling their strings. So, I'll ask you again. Did. You. Arrange. It?"

"No." He let his breath out in an annoyed spurt through his nose, flaring his nostrils in a way that reminded me of the highly strung Anglo-Arab horse, Zoot. "And perhaps *you* should not forget who is pulling *your* strings."

I ignored that crack. "You must have an idea who *did* grab her?"

"Logic would suggest it might be the same people who were trying to take her when you…intervened," Epps said carefully. "Too much of a coincidence for there to be more than one group behind the data breach and the initial kidnap attempt."

"No more of a coincidence than for *you* to be spying on Kincaid and then discovering somebody else was trying to do the same," I pointed out. "He must have more than one set of enemies? Present company excepted, of course."

"That he does," Epps agreed. Two could play at ignoring digs.

"If he's re-established trade with the Syrians, it's unlikely to be them."

"There are plenty of people in the Middle East who might be…alarmed by the prospect of Kincaid supplying them with chemical weapons."

"So, why is he doing it?"

"At a guess? Money." Epps came close to sneering. "A great deal of money. Most people find their principles take a back seat to greed."

I recalled Eric Kincaid's comments in the garage, looking at all those expensive examples of automotive art. "He's already a rich man," I said. "How much more wealth does he really need?"

"Since when did *need* have anything to do with it?"

"If it's so profitable, why did he stop dealing with the Syrians in the first place?"

"Let's just say there were some…shifts in policy."

I eyed him. "At whose behest? Yours?"

But he shook his head. "There's a limit to how much I can tell you, as you are well aware," he said. "For your own safety as much as operational security."

"You're hamstringing me here, Epps." I took a breath, looked him straight in those stone cold eyes and tried not to shiver. "Is Helena Kincaid your inside man? And I use the term in its loosest sense, obviously. Clearly she has daddy issues. It's just a question of how far she might be prepared to go with them."

But even before I finished speaking, Epps was shaking his head again. "That's not how this works," he said, showing me his teeth in a way that was more reminiscent of a guard dog than a smile. "You don't get to keep guessing until you happen upon the correct name. So, I can neither confirm nor deny that information."

"Thanks," I muttered, "that's very helpful."

"All you are required to do is keep a watching brief on the Kincaids and their household, and report back to me."

"Yeah, well, that's about to become a tad more complicated," I said. Not that it wasn't complicated enough already. I had a number of different routes I could take when I ran around the Kincaids' property each morning, knowing that Epps was monitoring the fitness tracker I wore. If I took one route in particular, he knew I needed to have a face-to-face meeting. Hence my unnecessary visit to the local supermarket.

"Complicated, how?"

"Mo Heedles told me yesterday that Kincaid has a trip to Europe planned, and after this scare, Helena's going with him, so that means I go, too."

"Europe?" he said sharply. "Have you been informed as to the location?"

"Not yet. But as soon as I know, I'll do my best to get it to you. Is this a major problem? I mean, Kincaid's business is all over the world. Surely you were prepared for something like this?" And when he didn't respond, I prompted, "Weren't you?"

"With enough of a heads-up, and depending on which country or countries you're visiting, I *may* be able to have some kind of back-up in place," he said at last, sounding uncharacteristically vague.

"When you put it like that, 'may' doesn't exactly sound very reassuring."

"Well, it's the best I got," Epps snapped.

I stared at him, realisation unfurling slowly inside my head. "You're off the reservation with this, aren't you?" I murmured. "Either the people further up the food chain don't *know* about this operation, or they don't know it might have gone sideways. And *you* don't want them to find out."

Eventually, he sighed. "On US soil I can...obscure whatever resources I channel into providing you with adequate support— lose them in other operations. In a foreign country, it's a whole different ball game."

"So, what do you suggest I do? Resign? Because, as I recall, you told me in no uncertain terms that if I wasn't spying on Kincaid for you, you'd ship me back to the UK on the next available flight."

"You could explain to Kincaid that you aren't able to leave the US and return to it until your resident status is reconfirmed," he suggested.

I stared. "And what's Helena supposed to do for protection in the meantime?" I shook my head. "That's not going to wash with Kincaid. Besides, if I can't do the whole job, why would he keep me on at all?"

He let his breath out down his nose, again like a horse. It was the only outward sign of his annoyance. "And you've picked up nothing so far?"

"No. But you expect me to work out if anybody has turned when you won't tell me who that 'anybody' might be. They're all playing their cards close to their chest. It's just about bloody impossible, Epps."

"I know," he said quietly.

I'd been so expecting him to argue that his admission took the fight out of me utterly.

I sat down abruptly, rubbed my face with my hands. For a moment or two we sat in silence except for the muted tweedling filtering through from the store. It was interrupted by an announcement over the PA trying to tempt customers with reduced items in the bakery department.

"I have to go, don't I," I said at last, more statement than question, and more to myself than to him.

"I can't offer you any kind of protection if you do."

"And I can't offer Helena Kincaid any kind of protection if I don't."

"She is not the primary focus of this operation and should not be your main concern." Epps rubbed a finger against the side of his temple as if dealing with me was giving him a headache. "This is why I dislike working with…" His voice trailed off.

"Women?" I finished for him.

"Amateurs." He scowled. "You just can't help yourself becoming too emotionally involved."

"Well, for the moment you're stuck with me so we both have to make the best of it," I said, more cheerfully than I felt. "If I can't work on who's on the inside, I'll have to work on who's on the outside instead."

"Meaning?"

"This trip to Europe may well provide the opportunity to flush out the people who went after Helena," I said, meeting his gaze as I spoke. He stared right back at me. No clues there, then.

"That course of action may have a negative effect on the integrity of my agent."

"And doing nothing may have a negative effect on the continued life of my principal," I said. I got to my feet. "Right at this moment, I know which bothers me more."

26

Mrs Heedles was waiting for me when I got back to the house.

"You do know that anything you need, dear, you can ask the housekeepers to pick up for you when they go to the market?" she said mildly, nodding to the brown paper sack of odds and ends I'd bought, almost at random, to justify my trip out.

"OK, um, thanks. I'll remember that next time."

"Oh, and he wants to see you," she said as I started to turn away. I glanced back, wondering if I'd undone all the good work towards earning her trust. She was frowning, but it looked more like worry than suspicion.

"Is everything OK?"

A quick smile came and went. "We traced the guns. The ones the men were using who attacked Mrs Kincaid on the road."

"Ah… Isn't that a good thing?"

"An excellent question, dear," she said. "But I'm going to let *you* ask it."

———

Kincaid was in his office. He stood by the window, staring out. Schade, predictably, was there as well. Instead of lounging in his usual place in one of the chairs by the desk, he was on the low sofa against one wall, tapping at the keyboard of a laptop.

Only Kincaid looked up when Mo showed me in.

"I understand you found out where those M4s came from," I said without preamble.

Kincaid nodded. "They were originally part of a US Army shipment, like I told you, but let's just say they got a little lost in the bureaucratic shuffle."

"And turned up where?"

"An Italian arms dealer based near Siena acted as the middleman. A guy called Ugoccione."

Something in his voice had me raising an eyebrow as I took a seat. "Someone you know?"

Schade gave a soft snort without looking up from his computer screen.

"Someone we know," Kincaid agreed flatly, which on balance didn't sound promising.

"And do you think he'll tell you who the buyer was?"

"If we handle him carefully enough," Kincaid said. "But it's not the kind of thing that can be done at a distance. For this it's gonna have to be face to face."

"Meaning, we're going to Italy?"

"Meaning, we were going to France anyway, but first stop is now *Italia*," Schade said.

"The one is not exactly on the way to the other," I pointed out.

Whatever reply he might have been about to make was interrupted by the office doors swinging open. Darius Orosco strode through, with Mo Heedles behind him. From her expression, I gathered she'd told him Kincaid was busy and had been ignored. It clearly did not please her.

"I'm sorry, Mr Kincaid. I—"

"It's all right, Mrs Heedles," Kincaid said. "Mr Orosco is family. He can drop in any time he pleases."

"Whether we like it or not."

He didn't add the words, but I heard them anyway. If the slight smile Mrs Heedles gave was anything to go by, she did, too. She nodded and went out, closing the doors quietly behind her.

Orosco strode towards the desk. Kincaid had turned away

from the window to meet him. I rose, stepping away from my chair so it didn't get in my way, just in case. To Orosco, it must have looked like I backed off from him. He flicked me a brief glance, filled with disdain, and kept moving.

"Eric! What's this nonsense I hear about Helena going with you to France, hey?"

"Italy," Schade said without looking up.

"*Italy*. What the hell…?"

Schade looked up briefly then. "Tomas Ugoccione supplied the M4s used in the ambush. We're going to ask him about that."

For a second, Orosco seemed lost for words, then he said, "And you think you're taking my little girl along for the ride?"

Kincaid paused a moment before he said, "That's correct. She is going. She didn't want to stay home, after all that's happened, and I confess I'd rather have her along with me."

Orosco shook his head a little sadly, as if at the naiveté of youth.

"Not happening."

Kincaid straightened a fraction and his eyes narrowed. "It's already been arranged."

"Well, you can just *un*-arrange it, then. My little girl is not disappearing halfway across the world with you, into who-knows-what kind of danger, when *you* need to have your head in the game."

"With respect," Kincaid said through his teeth. "I have no problem keeping my head in the game. And it's been decided— Helena *herself* has decided. Besides, the way things have gone down here, she'd be no safer staying here."

Orosco's eyes shifted to me again and his mouth twisted.

"Confine her to the estate and she'll be fine. Plenty to keep her occupied around this place while you're away, what with these damn ponies she's so keen on."

I tried to control my eyebrows, which were in danger of climbing into my hairline and ending up perched on top of my head. Kincaid's face was stony. Schade's attention was apparently totally absorbed by whatever he was doing on his laptop.

"She may be *my* wife, but she's *your* daughter," Kincaid said, and for a moment I thought he was relinquishing control. Then he added, "With that in mind, I doubt I could confine her anywhere without her breaking out and ripping me a new one. Too much of your blood in her veins for her to do it any other way."

The two men stared at each other. I could almost see Orosco wrestling with the knots Kincaid had just neatly tied him into. They weren't for coming undone.

"I've made it my life's work to keep that kid out of harm's way, Kincaid," he said at last, his mouth tightened into a thin line. "Be sure to do the same, or you'll answer to *me*."

27

THE GULFSTREAM private jet that Eric Kincaid had dismissed as being "a nice little family plane" was, in fact, a top-of-the-line G650ER. It had a range of up to 7500 nautical miles. More than enough to get us from the private airfield in New Jersey where we boarded, across to Europe without any need to stop and refuel en route.

There were seven of us on board, plus the crew. The Kincaids were in the aft part of the cabin with Mrs Heedles. She had spread a briefcase of paperwork across the wide table there and was going through it with Kincaid. Helena sat across the aisle, pretending to read a book—either that or she was a very, very slow reader. We'd been airborne for an hour and, so far, she hadn't turned a page.

But I guess being kidnapped can have that kind of effect on your concentration.

Helena was wearing an impeccably cut dark green blazer over slacks and a white shirt. She looked effortlessly stylish. I was not quite so stylish, but ever since I'd realised she preferred people to mistake me for her PA rather than her bodyguard, I'd tried to dress up a little. I was in black for the usual reason—it didn't show the blood.

Mid-cabin were the two extras on the security team for this trip, to act as drivers and general muscle. One was Lopez, now recovered from being drugged the night Helena was taken. The other was Chatty, who, I'd discovered, was an ex-US Deputy Marshal from Texas. His real name was Williams. I think he was more interesting when I didn't know.

He and Lopez were sprawled on the sofa, watching a football game on the big flatscreen that folded out of the cabinet on the port side. Both wore wireless headphones so the rest of us didn't have to suffer the commentary. Although they each twitched when play quickened, so far they'd managed not to forget themselves enough to stamp their feet or yell encouragement out loud.

Schade and I had the single seats in the forward part of the cabin nearest to the galley, on either side of the aisle. He was reading, too—an old paperback edition of William Golding's *Lord of the Flies*. In contrast to Helena's progress, he had almost finished the slim volume.

I was also reading—going over maps and ground plans of our destinations in both Italy and France. It bugged me, just a little, that Schade and the others appeared to be taking their job so lightly. I reminded myself that they'd worked for Kincaid a lot longer than I had. For all I knew, they'd been to all these places countless times before.

Eventually, he tucked the book into his jacket pocket and picked up the bowl of udon noodles the flight attendant served, using chopsticks without a fumble.

"Enjoying your book?"

He swallowed a mouthful of food. "Read it before."

"So, why read it again?"

He shrugged, and I saw his eyes skim across the occupants of the cabin. "It never does any harm," he said, "to be reminded of the savagery of human nature."

———

WE LANDED in the late afternoon at another small, private airfield, not far from Perugia in the Umbria region of Italy. There were no clouds visible in a brilliant blue sky as we taxied in. As soon as the flight crew released the door, fresh cool air gushed into the cabin.

We were not required to de-plane, line up with passports to clear Immigration, or drag our luggage through Customs. Instead, uniformed officials came to us. They climbed aboard, counted heads, counted passports, and when the number of one matched the other they handed them back with only a cursory inspection. I didn't bother asking how legit it all was.

As soon as we'd been cleared and the Italian officials departed, I heard the heavy thrum of a rotary wing approaching. A few moments later, a blue and white Sikorsky S-76 helicopter touched down less than fifty metres away. The co-pilot jumped out, all bouffant hairstyle and Aviator shades. Within ten minutes, our bags were transferred and we were buckled-in to the cabin.

The Kincaids sat in the two rearward-facing seats against the front bulkhead of the cabin. Mo Heedles and Schade took the two facing them, leaving me squashed into the back row with Williams and Lopez. They both took up more than their share of space, but at least I was able to elbow my way to a window seat on the starboard side.

As soon as he was in, Lopez reached below his seat and pulled out three small flat cases of a familiar style. I raised an eyebrow as he checked the contents and handed one to me. Inside was a SIG P226, two spare magazines, and a Kramer holster.

"What happened to it being a lifejacket that's usually under your seat?" I asked.

Schade gave me a wry look over his shoulder. "Different kind of life preserver."

The flight was short—less than thirty klicks as the turbocharged crow flies. The landscape beneath shifted from open farmland to thickly wooded hills. Valleys became delineated by shadows, roads hidden by the canopy. Buildings mostly had orange tile roofs, the occasional swimming pool, cultivated rows of vegetation that might have been olive groves.

We passed over a town I guessed from the maps I'd studied must be Torricella and then, almost without warning, out over aquamarine water, its surface like stippled glass. I craned in my seat and could just make out our destination—Isola Minore. The island was the shape of a comma, and tiny. The briefing file I'd read on the plane said it was around five hectares, which equated to a little over twelve acres total in size. The only buildings on it had been first part of a monastery and then a castello, before falling into ruin.

Tomas Ugoccione had bought the whole thing—island and property—five years previously. He was in the midst of a restoration that was as ambitious as it was costly. I gathered he could well afford it. And what better place, once the work was done, for a man in a very private business to carry it out?

As we approached the island, I could see a boathouse and a floating jetty jutting into the lake at the southwest end, at the narrowed tail of the comma. Above it was a sprawling building with a crumbling square tower in one corner, covered in sheeted scaffolding. We flew directly overhead. I looked down into the courtyard in the centre as it flashed below us, which appeared to be partly filled with rubble and a mechanical digger.

A moment later, we were clear of the house and pool area, and coming in low towards a clearing in the trees several hundred metres away. The pilot dropped us down neatly onto the concrete pad in the centre. Before he'd even powered down, several figures converged on the aircraft from both sides. They wore a uniform of dark blue polo shirts, tactical trousers, baseball caps, and body armour. Each man carried a machine pistol on a shoulder strap. Each had a handgun on his hip.

Whoever this guy Ugoccione was, it was clear he took his security very seriously indeed.

28

"Ah, *Erico*!" Tomas Ugoccione came striding across the terrace with hands outstretched towards Kincaid. "This is a surprise!" He was a small guy, deeply tanned and casually but expensively dressed in slacks and a pastel linen shirt. The shirttails hung loose, which might have suggested Ugoccione was carrying, but I got the feeling it was more likely an attempt to disguise a belly that could no longer be cinched-in by belt alone.

By comparison with Kincaid's square-jawed determination, there was something just a little soft about him. A little fake—an actor posing next to the real thing.

Only once the arm-clasping and cheek-kissing were complete did he turn to Helena and perform a sleek bow. "And *la signora*, of course. You look as lovely as always. Welcome to Isola Minore."

Helena murmured a polite but noncommittal response. Ugoccione greeted Mrs Heedles with something close to awe. She gave him a regal nod in reply. He glanced at me briefly, his eyes lingering as he tried to work out my place in the great scheme of things. From his frown, I gathered that he hadn't quite done so, but he nevertheless decided that I was not important enough to warrant individual attention.

Instead, he smiled at the group of us, all inclusive, and gave an elaborate shrug. "What a pity you have chosen this moment to visit."

Kincaid raised an eyebrow. "Oh?"

"Why of course," Ugoccione said. "Had you but waited until next spring—summer at the latest—you would have found this palace fully restored to its former splendours."

"Our business would not wait."

Ugoccione paused, gaze flicking over us. It might have been my imagination that it lingered on Schade, who slouched near Kincaid's shoulder, chewing gum, and on Lopez by the edge of the terrace. Both men's eyes were everywhere. Williams had stayed with the Sikorsky and the pilots.

"Come, please. We will talk." Ugoccione inclined his head to Helena. "Perhaps you would care for a tour of the finished rooms?" He put a hand to his chest, feigning modesty. "The decoration, even though I should not be the one to say so, is unrivalled. I am sure my *architetto* would be only too happy—"

"No," Helena said. The word reverberated, sharp and stark like clapped hands in an empty space. She softened it with a small smile. "Thank you, *signore*. I will stay. What we have to discuss concerns me, also."

Ugoccione's hands tightened, his mouth opened and closed. He took a sideways glance at Kincaid. Then he forced a smile even if his eyes were hooded. "Who am I to argue with *la bella signora*?"

He ushered us into a stone cloister and then through a pair of tall French windows that stood propped wide in the still air. As we followed him inside, I realised the windows had not been left open to vent the heat of the day from the old building, but to allow some warmth to penetrate the thick stone walls. The air inside was soft and chilled, without the slightly metallic tint of air conditioning.

Ugoccione led us up a magnificent stone staircase and across the open landing. It was tempting to gawp at the vaulted ceilings we passed underneath but I managed to keep my eyes—and my mind—on the job. Even with half their ornate artwork missing, the plaster patched with blank new sections or, in places, still hanging down in ribbons of horsehair and splinters, it was a stunning building. Restoring it, I reckoned, was an undertaking that could take a lifetime.

I thought of Ugoccione's claim that it would be finished inside the next twelve months or less and wondered just how much money he was throwing at this project.

We passed through an open archway out onto a loggia that ran along the length of the upper storey, overlooking the central courtyard. I checked rooflines and the dark shadows concealed beyond open windows but there was nothing to cause me undue alarm.

As we walked alongside the courtyard, I glanced down and saw the same pile of building rubble I'd noted from the air. Workmen came and went, carrying tools, or plans or timber. Interspersed among them were the guards with shades and machine pistols. It seemed excessive for someone on his own private island. What was he expecting the workmen to do—make off with the silver? I caught Schade's eye but he gave me nothing in return.

Ugoccione walked briskly ahead, a man with purpose. He threw open another set of doors and stepped inside. All his movements contained flourish, like a stage magician trying to direct attention away from the trickery going on behind the scenes. It did not make me feel more relaxed.

We followed him into a room that was big enough to play basketball in, not least because of the height. It had a grand central table surrounded by high-backed chairs, more suited to the boardroom than the dining room. Either that or some secret order of the Illuminati. An antique desk was slanted across one corner, opposite a line of windows that looked south across the lake. It was an impressive room for a study, but with a view like that who'd ever get any work done?

Ugoccione gestured to the board table and spoke to one of his staff in rapid Italian. The man nodded and left, closing the doors behind him.

"Please, sit," Ugoccione said. "Refreshments will be here presently."

Ugoccione took the seat at the head of the table, clearly determined to set the tone of this meeting. Kincaid calmly pulled out a chair halfway along one side for Helena, then sat alongside her. Mrs Heedles flanked him on the other side. Ugoccione hesitated, then scraped back his chair and moved down so he was opposite the three of them. The rest of us hovered. Schade and me around the Kincaids with Lopez by the doorway, and Ugoccione's guys behind him. I could almost hear the music to *High Noon* playing in the background.

"Now, *Erico*, please, *mio amico*, what is this about?"

Kincaid rested his hands on the tabletop, fingers apparently relaxed. I added him to my mental list of people never to play poker against.

"How long have we been doing business together?" he asked in a tone that was mild enough to be intimidating all by itself.

Ugoccione seemed to give every answer consideration before he spoke. A careful man, in a profession that gave him much to be careful about.

"You and me, personally? Not long. A few years."

It was Helena who cut in. "But you have been dealing with my family—first my father and now my husband—for more than a decade," she said. "Maybe closer to two."

"Indeed, yes, this is the case. I am honoured to say that Darius—your father—and I have been…associates for many years." His eyes flicked between husband and wife. "I confess I am a little…disconcerted to discuss our business arrangements in front of an audience," he admitted with what might have been intended as disarming candour rather than a snub.

"If I didn't trust my people, they would not be here," Kincaid said.

Ugoccione glanced sideways at Helena. "It is not a matter of trust, I assure you," he said. "But of keeping certain persons out of the line of fire, as it were."

"Yeah, well, it appears someone has already broken our non-combatant agreement."

"But…that's terrible!"

"It is," Kincaid agreed, no emotion in his voice. "And you will appreciate my concern when it was discovered that you had a part in it."

Ugoccione's face reflected an exaggerated confusion. "What

is this? What part? What are you saying?" His voice rose, but he remained seated and his eyes were calculating. He turned to one of his men. "Bernardo, did you know about this? Why was I not informed?"

The man stepped forward ducking almost into a bow. "We knew nothing of any attacks on members of the syndicate, *signore*," he murmured, not only loud enough to be heard across the breadth of the table, but thoughtfully in English, too.

I struggled to keep the impatience out of my face. Schade's slouch became even more pronounced. I was learning that the more relaxed he appeared, the more tightly wound he'd become. Looking at him now, I guessed he was close to furious.

Kincaid explained briefly, and without apparent impatience, about the attempt on Helena on the road. I was standing far enough to one side that, as he spoke, I could see at least part of Helena's face. Her expression was carefully blank.

"Fortunately," Kincaid added, "it was…foiled."

Ugoccione nodded gravely without asking for clarification. He was, I imagined, a man who did not want to know about the harsh realities. How else could he continue to ply his trade?

"We have an agreement. Surely, you know that I would never—"

"They were using Colt M4s," Kincaid interrupted, still calm and measured, "supplied by you." He made it sound personal.

Ugoccione sat back, looking from one face to another.

"*Erico*, please. You, of all people, know that I deal in thousands of units every week—every day. I cannot be held to account for the actions of each end user, just as you yourself cannot. It is a sad truth of the business we are in, *mio amico*."

Kincaid inclined his head slightly, allowing the point, but only *up to* a point. "I would take it as a sign of that friendship you refer to, to know who *was* the particular end user of that shipment, my friend."

Ugoccione gave an exaggerated shrug, his voice rising. "It could be any *number* of people. Do you know how long it would take to narrow down—?"

It was Mrs Heedles who interrupted sweetly, "Even with the serial numbers?"

Ugoccione took a moment to collect himself. When he spoke his voice was calmer. "You know that I cannot divulge such information. Absolute confidentiality is a part of my business, my reputation." He looked pained. "You must know this."

"Someone attacked my family when all of us gave our word that this was something we would never be party to."

"And I was not a party to it!"

"You know as well as I do that it was agreed there cannot be any connection, and yet there is." Kincaid's expression didn't alter. "The rules have already been broken."

Ugoccione eyed him in silence for a long protracted moment, then sighed mournfully. "You have the details?"

Mrs Heedles opened her notebook and passed over a sheet of the specs and serial numbers from the weapons recovered at the scene of the ambush. If it irritated him that his acquiescence had been so predictable, Ugoccione did not show it. He no more than glanced at the paper before handing it to Bernardo, who carried it to the desk and began tapping at a keyboard. Nobody spoke. After a moment or two Bernardo came back with a scribbled note at the bottom. Ugoccione studied this with more care, his lips pursed.

"Ah," he said, as if it had all become clear. "I am afraid to tell you that I knew no good would come of this, *mio amico*."

"Then why did you—?"

But Ugoccione was already shaking his head. "No, no, this is not my doing—it is yours. This consignment was bought for people who previously dealt with you, until you told them you no longer wish to do business."

"Who?"

Ugoccione laughed, short and harsh and without humour. "There have been so *many*? The Syrians. Who else?"

"I thought we had agreed that the Syrians were off limits."

I blinked, but kept the surprise out of my face. *I thought the whole reason I was here was because Kincaid was dealing with the Syrians...?*

Ugoccione laughed again. "*You* agreed. As for the rest of us..." A shrug.

"You cannot do business with everyone, *signore*. It's a case of deciding which relationships are in your own best interests."

"Indeed. I have no wish to endanger *our* relationship." Ugoccione paused, "But in this case I had certain...obligations. I am not a man who goes back on his word."

"Even to a regime that uses chlorine gas against its own people?" Kincaid asked.

"My heart bleeds," Ugoccione said, with every appearance of sincerity. "But the rebels, in their turn, have themselves used sarin nerve agent against their own *compatrioti*—their own government. Nobody comes out of this, as you might say, with the smell of the roses."

"Fuelling such a conflict is hardly productive," Helena pointed out.

Ugoccione spoke gently, his manner that of a father explaining the ways of the wicked world to a sheltered daughter. The patronising bastard.

"Maybe that is so, *mia cara signora*," he said. "But it is very profitable."

29

KINCAID GOT TO HIS FEET. His face was placid but there was a set to his shoulders that spelled trouble. He smiled at Ugoccione with every appearance of amicability, though. I doubt the other man saw the simmering anger beneath the surface.

"Thank you, *signore*, for taking this meeting at such short notice. I appreciate your frankness, and your cooperation."

Ugoccione moved round the table to perform another double-handed clasp in a show of sincerity. But his gaze did not hold Kincaid's for long, and when he stepped back he rubbed absently at the nape of his neck with one hand.

It was a surprise then, when the next moment he said, "You will stay for lunch, of course!"

Kincaid started to shake his head but before he could speak Ugoccione jumped in again, hands now spread wide. "I insist, *mio amico*. We came close to breaking a friendship today, with all that entails. Let us sit and eat together, as a sign of goodwill on both sides, yes?"

Kincaid hesitated. Next to me, Schade twitched. I glanced across. He was staring at Kincaid as if he could force him to make eye contact by will alone—no doubt so Schade could vehemently shake his head. Nice to know it wasn't only my instincts that were prickling.

In spite—or perhaps because—of that, Kincaid smiled. "Of course," he said. "We would be honoured."

Ugoccione's shoulders relaxed and his eyes brightened. "Good. This is good. Come, I have an excellent Brunello I think you will enjoy."

Kincaid pulled back Helena's chair for her to rise.

"I would like to freshen up before we eat," she said.

"Of course." Ugoccione gave her another of those conde-scending bows. "Bernardo, show *Signora* Kincaid the way, if you please, so she does not become lost." He turned back to Helena with a shrug. "This place, it is a maze. Sometimes I become lost even myself."

Bernardo moved to the door and indicated that Helena should go through. I let him follow her, then fell into step behind the pair of them. Bernardo heard my footsteps and paused, frowning. I gave him an innocent smile. "I need to go, too," I said. "And I'd hate to become lost."

Behind me, I heard someone clear their throat. Mo Heedles stood in the doorway. She gave Bernardo a bland smile of her own as she leaned in and said in a confidential voice, "When girls all live under the same roof, they tend to synchronise."

Bernardo had the look of civilian staff rather than security, but I would have been willing to bet everyone surrounding Ugoccione had to prove themselves capable of coping with any situation. Nevertheless, a dark flush seeped up the sides of his neck into his ears and he hurried forwards.

"This way, *signore*. Please…"

He led us along several corridors and down a short flight of marble steps before indicating a doorway. "I shall wait here to escort you."

I went in first. I would have preferred Helena to wait outside until I'd checked the room over, but both women followed me in. Inside, one wall held a marble countertop that held an ornate sink, also marble, with mirrors above. There was a gilded chaise longue under the window, and a single cubicle. I stuck my head through the door as much to see if they'd installed a gold-plated loo as to check for intruders. To my disappointment, the toilet was surprisingly utilitarian.

When Helena had disappeared into the cubicle, I edged closer to Mrs Heedles, cupped my hand around her ear and whispered, "How secure do you think we are in here?"

She drew back, her gaze assessing, then fished in her handbag for her smartphone. She pulled up an app and set the phone down on the countertop.

"Now? Very," she said then. "Unless, of course, Bernardo has his ear to the keyhole."

I opened the outer door a crack. Bernardo was a few metres away with his back half turned, but the way he was standing, the angle of his head, suggested he wasn't above a little eavesdropping, should the occasion present.

I gave him an apologetic smile. "I'm sorry, but you're out of toilet paper in here," I said sweetly. "Would you mind...?" And I watched him scurry away before closing the door.

I turned back to find Mo Heedles as close to grinning as she allowed herself. After a moment, she sobered, all business.

"Now, what's on your mind, Charlie?"

"What isn't?" I muttered. I took a long breath. "Look, you've been with Kincaid a lot longer than I have, but how far does he really trust this guy, Ugoccione?"

She frowned. "That depends on your definition of trust."

"Well, would Ugoccione lie to him?"

"Outright? No, I don't think so. By omission—by saying, or not saying, something he could slide out of later? Very likely." She paused. "Spill it."

"I know Ugoccione's English can seem a little hit-and-miss, but something he said earlier, it was just a little too carefully worded. It could be nothing, but it could mean something."

She made an impatient 'get-on-with-it' gesture with her hand, glancing at the door.

"OK. He said to Kincaid that the consignment 'was bought for people who previously dealt with you, until you told them you no longer wish to do business.' Those were his exact words, yes?"

"I believe so. And?"

"Bought *for* people," I repeated. "It implies that he didn't sell direct *to* the Syrians, but to an intermediary who purchased on their behalf."

"O–K," she said slowly, drawing out the word doubtfully. "Let's say you're right. Where does that get us?"

I shoved a hand through my hair. "I don't know, exactly. It's just…if Ugoccione is trying so hard to stay on Kincaid's good side, as he's making such a big song and dance about doing, why didn't he just give us the name of the intermediary?"

"If there *was* an intermediary."

"Granted, yes, but…why would the Syrians go to all the trouble of coming to the United States and attacking Helena— not to mention making a hash of it—over something as simple as a change of supplier? Ugoccione said himself, dealing with them is very profitable. It's not like they weren't going to find an alternative pretty quickly. Why would they give anyone else a reason *not* to deal with them?"

Mrs Heedles nodded slowly. "You make a good case, dear," she said. "Still doesn't mean the Syrians *weren't* behind it, though." She gave the ghost of a smile. "From my experience, they're not the most logical of people, nor do they take rejection well."

"The men in the ambush were not Syrian."

"Then there you are. They contracted out locally and someone ripped them off with inferior personnel. Not the first time that's happened."

I fell silent. It had been little more than a niggling uncertainty and there was no denying the logic of her explanation. But something didn't sit right, even so.

As I opened my mouth to speak there came a polite knock on the outer door. When I answered it, Bernardo thrust two loose loo rolls into my hands. They were pale pink. I wondered if he'd made the colour choice specially, or if they were the only ones at hand. I gave him a bright smile and shut the door.

Helena came out of the cubicle and began washing her hands. She kept her head down and her movements were jerky enough to be of concern.

"Are you OK?" I asked.

Her head shot up as if I'd yelled. Her eyes caught mine briefly in the mirror and drifted away again.

"Yes. Yes, I'm fine."

"You sure?"

"I said I'm fine! Don't fuss, Charlie."

I paused. "I'm guessing you heard all that?"

She shook the excess water off her hands and shrugged. "Not really."

The blatant lie threw me. We had not exactly been shouting but we hadn't been whispering, either. When I glanced at the older woman, her face was shuttered, offering neither advice nor encouragement.

As she turned to dry her hands on the fluffy towel provided, I saw Helena exchange a pleading look with Mo Heedles.

"Time we got back," Mrs Heedles said decisively, as if nothing had happened. "You know men—they can't be left on their own for long without breaking the furniture."

As Bernardo led us back to the study, I kept a surreptitious eye on Helena. Something had spooked her and she wasn't about to share with me what it might be. If I'd been hoping she might have begun to trust me a little by now, looks like I was bound for disappointment.

30

SAYING anything to Mrs Heedles had been a mistake, I acknowledged. For whatever reason, Helena knew more than she was admitting and Mo had sided with her. Bringing it up with Kincaid now would set the pair of them against me.

I tried to remind myself that my main concern was to protect Helena. But a big part of doing that was threat assessment—not simply the *when* and the *how*, but the *who* as well. It was all bound up together. The best way to prevent anyone getting to her again was to anticipate the next attack. Not knowing who was behind the last attempts made doing my job successfully difficult, bordering on impossible.

And the person who seemed most determined to stop me finding out anything of use was Helena herself.

It was frustrating enough to make me spit.

I managed to control myself through lunch on the terrace. Kincaid, Helena, Mrs Heedles and Ugoccione sat at a table overlooking the lake, under a canopy to keep the high sun off them.

Mrs Heedles may have dismissed my concerns, but she didn't exactly look relaxed. Mind you, neither did either of the Kincaids. Even Ugoccione seemed tense.

Schade, Lopez and I were given a smaller table at the other end of the terrace, further away than I would have liked. And not simply from the point of view of nosiness.

Schade and Lopez tucked in to their food with the concentration of men who couldn't be sure when the next meal was coming. I was too twitchy to do more than push a very good seafood salad about on my plate.

"Charlie, just sitting next to you is giving me acid reflux," Schade said at last. "Just chill out."

"Why should I be the only one?" I muttered. At his raised eyebrow I nodded to our principals. "I haven't seen a more uncomfortable bunch of people around a table since I last had lunch with my parents."

Schade shrugged. "Yeah, well, one wrong move could start a turf war." He abandoned his knife and fork and picked up a baton of raw carrot in his fingers, munching his way down it like Bugs Bunny, and just as unconcerned. "'Least Mr K got what he came for."

"Which was?"

"Who bought those M4s, of course."

I let out an audible breath. "I'm not so sure about that."

Schade motioned me to continue with the stump of carrot. Briefly, I ran through the same points I'd made to Mrs Heedles. As I spoke, I tried to keep my voice low enough not to carry and avoided the temptation to glance across at her, which would have been a dead giveaway.

"What do you think?" I demanded when I was done.

"About what?"

If I kept clacking my teeth together like this, I was going to need some serious dental work.

"About the guns being bought by a middleman," I ground out, "not directly by the Syrians."

"Well, *duh*."

"I don't understand." I slumped back in my chair. "If it was so obvious, why didn't Kincaid press him about who was the middleman?"

Schade had demolished two more sticks of carrot and turned his attention to the remainder of his veal. His eyes, expressionless behind the lenses of his glasses, focused on me without blinking until he'd chewed and swallowed. "What makes you think he doesn't know already?"

Before I could formulate any logical response to Schade's last statement, Bernardo came hurrying out onto the terrace. As I watched him cross to Ugoccione and bend to speak, my train of thought derailed, crashed and burned. There were no survivors.

Ugoccione had been slouched in his seat. Whatever Bernardo murmured in his ear had him surge upright as if someone had applied a cattle prod to his rear end. I was on my feet and moving before Ugoccione's chair finished clattering on the stone flags. There was no conscious decision-making process involved. It was all reflex.

Schade and I reached their table a moment later, with Lopez a few paces behind.

"What's happening?" Schade asked.

"The island…it is being assaulted," Ugoccione said faintly. The next second, his face went from pale to flushed as he turned on Kincaid. "Is this *your* doing, *Erico*? Is this how you treat your friends?"

Kincaid got to his feet, more controlled but no less concerned. He shook his head. "Nothing to do with me, Tomas. You have my word." He glanced to Schade. "Contact Williams. Tell him to brief the pilots. Wheels up in three minutes."

"No," Ugoccione said flatly. "Until we know what is going on —until *I* know—nobody leaves. *Capisce*?"

Kincaid didn't bother arguing. "Where are they?" he demanded of Bernardo. "And how many?"

Before Bernardo could answer, a rake of automatic gunfire stitched across the terrace, sending chips of stone spitting outwards.

I grabbed Helena out of her chair and spun her behind me, keeping a grip on the back of her neck to force her head down as we ran for the safety of the house. We didn't stop until we were two rooms deep, away from any windows. The outer walls of the old building were several feet thick. More than enough to act as a barrier unless they'd brought a tank.

"Well, I guess that answers the first question," Schade said. He had a hold on Kincaid's collar that mirrored my own on his wife. Beyond them, it was hard to tell if Lopez was covering Mo Heedles or if she was covering him.

"Where's Ugoccione?"

"They were right behind us," Lopez said.

Kincaid glanced at Schade, who read his intention at once. "No way, dude. Let his own guys take care of him."

"Oh, I'll *take care of him*, you can be sure of that," Kincaid said, putting a whole different spin on the words. "If that bastard's served us up like Thanksgiving turkey, I'm gonna make damned sure he's with us on the table."

31

WE FOUND them just inside the French windows. Bernardo was lying where he'd fallen between the doorway and a heavy table, deathly still. It was only the dark ooze from a wound to his leg told me he was alive at all. Hearts that have stopped beating no longer pump.

Ugoccione lay further inside, slumped on the floor with his back against an ornate chaise. He was clutching at his side, the pale linen shirt staining dark around his fingers. As soon as we appeared, though, he still had enough left in him to pull a gun on us.

For half a second, we all froze. Then Ugoccione let the muzzle droop as though he no longer had the strength to hold his aim.

"Come to finish the job, eh?" he asked tiredly.

"Don't be a goddamned fool, Tomas," Kincaid said. He covered the distance between them, keeping low, and gently nudged aside the bloodied hand Ugoccione had clamped over the wound. Schade, his own gun out, stuck close behind. Neither of them made any effort to disarm the other man.

"Please…" Ugoccione said. "Please… See to Bernardo…"

Mrs Heedles was already pulling on a pair of nitrile gloves. There must be a stock of them in that woman's handbag. She nodded to Lopez. "See if you can get him farther inside."

Lopez was ex-military and didn't argue. No point in treating the wounded if doing so exposed your medic and got them killed in the process. He cautiously stretched a hand to Bernardo's collar and unceremoniously dragged the man into better cover. I kept close to Helena and my eyes switching between possible breach points, of which this room had too many for comfort.

"He hit his head...when he went down," Ugoccione said, voice beginning to slur.

"Mrs Heedles is taking care of him." Kincaid had the Italian's shirt peeled back, revealing a matt of body hair, and was inspecting the wound. I didn't miss the way he glanced at Schade, his face grave. Helena snatched a silk cloth off the table, tipping a vase of flowers in the process. It glugged water onto the tabletop and cascaded over the edge like rain.

"Here, at least try."

She handed the cloth to her husband. He took it with a faint smile, wadded it into a makeshift dressing and pressed it to Ugoccione's side. The man was struggling not to pass out, jerking his eyes open as he fought to stay with us.

Mrs Heedles had improvised Bernardo's tie and a ballpoint pen into a tourniquet. She motioned Lopez to keep the pressure on while she retrieved a penlight—also from her Mary Poppins handbag—and shone it into Bernardo's eyes. She gently examined the back of his head with her gloved fingertips. They came away bloodied, but she sat back and nodded.

"Be thankful your man has a thick skull," she said.

"I am," Ugoccione murmured. His eyes fluttered closed again. "Thank you, *signora.*"

Schade's phone must have vibrated in his pocket. He answered it with a brief, "Yeah?" listened for a moment, then looked to Kincaid. "Pilots are getting antsy."

Kincaid held out his hand and Schade gave him the phone. "Williams? Tell them to be ready to leave the moment Fox gets to you with Mrs Kincaid. Understand?"

"Now, wait a goddamned minute, Eric—"

It was Helena who protested. If she hadn't, I may well have done so.

"I need you safe." Kincaid threw the phone back to Schade, who caught it without looking.

"I'm safe right here," she argued. "Either we all go, or we all stay."

Kincaid's eyes narrowed. A muscle jumped in the side of his jawline, but he held onto his temper and his tongue. He glanced at Mrs Heedles and gestured to Bernardo. "Can he be left?"

She shook her head. "It will take about ten minutes for his blood to clot," she said. "Until then, we need pressure on the wound or he'll bleed out."

Kincaid nudged Ugoccione, leaned down into his eye line to be sure he was paying attention. "Tomas? Do you have your own doctor on the island? Anyone with medic training?"

"*Si*," Ugoccione gave a faint smile. "Bernardo…"

Kincaid swore under his breath.

Somewhere outside came another burst of automatic weapons fire. It was close, and closing. Those of us who weren't already on the floor ducked instinctively below the level of the windows. Ugoccione grasped at the lapel of Kincaid's jacket.

"I am sorry, *Erico*," he said. "I did not know…" And he began to cough. There was blood on his lips.

"It's OK," Kincaid said. "Old friendships…they are not easily broken."

Ugoccione nodded briefly, and closed his eyes again.

"Eric? Is he…?" Helena's voice was a whisper.

Kincaid didn't look at her. "Charlie, please get my wife out of here," he said quietly. "We'll meet you at the airport. If we're delayed past our take-off window, don't wait. We'll rendezvous at the chateau in France."

I hesitated for a long moment before I gave a reluctant nod. It went against everything in me to cut and run, but my loyalty was to my principal—to keep her safe. Besides, hadn't the first rule I'd taught my self-defence students, back in the day, been that staying to fight was always the last resort?

Kincaid glanced at Mrs Heedles. "You, too, Mo."

"Don't be foolish," she said calmly. "In the absence of anyone better qualified, I'm the nearest thing you have to a doctor. You need me right here."

Kincaid nodded. He got to his feet, cupped Helena's face in his hands and kissed her.

"You are the world to me," he told her. "I *need* for you to stay safe."

"You know I'd die for you," she whispered.

"Ah, Helena," he murmured. "Without you, I'd have no reason to live. Don't you know that by now?"

He let his hands drop. I had to tug Helena's arm to get her to move. She kept her eyes on her husband all the way to the door, then finally turned away with something that sounded suspiciously like a sob.

As we ran through the castello, I was glad she was too embarrassed by her own raw emotions to meet my eyes. Otherwise I would've had to hide emotion of my own.

32

"You OK?"

We'd reached the last doorway. Beyond it lay open ground. My question to Helena was partly out of concern, yes. But it was also to gauge her focus on the here and now, and how much of a liability she was going to be.

I stopped raking my gaze over the landscape outside just long enough to glance at her over my shoulder. Her lips were folded tight together, lines etched deep between her eyebrows, but as she met my eyes her chin came up and she gave a short nod.

"Don't you worry about me, Charlie. I'm not about to go to pieces on you."

"Never thought you were."

She gave a soft snort but didn't call me a liar outright.

I took a few moments longer to check for signs of ambush. If I'm honest, I needed to clear the rush of memories out of my head, too. I'd spent a long time looking after people whose marriages were for the sake of appearances. Little more than mergers contracted for the sake of family alliances or to strengthen industrial dynasties.

Finding a couple who shared a genuine connection was a rarity that shook me.

Mainly because it reminded me of what I'd had with Sean.

And lost.

I took a steadying breath. "Move when I move, stop when I stop, and if anything happens, head for the helicopter and don't look back, all right? I'll hold them off as long as I can."

Without waiting for an answer, I stepped out onto another terrace—this one overlooking a walled garden rather than the lake—and set off at a steady pace between tall dense hedges that smelled like yew. The path underfoot was of white gravel, which was impossible to run along without making noise no matter how carefully you put your feet down. With Helena at my shoulder, I abandoned stealth in favour of speed. I was relying on the fact that the hearing of anyone who'd just been firing an assault rifle on full auto would be compromised anyway.

The gardens opened out into a complex design of low topiary. Box hedges about knee high that had been shaped and trimmed with geometric precision. Very impressive, but not much use for cover.

As we hit a turn in the path, I heard Helena gasp. The body of a man lay sprawled ahead of us. I approached with caution, although the amount of blood around the body told its own story. He was dark-haired, with a well-trimmed beard and a Mediterranean complexion, but he was not wearing the uniform I'd seen on Ugoccione's men. Whoever killed him had taken his weapon but left two spare magazines on his belt. Perhaps not surprisingly, I recognised them as belonging to an M4. I looked again at his features and wondered if they might lean more towards Syrian than Italian. I tried not to let the beard distract me. They were more popular in Italy since the last time I'd visited, but that didn't prove anything

I took in as much detail as I could about the dead man without doing more than slowing for a couple of paces, then took off running again. Helena stayed with me, stride for stride. I was thankful for her natural athleticism. It saved me having to carry her.

At the far end of the topiary garden was a narrow gate out into the wooded area that comprised the majority of the island. I opened it a crack and peered through.

A couple of guys were visible moving through the trees.

From their dress, they were members of Ugoccione's security patrol, but I ducked back out of sight anyway. My Italian wasn't up to complicated explanations and I didn't fancy having to try in a mixture of pidgin and mime.

Avoiding contact with anyone seemed by far the best course.

I kept an eye to the narrow gap between gate and wall until they'd passed out of sight, then we slipped through and high-tailed it into the trees.

It was around one in the afternoon, local time, so I knew if I kept the sun over my right shoulder we'd be heading roughly for the helipad. Even allowing for our increased speed, it took longer to reach it than expected. Long enough for the doubts to creep in, anyway.

Eventually, I caught sight of rotor blades through the trees, spinning lazily. We were approaching the Sikorsky almost directly from the rear. I dragged Helena down behind a small storage shed on the perimeter of the clearing and speed-dialled Williams. He picked up almost instantly.

"Charlie! Where are you?"

"Close by," I said. You can never be sure who might be listening. "Any trouble?"

"Not that we've seen."

"Good. We set to go?"

"Soon as you're on board."

"Coming in, your six o'clock. Try not to shoot either of us," I said, and ended the call.

Williams must have said something to the pilots because almost at once the engine note rose and the rotor speed picked up.

Helena knew the drill by now. The pair of us ran, side by side, for the starboard door. Williams was on the ball enough to swing the door open the moment we reached it and we jumped aboard. It was only as Helena slumped into her seat that I noticed her hands were trembling.

"You OK?" Even as I spoke, I was aware that I'd asked her that question once already, back at the castello, and asking her again now was not going to endear me. Sure enough, her head came up, eyes flashing. At least it took her mind off any residual fear.

She opened her mouth to snap at me, but before she could say anything, the pilot suddenly throttled back the engine and hit the kill-switch.

"Hey," I said, glancing over my shoulder. "Mr Kincaid said to go immediately."

"Maybe so," the pilot said, his Italian accent strong, "but these guys, they do not wish it."

I twisted, ducking to stare forwards through the narrow gap between the two rearward-facing seats and into the cockpit.

Through the canopy, I could see two men had moved out of cover and were standing directly in front of the Sikorsky. The first held an M4 assault rifle in his right hand. He was gesturing with his left—universal sign language for the pilot to shut down.

And just in case that message wasn't clear enough, the second man had a rocket-propelled-grenade launcher locked and loaded on his shoulder. He was pointing it straight at us.

33

OH SHIT…

I hit speed dial for Schade. He answered with a laconic, "Speak."

"We're under threat. Two bad guys with RPG. Repeat, with RPG. Take-off aborted."

"We're on our way," Schade said.

No sooner had he spoken than we heard the rapid rattle of automatic weapons fire. It came from the direction of the castello, muffled by the trees.

"OK, this may take a while. They got us pinned down in the house," Schade said, still sounding calm.

There was a pause, then Kincaid came on the line. "What do they want?"

"At a guess, this is capture not kill."

"I want better than a goddamn guess!"

"Well, that's the best I have. But if it was a kill mission, you'd already be able to see smoke from the burning wreckage," I said. Helena gave an audible gasp and I immediately regretted my snarky reply. *Ah, well.*

"Charlie, don't let them take her. Not again."

"I'll do what I can," I said and ended the call.

As the Sikorsky's engine died away, the man with the assault rifle shouted, "Bring out the woman. That's all we want." His accent wasn't American, but other than that I couldn't place it.

Over his shoulder, the pilot asked, "Which woman?"

"Well, that's the million-dollar question," I murmured. I glanced at Helena. "Take a look at these two guys. Do you know them?"

"Why would I?"

I suppressed a sigh. "Just take a look, Helena."

She did, just long enough to be sure, then shook her head. "No. Why?"

"Because if they're looking to kidnap you, we're going to let them."

"*What?*"

"Take off your jacket."

She hesitated a moment, then seemed to catch on. At least, she did as I'd asked without further argument. Physically, we were similar in height and build. My hair was cut in a shorter, more practical style, and was closer to red than blonde, but they'd asked simply for *the woman* and that suggested it might not matter.

I dumped my wallet and ID, shrugged into the blazer. If they did know what Helena looked like, they'd realise I wasn't her as soon as I stepped out of the aircraft. And if they didn't? Well, at least it might give me an opportunity to get closer to them— closer to that RPG, anyway.

"If you get the chance to take off," I said to the pilot, "then go."

He inclined his head slightly, as if wary of making any sudden moves.

Helena looked stricken, "Charlie—"

"Get out with me, keep low, get directly behind the rear of the heli," I said, cutting her off. "As soon as I start moving towards them, run for the trees. Stay in a dead straight line with the tail. The aircraft should shield you. I'll do what I can to keep their attention on me. Got it?"

She opened her mouth, closed it again, and nodded.

"One more thing—I need your watch."

We swapped my TAG Heuer for her diamond-encrusted rose-gold Rolex. I put my hand on her shoulder. "You ready?

She ducked out of reach. Her chin came up in a way I recognised and didn't like much. "Give me your gun." When I hesitated, she snapped, "You know the first thing they will do is search you and take it away. You're supposed to be me, remember? And *I* would not have a gun."

With reluctance, I handed over the SIG, complete with holster. She clipped the rig inside her waistband.

"OK, *now* I'm ready."

"If she is not out in five seconds, you all die," shouted the man with the M4. "One…"

"OK, OK, she is coming!" the pilot called, and didn't have to fake the concern in his voice.

I pushed open the cabin door. It hinged at the leading edge, providing a certain amount of cover from the two men. I stood behind it long enough for Helena to hop out behind me, crouching below the level of the glass, and scurry beneath the tail section.

I slammed the door shut, took a long breath, and walked forwards. The immediate shouts of denial and rage I'd been expecting did not come. I tried to keep my breathing steady, held my hands out to my sides where they could see them. The sleeves of the jacket rode up enough for the watch to be visible, too. I was hoping they'd take in the obvious signs and ignore the fact I didn't look like anyone's idea of wife to a billionaire.

As I walked towards them, I saw their gaze begin to shift. I stopped. Their eyes were back on me instantly. The man with the assault rifle was the one doing all the talking. He was tall, with long dark hair, loosely tied back, that looked almost glossy. His beard and moustache were neatly trimmed. The other man was younger and clean-shaven. The RPG resting on his shoulder meant I couldn't see his face clearly.

"Who are you?" I demanded, putting on my best American accent. Good enough to fool non-native speakers, if not for long. "What do you want?"

"Shut up and keep walking," the man with the M4 said.

I moved forwards again. The RPG, I saw now, was a Russian model. Old, but serviceable. It claimed a range of up to five hundred metres, but half the time you'd be lucky to hit anything at that distance, especially if the target was moving. A stationary helicopter, less than a hundred metres away, however, was pretty much a dead cert.

The projectile had a no-delay detonator at the tip, which was normally covered by a safety cap. Otherwise, if you dropped it, or tripped, it was game over. The man holding the RPG had removed the safety cap and had his forefinger wrapped around the trigger. His aim had not wavered from the Sikorsky. There was an air of quivering excitement about him, as though he'd been given a fine new toy and couldn't wait to play with it.

Both men wore dark civilian clothing but carried military weapons. I didn't recognise either. There was a chance they might have been part of the crew who made the attempt on Helena back on that rural road in New Jersey, but I'd no way to know for sure. The only one who'd got a look at me was dead. Certainly, neither man had posed as a waiter at the restaurant where the Kincaids attempted to celebrate their anniversary.

I kept my steps slow, as if reluctant. Rather, I was trying to give Helena a chance to get clear and the others to fight their way through.

As I edged closer, hands still outspread, the guy with the assault rifle said, "OK, do it."

I didn't need to be told who he was talking to. I stepped sideways, into the RPG's line of fire. The man moved left to open up a clear line to his target. I mirrored him. He began swearing at me in a language I didn't understand but didn't need to.

The flight crew of the Sikorsky took the hint. I heard the doors clang open to the airframe as they bailed out and ran, stumbling, for the treeline.

The man with the M4 dodged forwards and hit me with the stock of the gun. I'd been too focused on the RPG to mount a worthwhile defence. The blow smacked along the side of my jaw and sent me spinning, my vision crackling with stars.

As soon as I was out of his way, the guy with the RPG fired. I felt the flare of gases blast across me. A second later, the Sikorsky exploded with a concussive whump and a fireball that erupted above the trees and sent a pall of black smoke into that clear blue sky.

34

THE TWO MEN zip-tied my hands behind my back and hooded me. I acted as I hoped Helena would have done—scared but dignified.

They hustled me from the site of the burning Sikorsky to some kind of small utility vehicle nearby. We drove only a short distance—the island wasn't big enough to go far unless we did laps. I stumbled awkwardly as I was dragged across rocks and shingle, then dumped into the bottom of a boat. The ride over the lake was loud and rough enough for me to assume it was fast. I could still hear gunfire, growing fainter, as the island fell away behind us.

I tried asking the classic question, "Where are you taking me?" only because it was expected. I got the stock of the M4 in my kidneys for doing so. After that, I kept quiet.

It didn't take long to reach the lakeshore. The island was towards the northeast corner of Lago Trasimeno, but I had no sense of where we'd landed. The two men were joined by others. They transferred me to the back of another vehicle, larger this time, and more luxurious. I could smell air freshener or carpet shampoo—the kind of slightly chemical odour you get in freshly valeted rental cars. I hoped that wasn't to stop me picking up trace evidence of where I'd been.

The engine gunned. It was something powerful and quiet. I

guessed at a limo, by the space between the front and rear seats. They shoved me onto the floor and leaned what felt like the barrel of the assault rifle into my ribs to keep me there.

As soon as we were moving, one of the men made a phone call. He hit a stored number and spoke only to say, in thickly accented English, "We have collected the package. We will meet as arranged."

Apart from that, none of them spoke, to each other or to me.

I lay, half propped up against the rear seat, half on the floor, and concentrated on keeping my breathing steady, on trying to relax and be patient. Back when I used to eke out a living teaching self-defence, one of the things I had stressed to my students was to avoid at all costs being immobilised and taken from the point of abduction to a secondary location of their attacker's choosing. That the risk doubled if they allowed that to happen. I told them to do everything they could to fight back, to attract attention, to get free. And yet, here I was, breaking all my own rules.

But the further away we got from the island, the further away they got from Helena, and protecting my principal was my main —my *only*—priority.

What came next, I'd deal with when I had to.

I wasn't too worried about the zip-ties. They were tight, but I wasn't in danger of losing feeling in my hands unless I struggled. I knew I could get out of them when I needed to. No point in doing so yet, when all they'd do was cuff me with something I might *not* be able to deal with.

Still, I could feel the sweat soaking into my shirt, trickling between my shoulder blades and around my waistband. My heart caused the blood to thunder in my ears. Attempting to rationalise the dangers was one thing. Ignoring their effects on my subconscious was quite another.

The realisation made me angry and I clung to that, grateful for it.

We drove for some distance on a mixture of roads from slow and twisting to long, open stretches. I reckoned we'd been travelling for between half an hour and three-quarters when the vehicle slowed almost to a halt and turned sharply off the road. I could tell by the change in sound that we were now inside a building. The exhaust note reverberated against the walls, rumbling more loudly as the doors rolled shut behind us.

They dragged me out and up a couple of steps. Without my hands for balance, I tripped and almost fell. They hauled me up by my arms, their hands rough. I clenched my jaw hard under the hood, biting back the instinctive knot of panic that still rose up from deep in my psyche at having them touch me. I willed myself to be calm, not to lash out. There would be a time for that. It wasn't now.

The floor was hard underfoot, either wood or tile, and echoed with our footsteps as they hustled me through the building. Even through the hood, I could smell wax polish. So, a house or office rather than somewhere industrial.

The hand on my arm twisted and pushed. I braced myself for a fall, only to land on something soft that gave under me. A sofa, I realised as my bound hands came into contact with what felt like velvet.

"Stay!" someone ordered, as you would a dog. Their footsteps retreated. A door closed and there came the distinct sound of a key turning in a lock.

I pushed myself further upright, flexing my arms to test the tie-wrap fully for the first time. No weakness there.

Then, suddenly, I stilled.

There's something different about the atmosphere in an enclosed space like a room when there are two people in it. Some minute change in the vibrations, in the rhythm of your own breath. The echo of a heartbeat not my own.

Either way, I could tell I was not alone.

"Are you going to sit there in silence?" I demanded, remembering to maintain the accent. I pushed a touch of arrogance into my voice that I hoped would make me sound like an entitled daughter who'd grown into an equally entitled wife. "Or are you going to introduce yourself?"

If I was wrong about my fellow occupant and he or she was no more than a figment of my over-stretched imagination, well, there would be no-one there to laugh at my mistake.

But I heard a definite noise, then. A slither of clothing,

perhaps arms unfolding, or chair upholstery resettling as weight was lifted from it.

And I knew that I had not been mistaken.

"You have nothing to say? I'm disappointed." I paused. "And I'm starting to get bored."

No doubt about the sound this time. A grunt, or was it a stifled chuckle? Then slow footsteps, a measured tread.

The hood came off without warning. Static plastered my hair to my face. I shook my head, blew the hair out of my eyes with a snort like one of Helena's horses. The sudden light dazzled me and it took a moment to adjust.

The man in front of me was the bearded man I'd last seen ordering the destruction of the helicopter without a second thought, it seemed, for the people still inside.

He looked down at me, looming. I stared back up, refusing to play this game of intimidation by the rules. He was still in the dark clothing he'd worn on the island, perhaps further aiming to scare me. *To scare Helena...* I wondered briefly if it would have worked.

"Mrs Kincaid," he said, icily polite. "We have not, as you say, been introduced, but I am a long-time...associate of your family. My name is Khalid Hamzeh. I feel we know each other already."

A Syrian name.

"Mr Hamzeh," I responded, matching him tone for tone. "I'd offer to shake your hand but"—a shrug—"I find I don't wish to."

He smiled then, almost in spite of himself, half-covered it by strolling to the armchair opposite. I made a quick visual catalogue of my surroundings in the time it took him to sit down. We were in a large room with an open fireplace at one end, surrounded by sofas, and a long formal dining table at the other. Everything was in shades of cream or white. It looked put together but not lived in. An upscale holiday let, perhaps, rather than someone's home.

"Why am I here?" I demanded then, still keeping that slightly imperious note in my voice that Helena carried so well. "What can you possibly hope to gain by this?"

"At present? You are here as...insurance," Hamzeh said.

"And to ensure a little co-operation on the part of your husband."

"You must be aware that taking me will *not* make Eric more co-operative."

"Perhaps not, but he will at least be prepared to listen to what we have to say. Your presence will ensure we are able to discuss this matter in a…civilised manner."

I lifted my hands as much as I was able, behind my back. "You call this civilised?"

"I hope you will forgive me if I leave things as they are, for the moment," he said gravely. "I am not, by nature, a man who trusts easily. Particularly with those who have already shown themselves to be unworthy of that trust."

"Really?" I allowed my voice to drawl. "Well, trust is something that works both ways. And you have demonstrated quite clearly that you are not to be trusted."

He sat back, crossed his legs with a grace that was disconcerting. "You betray us and then seek to blame *us* for that betrayal?"

I had the feeling of stepping out onto a crumbling ledge, of inching forward and expecting the path to disintegrate beneath my feet at any moment. I'd never been so unsure of my ground.

"Betrayal is a strong word. Is that truly what my…husband, my father, have done?" It was hard to think of Kincaid and Orosco in those terms, much less to speak it, but if Hamzeh noticed any hesitation, he let it pass.

"When someone gives me their word, I expect them to keep it, with or without a written contract. Anything else *is* a betrayal."

"Really?" I said, affecting a careless tone. "I was given to believe it was purely business."

He raised an eyebrow. "You were 'given to believe'?" he echoed sharply. "You feign ignorance, when *I* was *given to believe* that American women were so much more involved in the business of their husbands—mere housewives no longer. Not so?"

What did I say to that? There was nothing I could say that wouldn't damn me—in his eyes as much as my own.

"Not always," I said at last, and didn't like the bitter taste the words left in my mouth.

He rose abruptly from his chair and though he turned away from me before he spoke, I heard the disdain in his voice, even so.

"How can an intelligent woman be so wilfully blind to the means behind the food that is put onto her table, or the clothes onto her body, or the roof over her head?"

It was Helena's life he described but I felt honour-bound to defend it.

"I tried to get out from under," I said steadily. "I failed."

"So now you simply accept your luxurious confinement, is that so?" he asked, stepping closer. "Like a caged bird content to sing for her supper. And what tune do *you* sing, Mrs Kincaid?"

He reached out and touched my cheek with the backs of his fingers, eyes fixed on mine as he softly swiped the pad of his thumb across my lips.

With a snarl, I snapped at him with my teeth, missed his flesh by a whisker.

He took a hurried step back in reflex. A surprised bark of laughter left him when I might have expected a back-hander across the face instead.

"I hoped to charm you into persuading your husband to reconsider his decision," he admitted, rueful now. "But I do not suppose my efforts would have succeeded."

"No. They wouldn't."

"A pity." His voice was casual but something in his face gave away a fleeting intensity.

"Why is this so important to you? Why not just find another supplier—one who is only too willing to accept your business?"

He shook his head, a little smile playing around his lips as if amused by this display of naiveté on my part.

"If it was a matter of nothing more than profit and loss, there was no reason for your husband to withdraw from our arrangement. It must have been a profitable exercise for him," he said. "But…my country has become increasingly isolated. Doors that once were open to us are now closed."

"Hardly surprising, when you treat your own people so appallingly. Human rights are an abstract concept to you, aren't they?"

"You may not like our leader," Hamzeh said. "You may not approve of his…actions, on occasion, but he keeps us strong."

"It is not a sign of strength to massacre and gas your own people."

"He keeps my country together," he bit out. "You Americans and your allies! You play at being the world's policemen, but you interfere in situations about which you know nothing—*less* than nothing. And chaos and death follow. Look at what has happened to Iraq. Look at Libya. And ask yourself, how much blood is on *your* hands?"

I kept my head up, met his gaze without flinching, however much I recognised more than a grain of truth in his words. "Less, I suspect, than is on yours."

He waved a hand, dismissive. "In personal terms, perhaps. But here we both represent something bigger."

"I don't represent anything," I argued. "Today, you were prepared to kill my bodyguard, my pilots, and for what?"

"Leaving behind no helicopter and no-one to fly it was a tactical decision. One your father, or your husband, would have made, also."

"I disagree."

His mouth twisted. "You have a sentimental view—it is a woman's weakness."

"Really?" I let my voice drawl. "I've always found a certain level of compassion inspires greater loyalty, but no doubt you know your own people best."

"And yet *your* people," he returned, "allowed you to be taken without a fight, in order to save their own skin."

That was a little too close for comfort. *Best not to go down that road.*

"Perhaps they know I'm a survivor."

"Perhaps so." He nodded, as if his argument had just been won, pulled back his sleeve, revealing a flash of a battered stainless steel wristwatch. "I must leave you, Mrs Kincaid. It has been…instructive. You are certainly not as I expected."

"Oh?"

"Yes… I expected more of the rose, perhaps, and less of the thorns."

"Well, I guess you can't have one without the other."

He moved to the door, knocked on it for whoever was outside to unlock it. While they did so he paused and glanced back, frowning. "I have spoken to your father often. I did not think his daughter would sound so...British."

Damn! I should have known I couldn't keep up an American accent for long.

But for that, at least, I could fall back on the truth.

"Oh, yes," I said airily. "I had an English nanny."

35

I WAITED a second after the door closed behind him, then rolled onto my back on the cushions of the sofa, wriggling my hands under my backside and tucking my feet through so now at least my arms were in front of me.

I got to my feet, stepping carefully to avoid making any noise on the polished tile, and prowled the room, looking for anything with a sharp edge or a point. They hadn't even left me a pen. Scanning, I saw a row of three metal candlesticks on the mantel-piece. I lifted one down and dumped the chunky candle it supported into the fireplace. Sure enough, there was a short metal spike that held the candle in place. I moved to the sofa, wedged the candlestick between my knees and shoved the spike into the plastic ratchet mechanism that held the zip-ties closed. It took a couple of clumsy attempts before I was able to push the locking tab open and loosen the tie enough to slip my hands out.

I rubbed my wrists as I looked around for anything else I could use as a slightly more discreet weapon. In a drawer of a side table I found an old-fashioned corkscrew. The T of the handle fitted neatly into my palm leaving maybe an inch and a half of curly metal protruding. Not perfect, but it would do. If I could get close enough to somebody, I knew I could blind, maim, or kill them with this. It was a comforting thought.

If Hamzeh contacted Eric Kincaid expecting to find him more

willing to negotiate because of my capture, he would be sadly disappointed. I couldn't even rule out that Kincaid would tell him he'd been conned—might boast of it, even. Which did not bode well for my long-term prospects. Or my short-term ones, come to that.

If I hadn't managed to get myself out of here before then, it was game over.

Outside the door, I heard new voices. Whoever it was, they weren't happy. I leapt for the sofa, then swore as I darted across to plonk the candle back on its mount above the fireplace.

I contemplated pulling on the hood again just to take the focus away from my hands, but dismissed the idea. Instead, I lay on my side and buried my face into the cushions, letting my hair flop forwards to cover what remained of my features. Still gripping the corkscrew, I shoved my hands behind my back, out of sight, just as the key rattled in the lock.

Footsteps entered and paused. A man's voice said roughly, "Leave us!"

The door closed again. The footsteps resumed, coming closer. I allowed myself to brace—it was what Helena would have done.

A hand grasped my shoulder, reached for my chin. His touch was not rough, but it still made me flinch.

The man said, "Hush. It's OK, Helena. It's all OK now."

As he lifted me and my hair fell away from my face, I recognised his voice. It took him a second in shock to do the same.

"But you're—"

I thrust off the sofa with my left hand outstretched—not the one with the corkscrew in it. I didn't need a weapon in order to punch him in the throat hard enough to silence him.

He staggered back, hands to his neck, mouth working soundlessly. I kept coming, grabbing both lapels of his jacket and using them to jerk his upper body down to meet my rapidly rising knee. The blow landed in the fleshy vee under his ribcage, blasting the air out of his lungs, leaving him winded and gasping. He crumpled.

I kept hold of his jacket to control the noise of his descent, spread it open once he was on the floor to pat him down. I took the 9mm Beretta out of the shoulder holster under his left arm.

By the time he'd got his breath back, I'd checked over the gun and wedged it against the underside of his right kneecap, leaving him in no doubt of my intentions.

"So, Mr Orosco," I said from between clenched teeth. "Are you going to tell me why you've just tried to have your own daughter kidnapped?"

36

Darius Orosco started to swear then, spitting out vicious words about what he was going to do to me. I jabbed the gun harder under his patella. All he did was sneer.

"Go ahead. Soon as you fire that thing they'll come running. They'll be all over you before you can leave this room, hey."

It grieved me to admit that he was right. I lifted the gun away from his knee and put it down on the sofa beside me. Orosco's disdain turned smug.

I rose, grabbed his right foot and lifted it sharply. The move flipped him half onto his side to avoid his knee flexing the wrong way. I braced my boot on his thigh and put about a quarter turn of twist onto his ankle. He went rigid, his knee a twitch away from exploding.

"How about now?" I asked. "If I break your leg and you squeal like a girl, they'll just assume it's me screaming."

Pride kept him silent. I notched it up a bit further, hardened the lock and felt the ligaments begin to quiver like high-tension power lines in a storm.

"Fuck you," he snarled.

"Really?" I said. "That's the best you can come up with?"

"Fuck you, *bitch*!"

I laughed without humour. "Did you know spiral fractures

are notoriously difficult to treat?" I piled on enough additional pressure to make him grunt.

"And so close to a joint...well, all kinds of complications are likely to ensue," I went on, my tone conversational. "*My* father was an orthopaedic surgeon, in case you were wondering."

I notched it up again and he couldn't suppress a groan.

"Factor in the poor blood supply to the lower leg and you may as well just go straight for amputation."

The groan became a whimper.

I held it, letting that sink in for a few moments, then said, "So, are we going to talk like adults, or do I need to *really* hurt you?"

"We talk," Orosco said between his teeth, but he still muttered, "bitch" after it.

As soon as I relaxed my grip, he lashed out with the foot I'd been holding. I blocked with my forearm and kicked him in the groin.

It took him longer to recover from that one. He didn't say much that was intelligible while he was doing so. Eventually, aware this was all taking too long, I hauled him into a sitting position and propped his back against the base of an armchair.

"Just breathe through it," I advised. "The pain will start to ease off in a minute or so."

He began hyperventilating like someone going into labour, asked sourly, "How the fuck d'you know that, hey?"

"You think you're the first bloke I've kicked in the balls?"

He glared at me but didn't try anything else. His colour began to normalise, his breathing slowed.

"OK," I said. "Are you going to tell me why the hell you kidnapped your own daughter?"

"Simple," he said, and the sneer was back. "I didn't trust *you* to protect her."

I eyed him for a moment, let him consider what he'd just said in light of what I'd just done. "But you trusted your bunch of thugs to grab her and bring her to you, alive and unhurt, when they didn't even know what she looked like?" I said. "You *are* aware they blew up the bloody helicopter we were in?"

For the first time, alarm flared in his eyes. "She wasn't...?"

I let him sweat a beat before I shook my head. "No, she got out—*I* got her out—in time. But don't you think it was overkill having your men shoot up Ugoccione's private island just so you could 'rescue' Helena?"

"You don't know what you're talking about," Orosco said. "What makes you think they're *my* men?"

"They grabbed me and brought me here. Now you've turned up and I don't see you with your wrists bound," I said shortly. "If they're not working for you, they give a damn good impression of it."

"I hear things in my line of business, and I got the capability —and the smarts—to react. Don't mean I ordered them in the first place."

"You knew before we left New Jersey that we were coming here to see Ugoccione, correct?"

He hesitated, but considering I'd been there when Kincaid told him, he had no choice but to admit, "Yeah. So?"

"*So*, you happened to hear—in the line of business, of course —that somebody was planning to hit Ugoccione. And then you trusted this unknown bunch of somebodies to kidnap your own daughter and, out of the goodness of their hearts, to bring her to you?"

"Easy to make the facts fit your own little theory when you don't got it in you to see the big picture, hey?"

"I guess so. Well, please excuse my tiny little brain and tell me why you didn't at least warn your own son-in-law he was walking into a war zone?"

"The kid talks good. Maybe I wanted to see if he really could handle himself when the going got a little rocky."

"When you *knew* Helena was with him?" I shook my head, more in disbelief than denial. "And what about Ugoccione himself? From what I understand, you and he go way back. Doesn't that count for anything?"

"Tomas is a switched-on kinda guy," Orosco dismissed. "He *does* know how to take care of himself."

I thought again of Sean, hit by a fluke shot fired by someone who hadn't even been aiming. It had changed everything.

"Bullets don't care about experience," I said bitterly. "Not when you walk into the path of one."

"Wait, you telling me they shot him? No way! They—"

His voice chopped off suddenly as his brain caught up with his mouth.

"By 'they', I assume you mean the Syrians?" I said mildly.

The look he threw me was vicious. "Can you blame them, hey? These are some very serious people. You can't just do business with a guy like Hamzeh one day, refuse to do business the next. Decisions like that have consequences. Kincaid knew damn well when he shut down the supply line Hamzeh wasn't gonna take something like that lying down."

"O–K," I said slowly.

He looked taken aback. "'OK'? That all you're gonna say?"

I shrugged. "It makes sense...but there is one more thing I'd love to hear you explain to me." I paused. "You see, we only just found out from Ugoccione that it was the Syrians who bought those M4s used in the ambush on your daughter. So, how is it that *you* seem to know all about it?"

37

"HEY, it wasn't *me* said it was the Syrians—that was all you."

Orosco's hesitation was momentary but there all the same. A fleeting behind-the-scenes mental scramble to review what he might have said—what he might have given away—and repurpose it for his own ends. He tried to hide the blip behind an exaggerated shrug, but it was too late.

"You didn't exactly look surprised."

"Hey, in this game you always gotta be a half-dozen moves ahead of everybody else, and I've been a player a *long* time."

Yeah, I'm sure you have...

"I don't suppose you'd care to spell it out for me," I said. "How you worked it all out?" *Preferably in a way that doesn't begin "once upon a time," and end with "and they all lived happily ever after."*

If I'd been hoping to appeal to his ego, I was destined to be disappointed. His face shut down. "I don't got to explain *nothing* to you!"

"That's true. You don't." I picked up the Beretta from the sofa, prodded him in the gut with the muzzle. "Come on—up. Maybe I can find someone you *will* talk to."

"Who—Kincaid?" There was an incredulity in his voice, a note of disdain. Whatever he thought of his son-in-law, I realised, he did not fear him. *Damn.* I switched tactics.

"No," I said. "Helena."

If that threw him, he didn't show it. "You think they're gonna let you just walk me out of here, hey?"

"No, but they'll let *you* walk *me* out."

"And why would I want to do that?"

I dropped the magazine out of the Beretta, began thumbing the rounds out into the palm of my hand, fifteen in all. Orosco watched sourly as I dumped them into my pockets and racked the slide to spit out the single chambered round.

"Because at the end of the day, we *are* both concerned with your daughter's safety. And that safety is in my hands."

"You reckon, huh?" he demanded. "Not if I have any damn say in it."

"You think Kincaid will listen to you?" I asked. "You may not want to tell me why you didn't warn him about the ambush he was walking into, but how are you going to be able to avoid telling him when you're face to face?"

"That's none of your damn business!"

I slotted the empty magazine into the pistol grip and handed the Beretta back to Orosco. He stared down at it in his hands, frowning, as if he wasn't sure why I'd returned the weapon.

I lifted one of the sofa cushions and grabbed the corkscrew I'd abandoned there. Palming it, I slipped my arm around his waist, inside his jacket. He stank of sweat overlaid with cologne. It made me wonder if he usually smelled that way, or if he'd come straight off his flight without a chance to shower. When he'd got his information about the attack on Ugoccione, and when he'd set off from the States, were questions I'd leave to Kincaid. Now, I tried not to cough as the man's failing deodorant caught the back of my throat.

"OK, *Daddy*, let's go."

He didn't move. I shifted my hand slightly, just enough for the tip of the corkscrew to tear a small hole in his shirt and dig into the flesh of his lower back. I felt him stiffen. I increased the pressure and twisted my wrist so the metal pierced the top layer of his skin. He flinched and tried to jerk away from me. I brought him up short.

"If I keep going, I will screw this thing straight through your kidney," I murmured. "Do you think, if I drive it in far enough, I'll be able to pull out the whole kidney in one lump? Maybe I'll hit your liver—bigger target than a kidney. Either way, puncturing it would be bad for you."

He didn't speak, but his body was taut as a wire. The side of his face had taken on a waxy tint.

"You're crazy," he managed then, almost a gasp. He tried to lean away from me, but all he could do was tuck his chin back. It was not a good look for him.

"No. What I am is focused." *Focused on getting back to Helena.* "Where's your car?"

"What makes you think I got a car?"

Give me strength! "Are you trying to tell me you took a cab here?"

"I was picked up."

"And these guys really don't work for you?" I demanded. "Tell them you need a car. Insist on it. Why the hell do you think I gave you back your gun?"

"Yeah, with no fucking bullets in it!"

I spoke through clenched teeth. "Be. Persuasive."

I turned him, edged him towards the door. He moved slowly at first, but it's amazing how easily someone can be controlled when you've planted the idea in their mind that you've skewered one of their vital organs and are about to yank it straight out of their body through the slit.

He was the one who reached for the door handle, pulled the door open. We passed through into a large hallway. High ceilings, more shades of cream, gilt-framed mirrors. In one of them, I caught sight of our reflection. I was tucked in close to Orosco's side, looking for all the world as if he was in charge and I was taking comfort and safety from him. I suppose in some ways I was—taking safety *away from* him, that is.

In my peripheral vision, I saw a man appear at the opposite end of the hallway. I glanced at him long enough to see that he did not immediately brandish a weapon at the sight of us. And to note with some relief that it was *not* Khalid Hamzeh, or the clean-shaven man with the RPG. Even so, I felt Orosco stiffen, felt the hesitation in him as he weighed up his options. Did he continue to play along, or trust this man, whoever he was, to come to his aid.

In the end, I think it was his pride that won out. He didn't want the loss of face that would come with admitting a mere girl had overpowered and disarmed him. Besides, I didn't know his relationship with these men. He'd denied they were working directly for him, so how had he persuaded them to grab Helena in the first place?

There would be time, I hoped, to find that out later.

"We're leaving," Orosco said gruffly. "I need a vehicle." Sneaking a sideways look, I saw the man straighten, standing centred in the hallway. He did not look inclined to let us pass unchallenged.

"The boss wants to speak with you first," the man said. His voice was accented, but it was hard to tell much with one ear pressed into the lapel of Orosco's suit.

"Later. I want to get my daughter some place safe." The lie tripped off his tongue without a hitch. Something to remember.

The man cocked his head on one side, regarding us. "She is safe here."

Orosco bounced a little on his toes, his chin jutting forward like a dog ready to fight. "She's safe where I say she's safe," he growled.

They faced off like that for several long seconds. It did not escape my notice that the man's jacket hung open, that his right hand twitched automatically towards the gun he undoubtedly carried beneath it. Orosco caught the move, too. He bristled. The Beretta was in his hand but, short of throwing it, there wasn't much he could do to force the issue.

I lifted my head a little, put a pleading expression on my face.

"I guess we could stay, Daddy," I said in a loud, whiny whisper. "But...my period just started. If maybe this guy would go out and get me some tampons...?"

Orosco's shudder was more or less mirrored by the other man, who jerked his head. "Go," he said, brusque. "I will tell him as soon as he returns. Do not be long."

Orosco hustled me past him. I kept my head down and appeared to be clinging on for dear life. Which, in a way, I was, holding the corkscrew embedded into the skin of his back. The wetness against my fingers could have been either sweat or blood.

We'd taken no more than a step past him when the man said, "Wait!"

My pulse rate accelerated wildly. If Orosco got any more tense he'd crack his spine. We turned as a single unit, like we were competitors in a three-legged race. The man was reaching into his jacket. I heard Orosco take an audible breath, start to react. I jammed the steel tip into his back a little harder, bringing him up short.

I'd seen a lot of people reach for a lot of weapons in my time. Half my career in close protection had been spent assessing body language, trying to identify the one threatening move amongst a myriad of harmless gestures. Nothing about this man's posture, the set of his shoulders, the tiny muscles of his face, told me he was about to go on the offensive. Orosco froze without completing whatever counter he'd been about to make.

The man withdrew his hand from his inside pocket. In it was a set of car keys.

"You will need these," he said.

38

WE STEPPED outside and I found myself in a narrow street with high stone buildings on either side. The street was flagged, barely wide enough for two cars to pass side by side. The buildings looked medieval. If we'd had more time I might have asked where we were. As it was, I had more pressing questions on my mind.

"So, where's this car?"

Orosco jerked his head to a side street. If anything, this was even narrower. Fifty yards along, it opened out into a wider space where half a dozen cars were parked up against the buttressed wall of what might have been a castle. I'd lived in New York for long enough for this blatant display of history to have the appearance of a movie set.

He thumbed the remote on the keys and the lights flashed on a little Fiat Cinquecento. His mouth fell open.

"What the fuck?"

I disengaged, picked the keys out of his hand. "I'll drive."

"Now wait a minute—"

"You happy with a manual transmission on something the size of a golf cart?"

His mouth clamped shut again.

"OK," he said. "You drive."

I pocketed the bloodied corkscrew and slid behind the wheel, clipping my seatbelt in place. The little Fiat cranked into life at the first turn of the key.

"OK, where to?"

"What the fuck do you mean?" he demanded sourly as he slammed the passenger door. "You were the one who wanted out of there."

"Yeah, well, it would help if I had any idea where we are."

"Place called Montisi," he said at last. "One-horse town. Doesn't even have a stop light."

I backed out and headed carefully along the side street. The car's mirrors barely seemed to clear the foliage from the flower pots on every window sill. At the end, Orosco reluctantly gestured to the left. With no better plan, I followed his directions, picking up speed as the street widened. Ahead was a junction with a main road. Blue signs gave distances in kilometres to Sinalunga and Trequanda. I recognised both names from studying the maps before we landed. Both were to the west of Lago Trasimeno by forty or fifty klicks. We were the best part of an hour away—further from where the Gulfstream had landed at Perugia. I put my foot down. The Fiat's engine note rose, but there was little noticeable difference in our speed.

"Do you have a phone?" I asked Orosco.

"Yeah."

There was a pause. I sighed. "May I use it?"

The sneer was back. He'd pushed one hand behind him, under his jacket. Now, he pulled it out and inspected his fingers. There was blood on them. Only a small amount, but blood nevertheless.

"You, lady, can go fuck yourself."

"Oh, so you'd rather your daughter was left unprotected?"

"Than be in the care of a psycho like you? Yeah."

"You arrange to have her kidnapped by a bunch of guys who are happy to blow up a helicopter in the process, and you call *me* a psycho?"

"If you hadn't stuck your nose in, she'd be safe with me right now."

I shook my head. Reasoning with him was impossible, and I hated the fact he'd reduced me to the level of a schoolyard squabble. Next thing you knew, we'd be insulting each other's mothers.

I shut up and drove, winding along fast twisty roads, keeping the Fiat hustling as fast as it could manage. Other traffic didn't seem to be in much of a hurry and I hopped past it whenever the opportunity presented itself. Maybe because of that, after about twenty minutes I noticed the big Renault doing the same in order to stay only a vehicle or two behind us.

It was hard to say if they were following. We were on a main cross-country route. Chances were that any traffic would be heading in the same direction. But it was the fact the Renault driver had overtaken the same vehicles I had—a couple of times in places that were marginal on safety. When there was only one car left between us, he suddenly seemed happy to stay in the line of traffic. Open sections came and went, and still he didn't move further up the line.

I jammed my foot down and bullied my way past the van ahead of us, despite the fact there wasn't really the room to do so, and the visibility was poor. The oncoming driver flashed and blew his horn, gesturing with an arm out of the window as we passed within inches of one another.

"Are you trying to fucking kill us?" Orosco squawked, knuckles white around the grab handle on the passenger door.

I ignored him, keeping one eye on the rear-view mirror. Sure enough, the Renault hustled past the car that had been between us, but stayed put behind the van. I caught enough of a glimpse to see there were men in both driver and passenger seats. I could see the outline of someone in the rear, too.

"We've picked up a tail," I said shortly. "Looks like your friends don't trust you to keep your word."

Orosco screwed round in his seat. "The Renault?" he asked a moment later.

"Uh-huh."

"Bastards."

"Yeah, that about sums it up."

He still had the Beretta in his hand. He glanced at it, then across at me. "You gonna give me the bullets back for this thing, hey?"

The words "rock" and "hard place" sprang into my mind.

"Take the magazine out and give me the weapon," I said.

He threw me a bitter look but complied. I wedged the empty Beretta under my thigh and dug in my pockets for the loose rounds, dumping them into Orosco's lap. He fumbled for them, feeding them into the magazine until it was full.

When he'd finished I held my hand out. Reluctantly, he slapped the magazine into it. I shoved that under my thigh and handed the body of the Beretta back.

"Now what?"

"If it comes to it, I'll give you the magazine back," I said. "But if you think I trust you with a loaded weapon before then, you've got another think coming."

If looks could kill, I'd have been ready for the pathologist's opening Y incision right about then.

"Bitch," he muttered.

39

WE DROVE into the outskirts of Trequanda on a road lined in places with cypress trees. Past fields scorched pale brown by the sun, through groves of vines laid out in neat, wired rows. Traffic ebbed and flowed. The Renault stayed with us, at least one car behind, sometimes two.

I considered my options, which weren't extensive.

At one point, Orosco asked, "Can't you lose them?"

"In this?" I threw him a disgusted look. "Not unless they run out of fuel or break down."

Equally, I didn't particularly want to let them follow me all the way back to the airport. It was not my preference to lead the bad guys directly to the people I was charged to protect, even if there might be more of us there to deal with the problem they presented.

That was assuming, of course, that Schade had managed to get everyone away from Isola Minore unscathed. If that were the case, I reasoned, he would not have waited for me, anyway. After what had happened, he could not afford to delay their departure, possibly putting both principals in further danger, just because one of their bodyguards had done the job they were hired to do.

I did not expect them to have made any moves to find me, either. For all they knew, I could be dead.

I tried not to give headroom to the thought that, for all I knew, *they* could be dead.

There was a truck up ahead. He was moving slowly and I was gradually reeling him in. I glanced in the rear-view mirror again. Now, a single car remained between us and the Renault—an elderly Citroën. As I watched, the Citroën's right-hand indicator came on. It slowed and turned off onto what looked more like a cart track than a side road.

"I don't like this," Orosco announced tightly.

I might not like *him*, but I couldn't fault the guy's instincts.

He ducked down a little to get a good view of the Renault in the door mirror on his side, bit out, "Gimme the mag."

I hesitated. In the rear-view mirror, I saw the Renault move up closer to our rear end when I'd expected—hoped, anyway—that they'd drop back further.

Orosco tried to reach across me, grabbed at my leg. I twitched reflexively, chopped down onto his wrist with the side of my fist. He punched me in the ribs. Not hard enough to make me lose control of the car, but hard enough to sting, then held his hand out.

"What, you think I'm going to shoot *you*? Give me the fucking mag."

Silently, I handed it over. Orosco palmed the loaded magazine into the pistol grip of the Beretta and pinched back the slide to chamber the first round. He made a noise of satisfaction in his throat while he did so, like a man having his first sip of beer at the end of a long day. It did not fill me with confidence.

"That's what I'm talkin' about," he muttered. Before I could do anything to counter, he'd opened the passenger door about a foot, twisted round in his seat to lean out through the gap, and fired three shots into the front end of the Renault.

My turn to roar, "What the fuck are you doing?"

He turned back, a feral grin on his face, letting the wind force slam the door shut again with a clang.

"Letting those bastards know they gotta back off."

I checked the road behind. The Renault *had* backed off, but not for long. In fact, his front end was now growing rapidly larger in my mirror as the driver floored the accelerator.

I stamped on the Fiat's throttle pedal. Once again, not much happened. I locked my arms to wedge against the steering wheel and just had time to yell, "Brace!" before they hit us.

The driver of the Renault was no amateur. It felt like he rammed into the driver's side rear corner of the Fiat hard enough to lift our rear wheels clean off the road.

As we thumped down I tried to keep the car straight, but it was way off balance. The Renault ploughed on, thudding harder into the same corner, shunting the rear end of the Fiat out to the left. I tried opposite lock to steer into the skid, but lacking the grunt to power out of it, we were pretty much doomed from the outset.

Skinny tyres howling in protest, the Fiat slewed violently to the right. I stamped on the brakes, but by now we were heading sideways towards the edge of the road. It dropped away at an alarming angle into a wooded embankment.

We bounced over the low kerb and launched into the trees.

Almost at once, the Fiat crunched into a low tree stump. Our own momentum flipped the little car up into the air. I let go of the redundant steering wheel, wrapped one arm around my head and gripped the seatbelt with the other, anchoring me. The car barrel-rolled several times. I shut my eyes to the kaleidoscope images of ground, leaves and sky flashing past. The noise was horrific—like somebody walloping a kettledrum with a broom handle. Broken glass, twigs, stones, and dry earth rained in around us.

The Fiat finally slammed to a stop with my side buckled around a tree trunk. The impact flung me about like a chew toy in the mouth of a big dog. Miraculously, we were the right way up. The engine had stalled. I reached automatically for the key and turned off the ignition.

The dust around us was so thick that I briefly feared the car was on fire. Sense kicked in. No smoke, no acrid smell of burning fuel and plastic. When I cautiously wriggled my arms and legs, they were still attached. The cabin had stood the abuse remarkably well, all things considered. At least nobody would need a hydraulic jack to get me out of the car, although using the driver's door was a non-starter.

I didn't think I'd been out of it, but when I glanced across, the passenger door was open. There was no sign of Orosco. I remembered him cracking the door to fire at the Renault. He might not have latched it fully—or put his seatbelt back on. Or there was a good chance he'd been flung out of the car as we rolled down through the trees. Either that, or maybe he'd got his wits about him far quicker than I had after the crash.

Like I needed to now.

Somewhere above me, perhaps at road level, I could hear voices, shouting.

Come on, Fox. Move!

I undid my seatbelt and scrambled across the broken glass littering the passenger seat. As I crawled out through draping foliage onto the banking, three shots cracked out in rapid succession. Someone else returned fire—a different calibre weapon firing a different load. I couldn't get a bearing on either. When I shook my head to clear it, I found myself on my knees.

There was a wetness in my hair that irritated. I lifted a hand to it and realised I was bleeding, but didn't remember hitting my head. It was high behind my right ear—the opposite side from the door frame and screen pillar. Was that how Orosco had got away from me? I wouldn't put it past him.

Right now, I couldn't work out who was shooting at who, but without a weapon of my own it was not a game I wanted to join in. I started heading downhill at an angle, away from the fight, hanging onto branches for balance.

I had no idea who the men from the Renault were. I couldn't rule out that they were part of the crew from the villa in Montisi, however unlikely that seemed. They'd let us walk out of there without argument, after all. And it wasn't as if I'd left behind the real Darius Orosco tied and gagged in a cupboard in his underwear.

Still, there was nothing to say they hadn't had a change of heart about letting us go. Maybe Hamzeh had returned and not taken our departure well. Or maybe these were men connected to Ugoccione, out for revenge for the attack on Isola Minore and intent on enacting that revenge on the first people to set foot outside the villains' lair.

Probably best not to find that out.

Behind me, I heard crashing through the undergrowth, running footsteps with little regard to stealth. Someone shouted, "Down there!"

I tried to pick up the pace, but my pursuers had not just rolled down a hill inside a tin can. It was almost a foregone conclusion that they were going to catch up with me.

What took me by surprise, though, was what happened when they did.

40

"HOLD IT! STOP RUNNING!"

I gritted my teeth and stumbled on.

"For God's sake, Charlie, will you just *stop*?"

Finally, I recognised the voice. I managed to slow my descent by aiming for a tree trunk and putting my hands out as a buffer. Even so, I nearly overshot, had to hang onto a branch. It spun me round to face the man chasing after me.

"*Parker*? But...what the hell are you doing here?"

Parker Armstrong hurried the last few strides and caught up with me. He was dressed like a tourist but carrying a Glock. He must have seen the way my eyes rested on the gun because he tucked it away in the small of his back before approaching.

"What do *you* think?" he demanded quietly. His gaze skimmed over me, made an instant assessment and plucked me off my feet with one arm under my knees and another around my back.

I went rigid in his arms. "Put me down."

It was more effective than struggling and shouting would have been but he didn't comply. He turned his head, stared at me.

"Just for once, Charlie, will you let me help you?"

But I couldn't quash the memory of his words at the apartment, or his actions since.

"Don't make me hurt you, Parker," I said tiredly. "Put. Me. Down."

He paused a beat, then let my legs slide out of his grasp, tilting me upright again, but kept a steadying arm around my shoulders. I didn't try to fight him on that. I wasn't sure I could do it without falling over, in any case.

We turned uphill and for a second I regretted not letting him carry me up there. Someone crashed through the undergrowth above us. We both tensed.

A man came half-running, half-bounding sideways down the slope. I recognised him as one of the new guys Parker had taken on over the winter. There had been quite a few personnel changes, even before the whole mess over Sean in the Middle East, the uncertainty over the Armstrong-Meyer agency itself.

"Boss," the man called, when he was near enough not to shout. "We lost him. Held up a passing car, threw the guy into the road, and took off."

"You didn't follow?"

"Front suspension's totalled," the man said with a shrug. "Damn French cars."

"OK, thanks."

"Great. That's just great," I said sourly. "I had him. You lost him."

Parker glanced at me. "From where we were sitting, it looked a lot more like *he* had *you*."

"Really?" I muttered, shrugging away from him.

We climbed in silence. It was only as we neared the top of the slope, where the Fiat had gouged ruts through the grass into the dark flesh of the earth beneath, that Parker asked, almost diffidently, "So, who was he?"

"Darius Orosco."

"Darius Oros—?" Parker broke off, eyes narrowing. "What the hell have you gotten yourself into, Charlie?"

"Nothing I wasn't only too aware of getting into, and perfectly capable of getting myself out of," I threw back.

We pushed through the forlorn curtain of snapped-off branches and stepped out onto the road. One of Parker's guys was trying to calm a middle-aged Italian man, dressed like a farmer, who was gesturing wildly and protesting at increasing volume about his hijacked car.

Another of Parker's men was inspecting the front end of the Renault. The passenger side wheel was twisted at an unlikely angle and jammed hard into the bodywork. Clearly, the driver was used to Yank SUVs that might have been constructed with offensive manoeuvres specifically in mind. Any normal vehicle would seem flimsy by comparison. He straightened when he caught sight of his boss.

"Alternate transport ETA twenty minutes, sir."

Parker nodded to him and turned to me. He gestured to the passenger side front seat. "Why don't you sit down while we wait?"

I'd had enough of being bundled into strange vehicles today, even ones that weren't going anywhere. "Thanks, but I'm fine standing."

He sighed. "Just pull that goddamned stick out of your ass and *sit down* before you fall down."

He sounded so exasperated, I eyed him warily. His expression softened, almost rueful. "You don't have to fight me on every single damn thing, Charlie."

"Really?" I murmured. "Only, nothing you've done recently smacks of having my best interests at heart."

He flinched. Infinitesimal, but there all the same.

"At least let me take a look at that wound."

I put up an experimental hand to my head. My fingers came away wet, sticky, and tinged with red.

"Oh," I said blankly. "OK."

Parker grimaced, whether at the obvious reluctance in my voice or the fact I seemed to have forgotten the head wound, I wasn't sure. But, he bit off whatever retort he might have made. Instead, he went to the rear of the car and retrieved a first-aid kit. It wasn't the usual perfunctory box of plasters and antiseptic cream. This was about the size of a briefcase and far more comprehensive than any rental car company might provide. Parker must have brought it with him.

"New office mandate?" I asked as he set the kit down on the roof of the car and flipped open the lid.

"Merely a sensible precaution on risky assignments."

"You're here working?" I frowned. "I hope you haven't had to leave a client unprotected for this."

He didn't respond to that right away, but gripped my upper arms and pressed until I subsided into the passenger seat. My acquiescence seemed to surprise him. I felt his eyes on me as he pulled on a pair of disposable gloves, parting the hair behind my right ear.

"We're here for *you*, Charlie," he said then, quietly. "If we have a client at all right now, you're it."

That threw me, held me still and silent while he crouched alongside me to apply kaolin-coated QuikClot gauze to the side of my skull, holding it in place until the blood stopped oozing. Perhaps that was why he'd said it.

It was on the tip of my tongue to ask if Epps was behind Parker's sudden appearance here in Italy. Epps had told me he couldn't provide overseas support. Had he called in favours from my former employer to cover that angle? Or resorted to blackmailing him, also? That *was* far more Epps's style.

In fact, I wondered if Epps had kept him in the loop right from the start. Was Epps the reason Parker had been so apparently vindictive about cutting off my lifelines, one by one? Had he been pressured into making it look good, in case anyone took an undue interest?

Or had he been pressured into making sure my options were so limited that I'd accept Epps's proposal regardless. It was a less appealing thought.

I scanned Parker's face, only a few inches from my own. His gaze was firmly on what he was doing. Too firmly. Then he flicked his eyes to mine and, just for a split second, I saw something close to shame.

And then it was my turn to flinch.

"I'm sorry," Parker said automatically. "I'm trying to go easy on you."

Yeah, well. It's a pity you didn't feel that way weeks ago…

I said nothing, just waited. A few moments later he sat back on his heels and stuffed the soiled piece of QuikClot back into its wrapper for disposal. He stripped off the gloves and folded them inside, too.

Then he sighed again, rubbed a hand around the nape of his neck.

"Look, I'm sorry, Charlie," he said, looking uncharacteristically uncertain. "I never meant to push you into doing anything…like this."

"Like what?"

He glanced at the guy nearest to us but his attention was still on the car. "Like working for the First Family of organised crime." Parker's voice had dropped to a furious whisper. "Eric Kincaid is bad enough, but *Darius Orosco*? Have you entirely lost your mind?"

"No, just my job, my home, and—I found out subsequently—my ability to easily replace either."

His head went back as if I'd punched him. "Hey, the job is all on you, Charlie. You know damn well I never wanted you to quit in the first place."

"And you know *'damn well'* why I did," I shot back. I took a breath, aware I'd let my voice rise, and lowered it again. "You *lied* to me, Parker."

I could have killed a man because of you. In fact, I suspect that you were rather hoping I would.

He shook his head. "I may not always have told you everything, Charlie, but that doesn't mean I flat-out lied to you."

It was on the tip of my tongue to tell him that lying by omission was still lying but suddenly I didn't have the energy to get into it.

"Why did you blacklist me?" I asked instead.

"Where did you hear that?"

"What's that got to do with it?" I paused a moment, decided to turn the screw. "Eric Kincaid told me, actually. I'd already turned down his job offer once. What prompted me to accept the second time was finding out how limited my options had become." *How limited* you'd *made them.*

Pain flashed through Parker's face. He disguised it with an edge of contempt. "So now you're working for a guy who sells arms to the highest bidder—including terrorists."

I was overcome with weariness again. All this verbal sparring with Parker would get us nowhere. It wasn't even fun.

"What Kincaid does with his business *is* his business," I said evenly. "But I'm not working for him—or for Orosco, come to that. I'm working for Kincaid's wife, Helena. Family members are considered strictly non-combatant, apparently—the arms-dealing equivalent of the Illuminati have a unilateral agreement to prove it. Something to do with honour among thieves and all that."

Parker digested this in silence for a moment.

"Tell me, why does a woman who's 'strictly non-combatant' have need of a bodyguard?"

I nodded. Parker's ability to cut straight to the heart of it, scalpel-sharp, like a surgeon making his first incision, was one of the things I liked best about working for him. *No, it was one of the things I* used *to like.*

"Because someone's broken that agreement," I said. "And if anything happens to Helena, it will start a war between the different organisations."

"If Mrs Kincaid is off-limits, as you say, who's foolish enough to go after her?"

"That's a very good question," I agreed, unwilling to give him anything more than I had already. "One I was trying to work out myself."

"And?"

"And I thought I might be getting somewhere." I gave him a rueful smile and dabbed a hand to the back of my head. This time, it came away dry. "But then some idiot ran me off the road and my best lead did a vanishing act."

41

———

By the time we reached the airfield near Perugia, the Kincaids' Gulfstream was long gone. No surprises there.

"What now?" Parker asked.

"France," I said. "I know where they're headed. I can pick them up there."

He glanced across at me, waiting for elaboration I was not inclined to provide.

We were in a replacement rental car—a big Mercedes this time. At my insistence, Parker had left his guys to sort out the wrecked Renault and brought me on alone. There was a slim chance the Kincaids might have waited for me. In that event, arriving with an entourage of obvious professionals was not likely to go down well.

As things turned out, it wouldn't have mattered.

"You'd have thought they'd leave some kind of message for you here," Parker said. "Tried to re-establish contact, at least."

"Would *you*?"

While we were on the drive over, I had given him a rough outline of what happened on Isola Minore. I left out certain strategic details but he got the gist of it.

"No point in making it easy for them to pick up the trail," I said. "If they had discovered I wasn't Helena and…disposed of me, then logically here would be their next port of call."

He shook his head. "I still can't believe you pulled that stunt. You took a hell of a risk, Charlie, and not just that they wouldn't know the difference. As soon as they'd gotten hold of you they might have killed everyone else—Mrs Kincaid included—to leave no witnesses."

"They tried," I said, remembering the scorching exhaust gases of the RPG skimming over the top of me heading for the Sikorsky.

She was well away by that time. I know she was…

"Anyway, Parker, don't pretend, in similar circumstances, you wouldn't have done the same thing."

"Maybe." His voice was dry. "But I can't say they would have believed *I* was Mrs Kincaid for very long."

Despite everything, I smiled. Maybe that was why he said it.

"Thanks, by the way," I said. "I appreciate you riding to the rescue, however it turned out."

"You're welcome." He fired up the Merc's engine. "I'm guessing you have the clothes you stand up in and not a lot else. You need to stop off at a mall before we hit the road?"

I twisted in my seat. "What do you mean, 'before *we* hit the road'? Where exactly do you think *we* are going?"

He shot a cuff, checked his watch. "It's probably eight hours from here to Geneva. We should be able to make it there in time for a late dinner, then go on in the morning." He put the car in gear and started rolling, apparently oblivious to my expression. "Where did you say in France?"

"I didn't."

He ignored the warning bite in my voice, shrugged. "OK, we'll work that one out tomorrow."

"Parker, stop—"

"We'll need to get you cleaned up if we're gonna get a room tonight without them calling the cops. That's a nice jacket, by the way."

I looked down, realised I was still wearing Helena's designer label. I hoped I hadn't got *too* much blood on it. *Ah well.*

"Parker, stop the damn car."

He shook his head. "Not if you want to eat overlooking Lake Geneva this evening. I know this fabulous hotel in—"

"*No!*" My turn to interrupt, close to a shout. "You are *not* driving me to France."

"No?" He ducked his chin back, gave a mirthless chuckle. "Charlie, you've got no money, no phone, no ID. So, how else you gonna do it, huh? How else you gonna get there, inside twenty-four hours, without my help?"

I didn't have an answer and he knew it. I slumped back in my seat, defeated and scowling.

"Yeah," he said, "I thought not…"

42

It must have been the bang on the head. There's no other explanation I can think of why I allowed myself to be sidetracked for so bloody long. Five hours, to be exact. We were somewhere between Milan and Turin on the A4—a six-lane *autostrada* through flat, fairly featureless scenery.

Darkness gathered, sucking the remaining light out of the day. I'd been dozing in the passenger seat. Suddenly, I sat bolt upright, causing Parker's hands to twitch on the Merc's steering wheel.

"You OK?"

"Yes… *No*… Parker, how *did* you know where to find me? And what did you mean when you said 'if we have a client at all right now, you're it'?"

"Epps," he said, confirming my earlier suspicions. Despite that, I felt the tug of disappointment. It's one thing to hope someone's come after you because they want to. Quite another to find out they didn't have a choice.

"When?"

"When what?"

"When did he…approach you?"

A last-minute manoeuvre by a car ahead and resultant bunching traffic took Parker's attention, so it took him a moment to reply. I tried not to betray how important that answer was to me.

"Yesterday."

"Right." I swallowed past the stone in my throat. It sank to my chest and lodged there. I kept my voice light. "You didn't waste any time getting over here, then."

"Yeah, well, Epps had all the arrangements in place. More or less." He grimaced. "We had Kincaid's flight plan to the airfield, but we were told you'd be going on by road. The helo threw us. We hoofed it over to Trasimeno. Arrived in time to see you being dragged out of a boat and bundled into a vehicle. We followed, were just working up a tactical breach when the two of you came out. The rest you know."

"I was hooded in the boat," I pointed out. "How did you know it was me?"

He glanced across and I saw the flash of his teeth in the glow from the car's instrument lighting. "I don't need to see your face to recognise you, Charlie," he said. "We've worked together long enough for me to know the way you move."

"Ah." It took conscious effort not to squirm in my seat. I grabbed for safer ground. "Is Epps still holding that cult business in California over you?"

Parker shook his head. "We closed out that tab a long time ago."

"So, what else does he have on you?"

"To get me to come after you, you mean?" Parker's gaze was on the road, but I caught the way the muscles tightened around his eyes. "He asked. I said yes."

"That's it?"

"That's it," he confirmed. "To be honest, I was glad of the excuse."

I gave a short laugh, devoid of humour. "There would have been easier ways to keep in touch."

He said nothing. The last pale pink band of sky at the horizon had disappeared. Any remaining warmth went with it. I shivered, flipped the heater control for the passenger side up a notch.

"Supposing that simply *keeping in touch* was…not enough?" Parker said quietly then. "Not enough for me, that is."

I sighed, rubbed a hand across my eyes. They felt full of grit. So did my brain.

"It all seems…a bit too little, a bit too late, Parker. I can't—"

"I did not send you out there to kill Sean." His voice was abrupt, almost fierce.

I froze, heart thundering. My mind did a fast rewind to another conversation I'd had with Parker, sitting in the belly of a C-130 Hercules. It seemed both a long time ago and nowhere near long enough.

"If Sean has gone after this guy for revenge, it's a one-way deal. You know as well as I do, he can't come back."

"You'd turn him in?"

"I couldn't do that to him. Prison would kill him. Better to give him another way out."

"One round in the chamber and tell him to do the honourable thing, you mean?"

"If he'll take that option."

"And what if he won't? After all, this is a man you think has gone 'clean off the rails.'"

"If he can't be reasoned with, then he has to be stopped. Like you said — Iraq's a dangerous place."

"Jesus, Parker. You're talking…assassination."

And he'd nodded as he told me he didn't think I was up to that part of the job.

The scene folded in on itself as rapidly as it had appeared. It left behind a buzzing in my ears and the agitated swirl of nausea high up under my ribcage.

"Didn't you? Funny, but that's not quite how I remember it went."

"I just…wanted you to think about Sean not being there anymore," he said. "About him being gone, and what that might…mean."

"Sean's been *gone* since he took that round to the head," I said bluntly. "The man who came back may have looked like him, and he may have sounded like him, but…" And suddenly that stone in my throat was making my voice hoarse, so I had to clear my throat before I could go on. "But it wasn't him. Not really. It was close, though. *Fuck*, was it close—close enough that I fooled myself. For a while…"

Eyes still fixed on the road ahead, Parker reached a hand across the centre console, palm upwards. I hesitated, but only for a moment. Then I put my hand into it. His fingers closed over mine, squeezed. I shut my eyes.

"I know," he said softly, and it might have been my imagination, but his voice seemed a little thicker than usual. "I know. We both did."

43

BECAUSE WE WERE in the European Schengen zone, officially we didn't need passports to go from Italy into Switzerland, but there was always the chance of a random spot-check. As we approached the Italian end of the Mont Blanc tunnel, I confess to a twinge of unease about my lack of documentation. Parker told me to relax and produced my spare passport, like sleight of hand, along with his own.

"You left it in the safe at the office," he said in answer to my unspoken question.

"And you only mention this *now*?" I'd assumed the spare was somewhere in storage with the rest of my belongings. I suppose it had been, in a way.

Because we worked occasionally in Israel as well as Arab countries, I'd been able to obtain a second passport. It had saved a hell of a lot of hassle in the past and looked like it was going to do so again.

He smiled. "Face it, if I'd told you back at the airfield, you'd have grabbed it and ran."

I said nothing. He'd got that right, so there was nothing to say.

Annoyingly, Parker looked in control, as though nothing would floor him. I felt in tatters by comparison, emotionally and physically.

It was only as we headed into the tunnel itself that I felt calm enough to return to an earlier conversation. "Before, when you said Epps asked you to come out here, and you said yes... Why?"

"Why what?"

"Why did you say yes? You couldn't have made your low opinion of me much clearer, when you came to tell me to get out of the apartment."

Parker sighed. "Not my finest hour," he agreed. "I was angry. I freely admit it. Angry, and disappointed, and frustrated. At myself as much as you. And Sean, of course."

"He let you down."

"He let us both down." He ran a hand across his face. "And I felt, by walking out, you were doing the same thing."

"So, what changed?"

"I realised...acting like I did... Well, I didn't behave any better, did I?" His smile was rueful. "I was trying to track you down when Epps reached out. Felt like a second chance."

"What did Epps tell you—about why I'm over here?"

"Not much. Does he ever?"

I thought of the few snippets of intel the Homeland man had fed me. "No, I suppose not."

"Care to read me in?"

"Not really my secrets to tell." I gave a shrug that was genuinely regretful—mostly. "I'm sorry."

"OK," he said. "How about I run some scenarios by you? Hypothetically speaking, of course. See if anything sounds...plausible?"

"This is not a game of twenty questions, Parker."

"It's a long drive and the scenery on this part sucks. Humour me."

For once there wasn't the usual congestion in the tunnel. Parker kept the Merc to a steady speed, just under the 70kph limit. It felt almost funereal. The overhead lights in the curved roof strobed past with hypnotic regularity.

Eventually, Parker said, "So, you're protecting Helena Kincaid because someone's broken this non-combatant agreement you mentioned. OK so far?"

He paused. I said nothing.

"Ah, you're gonna make me work for it, huh?"

The teasing note in his voice was at odds with our earlier conversation. He was distracting me from the topic of Sean, I realised, and was grateful for it.

"Hell, yes," I said.

He smiled. "Question is, why is Epps taking an interest—even unofficially—in organised crime infighting? Surely, he'd just let them slug it out and stand by to scoop up the last man standing?"

"Who said anything about organised crime?" I asked, deliberately playing devil's advocate. "Kincaid deals in arms. It doesn't necessarily follow that he's doing so illegally."

"Come on, Charlie, don't play dumb. Darius Orosco has a certain reputation. He'd sell his grandma an Uzi so she could blow his granddaddy away if he thought he'd make a dime on the deal."

"That's Orosco, not Kincaid."

"So?" He let out a brief, staccato laugh. "Meet the new boss. Same as the old boss."

"Is he, though?" I murmured. "That doesn't fit with what I've seen of Eric Kincaid. He's very different from his father-in-law. It was Kincaid who negotiated the non-com agreement in the first place."

"Something you would hardly need for a legit operation," Parker pointed out.

"But a good first step towards *turning* a business legit, perhaps?"

Parker sighed. "It still doesn't explain why Epps is sticking his nose in," he said. "His remit is *domestic* security, not international politicking."

There was no comment I could make that wouldn't be evasion or an outright lie. I knew very well where Epps's interest lay—his own undercover operative. And I was no closer to pinpointing their identity, never mind working out if the loyalties of that person had been compromised.

Parker took in my silence and glanced across. "You care to speculate on Epps's motives?"

"Hey, I was hired simply to look after Helena. She shops and lunches and rides her horses. As far as I'm aware, she has no part of the arms trade." That much, at least, was true.

"Well, that's a new development, too," Parker muttered.

"Meaning?"

He skimmed his eyes across my face again, taking a little longer this time. I preferred it when he kept his eyes on the road. Not just for safety's sake, but because he saw altogether too much.

"You think I would come out here without doing due diligence first?" he demanded. "A couple of years back, Orosco has a big health scare—his heart. Being the kinda guy he is, he tries to keep it hushed up, refuses to go see a cardiac specialist and almost leaves it too late. Then he has the surgery and comes back fighting fit."

I let my surprise show. "That's news to me."

But it probably explained why Orosco had given in quite so quickly when I'd threatened to skewer him, back at the villa in Montisi. Anyone who's stared their own mortality in the face tends not to take continued living for granted.

"Yeah, but before she married his right-hand man and allowed him to keep his empire neatly all in the family, the word on the street was that Orosco was grooming his daughter to take over."

44

"I DON'T KNOW where you heard that rumour, Parker, but it goes against everything I've learned about Helena." *Or learned from Helena herself, for that matter.* "She hates having her father interfere in her life."

"And yet she married one of his lieutenants."

I shrugged, remembering the story she'd told me about her previous fiancé. "Yeah, well, maybe it was a case of better the devil you know."

"Is that why you took this assignment for Epps?"

"Hm, like I had much of a choice." I kept my voice dry and level. "If I'd said no, he was going to deport me. And don't tell me he doesn't have the authority—this is Epps we're talking about."

There was a moment's silence, then Parker swore under his breath. "I'm sorry, Charlie. I didn't—"

His contrition sounded sincere but it had been a bitch of a day and I was bone tired. "What?" I demanded. "Didn't think? Didn't care?"

He shook his head. "No," he said. "If anything, I thought about it way too much."

A LITTLE OVER an hour after exiting the French end of the Mont Blanc tunnel and crossing into Switzerland, Parker swung the Merc to a halt in front of a distinguished looking hotel on the east side of Geneva. It was too dark to see if it was overlooking the lake, as he'd promised.

I'd dozed for the last thirty minutes or so, but he looked ready to drive through the night. Blearily, I checked the time. Had to blink a few times to get my eyes to focus on the face of my watch. *Helena's watch*, I realised. No wonder the face seemed unfamiliar. It was later than I thought.

"I'll go check in," Parker said. "You OK here for a moment?"

I nodded, watched him skirt the fountain in the centre of the forecourt and take the steps to the front entrance. He moved loose and easy, but I could tell from the angle of his head that he checked out every car, every corner and every shadow as he passed. He could no more turn off those instincts than I could.

I opened the passenger door and staggered out onto the gravel. The air seemed colder after Italy. It woke me better than a slap to the face. I tilted my head back and inhaled a couple of needle-sharp lungfuls. Above the lights of the building, I could just about make out the stars. I wondered if Sean was somewhere looking up at the same stars. I didn't even know what continent he was on.

Maybe it's time to finally let go...

Parker reappeared.

"Everything all right?" I asked, seeing his expression.

"They slightly screwed up the booking."

"How very unlike the Swiss," I said. "Do I need to arm-wrestle you for who has to sleep in the bath?"

He allowed himself a small smile. "Not quite that bad. It's a suite—two bedrooms. You OK with that?"

"Sure." It was nothing we hadn't done while working together before. Besides, I was too weary to argue. "Hell, that time in Buenos Aires, we had three teams working round the clock and hot-bunking it in one queen-size double, remember?"

"Yeah, I remember," he said. "And I never did like climbing into a bed that's still warm from the previous occupant."

I smiled as we grabbed our bags from the Merc's boot. At

Parker's insistence, we'd taken a quick detour through an outlet mall on the outskirts of Milan and I'd stocked up on the essentials, including a small backpack.

"The restaurant is finished for the evening, but they'll send something up," Parker said, holding the bevelled glass door open for me.

"Of course, they will," I murmured. His calm acceptance both amused and mildly irritated me. He took it for granted that if he arrived hungry, no matter what hour of the night, they would feed him.

Apart from his time in the military, serving his country, Parker's background was one of wealth and privilege. Maybe that was why he looked so at home somewhere like this, even dressed more casually than I could remember seeing him, in an open-neck shirt with the sleeves rolled back.

With uniformed flunkey in attendance, we took the mirrored lift up to the top floor and were shown into our suite. The man threw open the double doors with a flourish, earning every penny of the no-doubt generous tip Parker slipped him on the way out.

"I think I'm going to grab a shower and just crash," I said.

"When did you last eat?" And when I frowned, trying to pin it down, he added, "If you can't remember, you need food."

"Really, I'm fine."

He gave me one of his no-nonsense stares as he picked up the room phone. "I'll order down. If you want to waste it after it arrives, that's up to you."

It was easier to say nothing than argue. I went into the en suite next to my room and stood under a stinging deluge of hot water for as long as I could stand it, my hands braced against the tiles.

It was the class of hotel where there are heating elements behind the mirrors to keep them unfogged. When I stepped out of the shower, my reflection seemed to be everywhere, giving me an uncomfortable number of angles of my own naked body.

I towelled off roughly, trying to ignore the number of fading scars I possessed. A record of the violence done to me in the past. A reminder of the violence I'd done to others.

Afterwards, I looked at the meagre pile of clothes I'd laid out from the backpack. The thought of climbing back into my clothes again held no appeal. I shrugged into the oversize fluffy robe the hotel provided and padded out into the sitting room area of the suite.

To my left, the large flatscreen TV above the fireplace was switched to one of the twenty-four-hour news channels. The sound was muted, but a ticker-tape of the latest headlines scrolled across the bottom of the screen.

As I moved further into the room, I saw Parker over in the dining area, unloading covered plates from a service cart onto the table. Evidently, room service had arrived while I was attempting to drain the hotel's hot water supply.

Parker stood with his back to me, phone held in the crook of his neck while he worked. He, too, was wearing only the hotel towelling robe. My breath hitched, just a little.

He ended the call, turned to put the phone down and caught sight of me. He stilled, suddenly intent.

"You OK?"

"Yeah, thanks," I said, forcing my feet forwards. "Feeling almost human again."

"Good." His eyes, grey blue, skimmed over the robe and I resisted the urge to tug the belt tighter around my waist. "I was going to ask if you objected to me not dressing for dinner, but…"

"I think it's safe for you to take that as a no."

That quick flash of a smile again. The one that made him look boyish. The one that made him look far too good-looking for my peace of mind. Especially when he lifted the cover from the last plate, then licked his finger where something had spilled out.

"So, can I tempt you?"

"Sorry?"

"Food, Charlie."

"Um, yeah, sure. Now it's here, like you said, it would be a shame to waste it."

It wasn't the first time I'd shared a meal in a hotel room with Parker. We'd done so before, many times in many different corners of the world. Sometimes under stress, sometimes under more routine circumstances. But this felt different, all the same—

and not only because of how we were dressed. There was no team around us, nobody checking in, checking up.

Hell, I didn't even work for him anymore…

And that was the biggest difference of all.

The buzzing in my ears was back, but this time no nausea accompanied it. Instead there was an edgy anticipation that I recognised, in a detached kind of way, as the beginnings of arousal.

Nothing says you have to act on it, though.

We used the table as a buffet, filled our plates and took them back to the plush sofas. I tried to sit without flashing him. He gave me space, taking the other sofa. We ate in companionable silence and, finally, I began to relax.

"OK, you win," I said when I put down my empty plate on the side table. "I *was* hungry. Thank you."

"You're welcome. I asked them to send up a bottle of single malt Scotch, if you'd like a nightcap?"

My self-preservation instinct was telling me that this was a very bad idea. I knew I ought to decline, to say goodnight, walk into my bedroom, shut the door and go to bed. Alone.

But all the time I'd worked for Parker there had been a thread of attraction between us. A thread of attraction I'd never pulled, just in case whatever unravelled from it could not be put back together again. I admit I was curious to know if it would be enough to override the distrust that now lay between us. I doubted it would make things any better. Question was, would it make them worse.

Still, since when have I ever taken the sensible option?

"That sounds lovely," I said. "Why not?"

45

Parker cleared our plates while I remained slouched on my sofa. He always did strike me as very domesticated. When he returned, he carried two crystal tumblers, each containing a generous measure of whisky and a single cube of ice. He handed one over, clinked his own glass against the rim, and sat down next to me. Close, but not too close.

"Cheers," he said.

I lifted my glass in silent response and took a slug. It fired all the way down the inside of my ribcage. Suddenly, my reasons for caution, for *not* doing this, became a little less easy to discern.

Parker leaned his head back and put his bare feet up on the low table in front of us, crossing his legs at the ankle. He had tanned legs and well-shaped feet, only a light dusting of hair on his calves. Would it feel coarse or soft to the touch, I wondered.

He was longer and leaner than Sean, less overtly menacing, unless you knew what you were looking for. They both had the same knack for stillness. The same ability not just to look, but to *see*.

Perhaps that was why, as we drank our whisky in silence, I kept my eyes firmly on the news anchor miming on the TV. The ticker-tape announced violent protests in Paris, a new bombing raid in Syria, world leaders gathering in Germany for a summit on climate change. Between sips, I cradled my glass in my lap.

The ice had almost melted away. It could have been my imagination, but the room suddenly seemed overly warm.

Eventually, Parker sat forwards, set down his glass and reached for mine. It took a moment for my fingers to unlock enough to release it. He leaned across me to put the glass on the side table next to me. Close enough to see the fine lines radiating from the corners of his eyes. Close enough that I could tell he'd shaved as well as showered.

Instead of sitting back, he stopped, still poised half over me. His eyes searched my face. I'm sure he read it like an open book.

I cleared my throat. "This is probably a bad idea, Parker."

"Uh-huh," he agreed. "You're *probably* right." His hand came up to brush my hair away from my face. His touch was gentle. His eyes were on his fingers, tracing my hairline, the outline of my ear, the outside of my jaw. I shivered, teetering on the edge of indecision. It had been a while since anyone had needed me without underlying resentment.

My relationship with Sean was over. He'd made that more than clear, so I couldn't use it as an excuse anymore. My employment with Parker was over. I couldn't use that as an excuse, either. I was tired of doing the right thing. And a part of me wanted to know, wanted to feel, just *wanted*.

Just this once.

I circled his wrist with my fingers, allowing myself the luxury to explore. He was less muscular than Sean, but there was a corded strength beneath the skin that excited as much as it scared me.

My hands slid across his shoulders to the nape of his neck, tried to drag his head down to mine, impatient.

He blocked me easily, catching my wrists in one hand and levering both mine over my head, holding them against the back of the sofa. Momentary panic bloomed in my chest, a reflex I could neither hide nor control. I froze.

He pulled back a fraction and watched me quiver until the old fears began to subside. His body was a weight slanted over mine. The feeling of being pinned and helpless was illogical, I knew—I could have broken his hold in a heartbeat. Could have had him face down on the carpet in another. But right at that moment, that knowledge didn't make it all any less overwhelming. My heart slammed against my ribs. Surely he could feel it?

"Parker. Please—"

"Oh, I fully intend to please you, Charlie," he murmured. "You just have to let go and let me."

His lips were a fraction away from mine. His free hand tugged my robe free of its knotted belt and slipped inside. The softness of his seeking fingertips turned into the tantalising scrape of nails. My eyes went wide, then glassy, then blind.

He covered my mouth with his own and swallowed whatever noises I might have made.

Things got a little hazy after that. I vaguely remember him picking me up, as though I was some kind of lightweight, and carrying me into his bedroom. I'd expected the same kind of urgency that boiled through my blood. Instead, I found a tender intensity that drove me over the edge of sensation and almost ruined me.

———

I woke, in a bed not my own, a little after 4 a.m. the following morning. On the other side of the mattress, Parker was dead to the world. I couldn't hold that against him. By then, I reckoned he'd been asleep for less than an hour.

I lay semi-stunned, listening to his quiet breathing and trying to work out if I regretted what we'd done. After a few moments wrestling with my conscience, I came to the conclusion that I didn't. Not yet, anyway. His relentless pursuit of my pleasure, in which he seemed to take such delight, left me as shocked as it did satisfied.

I could not—*would* not—look too deeply into the implications of that.

It did not stop me, however, from lifting my passport from the bedside table and creeping into my clothes. When I stole into the dawn, that wasn't the only thing I stole. I also took the keys to the Mercedes.

46

DRIVING solo through the mountains from Geneva and over the border into France was an experience. One I might have enjoyed more had I not been dead tired. Or worried about the possibility of being stopped at any moment for driving what was, technically, a stolen car.

It was the reason I had not taken Parker's gun along with his keys. If I *was* going to be arrested, better for it to be for simple car theft rather than throwing in firearms offences as well. France may have been the land of *cordon bleu*, but I doubt that extended to prison food, even here.

Besides, I was hoping Helena still had my SIG and I could reclaim it when I reached them.

It was around five hundred klicks from Switzerland roughly southwest to my destination near Rodez in the *département* of Aveyron. After the first couple of hours, I reckoned that if Parker hadn't reported me by now there was a chance he wasn't going to. Either that or he was a far heavier sleeper than I realised. Still, every police cruiser I spotted on the *autoroute* made me nervous.

It occurred to me that the Merc was bound to have some kind of GPS tracker fitted. And it would no doubt suit Parker's purposes better to keep tabs on me privately, rather than involve the authorities at this stage. Even after last night, it was hard to know which way he'd go.

I confess I had absolutely no clue what to say to him the next time we met.

The long journey gave me the opportunity to reflect on the night before at some length. I found I was still without regrets. It had been a long time in the build-up and there's only so much foreplay you can stand. Besides, it had been good. Better than good, if I was honest. Parker always had been highly attuned to those around him. It was interesting to discover that sensitivity was not limited to his professional life.

Question was, where did we go from here?

Was there even anywhere *to* go?

————

THE ONLY THING I knew about the French part of the Kincaids' trip was the name of the place we'd been heading to and the man who owned it. I'd been planning to bone up on the rest during the flight from Italy. *So much for that idea…*

The Frenchman's name was Gilbert de Bourdillon. His home was a chateau in or near a village, both of which bore his last name. The de Bourdillons, I gathered, were an *old* family. In fact, they probably had their feet under the table well before a bunch of Norman toffs decided to hop across the Channel on the equivalent of a stag weekend and teach that English upstart, Harold, a lesson.

I'd entered the address into the Merc's satnav and followed where it sent me. But I was not wholly prepared for my first sight of the place when I arrived.

Chateau de Bourdillon was not simply a country house, as I'd expected, but a full-blown castle. A stout tower at each corner, crenellated walls, arrow slits, moat, drawbridge. The whole nine yards.

I braked to a halt, leaning on the steering wheel and taking it in.

"Now, that's what you call a nice little place in the country," I murmured under my breath.

The closest I could get, initially, was the end of the driveway. From there, a dead straight avenue of sculpted trees led towards the chateau itself, guarded by a pair of iron-studded gates about fifteen feet high. The gates were made of weathered dark wood —either old themselves or artfully constructed to look that way.

Their design was part practical, part decorative, with enough gaps between curving slats for me to take in the view of the castle itself beyond. On either side were enormous gateposts, topped by bears sitting up on their hindquarters and holding shields. The bears looked as though they were probably actual size.

Despite this history, the gates clearly had some kind of remotely operated electronic lock. Hidden in the creeper to one side was a camera. I climbed out of the car and leaned nonchalantly against the driver's door, staring up at it, until I heard a loud click and the gates began to swing very slowly open.

I slid back behind the wheel, suppressing a groan at the stiffness in my body. Surely it wasn't that long since I last had sex? Then I remembered that, in addition to two days of travelling, I'd also been in a fairly dramatic car crash less than twenty-four hours earlier, and put most of it down to that.

There were no obvious places to park in front of the castle, so I abandoned the Merc to one side of the moat. By the time I'd switched off the engine, a figure had emerged from the interior and was standing below the daggered tips of the iron portcullis, waiting for me.

Of all the people I'd been hoping to make up the reception committee, he had not been top of the list. In fact, the very sight of him gave me the feeling that perhaps my welcome was not about to be as warm and fluffy as I'd hoped.

Schade.

47

I CLIMBED out of the car, careful to keep my movements slow and predictable. It was like walking out of the western saloon and finding the lone gunslinger in the black hat standing waiting for me in the middle of Main Street. All it needed was tumbleweed and the jingle of spurs. I even imagined I could hear hoof beats.

Then I realised that I could—hear hoof beats, that is.

I turned, saw two riders on white horses approaching. I recognised Helena as one, not least because she yelled my name and urged her mount forwards from a sedate trot to a flattened gallop.

Well, at least someone's *pleased to see me.*

I stepped away from the car to meet her, which served the purpose of taking me further away from Schade at the same time. There was something about the way he just stood there that sent the hairs rising at the back of my neck.

Helena pulled up at the last moment, her face flushed with excitement. I didn't kid myself that it was entirely caused by sight of my prodigal return.

Close up, her horse was surprisingly small—almost pony sized—but with a well put together, muscular build. I knew I should probably recognise the breed, but for the moment it escaped me.

"Charlie! My God, I thought I'd never see you again." Helena jumped off the horse and grabbed me into a big hug. I was too startled to do much more than submit, although I did reach out and catch hold of a rein when the animal showed signs of taking off.

Helena stepped back. She was smiling. Then she punched me in the arm.

"Ow, what was that for?"

"Jeez, we thought you were *dead*. Couldn't you at least have *called* me?"

I never knew you cared.

I was saved from having to respond out loud by the arrival of the second rider, at a more dignified pace. He was a slim man with a rather large nose. He was wearing a tweed jacket and sat on his horse like he'd been in the saddle since before he could walk.

Helena turned to face him. "Gilbert," she said, pronouncing it 'Zhil-bere' in an exaggeratedly French style. "This is Charlie Fox. She saved my life—quite literally—in Italy."

The man dismounted and took off his tweed cap, revealing a curled wisp of hair on the otherwise bald crown of his head. He held out his hand.

"It's an absolute pleasure to meet you," he said, with an accent that owed very little to France but a good deal to Eton and Oxford. "Gilbert de Bourdillon. Your fame precedes you, Charlie. I can't wait to hear all about it—over breakfast, perhaps. Have you eaten?"

"Thank you, sir," I said faintly. "And yes, I would love some breakfast."

"Excellent. I'll just drop this pair back at the stables and be with you in a jiffy."

Helena started to protest, but he held up a warning finger. "No, no, wouldn't hear of it. By the sounds of it, you and your Charlie have some catching up to do. And all I have to do is deliver them. The stable girls will take it from there."

"They're beautiful animals, sir," I said, remembering my manners and, as inspiration struck, "Not Camargue horses, are they, by any chance?"

"Oh, well spotted. Yes, indeed. One of the oldest breeds in

Europe. I can see you know your horseflesh, Charlie. I shall look forward to chatting with you further."

He set off on foot, leading the horses, heading to one side of the chateau where I could see a cluster of buildings. They looked slightly less fortified than the main property.

Helena linked her arm through mine and turned me towards the chateau.

"Are you OK?" I asked, keeping my voice low. "Everyone got out of the Sikorsky before they blew it?"

"Yes, thanks to you. I don't know what I would have done if—"

"Don't," I said quickly. "It *is* what you pay me for, after all."

"I think that counts as above and beyond, Charlie."

I shrugged, then dug in my pocket and handed over the rose-gold Rolex she'd loaned to me. She took it with a nod, clutching it in both hands as if she thought she'd never see that again, either.

I hesitated about asking for my TAG Heuer. It was a good make, if nowhere near as expensive a piece of jewellery as the one Helena owned, but for me there was a lot of sentimental value in that watch. As it turned out, I didn't need to ask. She pulled back her sleeve and undid the clasp on the strap, dropping the watch into my hand.

I closed my fingers around it—a gift from Sean, just after we first arrived in New York. I couldn't bring myself to put it aside, no matter how painful the memories attached to it now. I was momentarily thankful I hadn't been wearing it last night.

As I clipped the watch into place, I nodded towards the Merc. "I have your jacket in the car, too, but it, um, may need dry cleaning."

"Keep it," Helena said. "It looked good on you."

"What about my SIG?" I asked. "Do you still have it?"

"I'm sorry." She shook her head, not meeting my eyes. "I had to leave it in Italy."

I grabbed the backpack from the boot. Helena fell into step alongside me and, unexpectedly, linked her arm through mine.

I glanced across at her, my stride faltering.

"Are you sure you're OK?" I asked.

"Of course. Why?"

"Oh, I'm not complaining, believe me. But let's just say you're not usually quite so…happy to have me around."

Helena was quiet for a moment. "You put your ass on the line to save mine. Don't think I don't know what a *hell* of a thing it was you did," she murmured. "I reckoned I owed you a little protection in return."

Before I could query that statement, she let go of my arm and walked on towards the drawbridge. When I followed, I realised that the main entry to the chateau was now deserted. Whatever Schade had been waiting for—whatever it was he wanted with me—he seemed to have changed his mind and disappeared.

Or perhaps he realised he'd missed his chance.

48

THE BREAKFAST our host had promised was served in a formal dining room on the first floor. The decoration went in for a lot of gilt detailing, huge faded wall-hung tapestries, and cherubs painted on the ceiling. There were fireplaces on both sides of the room, but they seemed to be blocked off with marble slabs. Food was being kept warm in polished silver chafing dishes with burners underneath, like a hotel buffet.

Helena helped herself to coffee and sat with me, even though she claimed to have eaten already, before she and our host went out riding.

Shortly after I'd begun to eat, the door opened and the man himself walked in, still in his riding clothes. De Bourdillon was accompanied by Kincaid and Mrs Heedles.

"Charlie!" Kincaid said, looking almost as happy to see me as his wife had done. He shook my hand vigorously. "I'm glad you're all in one piece."

"So am I. How's"—I broke off, realising slightly late that de Bourdillon might not be privy to the Kincaids' itinerary so far, finished with—"everyone else?"

"We all made it out unscathed," Kincaid said. The twitch of his lips told me he knew exactly what I'd done. "Mrs Heedles stabilised Bernardo and his people took him and Tomas to the hospital—over near Arezzo."

"Will they be all right?"

"So they reckon. It's a private hospital. The kinda place where money buys you a very good doctor and no questions asked."

"Well...that's good."

"What about you?"

"I'm OK, as you can see."

"Yes, dear, so we *can* see," Mo Heedles said, pouring herself tea from a bone china pot. "What we can't quite work out, though, is how."

Her face held only polite enquiry but the comment hung in the air between us, gathering weight.

I swallowed a mouthful of bacon, giving myself time to consider under the guise of good manners. "How what?"

Kincaid cleared his throat. "The last time you were seen, a group of Syrian mercenaries were loading you, bound and gagged, into a speedboat in Italy. You left behind your pocket-book, your driver's licence, and your passport." He spread his arms. "And yet here you are."

"It's a long story."

Kincaid put his elbows on the table and linked his fingers. "We have time."

I gestured to my plate. "Don't I at least get to eat before you throw me into the dungeons?" One of the things I learned in the army was never to pass up the opportunity to refuel. I glanced at de Bourdillon, who was sitting taking this all in with bright, inquisitive eyes. "I assume this place does *have* dungeons, sir?"

"Oh, naturally," he said. "Although considering that's where I lay down wine, I don't think being put down there would be too much of a hardship for you."

"Possibly not," I agreed. "The collective term for wines is a 'pleasure' I believe."

He laughed, a guffaw. I grinned back at him. Kincaid and Mrs Heedles, however, were not so easily distracted.

"Where d'you pick up the Benz?" Kincaid asked.

"Ah, I, um borrowed it."

He raised an eyebrow. "From who?"

"From my former employer."

"Armstrong?" His second eyebrow rose to join the first. "What's he doing in France?"

"He was in Italy, actually."

"OK, this I gotta hear."

I sighed and launched into my story, sticking as close to the truth as possible. I recounted the facts of my encounter with Khalid Hamzeh and Darius Orosco without offering my opinion on what any of it might mean. Either they could work that one out for themselves, or it wasn't something they wanted to hear at all. Either way, it was not my place to say it.

When it came to Parker, I left out any mention of Conrad Epps's involvement. And, of course, what took place between that nightcap in Geneva and my early morning flit. Kissing and telling was never my style.

"And he just happened to have brought along your spare passport?" Kincaid said, frowning. "Sounds like an intervention."

"After the way he behaved when I quit, it sounded more like a guilty conscience to me."

"For driving you to the dark side, you mean?" He eyed me. "You're not tempted to go back?"

Was I tempted? It was hard to reconcile the Parker who'd stripped away my every personal and professional lifeline when he threw me out of the apartment, with the same Parker who'd stripped me out of that bathrobe and then done things with his hands, and his mouth, and his body, that made my heart stutter just to think about it.

"Oh, I think that ship has sailed, don't you?" I said keeping my voice even. "I let him take me to what looked to be a very expensive hotel in Geneva and buy me dinner, then I not only ran out on him, but also stole his car. Not exactly in contention for employee of the month, am I?"

"I would say that depends on who you're really working for," Kincaid said, "doesn't it?"

49

AND SO IT BEGINS.

I schooled my face into careful blankness. "Forgive me, but *I* thought I was working for Helena."

"Yeah," Kincaid said dryly. "So did we."

"So, what changed?"

Almost on cue, the door opened and Schade came in. His gaze swept the corners of the room, like it always did, before settling on me. Behind him, came Darius Orosco. There was trouble in the bullish set of his shoulders.

"You shoulda been more suspicious of her right from the start," he said to Kincaid. "Right place, right time to stop that ambush back in New Jersey, hey? How d'you know she didn't arrange the whole damn thing in the first place?"

"If you think I'd be prepared to see people die—not to mention killing them personally—just to ingratiate myself, then you way overestimate my ruthlessness."

"*One* coincidence we mighta bought, but then your supposedly *ex*-boss swooping in outta the blue to rescue you yesterday? That was one coincidence too many, lady."

"But we *are* supposed to buy the coincidence of *you* being in the right place at the right time to swoop in and rescue your daughter—or someone you *believed* was your daughter—within hours of her being snatched?" I shot back.

"I've been in this business since before you were a twitch in your daddy's pants," Orosco said with a sneer. "I keep my ear damn close to the ground and I got the guts and the instinct to act fast when I hear something I don't like the sound of."

His eyes skimmed over Kincaid as he spoke, extending the insult to him by implication, also. I waited for Kincaid to react, to ask when, exactly, Orosco had heard about the proposed assault on Ugoccione's island. To ask why he'd taken action himself instead of—rather than as well as—warning anyone else of the dangers.

Kincaid said nothing.

Orosco nodded, as if he'd had a private bet with himself on that and was disappointed rather than surprised to have won.

"I got Mrs Heedles to dig deeper into this Armstrong guy," Orosco continued. Again, there was disdain in his voice. Clearly, he felt this was something Kincaid should have thought of himself. *If he was man enough for the job…*

Mrs Heedles threw out a look that hinted at apology before she said, "It would seem that Mr Armstrong is Homeland's go-to guy for operations that need an additional layer of deniability." She fiddled with the teacup in front of her, aligning the spoon on the saucer. "There was some business with a cult in California." Her eyes flicked to mine. "You may recall the one."

"Fourth Day," I murmured. "Yes, I remember."

How could I forget? When I untangled the chain of events that led to the Fourth Day cult, it had started with a mess my parents had got themselves into, and subsequently dragged in me, Sean, and Parker, too. We'd ended up beholden to Conrad Epps. Which, in its turn, had led me inextricably to this point, via tragedy, heartbreak, and several points of no return. Personal as well as professional.

Mrs Heedles cleared her throat. "And they're not the only federal agency with Armstrong-Meyer on speed-dial. You were involved with some government black-ops outfit in the Middle East just before you supposedly resigned, I believe? I haven't yet been able to discern which one."

"I *did* resign. There's no 'supposedly' about it," I said. "And I was hardly working for them. Let's just say that our objectives intersected. After that it was a case of 'if I can't control you, I might as well support you.' Something like that."

Orosco gave a grunt which eloquently expressed his opinion. Kincaid studied me for a moment longer, then said quietly, "You've gotta admit it looks bad, Fox. Either you level with us, or…" He shrugged. I could fill in the blanks myself.

The silence stretched and snapped between us. Eventually, I slumped back in my chair, let my breath out. "OK. The problem is Parker," I said flatly. "He has a bit of a…thing for me."

"A thing," Schade repeated. "Is that a reciprocal kind of *thing*?"

"I like Parker—a lot," I hedged. "He's a very decent guy but…it's complicated. I was involved with someone. Someone close to him."

"'Was'?" Kincaid picked up on the past tense more quickly than I would have liked. "Who?"

"The Meyer of Armstrong-Meyer. And before you ask, no, we're no longer together."

Orosco let out another grunt. "So you hop from screwing one partner to screwing the other."

I kept hold of my temper with an effort, flashed him a glare that should have flayed the skin off his bones if it hadn't been as thick as rhino hide. "Sean and I were together before we came over from the UK—before Parker offered him the partnership."

"And you came along for the ride, straight into a job on easy street. Slick."

"She's good," Schade said quietly, no trace of humour in his voice for once. "No way would a guy with Armstrong's reputation keep her on the books if she wasn't."

"She still got canned, though, hey?"

"I quit."

"Yeah, whatever you say."

"The reason Armstrong cut you off when you left—the non-competition clause, forcing you to vacate your apartment, recommending your gun permits were pulled," Kincaid said, almost to himself. "It wasn't just his professional pride you hurt, was it?"

"I don't know." I shrugged, said carefully, "I never gave him any reason, while I worked for him, to think there could ever be anything between us. He knew how I felt about Sean."

It was Helena who asked, "Ending things—with this guy, Sean—it wasn't your decision?"

I rubbed my temple. I needed a short sleep and a long shower, not necessarily in that order. "No. Sean was injured—shot. He was in a coma for a long time. When he came round"—I shrugged again—"well, things were never quite the same after that."

"I'm sorry, Charlie."

"Yeah, so am I."

"This is all very sad, dear," Mo Heedles said, "but what made Mr Armstrong come all the way over to Europe after you? Did you contact him?"

I shook my head, said dryly, "Apparently, he heard I'd fallen into bad company."

"Sounds like the dude has a major white knight complex," Schade said.

"Something like that…"

Kincaid sat back in his chair, suddenly enough for the others to glance at him. "OK," he said.

Orosco looked startled. "'OK'? Seriously?"

"Seriously, Darius. She's with us," Kincaid said. "I'm convinced. Let it go."

Orosco looked about to argue further, then changed his mind, tried for a casual tone as he clapped his son-in-law on the shoulder. "Sure, Eric. Whatever you say." But his eyes never left me, and their gaze was poisonous.

"We're meeting with our buyers the day after tomorrow," Kincaid said, talking to me directly now. "Helena's staying here, so I want you with us."

I shook my head. "Defence isn't good enough any longer," I said. "I'm not going to walk in there and wait for them to attack us, like last time. I want to be further out, picking off the trouble before it gets close enough to start anything."

"A sniper," Schade said. "You think we should put you in a position where you could have one of us in your crosshairs?"

"If you don't trust me enough to do that—to take the fight to the enemy—then I may as well leave now because, as far as I'm concerned, we're done."

50

I MAY HAVE SUGGESTED GOING on the offensive, but it was with defence firmly in mind that I took myself off on a tour of the chateau's exterior later that afternoon.

What I found was not encouraging.

From the front and sides, the building was very impressive, with the squat stone towers at each corner and numerous smaller turrets and castellated areas of rooftop which would provide excellent points for surveillance. Once the drawbridge was up, even with the moat drained and grassed over, it provided a stern and sturdy façade.

The long straight driveway and vast lawns worked in its favour, too, giving a clear field of fire with no cover beyond a low network of ornamental hedges for enemy forces. From ground level they might have worked, but a lookout in one of the high towers with a decent pair of binoculars would spot anybody approaching when they were still miles away.

Of course, the castle had been built with only the flight of an arrow to worry about, or possibly the arc of a trebuchet. I wasn't sure how well its walls—thick stone as they were—would stand up to attack from an automatic assault weapon or RPG, never mind anything heavier.

Still, the windows were little more than glassed-in slits until you got to the third floor. Most of the lower windows had iron bars surrounding them. It almost made me wonder if they were designed to keep people out, or to keep them in.

I kept walking, calculating the distance to the woods and the stable block, then turned to look at the rear elevation and stopped dead in my tracks.

"Oh…bugger," I said aloud.

As I should have realised from the interior, the rear of the chateau had been considerably remodelled at some point in its history. Where once might have been arrow slits and fortifications above the moat were now two rows of delicate French windows.

Those on the upper storey opened onto Juliet balconies with only faded wooden shutters to protect them. The lower storey windows led out directly onto a wide flat terrace. This had been created at the expense of the moat, which had been filled in and levelled.

Without doubt, this arrangement let in more light and air, but it also let in anyone who wanted to stroll across the grass and lightly tap out a pane of glass. It wasn't exactly the last word in high security.

I swore under my breath as I squinted upwards. The best I could hope for was that any would-be attacker would be blinded by the reflected glare of the sun from all that glazing.

The far left-hand of the lower French windows opened at that moment, and Gilbert de Bourdillon stepped out.

"Ms Fox. You do not look as though you entirely approve of my ancestor's embellishments."

"Architecturally, they do wonders," I said. "Defensively, though, I'm not so sure."

"Blame the Chinese," de Bourdillon said. When I raised an eyebrow, he laughed. "They invented gunpowder sometime in the ninth century, I believe it was, although it didn't make its way to Europe until the thirteen-hundreds. When it did, fortified domains such as this became somewhat redundant, I'm afraid."

"I suppose so," I said. "No point living in a cold, damp castle if it's not going to save you. Ah, no offence intended."

"Considering I have spent a good deal of my tenure trying to ward off the effects of just such cold and damp, none taken," he said equably. "Anyway, in the late eighteenth century, Philippe-Henri de Bourdillon was hoping to marry the rather beautiful daughter of an Italian nobleman, so the story goes, but the lady in question expressed doubts about coming to live here. He was so besotted that he had the entire south façade refashioned as you see it now, in time for the lady and her family to visit. But, apparently, she took one look at the front of the chateau and found it so forbidding that she refused to alight from her carriage."

"So she never got to see what he'd done in her honour."

"She did not."

"What a pity."

"Indeed it was. Philippe-Henri never married. On his death, the estate passed to the son of his younger brother, Bertrand."

"Do you know the entire family history by heart?"

"All learned at my mother's knee." He smiled. "Who was who, and who did what."

"What about you?" I asked. "Have you made any major modifications?"

"Improved the heating system, which was ancient and appalling. And I restored the stables, which had been turned into garaging. That kind of thing," he said. "There was always an armoury of sorts, in the cellars, but I suppose I returned that to its original use, also. Nothing major."

I nodded to the faded façade. "And what about the next generation? What do they have in mind for the place?"

The smile faded. I saw it fall away inside him, vanish from his eyes. "I'm sorry," I said quickly. "Of course, it's none of my—"

"They died," he said. "Car crash. My wife. And…my sons. Fifteen years ago. The older boy would have been twenty-one, this year."

I murmured another apology. He turned away to stare out over the gently rolling countryside beyond the chateau, though I doubted he saw any of it. His hands were clasped behind his back. The fingers gave a brief, convulsive clench.

"Now there's a cousin. South America somewhere. Distant, but his claim is valid, so the lawyers tell me." Disdain dripped from his voice. "He has announced his intention to turn the place into some kind of hotel and amusement park."

"Who inherits is your choice, sir, surely?"

"One would think so, yes," he said, without conviction. "But a thousand years of unbroken family line…is not something one can easily ignore…"

51

"HERE," Schade said, laying a canvas gun bag in front of me. "You want to be a sniper, you need the tools for the job."

I glanced up at him. It was the following morning. I'd spent a fitful night in one of the many guest rooms of the chateau. The bed was a full-dress four-poster. Its frame must have been ten feet high, even if the bed itself was barely long enough for me to stretch my legs out.

I'd read somewhere you're supposed to change your mattress every eight years. I doubted this one had been changed in the last eighty. Or maybe even eight hundred. It sagged unbelievably when I climbed onto it and the only way to sleep at all was to do so partly propped up.

Showing me the room, Gilbert de Bourdillon told me it was believed that in the Middle Ages the diet caused the aristocracy to suffer from almost constant acid reflux, to the extent where sitting up to sleep was a necessity. Either that, he said, or they thought lying flat should be reserved only for the dead.

The irony of that did not escape me.

Either way, the sagginess of the ancient mattress meant a half-reclining position was the best I could manage. Every creak and groan from the old stones and pipes and boards had me snapping back to wakefulness anyway.

When Schade knocked and strolled in, I'd been sitting on the floor, attempting to stretch out some kinks by introducing my forehead to my knees.

I uncoiled from the pose and reached for the zip on the bag he'd put down. Inside was an FR-F2 sniper rifle. I let out a low whistle as I slid the weapon clear of its cover, taking care not to snag the telescopic sight mounted on top of the receiver. The F2 was a tried and trusted weapon that had been standard issue to the French military for years. Chambered for the old NATO-calibre 7.62mm rounds, it possessed decent range and stopping power. It would have been nice to complement it with my SIG but you can't have everything.

"Very pretty," I said. "Where did you get hold of one of these? Although I don't suppose they're as rare over here as they are in the States."

"Our host," Schade said. "When it comes to his firearms, he's a connoisseur."

It had surprised me to discover that de Bourdillon, an aristo-crat whose family tree took up an entire wall in the library on the upper floor, was actually a fellow trader in arms. Mind you, his ancestors had found glory in more wars than I'd had dinners—of *any* temperature—so I suppose it wasn't as big a leap as all that.

I unclipped the small box magazine and worked the bolt to check the chamber was clear before lifting the rifle into my arms. Usually, such weapons are configured for blokes with a build far bigger than my own. I wasn't exactly petite, but I wasn't a gorilla, either.

To my surprise, the thin butt pad fitted comfortably into my shoulder and my right hand dropped onto the grip without a stretch. I raised an eyebrow at Schade. He shrugged.

"The dude likes to tinker," he said. "He sized you up 'soon as he found out you could handle a long gun."

I folded out the bipod legs mounted halfway along the fore-stock, set the rifle down carefully on the threadbare Persian rug and rolled into a comfortable sprawl behind it. With my cheek resting on the padded stock, the eyepiece at the rear of the sight was perfectly aligned.

I looked up, found Schade watching me without expression. "I'll need a few rounds to get my eye in."

"Wouldn't expect anything else," he said. "De Bourdillon has somewhere we can use to zero."

I sat back on my heels, suddenly cautious. "OK. When?"

Schade gave another shrug. "No time like the present."

———

SCHADE LEFT me to get ready. I changed into black jeans, boots, and a long-sleeve shirt—it was good to have access to my luggage again. I took the stone spiral staircase down with the F2 back in its bag, slung over my shoulder.

Voices led me to the dining room where we'd eaten after my arrival yesterday. It did not escape my notice that the conversation faltered as soon as I walked in.

I paused just inside the door, could almost taste the atmosphere. Mo Heedles and Schade were seated at the table. Darius Orosco was standing on the far side, leaning with both hands knuckle downward on the tabletop, as if arguing a point. All of them looked as though they had something yet to say and did not welcome the interruption. I thought briefly about offering to go out and come in again.

"You all set?" Orosco asked, but the question was directed towards Schade rather than me.

"Yeah, boss," Schade said.

"Are you sure you should be going, dear?" Mo Heedles asked me.

I lifted a shoulder to indicate the strap of the gun bag. "Schade's just taking me for some target practice."

She frowned. "But can Helena manage without you?"

"She didn't mention wanting to go out anywhere today."

"Perhaps you should check, anyway, just in case—"

"Leave it, Mo," Orosco cut in, his voice harsh. "Helena's fine. And if Eric wants this kid on board tomorrow, we gotta make sure she's up to it, hey?"

Mo looked about to argue further, but something about the way Orosco was glaring across the table changed her mind. She let it go with a glance at Schade and a murmured, "Well, if you're sure…"

"I'm sure, and I do not need you goddamn second-guessing me," Orosco snapped. In the light coming in through the tall windows, a fine spray of spittle flew from his lips. "*I* built up this goddamn business from nothing—*nothing*. You hear me? *I* did it. Without *Eric* and sure as hell without *you*. Just you remember that, hey?"

Silence followed his outburst. Mo, her pale cheeks flushed, seemed suddenly fascinated by the marquetry pattern around the edge of the dining table. Schade slouched in his chair, eyes on the portrait of some long-dead de Bourdillon on a prancing horse that hung behind Orosco on the opposite wall. He might as well have been considering the composition of the paint.

Eventually, I took a breath. "Well, then…shall we go?"

All three of them looked at me as if I'd said something out of turn, but nobody made a comment. The moment passed.

Schade got to his feet. "Sure," he said. "If you're so keen to get to it, who am I to argue?"

52

WHEN WE WALKED out of the chateau, our boots thudding on the wooden drawbridge, the Mercedes I'd 'borrowed' from Parker Armstrong was still parked where I'd left it the day before.

"We'll take your ride," Schade said. Considering we were loaded down with targets, weapons, a spotting scope, and an old olive drab ammo can almost full of 7.62mm rounds, I wasn't about to argue.

I fumbled for the button on the key fob to pop open the boot and we loaded our gear. Schade went for the passenger side, so I assumed that meant I was driving.

"Where are we heading?" I asked as I turned the key in the ignition.

"Far side of the estate. The land goes on for miles. Easier to go by road, though. Take a left outta the driveway and I'll tell you where to turn."

Rural French roads had a blanket speed limit of eighty-five klicks—a needle's width over fifty miles an hour. I kept to it. There was no way I wanted to have to explain our cargo if we were pulled over by the local *gendarmes*.

"I'm surprised nobody's come looking for this yet," Schade said, tapping the armrest to indicate the car as a whole.

"You and me both," I agreed.

"You think your old boss will have followed you to France?"

I hesitated a moment, then shook my head. No-one could accuse Parker of being slow on the uptake. Whatever mixed messages I might have sent by spending the night in his bed, I reckoned stealing his car and doing a runner pretty much said everything there was to say about the possibilities for any kind of a relationship.

Besides, if Parker had been inclined to come after me, he would be here already.

We drove for maybe ten minutes without speaking. Schade was slumped down in his seat, seemingly deep in thought. Then, finally, he said. "Just around the next bend, there's a turn on the left. You'll see a little shrine just before it."

I slowed, as instructed, and saw a gap between two open fields of a tall crop that might have been corn. On the corner was an intricate iron cross atop a stone pedestal. I took the turn. The road became single-track, the surface pot-holed and pitted, more gravel than asphalt.

We proceeded at a cautious pace, turned left again onto an even rougher track. Eventually, we reached the end of the road—quite literally. A gate blocked the way, hung with a sign in French that warned trespassers would be shot first and thrown off the land afterwards. Not in exactly those words, but that was certainly the gist.

We lugged our gear out of the car and humped it over the locked gate.

"This is all part of de Bourdillon's estate?" I asked as we struck out across a gently sloping field.

"Yeah, he tells some story about one of his forebears doing some king a big favour and being offered ownership of all the land he could ride around in one day, sun-up to sundown. Seems the wily old bastard kept a stable of fast horses. He lined 'em up in relays, like something outta the Pony Express, and ended up with one of the biggest estates in the whole of France."

"I bet that pleased His Majesty."

"I seem to recall him saying the next Duc—or Marquis or whatever he was—lost a whole heap of it, along with his head."

"De Bourdillon has a title?"

Schade shrugged. "Kinda goes with the territory, don't you

think?"

He stopped about halfway down the field, well out of sight of the road, and turned a slow circle. There were no signs of human habitation for as far as the eye could see.

"I'm guessing there aren't any public footpaths nearby, then?" I said.

"Private land for miles all around," Schade said. "Trust me. I've done a whole heap of live-fire practice here."

He loaded half a dozen ten-round magazines from the ammo box while I broke out the spotting scope and set it up. The best lie of the land was at ninety degrees to the lane we'd driven down on our way in. Ahead of us, the field dipped out of sight, then rose again. I used the laser range-finder component of the scope to note various features of the landscape and the distances.

"The F2 goes out to about eight hundred metres," I said. "Where do you want to start?"

He looked up, his hands continuing to thread rounds into the magazine by touch alone. "How long since you did any serious shooting?"

"With long guns? A while."

"We'll start at three hundred and play it by ear from there."

We left the ammo and the scope, but kept the rifles bagged and slung over our shoulders as we carried a pair of sturdy metal frames down range. The frames were free-standing, designed so paper targets would fold around the top and bottom, and clip on behind. The targets themselves were fairly standard, showing the black silhouette of a human head and torso with different zones marked out on a white background. I'd fired countless rounds into similar targets over the years.

The only difference here was that Schade had taped a rectangle of card onto each target. The card was roughly the dimensions of a paperback book, with the topmost long edge about level with where the collarbones of the silhouette would be. I didn't need to ask Schade what they were for. We were ignoring the usual scoring system and concentrating on that area at the top of the chest where a successful shot would immediately incapacitate an opponent, if not kill them outright.

We set our first target position at the distance agreed, three hundred metres. Side-by-side, about two metres apart. Schade didn't make small talk on the way out or back. I was aware of a prickle of nervous tension as we unsheathed the weapons, checked the sights hadn't been knocked out of alignment, and readied ourselves.

"You want me to spot for you?" I asked.

"Uh-uh. Ladies first."

I had a feeling he'd been going to say that. I suppressed a sigh, rolled my shoulders and sprawled behind the gun, keeping my arms loose as I wrapped myself around it. I reached up slowly and worked the bolt to strip the first round out of the magazine and feed it into the chamber.

Then I took three long breaths, feeling the way my body melded into the warm earth beneath and the mass of air above formed a blanket that pressed down softly over the top. With my left eye, I watched a ripple of light breeze stirring the grass between me and the target. And could sense, without quite knowing how, the moment it would fade to stillness.

I exhaled. Smoothly, gently, I took up the slight play in the trigger, felt the resistance build, then squeezed through it and beyond.

The butt of the rifle kicked hard into my shoulder but I hardly felt it. After a second, I operated the bolt again to eject the spent cartridge and feed in the next round.

I repeated the sequence four more times, five shots in all, without altering my aiming point from the centre of the white card. Then I lifted my head and glanced over at Schade, sitting with his eye to the spotting scope.

He kept me waiting a moment, then said in a voice that was almost rueful, "Well, I'll say this for you, Charlie—there ain't a whole hell of a lot wrong with the way you shoot."

"It's not exactly difficult with something this straight and this clean."

"Like I said, de Bourdillon is a connoisseur." He jerked his head in the direction of down range. "You want to go again? Just to make sure?"

I put another five shots into the same target at three hundred metres, the grouping as tight as before. The gun had no quirks I needed to compensate for. Neither, it seemed, had I acquired any bad habits since the last time I'd watched a target through a magnified scope rather than over the iron sights of a pistol.

I took over spotting duties while Schade put his first five rounds into the other target at the same distance. His grouping was a little baggier, but not by much.

"You're no slouch with a long gun yourself," I said when he was done.

"Yeah, well, you got your training in the military. I learned on the job. It's like the difference between going to college and having to compete for an internship, huh?"

I tried not to be offended by the implied snub. "I suppose you could look at it that way." When he didn't respond, I added, "Want to finish off that magazine and we'll move things out to four hundred?"

He nodded. I nestled behind the eyepiece of the spotting scope again, aware of an itch between my shoulder blades. Did he really think things had been so easy for me?

Maybe the remark affected his concentration as much as my own. As he fired the first of his next grouping, the rifle seemed to bounce in his grip and the shot went high and left. It missed the silhouette altogether and hit the top of the frame holding the target, skewing it sideways.

Schade swore under his breath.

"What happened there?"

"Dunno. Think maybe I didn't have the butt all the way into my shoulder. *Dammit.*"

"D'you want to use my target to finish off that clip?"

He frowned, as if still annoyed by the mistake. "I'd rather stick with my own." He let out an annoyed huff and put both hands flat on the ground, ready to lever to his feet.

"No, stay put—I'll go," I offered. "Then you don't have to let your breath steady before you can shoot again."

He smiled, the corners of his eyes crinkling behind the wire-rimmed glasses. "Cool. Thanks."

I left my rifle and the spotting scope, and jogged down the long slope of the field towards our targets.

I started having second thoughts long before I got there.

53

As soon as I reckoned I'd disappeared from Schade's view into the natural dip of the landscape, I ducked left and ran.

After maybe fifty metres, I dropped and low-crawled back uphill, now far enough outside his peripheral vision not to alert him—I hoped. As I reached the top of the crest I slowed, inching forwards on my belly, using the toes of my boots for purchase in the soft, dry soil.

The grass wasn't particularly long but it provided enough cover for me to get eyes on Schade without attracting his attention. He was lying prone behind his F2, face to the eyepiece of the scope. I could see from the way he was curled around the gun that he'd lifted the stock off the ground, pivoting the weapon downwards on its bipod legs. His aim was now on the area ahead of where we'd set out the two targets.

And I knew he was waiting for me to walk into his sights. Waiting for my back to present itself as the perfect target.

I knew then, too, that I owed my life to pride.

Not mine—his.

If Schade had 'missed' with his first round, I might not have suspected anything. Yes, there was an indoor range at the Kincaids' farm in New Jersey, but my practice session there had not coincided with Schade's. I had no real idea of just how well the man could shoot. Bodyguards are not usually called upon to act as snipers, after all.

It would not have been too difficult to believe that his first cold shot through an unfamiliar weapon might have gone slightly astray.

But he hadn't quite been able to bring himself to appear inferior in front of me. Not when I'd just given him a demonstration of my own skills. And not when his intention, clearly, was that I should not live to realise my mistake.

True, he hadn't given those first five rounds his best shot—in either sense. But then he'd pulled off the most skilful one of all. Hitting the narrow metal frame of the target, in exactly the right place to send it skittering out of alignment, was an impressive piece of marksmanship.

One day, I might even be able to appreciate it.

Right now, I was cursing both of us.

I glanced over towards the gate where we'd entered the field. It was maybe a hundred and fifty metres away, slightly uphill. The contours of the land meant I would remain hidden from view until I was perhaps fifty metres from it.

I slithered backwards through the grass, keeping it very slow and steady until I was well below his eye line. Then I scrambled to my feet, still bent low, and ran for my exit point.

By now, Schade would know something had gone awry with his plan. I should have popped up seconds ago—a nice fat unsuspecting target, filling the reticle of his scope. I was even wearing a black shirt that replicated the silhouette design, for heaven's sake! It was tempting to reach round, just to see if he'd taped one of those rectangles of white card to my back when I wasn't looking.

As I reached the final fifty metres of No Man's Land, I kicked down a gear and flat-out sprinted. I knew I was more likely to catch his attention by doing so—the human eye is attuned to movement—but it was a risk I couldn't afford *not* to take. I was just praying that by the time he *did* spot me, rose, twisted, lifted the F2 and re-aimed, it would be too late.

Too late for him, that is, rather than for me.

I was less than five metres from the gate when the first shot cracked out. I heard the high-pitched zip and whine of a high-velocity round passing way too close for comfort. Instinct made me want to duck my head, shy away, but I knew that was a pointless gesture. A hit just about anywhere was going to bring me down.

I'd been intending to vault the gate, had even visualised putting both hands on the top rail, springing up, swinging my legs over. Schade's second shot made me change my mind.

The round sliced into the ground barely in front of my feet, sending up a flutter of scythed grass and a divot of earth as it buried itself deep.

I took one last long stride and launched my body head-first over the top of the gate with my arms stretched over my head like a diver.

I didn't clear it as cleanly as I hoped, clattering my left knee on the top rail. Then I was rolling through the impact on the other side and up on my feet without missing a step.

The keys to the Merc were still in the pocket of my jeans. I fumbled for them, stabbed my thumb on the fob to unlock the doors, and hurled myself inside.

The engine fired at once. I jammed the gear lever into reverse and my foot down hard on the accelerator, both at the same time. The tyres scrabbled momentarily for grip on the loose surface, then the traction control system took over. Engine and transmission howling, I shot backwards up the narrow lane, eyes flicking between the gateway and my door mirrors as I fought to keep the car straight.

There had been a field gateway about a hundred or so metres back, I recalled. It wasn't exactly spacious, but wide enough for what I had in mind. Probably.

I shifted my hands ready, lifted off the gas, spun the wheel, and yanked the lever out of reverse, straight into drive.

The car dropped into gear with a clunk that would have made any Mercedes technician blench, but when I stamped on the gas again, the car leapt forwards.

I risked a quick look in the rear-view mirror. Schade must have been quick on his feet because I recognised his unmistakable figure standing in the centre of the gateway.

The rifle was still in his arms.

My heart rate shot up. The lane was dead straight at this point. He could have fired into the rear of the car as fast as he could work the action and there was nothing I could have done about it.

But he didn't.

As I stared in the mirror, transfixed now, he simply stood there. He had the butt of the rifle balanced on his hip, making no effort to aim or fire. I was too far away, and the car was rattling about too much, for me to see anything of his expression but his stance was almost relaxed as he watched me make good my escape.

And, just for a second, I wondered if his near-misses at me were just as skilful as his shot at the frame of the target had been.

55

IT WASN'T until two hours after my phone call with Parker that things started to happen. By then, the light was beginning to drop rapidly into dusk, the shadows lengthening as if the day was changing shape, elongating its way into evening. A trio of dusty old Land Rovers drove around from the side of the castle and pulled up alongside the drawbridge. The middle vehicle had a double horse trailer behind it.

Both Eric and Helena Kincaid walked out, looking their usual smart but casual, accompanied by de Bourdillon. He was dressed either like an eccentric duke or a penniless bohemian. There wasn't much to choose between the two.

I recognised Chatty Williams as he hopped out of the driver's seat of the middle Land Rover and opened the doors. The principals climbed in. The convoy pulled onto the driveway, moving slow enough for me to see the front and rear vehicles had two men in each—presumably de Bourdillon's own security personnel.

Of the occupants I could see, Lopez was the only man I recognised. He was in the front passenger seat of the lead Land Rover. I didn't spot Schade anywhere. The horse trailer had all its doors closed but I couldn't think of a reason he'd consent to travel that way.

I cursed under my breath as I thought of the distance to my

own transport. Too far to easily make in time to tail them…but I had to give it a go.

I launched out of cover and sprinted for the edge of the wood, keeping to the trees as I headed for the farmyard where I'd hidden Parker's Mercedes. If they turned left out of the gates they'd drive straight past me and I stood half a chance of picking them up. If they turned right…well, it was worth trying.

As I ran, I caught a last glimpse of the Land Rovers slowing for the end of the drive before they were hidden by the undergrowth. They were travelling at a leisurely speed, but even so, it took me longer than I would have liked to retrieve the Merc.

By the time I reached the road and braked to a halt in the farmyard entrance, there was no sign of the convoy in either direction. The light was in its final throes. Another twenty minutes or so and it would be dark, making any kind of search that much harder.

I sat there with the Merc's engine ticking over and swore again, more loudly this time. I had no idea of where the Kincaids and de Bourdillon were going. The horse trailer could have meant anything or nothing. Two chase cars and five men overall was not excessive, but it wasn't particularly low-key, either.

And surely, if they were planning any kind of risky excursion, they would not have left behind Kincaid's personal bodyguard—a man who was also his best security officer?

I put the car into reverse, preparing to hide it again amid the outbuildings and return to my nest in the woods. But as I did so I saw the nose of another vehicle appear from the gateway to the chateau.

I pulled back out of sight quickly, twisting the steering wheel to take the Merc behind a disused cowshed that would shield me from the road. I jumped out, leaving the engine running and the door wide open, and ran to the corner of the building, peering around the crumbling brickwork just far enough to see a big BMW X7 SUV that had moved out onto the road and was heading towards the farmyard. In the front seats were two men. There was still enough ambient light that I had no difficulty putting an ID on either of them.

Darius Orosco and Schade.

I hesitated a moment longer. I was one person with one vehicle—a vehicle known to both men. Using it to tail them, on the almost deserted French roads, was bound to get me spotted, despite the approaching darkness.

I couldn't guarantee Schade would shoot-to-miss a second time.

But this wasn't a truckload of AK-47s or RPGs we were talking about. This was chemical weapons with the potential to kill hundreds—thousands, even—with utter disregard for their military or civilian status. This was putting them in the hands of a regime with little compunction about using them and a terrible record on human rights.

I glanced at where the BMW was rapidly disappearing into the distance.

And I followed them anyway.

―――――

SCHADE CRUISED at a leisurely eighty-five klicks—bang on the speed limit. It made following them a relatively pedestrian exercise.

We drove south and picked up the autoroute, crossing the Bridge in the Clouds at Millau after about an hour. Standing a mile above the valley below, the bridge was a spectacular structure, even in the dark, with each of the seven vertical pylons lit gleaming white, topped by red aircraft warning lights.

I hung back as far as I dared on the road, occasionally varying the distance in the hope they might see my lights and assume they belonged to different vehicles coming and going behind them. Apart from a vague direction, I had no idea where we were heading. I brought up the satnav on the Merc's dashboard and zoomed out as far as I could. It didn't help me to guess at a possible destination.

Another hour followed of largely empty roads through sparsely populated countryside. Habitation thickened slightly as we neared the Mediterranean coast. The landscape flattened out into acres of rolling farmland, pale in the moonlight—more crops than livestock. It wasn't hard to realise why those involved with agriculture carried such sway with the French government.

South of Brignac, progress was slower. We drove through small towns rather than watching the clustering of lights pass from the autoroute. The scenery changed again, becoming more industrial than picturesque. This part of the South of France relied on commerce rather than pure tourism. The *Promenade des Anglais* in Nice, it was not.

Schade drove without pause or hesitation. Wherever we were going, I got the impression he was familiar with the route. Still, I found it hard to believe he hadn't spotted me loitering behind him.

The alternative, of course, was that Schade knew full well he was being followed and either didn't care or was leading me into a trap.

56

IN THE DARK, it was hard to tell when, about two hours after leaving the chateau, we finally hit the Med. The coast west of Montpellier was edged by a series of saltwater lagoons that formed a kind of intra-coastal waterway of linked canals and lakes.

It was the kind of area where I guessed there was a lot of pleasure boating and sport fishing. Where Schade and Orosco were leading me, however, there was little evidence of that.

They headed towards an industrial area and turned off the metalled road onto a hard-packed dirt track, bordered by scrubby grass and piles of hard-core left over from the construction. Either that or the moles around here were a force to be reckoned with. The track had chain-link fencing along one edge with scraps of paper and plastic trapped fluttering in the mesh.

A glance at the satnav screen told me we were almost out of land, never mind road. I pulled the Merc between a couple of shipping containers and left it, backed in for a quick getaway if need be. Continuing on foot, I picked my way carefully around the hard-core, careful where I stepped as much against potential injury as noise.

Maybe a hundred metres ahead, Schade swung the SUV in a circle and came to a halt. I ducked out of sight just before his headlights would have swept across me, stayed down until he'd switched them off, along with the engine.

We were in a dead-end yard with a couple of warehouses on one side and the water on the other. I could smell the salt on the breeze, hear the slap of water. After the air-con chill of the Merc's interior, the night felt muggy and warm. It seemed to clog in my lungs, making me sweat—I was blaming the humidity for that, anyway.

As my eyes adjusted, I took in more detail. Litter and lumps of rusted iron were scattered along the edges of the concrete yard. When people abandoned such crap, I wondered, who did they think would clean it up? Or did they simply not give a damn?

Orosco and Schade made no moves to get out of the big BMW, clearly waiting for someone or something to happen. I brushed the dirt off a lump of stone and perched on it, prepared to wait, also. There were few clouds and we were far enough away from the streetlights for me to be able to see the stars.

Once I'd exhausted the few constellations I could recognise, I passed the time gathering a little pile of detritus at my feet— stainless steel washers, half of a ratchet-strap used for tying down cargo, plastic banding tape, rusty nails, and a dented tin with half an inch of paint set solid in the bottom. Every now and again, I stretched each leg out and tried to ignore the fact my backside had gone numb.

Eventually, there came the rumble of a diesel engine from back out on the road. It gradually gained in volume as it neared, lights sweeping across the piles of rubble and the warehouse walls.

A few minutes later, a big articulated truck crawled along the track and into the yard. The driver swung the rig into a wide slow turn until it was facing the way it had come, and came to a halt with a final hiss of air brakes.

The engine shut down and the cab door opened. As the interior light flicked on, I could see only the driver inside. He climbed down slowly, careful to make no sudden movements. The truck had French registration plates and the container it was hauling carried the name of a national auto parts distributor.

I did not think it likely that the contents entirely matched the label.

Orosco and Schade met the driver halfway. He paused as they approached, glanced from one to the other as if uncertain who to address. Orosco cut a thickset figure in a cashmere overcoat that I'd never be able to afford, even on the salary Kincaid had been paying me. Considering Schade's entire outfit probably cost less than one of Orosco's shoes, it should have been obvious which of them was in charge, but Schade had a thoroughly dangerous air about him that the driver couldn't fail to pick up on.

"Monsieur Kincaid?" I heard the driver ask, glancing between the two of them.

Orosco didn't answer, just stepped forward. The driver hesitated a second, then shrugged and looked away, not keen to prolong eye contact. A means of demonstrating his see-nothing, hear-nothing attitude, I guessed. Neither Orosco nor Schade offered to shake hands. They both wore gloves they did not take off.

The driver led them straight to the rear. I saw him swing open one of the container doors but had no view of what lay inside. Orosco stayed on the ground with the driver, but Schade climbed up. He spent long enough checking whatever was in the consignment for Orosco to start fidgeting.

"There some kinda problem?" Orosco called up to him.

As if deliberately playing on his nerves, it took Schade a moment longer to answer. He jumped down, wiping his hands before he spoke.

"'S'all cool, boss. Just being careful."

"Well, be careful *faster*, dammit."

Even in the dim light, I saw the driver tense as Orosco reached inside his jacket. His unease did not diminish when Orosco pulled out a fat envelope and handed it over. The driver peered inside quickly, at what I assumed were banknotes, but he did not risk the insult of counting them. He looked about to say something, changed his mind at the last moment. Instead, he stuffed the envelope into his pocket, surrendered the truck keys, and walked quickly away.

I kept an eye on the man as he hurried out along the track. If he'd been paying more attention, he might have been able to spot me crouching among the rubble. Indeed, at one point his steps slowed. I froze, but then came the flare of a match, illuminating his face and the hand cupped around a cigarette. After that, I knew his night vision was blown. He walked on, stumbling a little on the uneven ground.

Schade closed up the rear of the truck again and he and Orosco got back into the BMW.

It didn't take a genius to work out that something very shady was going on. Kincaid appeared to operate mostly above board, but Orosco was clearly no fan of the direction his son-in-law was taking the family business. And I reckoned this indicated where Schade's real loyalties lay, failed assassination attempt notwithstanding.

The goods might have been delivered in a nondescript wrapper, but to a deserted location in the middle of the night did not smack of anything remotely legal. So, the likelihood was, Kincaid was being deliberately kept out of the loop. The fact the driver had been expecting him, rather than Orosco, seemed to confirm it.

And as Kincaid was still, technically, my employer, I reckoned a little light sabotage was called for.

I got quietly to my feet, stepping over the pile of scrap I'd gathered to pass the time. Then I paused before picking up a handful of the rusty nails.

I approached the far side of the parked truck by a circuitous route, keeping well out of sight of the BMW and its occupants. The first thing I checked was the rear doors of the container, but even if I could have opened them without being seen, the latches were secured with hefty padlocks.

Scratch that idea.

Instead, I worked my way along one side, wedging a nail, point upwards, between the concrete and the tread at the front of each tyre. I guessed they were more likely to drive out than reverse when there was no obvious reason to do so, but I added my last couple of nails to the backs of the wheels under the rig itself, just in case. I knew truck tyres were inflated to an incredible pressure compared to those on a car—over a hundred psi. As soon as the truck moved off, it was probably going to suffer multiple blowouts. Maybe not immediately, but enough that it would not get far. Or so I hoped.

I hesitated a moment. Thinking about it, I had no idea how far the truck *might* be able to travel. The nails would eventually cause the tyres to deflate, but because they were solid, they might also plug their own holes. The spikes on a police stinger, I knew from experience, were hollow so the air would come out immediately.

As I stood, gazing at the huge truck, something an old biking mate of mine once told me came drifting back to mind. I made my way back into the rubble and returned with the half a ratchet strap coiled in my hands. The ratchet itself was missing, leaving only the hook and a longish length of dirty canvas strap with a frayed end.

I tiptoed to the front of the trailer where it was connected up to the cab and located the red brake line. I looped the hook around it and back onto the strap, then ran the loose end down to one of the inside wheels, where it would be less likely to be spotted. I wedged the strap firmly under the tyre. It was the best I could do, with what I had at hand, to slow them down.

Another twenty minutes of inactivity inched past, during which time I returned to my uncomfortable lump of stone and the two men lounged in comparative comfort inside their luxury SUV.

I envied them the plush leather seats, even if they didn't start the engine or switch on the lights. I couldn't see more than the odd glimpse of the interior through the front screen, but it didn't look like they talked much to pass the time. Orosco liked the sound of his own voice. Schade, on the other hand, valued silence.

I would have put money on Schade winning that one.

Suddenly, more headlights—two sets this time—turned off the road and onto the track. They were moving a lot faster than the truck had done, suspension crashing as they thundered past and sending up a swirl of dust into the air.

I covered my nose and mouth with the sleeve of my shirt.

The last thing I could afford to do right now was have a coughing fit.

I fished my smartphone out of my pocket but hesitated over waking it up. The light from the screen would give away my presence and position. Much as I wanted some evidence of what was going on, I knew I couldn't risk it. Reluctantly, I shoved it away again.

The two vehicles braked to a halt in the yard. I saw the pair were big Nissan double-cab pick-ups, their paintwork dark and gleaming. They pulled up side by side, at right-angles to the BMW. For a moment or two afterwards, nobody moved. I peered at the glass but both had tinted windows so it was impossible to see inside.

The doors on the BMW opened. Orosco was first out, as if he couldn't wait to stamp his authority on the deal. As he stepped down onto the concrete, he did a little rearward jerk of his shoulders that pushed his chin out at the same time. Perhaps he thought it made him look more determined, a tougher proposition. What spoiled it for him was then having to wait, not patiently, while everyone else debussed.

Schade followed suit more slowly. Then the doors on the Nissans opened as if choreographed. Four guys got out together. They were dressed in variations on a theme in black. Although their hands were empty—as far as I could tell—their jackets were unzipped or unbuttoned. They were all dark haired and olive skinned. Two had moustaches, one a beard, one was clean-shaven.

They all took their time checking out the surrounding area. I concentrated on staying very quiet and very still, merging my body with the landscape around me.

After a couple of elongated seconds, the bearded man detached himself from the group and came forwards. His body language was open and unthreatening. It was only as Orosco moved to greet him that I recognised the man as the Syrian, Khalid Hamzeh. After that, it didn't take me long to identify the clean-shaven guy as the one who'd fired the RPG at the Sikorsky, back on Isola Minore.

The two of them shook hands, Hamzeh clasping Orosco's

forearm with his left. Whatever explanation Orosco had given the Syrian for our abrupt departure from the house in Tuscany, it had clearly not affected their relationship.

My mind raced. Hamzeh had complained about Kincaid cutting off his supply line since he'd taken over the business. With this clandestine exchange, it seemed that Orosco was determined to maintain the status quo. Why was he so determined to supply chemical weapons to these people, when his son-in-law was so equally determined to break that trade? Or was that fact alone enough of a reason?

When they spoke, the two men were close enough together not to be loud about it. From my vantage point, I could hear their voices but not the words. The tone sounded amicable enough, though.

I scanned back across the other men, the vehicles, the open ground surrounding them. They were tense, but only in the way professionals are—alert to the possibilities.

Hamzeh gestured to the container. Orosco shrugged his agreement and led him and Mr Clean-Shaven to the rear with Schade, who unlatched the doors. Nobody even glanced at the area behind the cab.

Moustache One and Moustache Two took up a halfway position at the front of the truck, where they could keep a watchful eye on proceedings but also see their own vehicles.

Whatever brief inspection of the merchandise Hamzeh carried out must have been satisfactory. He climbed down from the back of the truck and shook hands with Orosco again. The two of them walked back to one of the Nissans. Hamzeh produced a slim laptop from inside and flipped open the lid. The glow from the screen lit up both their faces. Hamzeh spent a little time tapping at the keys, then swivelled the laptop towards Orosco for him to check. A money transfer, I assumed. Whatever happened to briefcases filled with real cash?

After a moment, Orosco nodded and Hamzeh snapped the lid of the laptop closed. Schade handed over the truck keys. Hamzeh threw the keys to Clean-Shaven, who caught them one-handed. There was more brief murmuring, then Moustache One went with Clean-Shaven to the truck, while Hamzeh and Moustache Two got back into the Nissans.

I didn't need to stay for the rest, especially as I had a good idea of what was about to happen. They would want somebody to blame, and I'd rather it wasn't me.

I crawled backwards from my position, keeping low among the rubble until I was far enough away to hurry back to the Mercedes. I realised that as soon as I started the engine, they would hear me. I climbed in, set the key in the ignition and waited, window down, for the right time to make my escape.

The truck engine started with a roar of revs, louder than the other vehicles. I reached for the key but already I could see lights as one of the Nissans turned onto the track. If I moved now, they'd see me.

Shit.

The truck must have tried to pull in behind the pick-up. It barely made a few metres before there was an explosive bang and everything stopped. The Nissan on the track braked hard and I heard the transmission whine as it slammed into reverse. There was shouting and then, almost inevitably, the first shots.

I cranked the Merc's engine and had just reached for the gear lever when the barrel of a semiautomatic was thrust through the open window and placed, quite carefully, against the side of my head.

57

VERY SLOWLY AND SMOOTHLY, I moved both hands to the top of the steering wheel, where they could be seen. The muzzle of the gun nudged my temple and a voice growled, "Keys!"

With a sinking heart, I reached down again, switched off the Merc's engine and removed the key, all without moving my head by more than a millimetre.

A gloved hand extended through the window. I dropped the key into it and the hand withdrew. So did the gun. It took me a second for that to register, another before I could unfreeze my muscles enough to act.

By that time, the passenger door opened and a man slid into the seat. He was still holding the gun, and it was still pointed at me. For the first time, I turned my head far enough to look at him.

"Hello, Schade."

He handed the Merc's key back to me. "Don't just sit there, Fox. Drive."

A hundred questions ran through my head but now was hardly the time. The shooting in the yard behind us seemed to have stopped. Considering Orosco was one against four, I didn't think that boded well for him.

I fired up the engine, rammed the car into gear and took off. I didn't switch on the headlights until we were back out on the road. Nobody shot at us, as far as I could tell. Nobody seemed to be pursuing us, either.

Curiosity got the better of caution. "When…?"

"Did I spot you? About ten minutes after we left de Bourdillon's place," Schade said. He saw my face and added, "Don't feel too bad. I knew we were being tailed, but I didn't know for sure it was you until we got to the lights on the bridge at Millau and I got a look at the Benz."

"Yeah, well, trying to follow someone solo is a bitch."

"You got that right," he said. "Nice stunt with the truck, by the way. Where'd you learn that?"

"Long story."

"Long drive. Shoot."

I eyed the gun he was holding loosely in his right hand but didn't comment on his choice of words.

I sighed. "OK, I'm a biker. Occasionally, big trucks like that cut you up in traffic. A mate of mine who used to work for a haulage company told me there's usually a safety for the trailer brakes at the front of the unit. He said you catch up with them at the next lights, then ride alongside and thump the trip switch as you go past. Locks the brakes on the trailer. Or you can disconnect the red hose—same effect."

"But that's not what you did back there, otherwise we woulda heard the air escaping from the system."

I shrugged but there was nothing to be gained by not telling him. "I tied a line around the hose and tucked the other end under a wheel. As soon as he set off, it tightened up and yanked the fittings off the end of the hose."

Out of the corner of my eye, I caught a flash of teeth. "That is very cool."

"He's, um, going to have half a dozen flat tyres to deal with as well."

Schade shook his head and laughed outright.

"Shit, Charlie. I *knew* I liked you." But the barrel of the gun never wavered.

"Didn't stop you taking a pot-shot at me yesterday, did it?"

"Yeah, stopped me hitting you, though. You gotta give it that."

I'd already guessed as much but it was always good to have a theory confirmed. I eyed the gun again.

"And now?"

"And now…you concentrate on the road."

"I'm a woman," I pointed out. "Multi-tasking is in our DNA. I can talk and drive at the same time."

"Well, I'm a guy, so I can't talk and *not* shoot you unless I think *real* hard about it."

I wasn't inclined to argue the point…for the moment, anyway. Silence fell, broken only by Schade with the occasional instruction to take this turn or that. It soon became apparent that we were heading back north.

After half an hour or so, I risked trying again. Schade was twisted slightly towards me and slumped down in his seat in his usual rumpled pose. I wasn't foolish enough to imagine it meant he wasn't paying absolute attention to any false moves I might try. Which was precisely why I didn't try anything.

"Who are you really working for?"

He didn't answer right away. For a while, I didn't think he was going to.

"I could ask you the same question."

"Helena Kincaid."

I hesitated only for a fraction of a second before I spoke but knew he'd caught it by the dry tone of his response.

"Uh-huh."

"Her safety is my main—my only—concern. What about you?"

"Oh, I work for the only person I know I can trust," he said. "Me."

"That must make life tough. When do you sleep?"

He shook his head. "Don't go trying to psycho-analyse me, Charlie. Better minds than yours have tried and failed."

I ignored the warning, pressed on. "Well, I thought you were supposed to be working for Eric Kincaid, but tonight you were down here with Darius Orosco, so let me phrase it differently. Which of them *thinks* you're working for him?"

"Now that is a good question," he agreed. "And I guess I woulda said Orosco…right up to the moment back there when he pulled a gun on me."

58

We arrived back at the chateau just as dawn was beginning to lighten the eastern horizon. After a day lying in a wood, without food, followed by a night spent mostly behind the wheel, I was desperate for a shower, coffee and breakfast.

I thought it highly unlikely that any of those things would be on offer.

Schade had not expanded on his cryptic comment about Orosco's behaviour back at the industrial yard. In fact, he'd refused to say much more at all. It didn't matter how much I'd verbally poked and prodded him. His manner was calm yet implacable, as if he wasn't happy about delivering me to my own execution, but was determined to see it through anyway.

It was not altogether reassuring.

We pulled up next to the drawbridge, in much the same location as the last time I'd arrived. I turned off the engine and waited.

Schade didn't make any immediate moves. Then he tucked the gun back into the rig under his jacket with a sigh that sounded almost regretful.

"OK, let's get this over with."

"Get what 'over with,' exactly?"

He didn't reply to that, simply gestured for the ignition key. Without any viable alternative, I handed it across.

"Just out of interest, wouldn't it have been easier to shoot me and dump my body in the Med before you set off, rather than drag me back up here?"

But he just gave me a brief, impassive glance, eyes blank behind the lenses of his glasses, and climbed out of the car.

Without the key, I wasn't going anywhere. Hot-wiring something as complicated as a new-model Merc was beyond my skillset. I sighed and got out after him.

We made it as far as the inner courtyard of the chateau before Eric Kincaid appeared from the main doorway. I guessed he was surprised to see me. Not because of anything in his face, which remained almost as expressionless as Schade's had been, but because his first reaction was to pull a gun on me.

When he spoke, though, it was to Schade.

"I thought you said she took a shot at you and high-tailed it?"

I glanced across at Schade myself. "*I* took a shot at *you*, huh?"

"Yeah, like they were going to believe I missed."

"Oh, so it was OK for *me* to miss?"

He shrugged. Kincaid let his arm drop but did not put away the gun.

"What happened?"

"She threw a spanner in the works," Schade said. "Told you we shoulda brought her in on it."

"Should have brought me in on what?"

Kincaid ignored me. "What *happened*?" he demanded again, through clenched teeth this time.

Schade sighed. "She sabotaged the hand-off with Hamzeh."

"How bad?"

He cracked a smile. "Oh, she's thorough, I'll give her that."

"So they know. *He* knows."

"Yup. That's about the size of it."

Kincaid swore under his breath. My temper snagged and tore.

"Will somebody—please—tell me what the *fuck* is going on?"

Both men stared at me for a few moments. Then Kincaid finally put away the gun and nodded towards the doorway leading to the stone steps. "Come on," he said. "Let's grab us some coffee. You're going to need it."

He led the way back to the dining room on the next floor. The staircase was lit from wall sconces that must have been designed originally to hold flaming torches. Now, low-wattage bulbs threw out a feeble glow. I paused to allow Schade to go ahead of me, but he waved me on with a knowing look.

Yeah, I don't trust you further than I could throw you, either...

Upstairs, we sat around the large table again. Schade poured three coffees from the pot on the side. Either they were expecting us, or they kept it going all night. With the lights on in the room, the sky outside the window looked a deep, starless black.

"Darius was doing a deal with the Syrians," Kincaid said at last, his voice flat. "He thought he was handing over a truckload of merchandise—"

"What kind of merchandise?"

He shrugged. "You don't need to know the details."

"Oh, I really think I do," I said. "I mean, we already know they have RPGs and assault rifles, so what else are you supplying that's so hard to get, they're hell-bent on seeing this deal through? Why can't they simply buy whatever it is somewhere else?"

Schade flicked his eyes to Kincaid. "Told you she was good, dude."

"First off, *I* wasn't supplying them with anything. The relationship was in place when Darius was in charge. I've been trying to wind it down ever since I took over."

"Why?"

"Because, however much Darius wants the profit, I...have no desire to deal in NBC equipment."

NBC was a military acronym. It stood for Nuclear, Biological, or Chemical. I'd done all the drills back in the Army, struggling to run in full NBC suit and gas mask. They'd made us practise getting the mask on and changing canisters inside a chamber flooded with CS, just so you knew when you'd got it wrong.

Even though it was what I'd been expecting, hearing it put like that gave me a jolt that must have shown in my face.

"But you knew what Orosco was planning to do," I

murmured. I remembered Schade's apparent inspection of the goods in the container when the truck first arrived, glanced over at him. "What *was* in that truck, by the way?"

"Well...auto parts, mostly," Schade said, deadpan. "With one crate of dummies in case he wanted a look-see himself before the hand-off."

"You took a risk, even so."

"Darius doesn't like getting his hands dirty. And he trusted me."

I noted the past tense but didn't comment, asking instead, "How long were you *hoping* it would take before Hamzeh realised he'd been had?"

"They were intending to ship out of a port in southern Italy where they've paid off the right people. It's around fifteen hundred klicks, and getting there to make their scheduled departure was going to be tight," Schade said. By the way he smiled, I knew the timing had been no accident. "They were gonna tag-team drivers, hit the road non-stop. No time to start fully inspecting the load, even if they'd had a secure location to do it."

"So, maybe eighteen hours?" I murmured. "Time enough for you to do your own deal tomorrow and get out of here."

Kincaid cleared his throat. "We already did the deal," he said. "This evening."

I nodded slowly. Everybody lied to everybody else until it was normal—expected, even. I thought of the little convoy I'd seen departing, apparently innocent, with horse trailer in tow. The upper rear doors had been closed, I recalled. I should have known they didn't have any horses with them.

"What were you *expecting* to happen, once the Syrians *did* realise they'd been had?"

Kincaid shrugged. "Threats and posturing on their part. An apology and a refund on ours. And a very definite end to any business relationship between us."

"How very civilised," I murmured. I glanced at Schade. "When you first got in the car, you told me Orosco had taken a shot at you. Surely he didn't know, at that stage, the cargo wasn't genuine?"

Schade took a long swig of coffee and shook his head. "No,

but you gotta hand it to the guy, he sure thinks on his feet," he said. "As soon as your booby-trap was sprung, either he thought *I'd* rigged the truck or he was just trying to save his own skin. What better way to pass the buck and convince the Syrians that he was just as much a victim as they were?"

"Any chance that worked?"

Schade shrugged again. "If he's still alive, yeah, it probably did."

"But, if he *is* still alive, that would mean the Syrians believed him, wouldn't it?" I asked. "And I shouldn't imagine he's going to be exactly thrilled about what's happened. So, what's to stop him leading them straight back here?"

A muscle jumped in the side of Kincaid's jaw. "That's not the way we do business."

"It might not be how *you* do business, but are you sure the Syrians have read the same rulebook?"

I knew, without having to mention it, that he was thinking back to the ambush on Helena on the road back in New Jersey. That attack had not been the start of things, not by a long way, but it had marked my entry into the game.

He glanced across at Schade. "Call the pilots. Tell them to have the jet fuelled and ready to go, soon as we get there."

Schade nodded, already turning away with his phone in his hand, dialling.

"So, where does this leave things between you and Orosco?"

Kincaid shrugged. "He's family. We may have our…disagreements, as all families do, but when it comes to it, we stand united."

"For people who are supposed to be all on the same side," I said at last, "you certainly seem to keep a lot of secrets from one another."

"Everybody has secrets, Charlie. Even you," Kincaid said. "It's no secret that since I got…involved with the company, I've been trying to take it in a different direction."

"One your father-in-law doesn't like." It didn't need to be a question.

"He makes his…disapproval kinda clear."

I took a sip of my coffee. It was dark and bitter, but coffee had never tasted so good.

"Why do it, then?" I asked. "Why make your life difficult and have him go off and, from what I can gather, do deals that are both behind your back and under the table, putting everyone in danger in the process?"

Movement caught my eye. Maybe if I'd been less tired I would have caught it sooner. Next to the tall windows were doors leading in from the anteroom where food was brought up from the kitchen. They were standing open. I should have checked there was nobody lurking on my way to sit down. Like I said, I was tired.

Now, Helena Kincaid walked in, fully dressed and alert, with Mrs Heedles at her shoulder. If it was any consolation, Kincaid looked as unsettled to see his wife as I felt.

She stopped next to my chair. I looked up at her warily, unsure of my reception.

"You want to know why," she said to me. "It's because I asked him to."

59

"That kind of answer causes only more questions," I said.

Schade returned just as I spoke. He pointedly flipped back the cuff of his jacket and checked his watch. "Well, ask 'em when we're in the air, dude, 'cos we need to get gone."

Kincaid put down his coffee cup. He looked as tired as I felt. Helena cast him a concerned glance. "I'll speak to Gilbert and make our apologies."

"There is no need." It was de Bourdillon himself who spoke. He followed Schade in. "I understand your position completely."

"I am sorry," Kincaid said as they shook hands. "We thought only to out-manoeuvre Darius. Now it seems we must also out-run him."

The Frenchman smiled. "Then I will wish you *bonne chance*, my friend."

He and Helena exchanged cheek kisses that ended in a hug. He shook with Schade, and with Mrs Heedles, giving her a slight bow and a solemn, "*Madame.*"

She inclined her head, responded with regal gravity, "*Monsieur le Duc.*"

Schade's phone beeped. He checked the screen. "Vehicles are waiting out front."

He headed for the door. The others followed. By luck, Mrs

Heedles was just ahead of me. I touched her arm and she paused expectantly.

"You knew, didn't you?" I said, keeping my voice low.

"Knew what, dear?"

"What they had planned—when I went out to test that rifle yesterday morning. You tried to warn me."

She nodded, eyed me for a moment. I could almost see her debating on giving me the whole truth or just a version of it. Shame I didn't know her well enough to tell the difference.

"Of course," she said. "And for what it's worth, Charlie, I'm glad they failed."

"Was it Orosco?" I demanded quickly. "Or Kincaid?"

She blinked. "Well, I wasn't in the room—or supposed to be within earshot, for that matter—but I believe they were both present when the idea was…put forward."

I glanced at the now-empty corridor leading to the main stairwell. We only had another moment or two before people started to wonder where we were. And what we might be discussing.

"So which of them was it who told Schade to get rid of me?"

"Neither," she said. "Mr Schade suggested it himself."

60

By the time we caught up with the others as they crossed the drawbridge, I still hadn't processed that information. I purposely kept my expression blank when Schade glanced over at me. His eyes flicked to Mo Heedles but didn't get much traction there, either. If he inferred anything from that—or from the way we'd walked out together—he made no comment on it.

Lopez and Williams had pulled up by the moat in a pair of Land Rover Defenders. They looked to be the same vehicles I'd seen the day before, but this time there were no horse trailers in sight.

A couple of members of de Bourdillon's staff appeared with our bags. I'd never got used to having complete strangers unpack and repack for me. Usually, I planned ahead well enough to do it myself. Now wasn't one of those times.

Chatty Williams grabbed my bag along with Helena's and placed them inside the rear of the second Land Rover. From the luggage that Lopez stowed in the lead vehicle, I gathered that Mo Heedles intended to travel with Kincaid and Schade.

Helena herself was standing with her hands wrapped around her upper arms. She seemed quiet and withdrawn. Dawn had crept into the eastern sky, which was lightening by the minute. There was a curious lack of dew, but that didn't mean it was warm out there.

Kincaid moved to her side, hugged her to him as much to impart reassurance as heat, I guessed. She gave him a brief, distracted smile and he kissed the side of her temple.

"I'll see you at the plane," he said. A promise.

And to me, "Take good care of her."

A warning.

"It might help if I was armed."

Kincaid hesitated, frowning. It was de Bourdillon who said, "Let me take care of that for you." He disappeared inside.

Schade took the opportunity provided by the pause to dump a comms set in my hands. An earpiece and mic with a wire to a pack that clipped to my belt.

By the time I'd got it fitted and comfortable, de Bourdillon had returned. He had a long gun on a strap over his shoulder and a flat gun case in his hands. He flipped the case round and opened it towards me as if offering a duelling pistol.

Inside was a SIG very like the one I'd left behind. I picked the gun out of its foam bed, pulled back the slide enough to check the chamber and dropped the magazine into my palm.

"Thank you, sir," I said, laying the gun back into its bed.

De Bourdillon closed the gun case. He dug a box of 9mm rounds out of his pocket, placed it on top and handed over both.

"And I thought this might come in handy," he said, unslinging the long gun. "One never knows."

I'd already recognised it as the FR-F2. Probably the same weapon I'd been testing with Schade on the far side of the estate. It felt strangely familiar in my hands.

"Sir, I'm not sure—"

"It's merely a loan rather than a gift, I'm afraid," he said quickly. "Take it with you as far as the airport, anyway. If you don't have need of it, well"—he shrugged—"think of it as carrying an umbrella in the hopes that it will not rain."

"Well…thank you," I said again. "How do we get this back to you?"

"Oh, just leave it in the Land Rover. My chaps will be across to collect the vehicles later anyway, soon after you've departed."

The rifle might as well have been an umbrella, for the casual way he spoke of it.

Another box of ammo joined the first. The 7.62x51mm old NATO rounds were significantly heavier than those for the handgun.

There were further hurried goodbyes, during which I carried my new arsenal over to the rear Land Rover. There appeared to be genuine affection on the part of de Bourdillon for the Kincaids, and a certain amount of awed respect for Mrs Heedles. She had that effect on people.

We climbed into the vehicles. Mrs Heedles took the front seat alongside Lopez, leaving Kincaid and Schade in the rear. I expected Helena to take the rear seat of the second Land Rover, but she hopped into the front. With Williams behind the wheel, that left me in the back on my own. I was starting to feel ever so slightly got at.

Still, at least it gave me the space to spread out and load my weaponry. I laid the rifle carefully across the bench seat, unclipped the ten-round box magazine and started to feed in the long rounds. Better to get that out of the way first, I reasoned, before we hit the public road. It would have been better still to do it before we set off at all, but I wasn't given that choice.

Lopez set off, sweeping around in a wide arc and heading for the driveway. Williams followed. The driveway was dead straight between the avenue of tapered bushes, but gravelled rather than paved, so we were travelling at a moderate pace.

I finished loading the FR-F2 and clipped the magazine back in place. Ahead, Lopez began to slow for the gates, which were already swinging open.

Suddenly, the Land Rover he was driving swerved right, bounced two wheels onto the grass and accelerated hard. A moment later, it hit one of the massive stone gateposts, hard enough to lift the rear end off the ground and slew it sideways.

Williams stamped on the brakes of our Land Rover, cursing.

I keyed the mic. "Schade! Lopez! Status?"

As I spoke, I was twisting in my seat, scanning the distant trees, knowing how good the cover was that they provided. Knowing anyone could be hiding out there.

Knowing somebody was.

"Sniper fire. Trees. Ten o'clock," Schade said, his voice tight but controlled. "Lopez is down. So's Mo. Get her out of there, Fox!"

61

I DIDN'T NEED to ask who he meant. I didn't need to tell Williams what to do, either. Before Schade's message was over, he'd already thrown the Land Rover into reverse gear and sent us rocketing backwards.

The acceleration slammed me against the seat-back in front of me. I bounced off the headrest, wedged an elbow into the upholstery. The rifle pitched towards the footwell. I grabbed it, cursed as I heard the box of 9mm ammo tip out and scatter.

Twenty metres back, Williams grappled with the wheel to chuck the Land Rover into a rapid J-turn. It scrabbled for grip—not the most agile of vehicles to carry out such a manoeuvre. Gravel pelted up into the wheel-arches like hail as we skidded sideways and round.

As soon as he was facing away from the gate, Williams hit the throttle hard. We lurched forwards again, the transmission whining as it tried to make good on his demand.

Helena was screaming. It took a moment for me to realise that she was screaming for us to stop.

Her words registered with Williams a fraction later. He lifted off automatically. An ingrained response.

I growled, "Don't you dare."

"You work for me, not her," Helena yelled, hitting him on the shoulder with her clenched fist. "You damn well do as I say."

Williams didn't brake, but he didn't accelerate again either. We were coasting. He glanced back over his shoulder, the conflict of orders crumpling his features into a scowl. He knew we were both right and that didn't make it any easier deciding which of us to obey. In other circumstances, it might almost have been funny.

Helena twisted in her seat to glare at me, desperation in her face.

"Charlie, *please*. You have to help Eric!"

"He's got Schade," I said.

Besides, last time I delegated your safety to someone else, they lost you.

I didn't say the words aloud, saw from her expression that I didn't have to.

Her eyes flicked beyond me, through the rear window to where the other Land Rover was still buried nose-first into the gatepost. Schade had Kincaid out of the vehicle and bundled down close by the front wheel, but they were clearly taking incoming fire.

I let my breath out, fast and annoyed, and scooped up the rifle and the box of rounds that went with it.

"Get her inside the chateau and bloody well keep her there or you won't have to worry about anyone else," I told Williams. "Because I'll shoot you myself."

62

I BAILED out of the Land Rover while it was still moving. I hit the grass at the side of the drive in a half-roll, keeping the rifle clear of the ground, and scuttled deeper into the grass. I watched Williams make it all the way to the chateau, saw him hurtle around the side of the moat and knew he was probably heading for the line of French windows at the rear as his point of entry.

It was a better idea than stopping and then having to make an exposed run across the drawbridge.

Only when they had disappeared from view did I raise my head, moving slow and careful, and focus on the other Land Rover.

I could still hear sporadic shots, close and loud enough to make me cautious. And frequent enough to keep their heads down behind the vehicle. It made me wonder what their plan was now. Remembering the RPG that Hamzeh's guy had fired at the helicopter, I wasn't sure I wanted to find out.

A part of me was tempted, briefly, to leave Schade to cope on his own. If what Mrs Heedles had said was true—that he was the one who'd suggested taking me out during our zeroing session —then he could fight his own damn battles.

But that wasn't going to help Eric Kincaid. Nor was it going to help Mo Heedles or Lopez.

"*Down,*" Schade had said. Did that mean they were injured?

Or dead?

I eyed the vehicle again but could see only Schade and Kincaid. Surely he would not have left them inside unless…?

Taking out the driver, I knew, was the best way to send a vehicle off the road. The way the Land Rover had crashed, it was as though Lopez had all his strings sliced through at once, completely losing control. And if they'd stitched fire across the front windscreen, that would have taken out the front-seat passenger.

No, I wasn't prepared to leave the unknown gunmen to finish off the others as well.

Keeping in a low crouch, I ran alongside one of the neatly trimmed hedges that bordered the drive, using that cover to zigzag my way closer to the treeline.

I tried to recall the landscape inside the woods in as much detail as I could manage. I'd scoped it out myself with some deliberation and picked what I felt was the optimum position for concealment and field of fire.

No reason to suppose this shooter wouldn't have done the same.

And come to a similar conclusion.

I threaded my way through the trees, putting my feet down with moderate care, wary of stampeding through the under-growth like the wild boar I'd almost encountered.

I was prepared to sacrifice absolute silence in favour of speed, though. Either the shooter had ear protection, or he'd just experi-enced continued gunfire. Whichever was the case, it meant he wasn't going to hear every little crackle of twigs on my approach.

As I neared the spot where I'd made my makeshift hide, I slowed, bringing the butt of the F2 up into my shoulder but keeping the muzzle lowered and my finger alongside the guard. Out on the driveway, I could see the outline of the Land Rover, its front end ripped and distorted from the impact with the stonework. It was a wonder the full-size stone bear hadn't toppled off the top of the gatepost and crashed down on top of them.

The front glass of the vehicle was crazed but I couldn't see inside. Nor could I see any sign of Schade and Kincaid behind it.

I waited.

Nothing.

After maybe twenty seconds that felt no longer than an hour or two, there was no further gunfire. I keyed the mic on my comms unit and whispered into it.

"Schade? You still there?"

"More or less," came the response through my earpiece. He still sounded casual, even now.

"I need you to draw fire."

There was a pause. Then a sigh. "If you insist…"

He didn't hesitate beyond that brief silence, even though he must have realised that I knew he'd been the brains behind the attempt on me, not simply the brawn.

A second later, his head popped up from behind the Land Rover's bonnet. It should have been a rapid up-and-down-again, little more than a bounce, but he held it for a beat. Then two. And three.

It was so blatant it was provocation, a case of whose nerve was going to break first.

Ahead of me and off to the right, I saw movement in the leaf litter. A figure started to rise up onto one knee, head tilting towards the sight on the rifle he carried. He was lining up on Schade, who was still exposed.

Good God, man. Are you trying *to get yourself killed?*

Without time for hesitation or regret, I swung the barrel of the F2 up so my eye fell in behind the scope, slipping my right forefinger inside the trigger guard. The back of the man's neck dropped dead centre into the graduated markings on my reticle. My target was less than a hundred metres away from me. I'd set up the sight for three hundred and had to assume it hadn't been altered since. Calculating the offset was instant, a muscle memory.

I squeezed the trigger.

The rifle kicked hard into my shoulder, momentarily disrupting the sight-picture. When I reacquired the target, he had splayed forwards and now lay sprawled motionless amid the moss and the leaves.

Nevertheless, I approached him with caution, working the bolt to chamber another round before I did so.

I didn't need to get too much closer in order to recognise that had been an unnecessary precaution. A relatively small entry wound was visible in the hairline at the back of the man's skull. He was lying face down, for which I was grateful. I knew well enough what effect a high-velocity round would have as it exited. I didn't need to see it again.

I patted him down, found a wallet in his side pocket that contained a wad of euro currency but no ID. I left the money where I found it. It was no use to him now, but I wasn't about to steal from the dead.

I had intended to take his weapon with me—that didn't feel like looting. It was simply good tactics not to leave something behind that another enemy fighter could easily pick up and use against us.

But when he'd dropped, the man had fallen on top of the rifle he'd been using. I couldn't bring myself to kick his corpse aside to get to it. If that made me a hypocrite, so be it.

I keyed the mic on my comms unit. "The sniper is down. I'm coming out. And this time, Schade, try not to shoot at me."

63

LOPEZ WAS DEAD. I didn't need to check the pulse in his neck to know for sure. Not when he had at least two bullet holes in his skull and had redecorated the back of his seat with brain matter.

Mo Heedles hung forward against her locked seatbelt, her body limp. Her face and upper body were bloodied. I checked her over quickly but found no obvious wounds.

Schade appeared in the open driver's doorway. He nodded to the state of Mo.

"She hurt? Or is that mostly Lopez she's wearing?"

"Lopez," I said. "I don't like to move her without knowing if she's damaged her neck or spine."

"We leave her here, she's likely to end up dead anyhow."

"She comes with us," Kincaid said, his tone allowing for no argument. "We carry her if we have to."

I could have pointed out that carrying her ran the risk of making whatever injuries Mrs Heedles had suffered far worse, but they knew that anyway. Instead, I said, "Call Williams, then, and get him back out here. She needs medevac. The Land Rover makes sense."

Schade spoke without pausing in his constant scan of the treeline. "If it turns into a casevac, we can't afford to lose another vehicle."

I'd been out of the army for a good few years, but you never forget the difference between the straightforward evacuation of casualties, or medevac, and a casevac—casualty evacuation under fire.

When Kincaid hesitated, I glanced at him. "You'd rather lose another employee?"

He said to Schade, "Call him."

"I've tried, dude. He's not answering."

Which opened up a whole new list of concerns.

I took in a breath, gauging the distance to the chateau from here. Why the hell did aristocrats have to build their houses so damn far away from the front gate?

Kincaid opened the rear door of the Land Rover and dragged a long wool overcoat out of his suitcase. I was suddenly reminded of the one Orosco had been wearing, back at the port.

The coat came to mid-thigh on someone of Kincaid's frame, but when we carefully lifted Mo Heedles out of the Land Rover and onto it, the material enveloped her, head to knee, like a blanket.

She wasn't a big woman. Either of the two men could have slung her over their shoulder and made it to the house without having a coronary on the way. It would not be comfortable, however—least of all for the casualty. Using the coat as a makeshift stretcher meant not making possible spinal injuries worse.

Kincaid gathered the sleeves across her chest and knotted them.

"If you two can carry her, I'll stay out here," I said, nodding towards the buckled gate, the front end of the Land Rover still embedded halfway into it. "We'll need some kind of early warning system if Hamzeh turns up."

No, when *Hamzeh turns up.*

I reached for the F2, which I'd stood on its butt by the Land Rover door while we manoeuvred Mrs Heedles out. Schade caught my sleeve.

"I'll stay."

I stilled, glanced down at the hand on my arm. Schade didn't remove it. He continued to meet my gaze, his head slightly tilted and nothing in his face.

"One or other of you stays—I don't care which," Kincaid said through his teeth. "Just make a fucking decision and make it fast."

Divining the reason for my reluctance, Schade stepped in closer. "Come on," he murmured. "I'm not gonna risk taking a shot at you while you're carrying Mo."

"You mean *another* shot."

He shrugged, part acknowledgement, part irritation. "You still think like a bodyguard, Fox. I don't have that problem."

"OK." I let my breath out in an annoyed huff and turned to Kincaid. "Schade stays."

Kincaid picked up Mrs Heedles' upper body by the sleeves of the coat, leaving me with her legs. Another advantage of buying quality clothing, it seemed, was strong stitching. With her slung between us, we set off at a brisk walk, falling into step. As fast as a trot but less of a rough ride for the casualty.

It was only when we were halfway along the drive that I realised something was different about the front façade of the castle.

"They've pulled up the drawbridge," I said. "I didn't think that even still *worked*."

"Oh yeah. Gilbert has been known to use the traditional methods of deterring uninvited guests."

"Does that apply to us, or Hamzeh?"

To that, Kincaid made no reply.

As we rounded the northeast corner, I was acutely aware of the blank eyes of the arrow slits and barred windows, gazing down at us. The hollow of the moat, even devoid of water, made the walls appear taller and more forbidding.

Williams had abandoned the Land Rover he'd used to bring Helena back to safety on the grassy terrace near the French windows. It was slewed at an angle, the ruts in the ground testament to how fast he'd driven and how late he'd left his braking. No bad thing.

Mrs Heedles had not stirred or made a sound. I glanced down at her face as we hurried across the terrace. It gave me no sign—of reassurance or otherwise. The blood had dried dark against her pale skin. I remembered Ugoccione's fear when

Bernardo was injured, back on Isola Minore. It was Sod's law the medic always went down first.

The far left-hand French window opened as we approached. I felt a lift of relief at the prospect of help close at hand.

The feeling did not last long.

The figures who came out did not have the air of rescuers. They came out armed and ready, assault rifles pulled up into their shoulders. They split right and left, covering not just us but the area around and behind us, too.

I recognised both the men instantly. One was Mr Clean-Shaven from the truck ambush. The other was Khalid Hamzeh.

Eric Kincaid, ahead of me, came to an abrupt halt. I had no choice but to follow suit. And I realised that Schade's position out on the driveway might not be to prevent our enemies from arriving, after all. Patently not—they were already here.

But Schade *might* have chosen his position precisely to cover their escape.

64

"MR KINCAID. MRS KINCAID," Hamzeh greeted us. He gave me a bow that was more than a little mocking. "Or should I say Ms Fox? It is so hard to keep track."

I made no reply to that. There were any number of ways he could have found out who I was. After the incident at the dockside with the truck, when Schade had commandeered me to drive him back north, Hamzeh had got hold of Orosco, clearly. And he'd talked.

He probably didn't have much of a choice.

Just as the thought formed inside my head that I wondered what they had done with Orosco afterwards, the man himself appeared. He stepped out through the French windows. I guessed whose side he'd plumped for by the fact he was unmarked and did not appear to be supervised or restrained. Hamzeh and Clean-Shaven ignored his arrival. They were still scanning the area for other dangers.

Under the guise of shifting my hold on Mrs Heedles' legs, I shuffled half a step closer to Kincaid. Unarmed against at least two opponents who *were* armed—even discounting Orosco—there wasn't much I could realistically do. But it was ingrained in me to try.

"What in the hell do you think you're playing at, Darius?" Kincaid asked, his voice more wearied than angry.

"Could ask you the same goddamned question, Eric. We had a deal going, hey? You messed it up."

Kincaid shook his head. "In this case, there is no 'we'. *You* made a deal you knew I would not approve."

Orosco stalked forwards, hands clenched and chin thrust out. "Who the *fuck* are you that I need approval for *anything* to do with my own fuckin' company, hey?"

Kincaid stood his ground without flinching, even when his father-in-law got right in his face. When he replied, his voice held a deadly calm.

"I'm the man you signed over control to." He paused. "*Complete* control."

"Yeah, when I thought I was—" Orosco broke off sharply.

"When you thought you were dying," Kincaid finished for him. "So, either I am competent to take the reins, or you didn't give a damn what was gonna happen to your organisation after you were gone. Now *that* is not reassuring for the people you do business with, is it?"

Orosco scowled and said nothing. Kincaid nodded as though he'd spoken and turned to Hamzeh.

"We will, of course, return any payment made."

But the Syrian shook his head. "Things have gone too far for that. Blood has been spilled."

"On both sides," Kincaid said pointedly. He shifted his hold on the overcoat to reveal Mrs Heedles' face. She was still unconscious and looked terrible. "I trust you have no objection to us taking her inside and making her more comfortable?"

Hamzeh stared down at her for a moment without expression, then stepped back, which we took as acquiescence. "And my own man?"

Kincaid hesitated. "He did his job—and my people did theirs."

Hamzeh nodded. His eyes flicked to me. "Of course."

But as we moved to pass him, he muttered to Clean-Shaven, "*Raqib almar'a.*" I knew from time spent in the Middle East exactly what he'd said: "Watch the woman."

It wasn't the first time I'd heard it.

The younger man checked us over before we were allowed

in. I'd left the sniper rifle with Schade and the SIG in the Land Rover, so I had no weapons for them to find. Despite Hamzeh's order, his search of me was cursory. He paid more attention to Kincaid, who was obliged to give up a Beretta semiautomatic I didn't know he had. From the look on Orosco's face, he didn't know about that one, either.

Inside, the first thing I saw was the body of Chatty Williams, lying face down on the polished floor by the wall. A jacket had been draped over his head and shoulders. One sleeve was stained with blood.

Another of Hamzeh's men—one of the Moustache twins—was standing guard over Gilbert de Bourdillon and Helena Kincaid. They'd been made to sit on low sofas in the salon, but neither looked comfortable.

Helena's head snapped round as we entered, her mouth opening in shock at the sight of the burden we carried. I saw her eyes flick to the doorway, waiting for others who were not coming. I saw the moment the realisation of that fact hit, too. The way her shoulders drooped a fraction, then squared.

We laid Mrs Heedles gently onto another sofa. The room was large enough for five such pieces of furniture to be dotted about the place, fussy Louis XIV style, some foxed and faded, others over-bright to the point of gaudiness. Not somewhere to relax, regardless of the circumstances.

Kincaid would have gone to his wife, but Hamzeh stepped between them in warning, flicking his fingers towards an empty seat that was too far away for the couple to touch.

I crouched alongside Mrs Heedles, pulling undone the knotted sleeves of the overcoat. I checked her pulse again. At least it seemed stronger than it had been.

"I need to clean her up," I said. "I can't tell which blood is hers."

Helena gave a quiet gasp and I cursed myself for speaking without a filter.

Gilbert de Bourdillon half-rose from his seat, tilted his head towards Hamzeh. "Do you have any objection to my assisting the lady?" he asked politely.

Hamzeh's face was expressionless as he considered for a moment, then gave a curt nod.

The Frenchman returned the gesture, more elegantly, and rose. He came upright slowly, as though his joints ached, and shuffled across to an antique side table where a jug of water sat with glasses and a neat stack of linen napkins. His shoulders were slightly stooped, I noticed. Normally, de Bourdillon had a very upright posture and, despite his age, a sprightly manner. So, either they'd roughed him up a little on the way in—and there were no overt signs of that—or he was doing his best to appear no threat to the intruders. Was that down to self-preservation, or something more? The man had seemed no coward but I didn't know him well enough to be sure.

He brought the water and the linen across to me. As I reached for them he didn't immediately let go. My eyes jumped to his. The way he was bending over us, only I could see his face. Either he winked or he had a slight twitch in his left eye, and I understood.

"Thank you." I dampened one of the napkins and began wiping Mo's face.

The water revealed a bruise spreading outward from a dark vertical mark across her forehead. It went diagonally from the corner of her eyebrow up into her hairline and around her temple.

"How is she?" De Bourdillon sounded genuinely concerned for her.

I touched her head with experimental fingertips, feeling for any give in the skull beneath the skin. There didn't seem to be any. Still, I didn't like the fact she had not yet come round.

"Looks like she just hit the windscreen pillar in the crash," I said. "She's going to have a hell of a black eye when she wakes up."

When de Bourdillon looked relieved, I didn't have the heart to add, "*If she wakes up, and* if *she hasn't broken her neck...*" But I didn't say the words out loud.

Hamzeh, meanwhile, had been watching us in silence.

"So, Mr Kincaid," he said at last, "can I suggest that we complete our business without further...unpleasantness?"

Kincaid was sitting back in the corner of his sofa, one arm stretched along the back, legs crossed. Only the movement of his foot gave lie to his apparent calm.

"I'm afraid that will not be possible."

Hamzeh's face twitched. "That is not an acceptable answer. I have paid for the merchandise. You *will* deliver it."

"You will be compensated for any...inconvenience caused."

"No!" Hamzeh said, the single word suddenly loud and stark. "No refunds. No compensatory amounts. We made an arrangement. It *must* stand."

Kincaid tilted his head slightly to one side, as if assessing. "Like I said, that will not be possible. We have rules, particularly when it comes to family. By coming after my family, you have broken those rules."

"We had an agreement. Until you decided—*you decided*—without consulting me, to revoke that agreement. It could be argued that, by doing so, you brought trouble upon yourself."

"And *you*, Mr Hamzeh, caused troubles of your own by ambushing my wife."

"I wished only to get a message to her. To ask her to put our cause to you. What happened was regrettable, but I am told your men...over-reacted."

"So you thought you'd kidnap her instead?"

"That was not a kidnapping," Hamzeh denied. "It was...an extraction, from a dangerous situation."

Kincaid raised his eyebrows but kept his voice level. "On what planet does dinner and a cello recital qualify as a dangerous situation?"

"Planet?" Hamzeh frowned. "I do not understand. I speak of events in Italy—on the island."

"And *I* speak of events in New Jersey."

"That was not my doing."

"Then who was it?"

But Hamzeh shook his head. "Clean your own house, Mr Kincaid. You are in no position to ask me to do it for you."

"And you, Mr Hamzeh are in no position to refuse. Not when you want something from me."

Hamzeh gave a growl of frustration. He threw up his free

hand—the one not wrapped around the pistol-grip of the M4 he carried—and swung away, back-handing a large and intricately patterned vase off its pedestal. The vase dropped, bounced once and then shattered into fragments.

I saw Helena flinch at the sudden explosion of violence. Gilbert de Bourdillon closed his eyes briefly and swallowed. I wondered how many hundreds of years that particular vase had been in his family.

"Fuck's sake, Eric, just give the man what he wants, hey?" Orosco broke in. "You do the deal, like you shoulda right from the start, and we can all still walk away from this."

"Not all of us," Kincaid said quietly. "Like the man said—too much blood has been spilled."

"Exactly!" Orosco said, emphasising his point with a stabbing finger. "Why cause any more?"

"Because that would be allowing Mr Hamzeh to break the one rule that's most important to me. That's not how I do business."

"This is more than business." Hamzeh said through his teeth. "You made promises. I, too, have made promises—to people who have, in their turn, made promises. And so it goes on. Your lack of honour has resulted in my own dishonour. You *will* deliver."

"I cannot deliver," Kincaid repeated. "Because, even if I was inclined to supply you—which I am not—I am no longer in possession of the merchandise."

Hamzeh froze for a second that stretched into two, then three. His face hardened and he took a step back, bringing the M4 up into both hands.

"Then you are no longer of use to me."

65

"WAIT!"

It took me a second to pinpoint who'd spoken. My mind had been fully engaged with calculations of speed and distance, and angles of attack, and odds. How fast I'd have to move to get between gun and target. The impossibility of finding a blind spot that wouldn't allow at least one of Hamzeh's men a clear bead on me. The odds of me being able to stop any one of them from shooting Kincaid dead. Not to mention the odds of me surviving the attempt.

Not good, whichever way you squared it.

Gilbert de Bourdillon had retaken his seat but now he rose again with slow dignity.

"Please, wait," he said, more quietly this time. "I may have something I can offer you by way of…reparation, shall we say? Something of value."

Hamzeh eyed him with contempt. "You try to buy me with trinkets like some savage?" He waved a hand towards the shards of pottery from the vase he'd smashed. "I do not have either the contacts or the luxury of time to trade art for armaments!"

"Precisely. Which is why I am offering you the latter rather than the former," de Bourdillon said.

Hamzeh paused, frowning, although whether that was

because he was debating the offer or couldn't quite work out the meaning of the words, I wasn't sure.

"I'm sure Darius will be able to confirm for you that he and I are in the same line of business," de Bourdillon said. "I don't keep a full inventory here, of course—and nothing of a similar nature. But...I do have a few of the very latest heat-seeking Stinger missiles, man-portable, shoulder-fired, if that might be of interest?"

"Where?" Hamzeh demanded, but brought his weapon up when de Bourdillon took a step forward. "Ah, ah—no. Tell me, and we will check for ourselves."

"My dear *monsieur*, this place may be a thousand years old but I can assure you that the security systems for my storage facility here are state of the art. Without me, alive and kicking, you will not get past them." He flicked his eyes across the Syrians. "Perhaps one of your...associates would care to accompany me and take a look?"

Hamzeh exchanged a quick, speaking glance with his men, which somehow told me they were more than mere subordinates. He nodded, as if they'd discussed things out loud. "*I* will go."

When Moustache gestured to the rest of us, Hamzeh regarded us with narrowed eyes. When he spoke, it was in English, so there would be no confusion on our part, jerking his chin to indicate Eric Kincaid. "If they give trouble, kill this one first."

———

INTO THE SILENCE that followed de Bourdillon's departure with Khalid Hamzeh, it was Kincaid who spoke first.

"Was he telling the truth—about the kidnapping of your daughter?" he asked Orosco, his voice far too calm. The phrasing was deliberate, I suspected. 'Your daughter' rather than 'my wife.' A reminder of the relationship between Orosco and Helena, hammering it home.

Orosco wilfully misunderstood.

"Like the man said, it was an extraction. Things were—"

"Don't!"

The word snapped out across the space between them. Orosco flinched in spite of himself, as though physically struck by it, then scowled at his own response. Both Moustache and Clean-Shaven tensed, their hands tightening around their weapons.

"Just...don't. Don't lie to me," Kincaid said tiredly. "And, more important, don't lie to Helena. You owe her that much, if nothing else."

Orosco floundered for a moment in the face of his daughter's stony gaze.

"What? No! You got some balls accusing me of something like that, Kincaid." He tried on the different emotions of outrage and denial like costumes in a quick-change farce. "I mean, you think I'd lie to you, sweetheart? Aw, c'mon, hey? You're my little girl. You think everything I've done hasn't been with your best interests at heart?"

"You did, didn't you? You had me kidnapped from my own *anniversary dinner*, damn you." Helena's face paled. "You *bastard!*"

She scrambled to her feet, but Moustache moved to intercept her with a sharp rebuke that needed no translation. Clean-Shaven, I noted, stayed back near the open doorway, covering the approach and keeping his eyes roving across the rest of us, just in case. Whoever trained these guys had done a first-class job.

They were right to be distrustful of the show, even if it was more than an act put on to distract them.

Just for a moment, Orosco considered keeping up the pretence of ignorance but clearly decided it wasn't worth the effort. Not with so little likelihood of convincing anyone, least of all Helena. She stared him down with nostrils flared, her clenched hands trembling.

"Look here, kid, you were never in any real danger—"

"Well, that cuts no ice with me. You may have known it was all an act, but I damned well didn't! I'd just been ambushed on the road, remember? I'd just watched Ellis *die*. He had a wife and another kid on the way. I'd just seen Illya almost give his life for mine. I've had nightmares ever since. And now you tell me that because the danger to *me* was never real, it's all *OK*?"

"Sweetheart, that's just crazy talk. You're being a little over-emotional here, hey? That's all right. It's natural in this kinda situation. But later, when you've calmed down, you'll accept I've always done *everything* in my power to keep you out of harm's way."

"No, you've done everything in your power to keep me under *your* control."

"Now, sweetheart, you know that's not—"

He never got to finish his denial, and not because he had a sudden revelation about how patronising he was being.

A shot cracked out. In the doorway, Clean-Shaven spun with a cry and went down, letting go of the assault rifle to clutch at his leg. The weapon hit the door frame and clattered to one side.

The sound of the shot was loud enough to startle but at the same time way quieter than it should have been.

Outside.

The shot had come from outside. I was on my feet before Moustache had fully reacted to his comrade falling. Moustache wouldn't have been human if he hadn't twisted towards him, presenting his back to me. I knew I wasn't going to get a better chance than this.

I leapt.

66

Even as I launched, a part of me recognised the risk I was taking.

And the price of failure.

So, don't get it wrong, then…

I bounced one foot off the low seat of the nearest sofa, using it as a springboard, adding gravity to momentum. At the last moment, Moustache caught my attack in his peripheral vision and started to spin, eyes widening.

He was too slow.

I hit him with the side of my open hand as I came down, slashing into his exposed temple between eyebrow and ear.

The idea of the one-punch knock-out blow may seem like an urban myth but it isn't. There are certain strike points on the body that will do it, every time. It's as much about technique as brute strength. I'd spent a lot of time over the years learning where to hit people and how hard. Now, it was automatic.

A split second after I landed the blow, Moustache's body recognised his brain was no longer in charge. He continued to turn towards me, but by that time his arms were heavy and his knees had gone soft. I caught a brief flash of his expression, saw the shock and surprise in his dilated eyes.

He tried to bring the assault rifle to bear but couldn't control his aim. I stepped inside his guard and punched into the bicep of his right arm—knuckles into muscle—tripping out his brachial nerve. The muzzle of the weapon drooped as his arm went numb. He tried to tighten his hand around the grip. I chopped across his forearm, attacking the radial nerve leading down to his thumb. It sprang open like a busted lock and the gun tumbled from his nerveless fingers.

As soon as he was disarmed, I was on him. I grabbed his face, jerking his head away and down. His torso followed. I went down with him, swinging him into position so his right arm was braced into hyper-extension across my bent knee. As we landed, I shoved hard on his wrist.

And felt his elbow snap without a twinge of regret.

If you're going to take someone out of a fight, do it hard, do it fast, and make sure they stay out.

He let out a yell and began to struggle, still groggy from the initial blow but lent strength by pain and fear and a strong enough survival instinct to push and keep pushing.

I shifted my grip from his face to his neck, wrapping my arms around it and wedging them in tight. All I had to do then was squeeze, keeping my head tucked in so his flailing limbs failed to connect. He continued to thrash for maybe ten seconds, growing weaker all the time until finally he went limp.

Still I didn't release the hold. Ten seconds became twenty. I could have tried to claim I was making sure the threat was neutralised, but that would have been a lie. I'd seen Williams' body and wanted this man dead.

A hand on my shoulder jolted me out of it.

"Charlie, please—that's enough." Helena's voice. "He's gone. Let him go."

I released the choke hold and thrust Moustache away from me. He rolled bonelessly onto the carpet. I tried not to wince at the way his broken arm flopped. Over by the doorway, Clean-Shaven was sitting propped against the wall, bloodied hands clasped to his wounded leg. He stared at me with both disgust and horror. I looked away.

As I came to my feet, I noted without any pleasure that

Darius Orosco had managed to pick up the gun that Moustache dropped in the fight. He was holding it loosely but I didn't like the way his right fist was curled around the grip, finger close to the trigger.

Kincaid gave me a brief nod and headed for the doorway where Clean-Shaven's weapon had landed.

"Kincaid, hold up a minute," Orosco said.

My heart sank, as much at his tone of voice as the words themselves. Kincaid must have heard it, too. He paused, raised an eyebrow in the direction of his father-in-law.

I took a sliding step away from Kincaid. Orosco caught the movement and his mouth twisted into a sneer, as though I was trying to put distance between myself and a possible target.

I was—but not for the reason he assumed.

In a confined space like a room, with two distinct targets, a long gun is a disadvantage. And the further apart those two targets are, the less chance the shooter has of swinging around to hit both of them. Kincaid glanced at me and I saw he understood at once what I was doing, and why.

"Well now, Darius," he said. "Looks like you got a choice to make. But make it the right one because, if you don't, I think I can pretty much guarantee you won't live to regret it."

Orosco hesitated. His brain told him he was top dog and had been for his entire adult life. That Kincaid was no more than a hired hand who'd been in the right place at the right time, caught Helena's eye and got lucky. But at the same time, he knew Kincaid had been hired for good reasons and promoted for ones that were even better.

And as for me, well, he'd just seen with his own eyes exactly what I was capable of. His gaze flicked over me, laced with a lingering denial that bordered on panic.

How could he shoot either one of us without the other killing him?

The tension stretched between us, humming like railway tracks just before a high-speed train comes whistling through.

A shadow in the doorway snapped us out of it. Helena let out a gasp of surprise as a figure came through, casually scooping up

Clean-Shaven's weapon as he passed. He paused just inside, the barrel of the sniper rifle resting on his shoulder and the newly acquired M4 in his other hand.

"Hey," Schade said. "What did I miss?"

67

KINCAID GLANCED from Schade to Clean-Shaven, still sitting with his back against the wall and hunched over the bleeding wound in his leg.

"Oh, I'd say you didn't miss a thing," Kincaid said. "Unless you were aiming for his head."

"Dude, this is me you're talking to. I thought I better not kill him right off, just in case—"

"Schade!" Orosco barked. "Cut the crap and get your ass over here."

I was close enough to see Schade's eyes blank behind the lenses of his glasses. Just for a second I thought he wasn't going to comply. Then he looked at Kincaid with a flicker of something like regret, and moved across to Orosco's side. Was it my imagination, or did Kincaid's shoulders droop a fraction as he did so?

"Where the fuck d'you disappear to last night, hey?"

"Making sure I got back up here before you did, boss," Schade said, nothing in his voice. Orosco scowled for a moment longer, then clearly decided not to make an issue of it. He clapped Schade on the shoulder.

"OK, OK. Glad you made it."

"Yeah, well, I don't come bearing good news. The shipment is gone already."

"I know that. But where?"

"They sold it to the Kurds."

Orosco swore with heartfelt vehemence and turned on Kincaid. "You are *really* trying to screw the pooch, hey? Not good enough just to balls up the deal I had going with the Syrians, then you had to sell to the fuckin' *Kurds*?"

"Their need is greater," Kincaid said without contrition.

"Yeah, and their credit is fuckin' non-existent!"

Kincaid shook his head and said with satisfaction. "Paid in full."

Orosco's mouth gaped. "You gave 'em a deal, didn't you? Please tell me you did *not* give those fuckers a deal... You did. I knew it. I fuckin' *knew* it."

"It was all over before we even got to the coast," Schade said. "I doubt we'd catch up with 'em now, but I can try if you want?"

Orosco shook his head, even as Helena scowled at Schade. "Do you even know the *meaning* of the word 'loyalty'? We *trusted* you."

"The trouble with trusting people is that most of 'em let you down, sooner or later," he said evenly. "This is a business where loyalties are sometimes traded along with the merchandise."

"So, who *do* you trust?" I asked him with a hint of bite.

"Me," he said, as though the answer was simple. "That way, I'm never disappointed and I'm never surprised."

"And you never have anyone you can rely on when your back's against the wall."

"Hasn't happened yet." He cocked his head. "Tell me, Fox, who do *you* trust?"

I said nothing.

He nodded. "Yeah, thought so."

"Put down your guns!" came Hamzeh's voice from the inner doorway. "And if you hold your friend's life to be of any value, I would suggest you make no sudden moves."

I kept my body still but turned my head just far enough to see the Syrian had Gilbert de Bourdillon braced in front of him with a pistol to the back of the old man's skull. I saw Hamzeh's eyes rake over his fallen men.

"*Al'abalah!*" he spat at Orosco. As far as I could recall, it meant idiot or fool. I was surprised Hamzeh didn't call him something worse.

Orosco may or may not have understood but he flushed anyway. "Hey, chill the fuck out, Khalid," Orosco said. "I'm just takin' back control of the situation here."

"*This* is under control?" Hamzeh demanded. "Put down your weapons. I will not tell you again."

"OK, OK." Orosco huffed out a breath and loosened his grip on the M4 before dumping it onto the nearest sofa.

Schade stared at him blankly for a moment and I realised that, had Orosco not moved first, he would have stood fast, regardless how much that put de Bourdillon at risk.

"You heard the man, Schade. Put 'em down."

Schade did not look happy, but he let the M4 slide through his grasp until it landed, butt first, on the toe of his boot and from there laid it carefully onto the carpet. At the same time, he unshouldered the sniper's rifle and placed that weapon alongside the first.

Hamzeh prodded de Bourdillon further into the room and stepped clear of him. As he did so, he looked at Moustache, still on the floor where I'd left him.

"Who?" he demanded. Orosco nodded at me by way of reply. When Hamzeh's gaze sought mine again, it was narrowed and hard to read.

Then he said, almost abruptly, "Would you say that loyalty is a fluid concept for some people, Ms Fox?"

"For some, perhaps."

"You are a paid protector, are you not?"

I could see where this was heading but let it play out—to gauge the reactions of others, if nothing else. "I am."

"Then would you consider a…change of employer?"

"What—now?"

"Of course."

I glanced at Kincaid. He knew the circumstances that led to my present employment—or thought he did. As far as he was aware, I'd been backed into a corner and had allowed the prospect of a hefty paycheque to override any reservations I might have had about him or the business he was in. Now, I could read nothing from his expression.

Decoding his wife's features was easier, but not by much. Her face was tight with stress, that was obvious. But under it I thought I could detect a hint of resignation rather than resentment. Schade had changed sides—if he'd ever truly been on the Kincaids' side to begin with—and now she clearly expected I would do the same.

"Sorry," I told Hamzeh. "Once I've signed on to do a job, I like to make a point of finishing it, one way or another."

68

"That is a great pity," Hamzeh said. "For both of us."

"Oh?" I raised an eyebrow. "I assumed you would under-stand the position of someone with a sense of…dedication that's close to your own."

"You are right, of course," he said, even if his tone suggested he would far rather have been wrong.

"You have seen what I have to offer you," de Bourdillon put in, speaking stiffly to the man behind him, trying to keep his head very still. "I realised it is not what you were hoping for, but very desirable ordnance, all the same. Can I propose that you… take it and go?"

"Who will carry it—these men?" Hamzeh gave a harsh laugh as he gestured to Clean-Shaven and Moustache. "And who will carry them?"

"I have domestic staff, in their quarters here or at the stables. If you will vouch for their safety—"

"Even if we could load and transport the merchandise, our ship has departed. My people are dead or wounded. And my masters may believe already that we have betrayed them."

Clean-Shaven, his voice blurred with pain, blurted, "Khalid…*atarakna ya.*"

Leave us.

The pool of blood under his outstretched legs was wide and

growing wider, I realised. If something wasn't done soon, making a decision on leaving him behind would become academic.

Hamzeh silenced his protests with a single, sharp flick of his eyes.

"It is not enough."

"You'll have your money back," Orosco said. "You got my personal guarantee on it."

"Still, it is not enough!"

"Well, what the fuck else do you want, hey?"

"I want…*consequences.*"

"We also have two dead and another injured," Kincaid said, with a twitch of his fingers towards the body of Williams and to where Mrs Heedles lay, still unmoving on the sofa. "You are not the only one who has suffered."

"*You* are to blame for that. And yet, even if you were to repay your friend here, you walk away with no more than a small deficit in your profit and loss account. Where is the lesson in that?"

His voice, his tone, was making the hairs come up on the back of my neck. I stole a glance at Schade, just the slightest movement of my eyes without turning my head. I saw the same tension in his stance.

He feels it, too…

Time slowed. Between one tick and the next of the antique clock on the side table, I could feel the position of everyone in the room, could almost see the connected emotions swirling around them like smoke. Those out of the game—Clean-Shaven and Mrs Heedles. Those who could not be trusted—Hamzeh, Orosco, Schade. Those to be protected—Helena, Kincaid, and de Bourdillon.

Too many people… It's like Piccadilly fucking Circus in here!

I'd come over to Europe to safeguard Helena, whatever that entailed. My refusal of Hamzeh's offer was a renewal of that vow. I wasn't about to renege on a promise now.

I shifted my weight, trying to disguise moving half a step closer to Helena as no more than a nervous shuffle.

Hamzeh caught it, all the same. He gave a twisted smile. As

though I'd just bluffed a bad hand in poker and he'd seen through it and was about to play a royal flush.

"For every action there is an equal and opposite reaction," he said. "Is that not so?"

He lifted the gun in his hand, arm straightening as he did so. It was absolutely steady, without a hint of a tremble. I heard someone draw in breath on a soft gasp but didn't immediately register who.

Because it wasn't Helena in his sights.

It was Eric Kincaid.

69

Nobody moved.

Seconds passed like minutes. The muzzle of the gun was too close to Kincaid, and I was too far away to do anything. It didn't matter how many lightning estimates zipped through my brain. There was no outcome I could affect.

Helena had begun to whisper, "No, no, no no no…" under her breath, and I knew the gasp had come from her. Schade's jaw was set so hard his teeth were in danger, but he remained still. Orosco's gaze was hooded. Even so, I caught something slither behind his eyes.

You want this, don't you?

Hamzeh held his aim for another second. Kincaid stood, braced, as though that was going to make any difference. Still nobody moved.

Then, abruptly, Hamzeh lowered his arm.

"So, perhaps every reaction is *not* equal after all," he said lightly. "It appears that you would not be missed in all quarters, Mr Kincaid."

"Go," Kincaid said through his teeth. "Go now and don't give me a reason to come after you."

"Oh, it's too late for that, don't you think?" Hamzeh skimmed his gaze across both Orosco and Kincaid. "I have failed my masters and they are not forgiving. It is not only me, but also my family in Damascus who will pay the price of that failure. Why should you and your family not pay the same?"

He snapped his arm straight again, twisting as he did so. This time, the gun was pointing square at Helena's chest.

We all went rigid like he'd hit a switch that lit us up with high-voltage charge. A reflex action we could neither hide nor control. Hamzeh saw it and his mouth distorted into what passed for a smile.

"You see what happens when you play God, Mr Kincaid? You reach a crossroads. You make a choice. One action leads to another and the end result may turn out to be far from what you wished. All from one small, thoughtless decision."

"I'll resupply," Kincaid said without hesitation. "The full order—double the order. Just leave her alone. Helena has no part in this…business between us."

"Oh, I think she plays a vital role. Before, you wanted nothing more to do with me. But now, when you fear you are about to lose her, suddenly all is good between us? I don't think so."

"Leave her out of this… Please."

In taking a bead on Helena, Hamzeh had angled his body slightly away from Schade. I saw Schade's hand snake, slow and smooth, under the tail of his jacket. I forced myself not to react, not to betray that movement to Hamzeh.

Orosco, to his credit, waited until Schade had drawn and aimed before he cut in.

"You shoot my little girl, Khalid, and it'll be the last thing you ever do."

Hamzeh heard the ripe threat in the other man's voice and seemed aware, for the first time, of the mistake he'd made in part turning his back on Schade.

Schade took a step to the side that brought him fully into Hamzeh's field of view. The gun was a .40 calibre Glock, and the hand that held it didn't waver. Hamzeh eyed both with irritation.

"I should have made you strip."

"Let it go, dude. No way to win this one."

"Perhaps," Hamzeh said, "but sometimes simply 'not winning' is better than losing."

The tendons in the back of his hand began to bunch as his grip tightened. I didn't wait to see any more. I didn't need to.

The distance between me and Hamzeh was too great to bridge. Instead, I threw myself sideways at Helena, bowling her straight off her feet as the shot cracked out with jolting force.

Sheer momentum carried us over the low back of the nearest sofa. I was already spiralling in flight, so when we flipped over the top and crashed onto the floor behind it, Helena landed half-sprawled on top of me rather than underneath. I had one arm wrapped tight around her body and the other up high to shield her head. The force of the impact knocked the breath right out of me.

It was only as we hit that the pain, sharp as a razor, speared through my right side, just below my ribs. A scalding heat that flooded outwards in rapidly increasing gushes with every beat of my heart.

Fuck, I'm hit.

I shoved the realisation back down into my subconscious, rode over and through it. With a grunt of effort, I rolled Helena under me, keeping her head pressed down while I lifted mine. The pain was building faster now, vicious with it. I gulped down air.

Under the bench seat of the sofa I could see enough to know that Hamzeh was down. He lay crumpled, face turned towards us. His eyes were wide, but whatever had been behind them was already fading. As I watched, he seemed to sigh, his chest deflating for the last time as his final breath slipped away.

Jean-clad legs and booted feet stepped in close. Schade leaned down and placed two fingers against the empty pulse-point in the Syrian's neck for just long enough to know for sure.

"Helena!" Kincaid was bending over us. I dragged myself off to the side, aware as I did so that she made no protests or attempts to rise. Her shirt was greasy with blood. I got as far as opening my mouth to reassure him that it was all mine when it finally dawned on me that it wasn't—all mine, that is.

Oh shit…

Kincaid ripped open her shirt. Under it, her skin prickled with goose bumps. Her breath came in shallow, hard-fought gasps. Kincaid ran his fingers over her. As he reached her left side she cried out. He jerked his hand away as if he were the one solely responsible for her pain.

And I saw the puckered gunshot wound in her chest.

How…?

Dazed, I looked down at my own body. I *knew* I'd been in the path of the single round Khalid Hamzeh had fired at Helena.

And somehow he'd shot us both.

70

Helena was suffocating.

At a guess, the round had wedged somewhere in her left lung. Blood was leaking into her chest cavity, slowly filling the space she needed to draw breath. With infinite gentleness, Kincaid turned her onto her left side to give her other lung half a chance, murmuring to her all the time. There was a catch in his voice.

Orosco hovered, clearly wanting to shove Kincaid out of the way and take charge but clueless what to do for her. I'd no idea where Schade went.

"But…I got in front of her," I mumbled. "I *know* I got in front of her."

"You did, my dear. So you did." De Bourdillon was suddenly right by my side. He helped me to sit, carefully manoeuvred me so I was leaning against the sofa, and lifted the sodden tails of my shirt.

I looked down, saw a small ragged hole in the side of my stomach just below my ribcage, oozing blood. It burned like I'd been run through with a flaming sword. I couldn't suppress a groan. Not the first time I'd been shot, but it didn't get any easier with practice.

Carefully, de Bourdillon tilted me sideways, pressed his fingers round to my back. He reached an area where the skin was numbed but everything beneath it howled with pain. I hissed in a breath. My head was beginning to buzz, vision prickling. I blinked, took in more air.

I will not *pass out.*

"A through and through," de Bourdillon said. "You got in front of her, without a doubt. Had Mr Hamzeh been firing soft-nosed rounds, you would have stopped the shot with your own body, which I believe was your intention."

Orosco gave a harsh laugh. "Either that or the bitch pushed her into the line of fire, hey?"

"Darius, for once in your life will you just shut the fuck up," Kincaid said. "Gilbert, where's the closest trauma centre with an air ambulance?"

"I believe the nearest SAMU unit is in Rodez." He got to his feet. "I'll call them—"

"No way!" Orosco's order brought both men up short. Kincaid rose, stepped in close to his father-in-law.

"Need I remind you that your daughter may be *dying*. We need medics and a helicopter and we need them here now!"

"And by the time they arrive, she could be dead already. We take her. That way, we get her there maybe faster, and no cops. Schade's grabbing us a set of wheels."

I expected Kincaid to argue. Driving fast on rural roads could do Helena untold further damage. My money would have been on the local *Service d'Aide Médicale Urgente*. The French, I recalled, preferred to send doctors to the scene rather than stabilising the casualty for transport. It was Helena's best chance.

But if the cops turned out, too, there was no way we could hide the bodies before they got here.

"You're worried about saving your own *skin*?"

"Hey, I'm no good to her—or anyone else—rotting in some frog jail!"

Kincaid looked set to argue, but Orosco had snatched the pistol from Hamzeh's dead hand and he gripped it now with meaning.

Kincaid bit back whatever was foremost in his mind with obvious effort. He stepped back, lifting his hands, and said instead, "Tell Schade to hurry."

Orosco's shoulders came back, recognising the capitulation for what it was. He gave a short, triumphant nod, and hurried from the room.

As soon as he'd gone, Kincaid dropped into a crouch again, but this time his focus was all on me.

"Charlie, that bastard is going to kill her with what he's trying to do."

I gave a half-laugh that didn't quite come out right. "I know, but if you think I can do much to stop him right now, I'm afraid you're way over-estimating my abilities."

He shook his head. "Call him in. Just…call him in. I'm begging you. Before it's too late."

"Wait… Call who?"

Kincaid's face twisted. "He's got to be somewhere close by. He wouldn't let you come here without back-up… I *know* you're working for him."

"Who?" My brain was not firing on all cylinders. "You mean Parker?"

"No—Epps. *Conrad Epps.*"

71

To begin with, I said nothing. Which, I realised quickly, was a mistake. I should have asked Kincaid right off the bat what the hell he was talking about, or at least said who the hell is that?

But what I eventually blurted out was entirely the wrong question: "What do you know about Epps?"

With a grim smile, he said, "Just about all there is to know."

My brain made up for its earlier stutter by over-revving now. So Kincaid knew who I was and why I was there. Or, what he didn't know for sure, he'd guessed at and was probably pretty close to being right. It made some sense of why I'd been left behind in Italy, and why Schade had been told to get rid of me here.

But now he was desperate. Now, Helena's life was on the line and he was prepared to climb into bed with the devil himself to save her.

Which meant yes, he probably *did* know all there is to know about Conrad Epps.

I hesitated. If I told the truth—that I'd been more-or-less disavowed the moment I set foot outside the States—then my usefulness would be gone.

So, too, would any reason for them keeping me alive. And I wasn't in any state to do much about it.

I glanced at Helena. De Bourdillon had turned her onto her

left side and was supporting her there, trying to hold the pressure off the wound but let gravity keep her lung drained at the same time. If the way her whole body shook in his arms with the sheer effort of dragging in each breath, it was only partially successful at best. Her eyes were wide with panic, seeing nothing.

Kincaid was staring at me like he was willing me to give him what he needed.

"I'm sorry," I said. "There *is* no back-up. Not this time. It's just me."

I half-expected him not to believe me, but instead he gave a bitter smile.

"I guess that figures. He always was good at kicking you in at the deep end of the pool without asking if you could swim—or telling you about the sharks."

My mouth opened, closed and opened again as, *finally*, the pieces slid into place with a bloody great clang like a steel door.

"My God," I murmured. "Gone native...he was right about that. You went *so* native you married the boss's daughter. It's you, isn't it? All this time...you've been Epps' inside man..."

Kincaid said nothing but he didn't need to. I could see it in his face—a kind of relief that the secret he'd carried for so long, like a stone, could finally be set down. If only for a brief while.

"Yes," he said quietly. "But what use is any of it if I can't reach him when I most need his help?"

"Let me try to get hold of Parker," I said. "I don't know where he is, exactly, but he might have contacts here."

Kincaid reached for his phone. As he did so, de Bourdillon cleared his throat.

"I, ah, *may* have some assistance on the way," he said, almost diffidently.

"What? Dammit, Gilbert, when did you manage that?"

The old man looked almost embarrassed. "The alarm on my storage facility here requires a very specific entry code," he said. "Certain...variations on that code will still open the strong room but also send a silent alert to a monitoring service. Who, in turn, pass on a prearranged message."

"What kind of 'prearranged message'? And who to?" Kincaid

demanded. "Don't tell me that bastard has *you* working for him as well?"

"Not at all. But in this business one can't help hearing things... So, for some years now I have had a certain arrangement with the DGSI—the French intelligence service."

"Well, fuck me," said Orosco. I was suddenly aware of his footsteps through the floorboards under me as he stalked back into the room. He rounded the end of the sofa and came into view, glaring down at us. "Am I the only one in this entire fuckin' outfit who *isn't* a goddamn rat?"

As soon as he stopped moving, I was aware of a second set of footsteps, softer and more careful than Orosco's own. I turned my head just as Schade slipped around the other end of the sofa and took up a flanking position. Both men were armed.

"This is not the time for accusations, Darius," Kincaid said. "When we've gotten Helena to safety, then we can settle things—"

"No way. Car's outside. *I'll* get her to safety. You, my friend, are *done*. Done with me and done with my daughter." He lifted the pistol in his hand. "You got any last words for her, you say 'em now."

"Da–Daddy, no...*please*." Helena could barely speak above a rasping whisper. "Please, don't...hurt him... Don't..."

"Hush now, sweetheart. If he's undercover then this—you— has all been a game to him. He was just acting a part. He never wanted you, just what you could get him—closer to me."

"That's not true and you damned well know—"

"Shut up, Eric! I mean, is that even your *name*?"

Tears leaked silently from Helena's eyes as she lay there, still clinging onto life with a vibrating tenacity I could only admire.

"Don't...kill him!" she managed, almost choking with the effort. "Promise me..."

Orosco stilled for a moment, then sighed. "OK, sweetheart." He glanced across. "Schade, do us all a favour and take out this piece of trash."

Schade stood for a moment with no expression on his face. Kincaid got slowly to his feet and faced him, saying nothing.

With a grunt of effort, I rolled up onto one knee but Kincaid put his hand on my shoulder.

"Stay down, Charlie," he said. "I need you to be there for her later."

Helena cried, "*Eric!*"

Schade looked down briefly at the Glock in his hand, then opened his fingers and let the gun drop onto one of the empty sofas.

"Sorry, boss," he said to Orosco. "This time you're gonna have to do your own dirty work. I quit."

"You *quit*?" Orosco repeated, voice climbing. "You work for me, you don't just *quit*. Nobody quits on me."

Schade shrugged. "Whatever, dude. I'm outta here." He turned away.

"Hey, Schade!" Orosco called, and when the other man paused, glanced back, he brought his own gun up to bear. "How 'bout this instead? You're *fired*."

And he shot him.

Schade spun and went down. Orosco swung his gun hand back towards Kincaid, who dropped into a crouch. He might have been about to take his chances hand-to-hand, but he never got the opportunity. Another shot cracked out, ferociously inside the room. Orosco froze.

I flinched and at first saw nothing amiss. Then Orosco's fingers lost their hold on the gun. It bounced on the carpet and came to rest near his foot. He looked down at the slice of shirt-front that was visible between the lapels of his jacket. Slowly, a bloom of dark red started to creep across the white fabric, moving left to right. It spread towards the line of buttons, swamped and overtook them.

Orosco stared at the stain as if he couldn't believe what he was seeing and couldn't understand where it had come from. He made a sound that was almost a giggle.

"What the fu—?"

Then his knees gave out.

He twisted and dropped like a rock. If I had to guess, I'd say he was dead before he finished falling.

Kincaid straightened slowly. I checked his hands but they

were empty. Same with de Bourdillon and even Helena. Gripping the back of the sofa, I managed to haul myself to my feet without groaning. Schade was slumped on the carpet, clasping bloodied fingers to his left shoulder. He caught my eye and jerked his head towards one of the other sofas.

I followed his gaze. On the sofa lay Mrs Heedles. The coat we'd used to carry her was pushed open. Her forehead was a mass of bruising and one eye was swollen shut. But in her right hand she had a firm grip on a SIG semiautomatic that looked strangely familiar to me.

Kincaid moved over to her quickly, peeled the gun from her nerveless fingers.

"Mo…" His voice was full of wonder. "Thank you."

"Tell Helena I'm sorry—I've made her an orphan," she murmured, letting her good eye blink closed again. "But I was damned if I was going to let that bastard make her a widow."

EPILOGUE

THE STEPHENSONS' farm in New Jersey looked much the same as the last time I was there. Hard to remember it was only a few weeks ago.

I parked my rental Buick on the grass near the front porch, got out and took a moment to stare across the mirror-flat pond to the dense trees beyond. If there were watchers in those woods, I'd never spotted them before and didn't expect to do so now.

When I climbed the couple of steps up onto the porch there was only a slight hitch in my stride. The bullet track through my waistline had done remarkably little lasting damage, all things considered. It had hit no bones, passed through no vital organs, singed no nerves. It wasn't surprising that I hadn't done much to slow it down on its way into Helena Kincaid's chest.

The door was opened quickly to my knock. Lorna and Frank stepped out together, coats on. Lorna had her bag slung over her shoulder.

"You're not staying?" I asked, once the greetings were over.

"I don't think there's anything to be said that we need to hear," Frank said. "Coffee's in the pot. Make yourself at home."

"And watch out for those kittens," Lorna added, kissing my cheek. "They're adorable, but they do like to climb and their little claws are sharp as needles."

"Don't suppose we could talk you into taking one?" Frank

asked. "Another week or so and we'll be needing good homes for them."

I shook my head, half regretful. "For that I'd need somewhere to call a home—not to mention a means of putting kibble on the table. Neither are on the horizon at the moment."

"It'll come right for you, Charlie," Lorna said. "I have no doubts about that."

"Thank you. I wish I had your confidence."

She patted my arm and went down the steps. Frank nodded to the front door.

"We're over to the neighbours' for supper, so we'll be back late. Lock up when you're done."

"Yes, sir."

He patted my shoulder as he passed. I was beginning to feel like one of Helena's horses.

I stayed on the porch until the old GMC truck had rumbled over the plank bridge and disappeared into the woods before I went inside and shut the door. The quiet calm of the house wrapped itself around me.

I moved through to the kitchen. The box of the tabby cat with the white bib was still by the stove. The corners of the box looked a little more chewed. She was just the same but the kittens had doubled in size. If the way they leapt and rolled and tore about the place en masse was anything to go by, there were *way* too many artificial additives in their diet.

I left the tsunami of fur and took coffee through to the sitting room. There, I stood looking out of the long windows and waited.

I'd been back Stateside less than twenty-four hours. The French authorities, despite de Bourdillon's intervention, held me under a kind of hospital house arrest while intercontinental, inter-agency bureaucracy slowly sorted out the mess. Eventually, after what amounted to a debrief by a chic woman from the *Direction Générale de la Sécurité Intérieure*, they told me I was free to go. And escorted me to the nearest airport, just to make sure.

I flew to the UK, stayed with friends while I picked up strength and came to terms with the fact that, yet again, I had blood on my hands. Not only at a distance, either, like the sniper in the woods. Up close and personal. Blood I'd been able to feel the moment it stopped circulating.

Maybe that was why I didn't go home. My father's previous warnings about the ease with which I seemed capable of taking a life still rang in my ears, even after all this time.

Then, only yesterday, I received a cryptic summons from Epps. Not one I thought it wise to ignore. Not when it came with an e-ticket, a departure time, and a warning.

So here I was, back in New Jersey, hot off a plane into Newark.

I made only one detour on the way out to the farm—to the Kincaids' place. I hadn't been in contact and wasn't sure of my welcome, or what I might find.

Considering I arrived uninvited and unannounced, I was allowed through the main gate with the minimum of fuss. A stern-looking woman I hadn't seen before patted me down in the grand hallway, then jerked her head towards the door to the drawing room.

Not much had changed inside. More in hope than expectation, I glanced behind the door, to the place where Schade had been lounging against the wall, the first time I met him. He wasn't there. On balance, I would have been more surprised if he was.

Helena Kincaid was propped on the sofa in front of the fireplace, supported by cushions. Meds of various types and a water jug stood within reach on the low table nearby.

"Charlie, how lovely," she said, holding both hands out to me. I let her clasp mine and bent to kiss her cheek.

"I'm glad to see you," I said, and meant it. They hadn't told me much more than she had survived her injuries. After the revelations of that last day, I feared her marriage might not have been so fortunate. "How are you doing?"

"Good, I guess." She eased herself a little more upright, half smiled. "I'm a very impatient patient, though."

"When did you get back from France?"

"The doctors OK'd me to fly a couple of days ago. They did an amazing job, so I understand—even gave me a souvenir."

She picked up a clear pot that I'd mistaken for another pill bottle, handed it across. Inside was a slightly deformed copper projectile.

"I'm sorry it got through to you."

"Don't be. They told me if it had hit me at full velocity, well..." She shrugged. "Maybe you should be the one to have it."

They say you don't see the bullet with your name on it. I kept the one that had—technically, briefly—killed me. Another time, another place. I'd contemplated getting it drilled for a necklace. I suppose if I accepted this one, I could turn them into earrings.

I put the pot back on the table. "I have others."

Helena's face twitched. "Ah, yes. In your line of work, I'm sure you do."

A door at the far side of the room opened and Kincaid himself stepped through. I'd been wondering how to bring up the subject of Helena's husband and where his loyalties lay. It seemed as though he was going to do it for me.

As he approached, the look that passed between them was intimate, but something more than that. The bond of soldiers who've been through combat together and emerged not quite unscathed. Something loosened between my shoulders.

He shook my hand, looked me straight in the eye.

"We are more grateful to you than we can ever say, Charlie."

"It was what you hired me for."

"We both know that looking after Helena was never your primary objective. When the bullets started flying, it would have been all too easy for you to step back."

"No, actually, it wouldn't."

Kincaid nodded, like he got it. He put a hand on his wife's shoulder. She reached up to cover it with her own.

I wanted to ask about Orosco's death, about Kincaid's double life, but didn't know how to start.

"How's Mrs Heedles?"

Kincaid smiled. "Still in France. She had a concussion that's taking a little while to get over. Gilbert invited her to stay on at the chateau to recuperate."

"I think he's sweet on her," Helena said in a mock whisper.

"That's because as long as I've known you, you've always been a romantic at heart, darling."

"The gun she used," I said, choosing my words with care. "You told me you left it behind in Italy, but it was mine, wasn't it?"

Helena nodded, almost shame-faced. "After what happened, I thought I might need it."

"When did you give it to Mrs Heedles?"

"Just before we left the chateau—that last time. I realised that, if I had it, I might actually have to use it. I wasn't sure I had the courage for that. And Mo is an excellent shot."

"So I saw." I paused. "Speaking of which…"

"My father?" Helena put in. "That's OK. You wouldn't be human if you didn't ask. Although, I have to admit there were times when I wondered if you *weren't* entirely human."

"Thanks—I think."

"You want to know how I can love someone who only came into my life to bring down my father?"

I blinked. "Basically…yeah, that about covers it."

"Because I knew—almost from the start." She smiled up at Kincaid, then met my gaze while something hardened in her voice. "It meant Eric was the one man that bastard could never own."

There wasn't much I could say to that. I didn't try. We said our goodbyes and Kincaid saw me out to my rental car at the front of the house.

"What happened to Schade, by the way?"

"Nobody knows. By the time the French authorities arrived, he was in the wind."

"And you've heard nothing since? He was wounded, after all."

"Gilbert told us his local veterinarian reported a break-in the same day, so I'd guess he fixed himself up." He paused, as if about to say more. I raised my eyebrows and he sighed. "And I had a call, saying we had nothing to fear from him."

"What did you say to that?"

"I offered him his old job back—with a hell of a raise. He said maybe one day and that was it." He stuck his hands in his pockets and eyed me. "I don't suppose there's any use me making you the same kinda offer?"

I shook my head. "I *am* tempted, but I don't know what my plans are yet. Until I've met with Epps, I don't even know if I'm allowed to stay over here."

"The offer's on the table." Kincaid smiled. "As for Conrad, he may just surprise you. He did me…"

———

I'D FINISHED my coffee and helped myself to a refill before I heard the distinctive sound of a vehicle coming over the plank bridge, like someone running a finger along the keys of a dead piano. A glance out of the window showed a dark SUV with heavily tinted glass approaching the house. It was so nondescript it could only be government-issue.

I stood back, concealed in the shadows, and listened to the engine note die away. Doors opened and closed, hard-soled shoes sounded on the wooden steps to the front door. If I'd expected them to knock, I would have been disappointed. I did not expect it.

The front door opened and closed, then came the murmur of voices. No doubt Epps telling his security detail to wait in the kitchen. I gave brief thought as to how they'd cope with the feline circus going on in there, then turned towards the door and squared my shoulders.

Conrad Epps paused for a moment, owning the doorway. He greeted me with a nod towards my stomach as he unbuttoned his overcoat. "How is it?"

"Healing cleanly, thanks."

"You took a chance."

"I took lots of them. I hope, from your point of view, it was all worth it."

"Khalid Hamzeh is no loss to anyone, if that's been on your mind?"

I shrugged. "Why would it? *I* didn't kill him."

He ignored that. "And neither is Darius Orosco."

"Hm, I didn't kill him, either, I'm afraid."

His eyes narrowed. "Yes, there seems to be some confusion about who did."

"Well, it was a confused situation."

He waited for me to expand further. I had no intention of doing so. When that became apparent, he sighed, folded the overcoat onto a chair back and took a seat. Away from the windows and with direct eye line to the doors. Old habits…

"We spent countless man-hours and countless thousands of tax dollars gathering enough evidence for a racketeering charge against Orosco," he said without expression. "All of which died a death the moment he did."

My heart rate started to pick up pace, my skin flushing as my body primed itself to flee. An instinctive response to danger. I locked my knees to stop them trembling.

"Look on the bright side," I tried. "At least Eric Kincaid survived."

"Yes, he did," Epps said heavily, not looking particularly happy with that result. "He not only survived, but he is now the undisputed head of one of the largest arms dealing operations on the East Coast, with reputation and influence all over the world."

It took me a second to match the upbeat words to the down-beat tone. I frowned. "You mean—?"

"I mean that I could not have planned for a better outcome. Had we succeeded in bringing down Orosco, Kincaid's useful-ness as an undercover operative would have been finished. He would have had to hide out with twenty-four/seven security until the trial, then spent the rest of his life in Witness Protection. Maybe even undergone surgery to alter his appearance."

"And now?"

"Now he gets to carry on hiding in plain sight with his remarkable wife."

"And maybe *you* get to have a little influence over who he does business with," I said slowly. "The Kurds, for instance?"

Epps didn't show surprise but he came close to it then. "I can neither confirm nor deny that allegation," he said, very formal. The corner of his mouth cracked into the hint of a smile. "But we did shit on them from a great height during Desert Storm."

"So you're *happy* for him to sell them chemical weapons?"

"If that's what he'd sold them, no I wouldn't be happy about that at all. Fortunately, his deal with the Kurdish forces involved vaccines, antidotes and NBC protective equipment, not the weapons themselves." Epps rose, reached for his coat and looked almost disappointed as he said, "All in all, a positive outcome."

I hovered. "May I take it, from all this, that you're *not* about to have me deported?"

"You may. What you choose to do with it is up to you." He turned up his collar, buttoned the front of the coat, and called over his shoulder. "OK, she's all yours."

The kitchen door opened and closed and a second man stepped into the room.

"Hello, Charlie."

"Parker," I said. My heart had begun to settle. Now it kicked off again. We stood there for a week or so without saying anything else.

Parker cleared his throat. "Would you give us a moment, Conrad?"

"I'll wait outside." Epps nodded to me. "You did some good work, Fox."

Don't spoil it now.

I heard the words as if he'd spoken them, and wondered how he considered I might do that. I wasn't about to ask.

When the front door closed behind him, Parker said, "It's good to see you. I'm glad you made it through."

"So am I."

Another week passed. Or maybe it just felt that way.

I sighed. "Why are you here, Parker? What do you want?"

"What I want…is for you to come back."

"To the agency?"

"To me."

I took a deep breath. "I…can't do that. I'm sorry."

"I understand. It's too soon. Maybe—"

"No, you don't understand. You…me… I can't do any of it. I'm not saying I don't want to. Jesus, Parker, you caught me at a moment of weakness and I gave in to it. But that doesn't mean it would work, mixing professional and personal. Not day to day."

"It worked for you and Sean."

"No… No, I don't think it did. Not in the end."

"Oh, come on, Charlie! He was shot in the head. His whole personality changed."

"Even if that *hadn't* happened, too much other shit went on. Trust issues. Bad stuff that would always be there between us, eating away. Eventually, there wouldn't have been enough of the good left to hold us together."

Parker's smile was bitter. "So, it's not me, it's you, is that what you're saying?"

"It's both of us. I can't bring myself to trust you a hundred percent, not after what you did."

"I thought we went over this already. I *didn't* tell you any lies about Sean."

Yeah, but you held back truths, and that still counts…

"I'm not talking about that. I'm talking about evicting me from the apartment, blacklisting me, then being only too ready to believe I'd turn criminal."

"Even you have to admit it looked pretty bad."

"To an outsider, maybe. But to someone who knew me well— someone like you? It shouldn't have done. You should have trusted me, and you didn't."

"I was worried about you—what I might have inadvertently made you do. And I'm sorry. More than you'll ever know." He moved closer, smoothed my hair back from my face with gentle fingers. "Let me make it up to you, hm?"

I stepped back and his hand fell away. "Actually, I've decided to go home for a while."

"Back to the UK? You're kidding me. I thought the whole reason you agreed to work for Epps was because you didn't want to leave?"

"I didn't. But not wanting to be thrown out is not the same as going of my own free will."

"Sometimes I think, if there's a stubborn option, you take it just because you can."

"Free will is a wonderful thing."

"Not if it forces you to make decisions that are not in your best interests."

"Not in *my* best interests, Parker, or not in yours?"

He gave a rueful smile. "Can't they be both?"

"They can. But, in this case, I don't think they are."

"Come on, Charlie. You know how it is between us. Even you have to admit it was good—too good to throw away, hm?"

I shook my head. "What happened in Geneva…well, it was probably a long time coming. But it was more like an end than a beginning. It has to be, if either of us are going to move on from this. I'm sorry."

"You're wrong." He stepped back. Something hardened in his face, around his eyes. It sent a trickle of unease down my spine. "This isn't over between us, Charlie. And sooner or later you're going to realise that with me is where you belong…"

————

AFTERWORD

Liked it?

If you've enjoyed this book, there is no greater compliment you can give an author than to leave a review on the retailer site where you made your purchase, or on social media. Doesn't have to be long or in great detail, but it means a huge amount if you'd write a few words to say what you liked about it, and encourage others to give my work—and Charlie Fox—a try. Thank you so much for taking the time.

I'm only human…

We all make mistakes from time to time. This book has gone through numerous editing, copyediting, and proofreading stages before making it out into the world. Still, occasionally errors do creep past us. If by any chance you do spot a blooper, please let me, the author, know about it. That way I can get the error corrected as soon as possible. Plus I'll send you a free digital edition of one of my short stories as a thank you for your eagle-eyed observational skills!

Email me at **Zoe@ZoeSharp.com**.

ABOUT THE AUTHOR

Zoë Sharp opted out of mainstream education at the age of twelve and wrote her first novel at fifteen. She created her award-winning crime thriller series featuring ex-Special Forces trainee turned bodyguard, Charlotte 'Charlie' Fox, after receiving death threats in the course of her work as a photojournalist. She has been making a living from her writing since 1988, and since 2001 has written various novels: the highly acclaimed Charlie Fox series, including a prequel novella; standalone crime thrillers; and collaborations with espionage thriller author John Lawton, as well as numerous short stories. Her work has been used in Danish school textbooks, inspired an original song and music video, and been optioned for TV and film. To find out more, please visit her website: **www.ZoeSharp.com**

facebook.com/ZoeSharpAuthor

twitter.com/authorzoesharp

ACKNOWLEDGEMENTS

Barbara Zilly
Caroline Moir
Derek Harrison
Eric Kincaid
Dr Heather Venables
Helena Hoare
Hermann Schade
Jane Hudson
Jeffrey Siger
Jill Harrison
John Lawton
Lewis Hancock
Libby Fischer Hellmann—US-to-UK translation
Liz Graham-Yooll
Mo Heedles
Pippa White
Robert Etherington
Tim Winfield
Tony Walker

THE STORIES SO FAR...

DIE EASY #10: A deadly hostage situation in New Orleans forces Charlie to improvise as never before. And this time she can't rely on Sean to watch her back.

ABSENCE OF LIGHT #11: In the aftermath of an earthquake, Charlie's working alongside a team who dig out the living and ID the dead, and hoping they won't find out why she's *really* there.

FOX HUNTER #12: Charlie can never forget the men who put a brutal end to her army career, but she swore a long time ago she would never go looking for them. Now she doesn't have a choice.

BAD TURN #13: Charlie is out of work, out of her apartment and out of options. Why else would she be working for a shady arms dealer?

TRIAL UNDER FIRE #0: The untold story. Before she was a bodyguard, she was a soldier... (Coming soon)

FOX FIVE RELOADED: short story collection. Charlie Fox in small bites, with sharp teeth. (Coming soon)

standalone crime thrillers

THE BLOOD WHISPERER Six years ago CSI Kelly Jacks woke next to a butchered body with the knife in her hands and no memory of what happened. She trusted the evidence would prove her innocence. It didn't. Is history now repeating itself?

AN ITALIAN JOB (with John Lawton) Former soldiers Gina and Jack are about to discover that love is far deadlier the second time around.

DANCING ON THE GRAVE A sniper with a mission, a CSI with something to prove, a young cop with nothing to lose, and a teenage girl with a terrifying obsession. The calm of the English Lake District is about to be shattered.